MW01427751

AN UNFINISHED SUNSET

The Return of Irish Bly

AN UNFINISHED SUNSET

THE RETURN OF IRISH BLY

WILL IRBY

MacGuffin Books LLC

MacGuffin Books

Published by MacGuffin Books LLC
MacGuffin Books are designed and distributed by Mill City Press.

© 2018 by Will Irby
Premiere Edition
MacGuffin Books, Kendal Norris, editor
Cover art by Adbiz, Sun Valley, Idaho

All rights reserved solely by the author. The author guarantees all contents are original and do not infringe upon the legal rights of any other person or work. No part of this book may be reproduced in any form without the permission of the author. The views expressed in this book are not necessarily those of the publisher.

MacGuffin supports copyright. Copyright encourages creativity, gives expression to diverse voices, promotes free speech, and cultivates a vibrant culture. Thank you for buying an authorized edition of this book. No part of it may be reproduced, copied, scanned, or distributed in any form without permission. When you support copyright, you support all writers and publishers of books for every reader.

This is a work of fiction. Names, characters, places, and incidents are either products of the author's imagination or are used fictitiously. Any resemblance to actual persons (living or dead), businesses, companies, events, or locales is entirely coincidental.

Printed in Canada

ISBN-13: 9781545612880

PREFACE

THIS STORY INCLUDES FOLK histories, anecdotes, and recollections both real and imagined. All manner of musical and literary allusions are presented without scholarly citations. Masked by the narrator to appear as passages of authentic experience, these *reveries* (as the author refers to them) are meant to enlarge the reader's understanding of relationships among the various characters and events. Apropos of William Faulkner's oft quoted proclamation, "The past is never dead. It's not even past," the subchapters reveal these reveries in the simple present tense. They are preceded by individual chapter sections written in the past tense. Consequently the subchapters set up something of a looking glass conundrum whereby the past may well reflect the present or vice versa. Whether the stories convey accurate recollections of authentic experience, illusions, delusions, or mere vagrant imaginings, as vignettes, each one has the intended effect of dreams bearing their own times and places. There are surely simpler, more linear ways to tell a story. But the reveries suit quite well our wayward narrator, Irish Bly.

Prologue

> There is some thing under these false names
> and showes that hath been done truly.

—from *Willobie his Avisa* by Henry Willobie (1575–1596)

SPRAWLING OVER THE CHALKY green water of Pigeon Key, US 1 spans the Seven Mile Bridge alongside an archaic remnant of the enduring Overseas Railroad trestle. A sunburnt-orange pickup with pale blue doors passes now, coming up out of the lower Keys. Decades of junkyard restorations have rendered the truck of no particular vintage, though it sports the hood ornament of a heavy duty '64 Ford. Even more conspicuous are the truck's high, colorful sideboards. These support a faded army surplus tarpaulin shading the slat-wooden crates of the driver's prized cargo in the bed beneath. Absent air-conditioning, the windows are down. Shocks of gray hair protrude like goats' ears flagging beneath the wilted brim of a sweat-stained panama hat. The driver's wide grin is as prominent as the front grill on the old truck.

In its various shades and conditions the iconic vehicle has rambled into Florida lore. It's a curious mainstay known to generations all along Florida's old roads—those weary byways left increasingly derelict by the interstate highways and turnpikes. No time or place now for folkways or homegrown produce of the type this truck features.

As to that, its carnivalesque signage, sporting cartoonish renderings of bees buzzing about the old-style wicker image of a coiled hive, promotes the aging peddler's products. The identity of both his person and product branding (as much as is publicly known) is foisted in a bold, iconic banner script across the panels: *Henry of the Hive.*

Chapter 1

I cannot rest from travel; I will drink
Life to the lees. All times I have enjoyed
Greatly, have suffered greatly, both with those
That loved me, and alone; on shore, and when
Through scudding drifts the rainy Hyades
Vext the dim sea. I am become a name ...

—from *Ulysses*, Alfred, Lord Tennyson (1809–1892)

Deep within the palmetto thicket I raised myself slightly and blinked before the slumbering gaze of morning. The mosquitoes had found me in the night. Even before the rain stopped entirely, they'd descended over me in a prickly nausea. They matted the bloody bandage over my shoulder, their frantic buzz like bees at a disturbed hive. I'd tried to sit up, but my head was too heavy with that awful buzz—bursting and breaking up like the frenetic sounds of a shortwave radio.

The shortwave in my feverish brain tuned to data bursts resembling those between merchant vessels on the sea at night. Random voices crackled in abrupt electronic exchanges, their number and volume shifting with the dispatch of diving mosquito squadrons. Then, as the exchanges intensified, they suddenly scattered. In the delirium of my mind's eye the winged sound shaped a school of flying fish racing outward over the surface sheen. Their silver fins lifted in mass flight before a great white sun on the horizon. When the sun was sated with the fish's mind-numbing buzz, it solidified to appear as a radiant white microwave dome emanating a monotonous drone over the dark magenta sea. Out of that dreaming emerged a Spanish-speaking female voice repeating a number sequence. Her mechanical repetition of the numbers continued in the same anesthetizing monotone and sequence of numbers—seven numbers said in Spanish over and over again.

Then came the vocal eclipse of another woman's voice, this one in English, singing loudly and boldly, as though her song came from a deep well or cave. I managed to sit up enough to see out of the palmetto thicket. A weathered house stood in the early light across the sandy yard. It was a sun-bleached shanty on the cusp of a vast marsh. In the side yard a large woman was hanging clothes on a line. And she was singing. It had been her song swelling in my uneasy drowse that woke me from the dark monotony of the *números* and drew my cold eye to the light of day.

> *There's a mighty wave crashin' 'round my head.*
> *It's chokin' my throat and wishin' me dead.*
> *But that won't scare me and I won't dread—*
> *Just surface and roll to the shore instead.*
> *Roll with me, Lord, to the shore ahead.*

The rough-cut timbers of the house had long silvered in the sun and salt air. Storm winds had bent and twisted the rusted roof tin at its eves. Still, all in all, the place showed a steadfast character, and the woman's song was strong in the breeze riffling the grass in the manner of a prairie wind over wheat fields. These gave me hope—the sturdiness of the house and the strength of the woman's song. I watched her thick arms rise again to pin white sheets to the line. They flapped and lifted in the breeze, opening a vista to the Gulf. I could see out over the needle rush to a long rickety dock. A tidal creek meandered past in the needle grass. All along the coastline after that lay the vast marsh, dappled with small cedar islands where palms stood against a sullen sky bending to the horizon.

A stabbing pain struck behind my swollen eye. The entirety of all I surveyed froze in the instant. I saw the old house melt against the panorama of the marsh like a frame of film caught up in an old movie projector. The scene mottled and speckled as it dissolved,

Chapter 1

burning to oblivion out of an expanding aperture of blinding white light. I fell back and dreamed again.

1.1

Key West

A buzzing comes across the sky. The red biplane rolls inward over the turquoise water, past a wispy pine isle and a scattering of sailboats close by. Deep-sea fishing boats make froth lines as they enter the channel below. A windjammer heads out for a sunset cruise promising a marmalade sky. The buzz hardens into an immense whirling sound above the yachts and sport fishers at the marina docks—the plane now racing its elongated shadow over the waterfront restaurants and bars. A man on bicycle coming round by the schooner wharf looks up with the *whoosh* of the plane already over the tall palms and roof tin, disappearing then in a muted drone down toward the Southernmost.

Irish Bly, a character in his own story now, rides his rusty bicycle with a loose chain that clanks through the quiet streets of Old Town. His salt-and-pepper hair long, he rides with a ball cap on backward, shirtless and no-handed. His sun-burnished arms—tattooed and scarred—extend wing-like to tilt for balance as he leans up a lane off William Street.

Bly keeps a bamboo-shrouded bungalow here. It's a small place with a tropical yard bright with bromeliads. Some shipwright fashioned and fitted the house from Bahamian boards long before hurricanes had names. Bly keeps the place neat and keeps himself trim. He makes coffee before daylight and does some of his best thinking while making his bed with tight military corners. He hasn't always made his bed or even lain in it, having at times not made it that far from the bars or bawdy houses or car when he had one.

Bly is a barnacle man. He does skilled, difficult work, using diving gear over at the marinas, going under with a hand scraper to clean the hulls of world-class boats. He likes the work, though it's patchy and occasional. It suits him now to feel the hull clean and smooth, to see the job complete, finished. Irish Bly (as he calls himself) rides with the attitude of an old fighter in perpetual training for a promised comeback. Anywhere else it would be a comeback that never quite seems to *come back around* from glory days that never really were. But this is Key West.

A pastel-pink vintage Citroën with the top down is parked awkwardly by Bly's bungalow. On his front porch swing two older women, dressed in black and white, glide up and back again. Lifelong companions, Consuela Doge and C. C. Moth, the "Sisters," as they are known, croon in duet sing-song from the swing as Bly rolls past, "IrRrrish! We have busSssiNesss!"

It's what they call it now, *their* story or *business*—their Mirror of the Jaguar Night. And in that business there is Mexico, the ancient *Mexica* in the time of Montezuma and Cortés. There is Cuba and Key West of course because they brought the business to Key West from Cuba after Batista's fall and Castro's rise. They carried their yarn as one might transport a medieval ampule filled with some enchanted scent from a secret garden they were anguished to abandon long ago. It's melodramatic to say such things, but then that is part of who the Sisters are.

High-strung, edgy women who, despite their considerable conceits and arrogances, never mean to injure anyone with their tall tale. Rather, they simply intend to draw those they select into their own story even as lonesome children sometimes do with a delightful fib about an imaginary friend they want included at the table. To the Sisters Irish Bly seems a perfect fit.

It's late in the afternoon. Irish leans his bike against the thick tentacles of a banyan tree in the backyard. Speckled chickens scurry expectantly toward him. He pulls on a faded red lifeguard T-shirt wrapped around a bottle in a paper sheath in his bicycle basket. Come Friday, Bly will always have a bottle of the cheapest good wine he can find. There's usually a sensible buy over at Fausto's on Fleming. He'd gotten that done in the early afternoon. Now he takes the bottle, twisted tight in its thin paper sack, back around to the front porch. The Sisters are waiting impatiently with flamingo-pink plastic Fantasy Fest chalices in hand. This is not their first Friday on Bly's porch swing, although on this afternoon they've brought their own. It's a globular bottle presented and placed on a side table. It is unlabeled, with nothing to hint at its golden liquescent content except a cork sealed with beeswax.

"Ladies," Bly greets them both with a lift of his tattered baseball cap, bringing its bill around. Sewn into the front of it is what remains of a threadbare Vietnam War-era river patrol boat patch.

Doge, the larger woman of the two, surges immediately into conversation, as if the very same one had been going on without interruption since last they spoke.

"Irish, we wonder, do you know that if you go into a very dark room on a sunny day and make a small hole in a covered window—"

"And look at the opposite wall, you will see something magical?" the petite Moth continues excitedly.

"Magical?" Bly locates his corkscrew by a geranium blooming in the door-less antique chifferobe he'd repaired with shelving for potted plants.

"Oh, and by the way, it's our treat today," Doge snorts, extending the globular bottle. "Our treat, Irish. Henry of the Hive's been around."

"Yes," Moth affirms flowingly. "His finest mead. Nectar of the gods. Notice its splendid color!" Then, as if the mention of color has prompted her back on course about the Mirror, Moth surges ahead, "But of the camera obscura we see something really marvelous, don't we? There, in full, vivid color and exact movement, is the entire surround of the world outside that miniscule window."

"Except upside down," Doge clarifies drily.

"Upside down?" Bly carves the wax away from the neck of the mead with a boatswain's knife from his pocket. He then works the cork from the bottle of mead. The scent of a musty old volume from a long-neglected archive will misrepresent its smooth clover honey taste.

"Old Henry ..." Irish says half aloud.

Some months before, oddly enough, he roared up on Henry of the Hive. It had been a good day spent on the perpetually-under-repair Harley he kept beneath a waxed tarpaulin in the backyard. Like most anyone accustomed to Florida's back roads, he knew Henry's truck trudging along. He could recognize Henry's signature wagging wave and possum grin in the zoom past. There was something else, Bly begins to recollect, but Doge has savoured her first deep sip and steams on in real time.

"Light travels in a straight line, you see?" she says, stridently back on point. "So when rays reflected from a bright subject pass *through* the small hole, they don't scatter, do they?"

"I didn't know!" Bly concedes with mock delight in his inquisitiveness.

He pours again from the bottle into each of their ready cups and then into his own, a thick coffee mug from an old Navy mess he keeps up in the peeling chifferobe.

"No, indeed. The rays don't scatter," says Moth spritely after her next slow sip of mead. "They cross and re-form as an upside down image on a flat surface that must be offered parallel to the hole."

"This is the camera obscura!" Doge announces regally.

"Sounds familiar."

The mead was truly smooth and went down easily, with maybe even an orange-blossomed hint of Henry's fermented honey lingering at the tip of his tongue. In any case, absent the scent, each sip enticed the next.

"I think I read about those camera obscura devices—something relating to the painter, Vermeer, and how he worked with light? Controversial, wasn't it?"

"We all have our tools," Doge insists. What we make with them means more than the instruments themselves. There, that dispenses with that. Enough of Vermeer."

"Don't get her started on Caravaggio," Moth cautions and empties her chalice.

"But do you know, or do you not, of the grand Camera Obscura in Old Havana?" Dodge demands. Before Bly can answer, she adds, "It's quite large and most impressive."

"Yes," Moth affirms. "At the corner of *Plaza Vieja*, the Old Plaza. Up on the roof. There's a dark room at the top, you know? The Camera Obscura is there, each image, each color so vivid and so marvelous!"

"But upside down," Doge reiterates over the last of her mead.

"Can't say I've seen it." Bly sits barefoot on the top step.

Chapter 1

"Well, it's time we told you about it, Irish," Doge says in her confidential tone. "*That* is how to see *La Malinché*, the grail of our tale, this Mirror of the Jaguar Night. It is the way to see it, and we shall tell you exactly when and how to do so soon enough."

"Yes, the Camera Obscura," Moth says with a sigh. "There, now we've told you where to find the key. The rabbit warren, as it may be," she avers, having emptied her cup a second time.

"Well," Doge states sternly, "we'll have more business later, Irish." She extends her chalice and adds, "A drop for the dusty road."

Bly pours a jigger-full more. Doge downs it and says, "Now we really must go. She takes possession of the bottle then. "The bottle goes with, matey. Too much mead may make you a dull boy, Irish, and not the dreamer we need."

With a solemn cast of her gray eyes down the dry bottom of her cup, Moth sighs, "My, my, Henry's mead. There's a fine line, you know, and mead makes that distinction best. Nature to culture," she opines. "No one knows better the alchemy of such things than does that old goat, Henry of the Hive."

Doge huffs impatiently. The Sisters are always in a hurry, if only to wait. And they've been waiting quite some time to determine that Irish Bly is, as they declare in departing, "Our man. You, Irish Bly, are our man for Havana indeed," Moth reasserts.

And so they are off, the pale pink Citroën edging out from the house tentatively at first and then posthaste. With Consuela Doge at the wheel, it gains speed down the hedged lane before bucking to an abrupt stop back on William. Midway the Citroën makes a sharp right and disappears up the otherwise quiet street, driven more like a Porsche than the sedate, dated French car.

Irish Bly sits on his broad front steps, his Fausto's bottle uncorked in a baggy pocket of the faded military fatigues that he wears chopped above his knees. Bly knows he's been brought in somewhere in the middle of this tale the Sisters tell. They have a part for him going forward. But it's not exactly clear what that part is. It's their tale, and they tell it incessantly, excitedly, as if just learning of it themselves—verse by verse—from some fellow travellers on their way to Canterbury. It's that curious. So they recount their tale over and over again as time bobs along, much like waves that wash up and slide back across the sand, up and back again differently each time. On this day, however, an old bottle of memory has washed up in Bly's thoughts at the mention of Henry of the Hive, and he takes it from those sands of time.

His mind's eye harkens back to a photograph in the stacks of neatly labelled and stored boxes in the bungalow behind him. Cameras—all sorts of cameras—are part of his experience, and some rather rare ones now remain in his collection. The photographs, where there is apparent virtuosity (even if demonstrated entirely by chance), are among his greatest treasures. That is, Irish has long mastered the ultimate technique for capturing the amazing moment in a photograph. He takes lots of pictures, or so it has been his habit. In this one, however, a young woman sits cross-legged on the bow of a skiff. The photo is in Polaroid hues, one of the first Bly took. Her thick blond tresses reflect the sun, though the light is no more radiant than her magical smile. Past the smile one notices that the girl is taut and lean, yet not frail, and the glint of her eyes touches a chord tolling a deep inner strength. Scrawled in Bly's self-styled calligraphy on the back of the photo is the girl's name. He has written simply: *Grace*.

Bly is remembering himself back in the stained passenger seat of a greasy work truck returning at dusk from the Florida state prison at Raiford. Grace, as she had insisted, was driving her father's vehicle. She'd met up with Irish mere days before he was to board a Pan Am flight for Viet Nam. He was waiting there at dawn by the lighted phone booth at the Pure Oil station out on Highway 41. The Pontiac GTO he'd already sold to a friend was parked close by. Bly had worn his dress blues brandishing a boatswain's patch on his jumper, a few routine service ribbons, and his coveted River Patrol Force breast insignia. Not that he'd wanted to wear his uniform, but it was on Grace's insistence that he'd knotted his tie with a perfectly square knot and donned his "Dixie cup" sailor's hat.

By some sad irony Bly was recently returned from California, having completed training on the Sacramento River delta—close enough for government work to the Mekong. Despite some earlier snafus, he'd managed to maintain his rank and be transferred to training in the *Brown Water Navy*. Specifically, this meant the operation of patrol boats or river craft known in naval nomenclature as a PBR (patrol boat, river), which, not so ironically, corresponded with the popular acronym for his choice of beer at the time: Pabst Blue Ribbon.

Grace's mother and sisters watched them coming back on the sand road from the highway, up through the rough pasture, round the massive tangled char of a burnt oak, and then on to the house shin-deep in weeds. When they came in, her mother and sisters didn't know how to look at her or what to ask. They ignored Bly, not with malice but with an ignorance of what to say.

Grace was the youngest, scrawny and towheaded like the others, but she was always a *feist*, her daddy had said. So she had been the one to go that day because she had always been the one to go with him. She was the one who learned from him how to keep the truck running and when to pass the right tool while he worked on diesel engines in the logging woods. It was from her daddy that she learned to filet catfish and sense when the hounds were on a buck or chasing a doe.

Few words were spoken when they did these things together. There was no need. The father and daughter seemed instinctively to protect the quiet space around the other, the space that insulated each from sharp remarks and resentful looks otherwise ample at home. Between those newspaper-chinked walls there had long been the ricochet of comments edged with disappointment or reproach. Apart from the endless grinding chores that never seemed to catch up with their household needs, Grace had long ago confided to Irish the vast disparities of their two different lives.

Nevertheless they'd become true friends, and Grace was the first to consistently call him *Irish Bly* by name, exactly as he had first proclaimed himself to her on the banks of that river during their adolescence. The two had often talked on the bluff well into the twilight with their arms folded about their knees, the last of that day's sun fading from water darkening before them. Grace had explained to Irish how she never understood her mother's clear resentment of her father. Nor did she comprehend the dour contagion of those sullen resentments, protracting to her sisters who seemed to feel disadvantaged and disgraced by their father's rough calluses and greasy fingernails. So Grace was pensive and quiet, on guard much of the time, except with her daddy and when she escaped to swim and play on the narrow winding river that was the ribbon binding up the spirited friendship between Grace Briarly and Irish Bly.

Still, first and last, she was a daddy's girl. The two islands that were their souls were inexplicably linked by temperament and conviction in the wash of emotions that rippled through their troubled home. Grace came to think of her father's boundless heart in terms she'd borrowed from something Irish had once read aloud from a book about seagoing. It was something to the effect that the same serene water that might bring a sailor safely to port could also rise up fiercely to thrash him against the rocks. Her father's heart was like that, she said.

Now her father had risen fiercely. He'd taken lives, and he would lose his own. She would be the one to see him to that end. Just as they had once shared the same rope swing over the river, Irish would share this ordeal with her.

As she drove she told him that when she was leaving that morning, her sisters had stood speechless in their flannel nightshirts. They merely mimicked their mother's expression of angst when she said bitterly, "I don't know, I just can't. I just can't ... go." This is what the man's wife of more than thirty years wailed as Grace went out alone into the dark to the truck. "He was a hard man!" That was all her mother would say after that. "Just a hard, hard man."

The victims' families had filed in apart from where she and Irish, removing his sailor's cap, were shown to go. The pinstriped-suited prosecutors and some of their burly detectives in rumpled blazers, who'd testified at the trial, comforted the affluent, well-dressed gentry as they went in through the block.

But the investigator for her father's pro bono appellate attorneys waited alone for Grace. This was the same man with a limp and prosthetic shoe who'd come to her house days before to personally say that the state's governor had refused any stay. Briarly waited now like a mourner himself, with his head down, not knowing

Chapter 1

exactly for whom he waited, though he somehow expected it would certainly be this one coming in now—his daughter, Grace.

The investigator looked up and saw her walking toward him, a prison guard and Bly flanking her between the distance of the road and the high fence crowned with razor wire. The investigator's silent embrace was courteous and kindly, a deeper warmth emanating through the tightening of his fingertips over the petite blades of Grace's taut shoulders. He shook Irish's hand firmly with the consoling two-handed grip of a fellow pallbearer. He did not ask by what relation or connection Bly came. Beyond the tall fences behind them the protestors and vindicators raised their shrill, quarrelsome voices, weightless beneath a leaden winter sky.

Grace, Irish, and the investigator were the only ones then to enter the other room, stale and vacant but for the viewing lines of blue chairs across the cement floor. The guard waited uneasily behind them by the door. There was only the glass in front, the same glass through which the victims' relatives also saw the brawny, rough-cut man being brought in. His thick hair, the flaxen color of old gold with a curly forelock over his corned beef complexion, had been shaved cleanly. This was the same man—one and the same—though seen so differently by the two groups gathered to witness his death.

For Grace, there was still the dark, unexplainable gulf between her daddy and the man standing squarely now before the unsympathetic, stony-faced patricians on the other side of the partition. Those people saw only blood on his big, hardened hands. They had no knowledge, as she did, of the man who would carry vegetables from his garden to elderly neighbors down the road. They knew nothing of him as the father who'd once taken up a shovel, without a moment's hesitation, to save her from a rattlesnake poised to strike.

Those sons who paraded about the county with such local prominence, roaring around in their expensively customized trucks, had made a carnal, threatening advance on his daughter. So he'd dealt with them no differently than he had the rattling snake. He'd taken up the same shovel. The snake was as dead now as were the other two, rotting away in the same good earth.

This was her daddy who had patiently taught her to swim in the river where she and Irish later sailed from that rope swing to board an imaginary French corsair laden with jewels and caches of gold coin. She remembered her startlingly blue-eyed father earlier then, standing waist-deep out in the cold water saying warmly, "Come on. Come to me now like I showed you. Swim, baby girl. I'm right here for you."

Grace folded her arms over her chest and began to shiver, just as she had back then, before she knew she trusted him enough to let go. Irish raised his hand to her shoulder, the piping over his turn cuff resting on a limb hard as the bone beneath the pink sweater she wore over her best blue jeans. Grace saw, but she did not see the preparations taking place. Her father saw, but he did not look to see, nor did his eyes reveal that he knew he would soon see no more.

The warden asked if there was anything he wanted to say. The hulking man did not answer but, suddenly and astonishingly, began to sing. He sang, his voice a deep, wonderfully rich baritone:

> *Amazing grace, how sweet the sound*
> *That saved a wretch like me.*
> *I once was lost but now am found,*
> *Was blind but now I see.*
> *T'was grace that taught my heart to fear*
> *And grace my fears relieved.*
> *How precious did that grace appear*
> *The hour I first believed.*

The execution team closed in as the warden retreated. The prisoner paused to swallow deeply before setting his square jaw. The executioners began strapping him into the electric chair—*Old Sparky*—with belts that crossed his barreled chest, groin, thick legs, and muscular arms. A metal skullcap-shaped electrode was then attached to his bare scalp and forehead over a sponge moistened with saline. He sang out louder:

> *Through many dangers, toils, and snares*
> *I have already come.*

Chapter 1

> *T'was grace that brought me safe thus far*
> *And grace will lead me home.*

The girl's face fell to her frail hands. Her father's voice also fell.

> *The Lord has promised good to me,*
> *His word my hope secures.*
> *He will my shield and portion be*
> *As long as life endures.*

Someone unseen and unheard evidently instructed that the microphone be cut off. An additional electrode was moistened with Electro-Crème and attached to his sturdy leg where it had been shaved for that purpose. As the execution team withdrew, his lips shaped the words firmly, silently to these, his last:

> *When this flesh and heart shall fail*
> *And mortal life shall cease,*
> *I shall possess within the veil,*
> *No ... less ... days to sing God's praise*
> *Than when we've ... first ... begun.*

The first of two jolts of a thousand volts each hit like a blazing freight train. It took two to kill him as he writhed and stiffened and his head smoldered, his square-jawed face distorted. As those still waiting their turn on Florida's death row would say, Clayton Briarly *rode the bolt* that day.

"It ended that way," Grace said later with Irish at her side.

"That ... that's what he did?" her oldest sister asked incredulously. "He sang? Daddy sang?"

"A song?" her other sister asked, confused. "You mean Daddy sang a hymn like that? I never even heard Daddy sing nothin' before!"

"Well, he did," the youngest of them said resolutely. He sang "Amazing Grace."

"Dear God! Daddy sang that?" the oldest yowled. "Mama, did you never hear Daddy sing?"

An Unfinished Sunset

The woman watched solemnly out the window past the dented work truck, her eyes fixed on the burnt oak out in the gloaming, the one that was set afire the night the sheriff's men took her husband away. There had been yelling and venomous curses of young voices coming from the charred shadows beyond that horrible flame rising in the night sky. She could still see the burning tree and hear the angry voices that would return.

"Mama?" the other girl asked again. "Do you hear? Did Daddy ever sing like that?"

The woman did not look away from the burnt tree, now released from its gnarled, tortured shape to the night.

"No," she answered softly, "I never heard your daddy sing afore. Not once in all his born days did I ever hear that man sing."

~~~

Alone now, out on the mossy fractured steps of his unpretentious bungalow off William, Irish sits. There's that photo of Grace Briarly on the bow of a wooden boat back there somewhere. And elsewhere in another box were most of the letters Grace had written to him almost daily while he was "in country," up river on the Mekong.

There is this too: a mysterious thread left unraveling to this very day. In his recollection of that night after the execution Grace had returned him to his car parked at the Pure Oil station out on Highway 41. A round-faced fellow at the pumps was filling his sun-bleached truck with gas. While Grace offered Irish her firm (if sisterly) embrace at the battered tailgate of her daddy's truck, the man at the gas pump touched the wilted brim of his sweat-stained panama hat. He removed the hat while Grace acknowledged him with a nod from Irish's shoulder. The man covered his heart with his hat. It was a kindly gesture, accentuated by a compassionate nod in response—some enigmatic consolation from this ubiquitous fellow she knew only by the tattered moniker broadside his truck. Irish turned Grace slightly in the arm of his embrace and, in that moment of recognition, brought a solemn salute to his sailor's cap. It was a salute to a man he knew far better than some mere recognition of the moniker mounted on those decorated sideboards announcing *Henry of the Hive*.

1.2

They are not biological sisters, Consuela Doge and C. C. Moth. Nor are they sisters by solemn vow, committed to some sacred order or other. They are older American women. Earlier expatriates, actually, because they'd lived abroad since Radcliff (the sister of Harvard in those days). They have *old money*. Not as much as rumored perhaps but enough to live quite well their repetitiously refined lives. The Paris years had been first, then Rome, and Barcelona after that. They'd gone to Cuba in the early 1950s, well before the Revolution waded ashore.

Oddly enough, except for the faint crow's feet about their eyes, they appear today much as they did all those years ago strolling the Prado down in Havana. It was there they'd received their blithe sobriquet, *Las Hermanas* (the Sisters). They had, you see, the habit of a leisurely Sunday walk in the afternoons in *Habana Viejas*, the old section of the city where the Prado cascades in a linear succession of parks down the *Paseo de Marti*. Adorned with its marble flourishes, the tiled median passes through a laurel canopy dividing the boulevard down to the harbor. It's a place made to promenade for the centuries.

The Sisters once walked erect in their broad hats, gesturing kindly as they went, dressed always in black and white. Or white and black perhaps but always the opposite of each other. In this fashion they brought to mind a pair of nuns. Most speculate that the Sisters' moniker (Las Hermanas) came from this association.

Not surprisingly, however, given their avant-garde fascination with emerging luminaries in Cuban art and politics, the Sisters briefly became *Fidelistias*. On that fateful New Year's Eve in 1959 when the Revolution rolled in, they'd popped champagne corks beneath their crystal chandelier while other wealthy Miramar neighbors stuffed suitcases and stampeded through the eerie electrical smoke for the airport or first ferry boat out.

But a few short months later, Doge and Moth were themselves in trouble with the Revolution. They'd scurried then like hissing geese in a night flight back across the Florida Straits to land in the Keys. There they settled in Key West, down by Mile Zero, at the old Moth seaside Mediterranean manse built by C. C. Moth's grandfather. He was the immigrant inventor of a patented wire fastener used extensively (well into the twentieth century) by the fruit and vegetable companies importing from the Caribbean and South America. Other discreet Moth fasteners of diverse descriptions, particularly those patented for girdles and later braziers, made millions more.

The Key West house is quite as Old World charming as was the Doge manse down in Miramar, that plush suburb of Havana in which the aging Wilmot Doge had secluded himself in his last days. Shipping money built that one, the Havana house. Doge built the Key West place with a 1932 windfall from his banana fleet, laden with those tropical fruits stored securely in Moth crates.

Anyway, the interesting old Key West house the Sisters now inhabit has long intrigued passersby even if they're unaware of its curious history. Captivated by its charm, rented scooters pull over, their inquisitive riders peering through the corroded iron gate still bearing the Moth emblem in spoiled brass. Through the gate, down a short lane of slender cypresses, stands the two-storied ochre house, perpetually haunted above its towering terracotta-tiled roof by a confusion of gulls.

Then too you sometimes see the Sisters in town, bustling around in their hard to miss pink Citroën convertible. Not surprisingly, Doge and Moth are quite as devoted to their Sunday strolls these days as they had been to their Prado walks down in Havana. Now, it's Sundays at the evening sunset celebrations on Mallory Square, every bit as elegant as they once were in their Havana promenades. They are, to put it politely, *local characters*—often photographed though seldom approached.

Bly also makes the Square a haunt of his, but his perch is typically over with that small tribe of bums that congregates with contraband in their matchboxes and wine in their power drink bottles. As it happens, it was on Mallory Square, where a juggler did his tightrope act against a fiery sunset, that one of Bly's more curious early encounters with the Sisters occurred.

The encounter wasn't by mere happenstance. There had been a brief introduction some weeks earlier at a social event, a little soirée at one of the grand houses over on Whitehead Street. The host was the notorious Bertrand Oliphant. The suave older gentleman (though appearing disinterested in their question) made a discreet nod toward a Bly out on the patio. The Sisters thought his salty, sun-burnished, rather piratical appearance rendered him appropriate in response to their confidential inquiry.

In a stage whisper behind his slender hand Oliphant confided, "He goes by *Irish Bly*. He goes down to Cuba."

He goes down to Cuba. There's a certain way this is sometimes said in the Keys. It's the way Oliphant said it, in a tone implying some concealed purpose for the going. Smuggling usually.

1.3

So here they are now out on Mallory Square. Know that it's entirely characteristic (however peculiar) for either Sister to begin a conversation quite abruptly, exactly as Consuelo Doge does when approaching Irish Bly: "There is a mystical cave we know of in the hills of *Malinalco* in Mexico."

That's what Consuela Doge says first—this about the cave—when she and C. C. Moth sidle up to him on their chance encounter at the twilight carnival out on Mallory.

"There's more to this, I presume?" Bly asks, amused.

"Oh indeed," Doge replies. "An obsidian mirror known to treasure hunters worldwide as La Malinché—the same appellation used for the captain's woman, the native girl who would make the object itself a gift to Hernan Cortés, the bloody conquistador of the Mexica people."

"And later, the volcano above the valley of the Mexica, that was named Malinché too," C. C. Moth adds sweetly. "For it has always loomed large over the place of *many* mysteries."

"I like mysteries," Bly acknowledges casually.

"Well yes," Consuela hurries on. "So now to this obsidian mirror crafted in Malinalco in the time of Montezuma before Cortés. This dark glass was made in the bowels of the sacred cavern, said to be a magical site devoted to the cult of jaguar warriors."

"Jaguar warriors?" Bly repeats emphatically with a nod.

With a stern nod of her own, Doge responds, "The mouth of the cave gaped then, even as it does today, like the jaws of a great serpent. Deep within its smoky den sorcerers plied their crafts, skilled in the use of both healing herbs *and* hallucinogens—potions for questing, bravery, love, and the elimination of pain."

"I'm listening ... seriously."

"Morning glory seeds," Moth offers with a wink, "mushrooms, peyote buttons, the extracts from the *Bufo* toad, and the like. Also laboring among their dwellers were fantastic metallurgists, craftsmen of precious metals. It was by these skilled sorcerers that the prized obsidian Mirror of the Jaguar Night was made."

"Made for what purpose?" Bly wants to know.

"Made as a gift to Montezuma," Doge announces, "one he shared with his favorite concubine in their temple chambers."

"But it was taken later by this Malinché, the native guide and lover of Hernán Cortés, the *caudillo* or conqueror of the Aztec Mexica," Moth hurries on. "That is how the Mirror came to his greedy armored glove!"

On a park bench just vacated by an eco-tourist couple in spongy sandals Bly sits between the two women. An eager Doge reveals more.

"She, Malinché—whom Cortés called *Dõna Marina*—gave to Cortés the Mirror at his final departure from Mexico. Malinché knew she would never see Cortés again except as he might conjure her in the Mirror she took for him on the Night of Sorrows, that dark business *we* call the Jaguar Night."

"So," Moth insists next, "the Mirror would ultimately be included in the inventory of a secret treasure that Cortés intended to conceal from his king on returning to Spain."

"And that was about the tribute, the taxes, I assume?" Bly surmises.

Chapter 1

"Ah yes, but his rather substantial retirement fund, so to speak, disappeared in a storm on the homeward voyage," Doge divulges. "It was lost for centuries until a *Cubano*, fishing with a hand line from an inner tube, saw deep into a donut-like hole in a coral reef. There lay the lost Cortés treasure exactly as it had rested in obscurity for centuries in the sparkling sands off Cayo Coco."

"The Mirror was there!" Moth proclaims. "We didn't know about it then, but we know quite a bit about it now, don't we, Sister?"

Doge eagerly agrees, "Oh yes, as much as anyone, I should think. In fact, though the Mirror has long since been obscured again and we can't yet determine exactly where to look, we jolly well know *how* to look."

"How?"

"Not so fast, Mr. Bly," Moth admonishes. "First there's something else we now know—know about you, sir."

"And that is?"

"That is," Doge answers sternly, "we also know that you—how shall we say—*you* go down to Cuba."

"And?"

Doge glances over at Moth and then, in a hushed tone directed at Bly, inquires, "Do you know Havana's Chinatown, Irish? The *Barrio Chino de La Habana*?"

"Yes, well, a restaurant down there. The Fan-Tan, I believe."

The Sisters look back at each other with great satisfaction on their cherubic faces.

"Oh, we *really* must tell you more!" Moth insists. "You are most certainly our man."

The Sisters will do just that on their terrace the very next afternoon. But momentarily, the big voice of the soulful singer, Rachel Perl, begins to fill Mallory Square.

Chapter 2

Wandering, dreaming
In fever dreaming that dreams
Forever wander.

—Matsuo Basho (1644–1694)

I HAD A NAUSEATING GASH above my right eye, caked with clotted blood and mud. It must've happened when my boat plowed over the creek's bank in the rain sometime the night before. Now I couldn't move my left shoulder. Pain from the bandaged wound gnarled my fingers into a frozen fist. The wound oozed blood again through the dirty fabric of my shirt. I felt weak lying there in the palmettos, as tangled up as the tattered net of my thoughts. I tried to think where I came ashore. By what inlet? By what light? I was recollecting some things—staccato images of desperate spots of time, disparate and non-sequential. Nothing connected the dots from the dark, stormy Gulf to the place where I now lay.

Then the woman was singing again. I rested with her song settling in me warmly while I struggled to visualize her fully in the muted, dense hues of an old Polaroid photo.

I caught the regal lift of her head. I heard and saw the breeze flapping the white sheets before the broad expanse of marsh. I strained to roll onto my good arm and lever myself up to call out.

No. It would be better to stand and announce myself as benignly and courteously as possible. The woman would see me at once, openly bent and wrenched of any danger to her by the helplessness of my easily observable wounds. Then I thought to myself,

Chapter 2

Maybe I can't make it to stand? There was so much blood loss from the injuries sustained in being thrashed around in the stormy seas that washed over my open boat. And my head was throbbing intensely by then.

In that throbbing I heard the rapid footfall of a child racing up and down, down and back up the golden oak stairs of a great house. I listened to the illusory footfall with another strange wave of warmth coming over me. The pain was pulsing from the gash above my blackened eye, swollen nearly shut and blurring my vision. I considered queasily that I might have internal injuries too. In those same Polaroid hues I saw myself suddenly out on the bow of a Navy river patrol boat, wearing sunglasses and a sly-dog smile. But I was dumbstruck now, pummeled by the fact that I had actually been shot.

This was something new. Disregard the times I'd deserved to be shot. Several times, astonishingly, I'd been too close to miss yet had survived without a scratch. I'd been cut, but that was by a drunken chum down on the docks—nothing like what a bullet could do. So that long run of luck had finally played out. Now I lay dying.

I heard again the snap of a bed sheet in the wind over the sunburnt yard. Behind my gritty eyelids I saw the flash of a shot in the dark. Discharged light coming, expanding slowly like skillfully blown glass. That image shattered then, showering brightly over the cobalt sea in my feverish dreaming. While the dispersion of star-like specks settled over the water, I blacked out into the muck and palmetto root. Just before oblivion I saw myself descending deeply into darkness while the last of the luminous glass floated on the surface above me, extinguishing itself one twinkle at a time.

2.1

Rachel Perl is a busker, a street musician with a big voice and a tiny brass band out on Mallory Square. Three Bulgarian brothers compose the group. They perform in newsboy hats and roll their suspendered trousers above their ankle boots and limp socks for that *Little Rascals, Our Gang* effect.

An Unfinished Sunset

While working in the immense steamy kitchens of one of those big cruise liners, the Balassi brothers had jumped ship to make a new life for themselves in the tropics. Why Key West? With a shared reminiscence of the frozen, forested mauve of their motherland as a chilly backdrop, the Balassi brothers reply in the unison of a Slavic accent, "It was cold there."

"Cold," the youngest repeats, resting a worn trumpet against his knee.

"Very cold," the middle brother agrees, his trombone across his chest.

"The cold, this is why. In this place, all the time we are warm," elaborates the eldest whose flugelhorn is particularly suited to Rachel's Perl's bluesy melodies and the rousting street-jazz solos she does on the Square.

Rachel is a young Quaker woman down from the north country, or so she says. She looks Spanish or Portuguese perhaps but isn't. Though she's fluent in Spanish, she sometimes speaks of being a remnant of Romanian descent. Anyway, up the line her parents had settled in as caretakers of a Minnesota lakeside resort. They'd declared themselves Quakers by then, and so they were. And so she would be, this Quaker girl—a gypsy maybe—with large Spanish eyes and an enormous, fathomless voice.

Rachel sometimes wears ribbons and seashells in her thick dark hair. She prefers those peasant skirts sold on the island, the ones made of gauzy batik. She plays any stringed instrument by ear. Anything with strings she plays amazingly and sings boldly with the voice of an angel who smokes a little.

Later at night she often performs blues numbers alone down on Duval. She jams on her acoustic guitar at a spot away from the blaring din of open-air bars up at the rowdy end of the street. This is down past the guy with the green iguanas and albino python, after the fellow with a cursing parrot on his arm, by the menagerie of shopping stalls where a dark-skinned man in a white shirt rolls cigars. Rachel's spot is just past that old Southern Cross Hotel sign. It's there, in the pool of little lights, that the sidewalk is good for spreading her sand.

Chapter 2

Rachel Perl's leather-soled Mary Janes make a scuffing, brush-like sound over the sand. Her shoes shuffle forward and slide back in perfect percussion to the melodies she makes. From more than a block away you can hear Rachel well before you see her. Whether in the heavy drift of passersby down Duval or coming up by another way, the sunburned tourists in boozy clusters bob up and down with the heartfelt wallop of her spellbinding notes. Some stand with mouths agape that such amazing sound comes from one so rapt and small. The wispy smoke—a fragrant scent of orange blossom adrift from the burning stick of incense stuck in the headstock of her guitar—further blesses those walking in the night breeze. But it's Rachel's big, earthy voice that attracts the cash, as true orange blossoms do the honey bee. The bills drop aflutter to that old buckaroo straw hat at her dancing feet.

Locals too are now fans. Among the more prominent Key Westers thrilled by Rachel Perl's unique voice is a distinguished-looking older gentleman, the celebrated Key West restaurateur and prominent socialite, Bertrand Oliphant.

Consuela Doge will infamously snoot later to a *Times Picayune* reporter, "Anybody who is anybody on the island knew Bertrand Oliphant. And Bertrand knew everybody, whether they were *anybody* or not."

Virtually all secrets in Key West come to Bertrand Oliphant. They're laid before him like lingerie by tawdry dancers from the clubs or delivered in private soliloquies behind the willowy, bejeweled hands of the wealthiest women on the island. He is their confidante and welcomes their confessions in a near-priestly manner. Many of the prominent women depend on his advice in both personal and social matters. In desires as diverse as the selection of proper stationary or miraculous cosmetics or the securing of a secret offshore bank account Bertrand Oliphant knows immediately and precisely that which he deems to be "correct."

With men he primarily talks business or politics down at the Blue Rendezvous, his popular waterfront restaurant and bar on the Key West Bight. He has an uncanny command of extensive, accurate facts about each. Even his most astute and accomplished patrons remain continually surprised by Bertrand Oliphant's breadth and depth of information. Local luminaries and the occasional celebrity in town, shopkeepers, sandal and soap makers, painters, buskers and street poets, hotel clerks, jewelers and exotic bird handlers, pole dancers and dry cleaners, even off-duty cops, Coast Guard officers and Navy pilots—these and more might be included in the mix of Bertrand's legendary house parties. He holds them at his elegant old home on Whitehead Street where he often graciously plays his grand piano for assembled guests. Sometimes Rachel Perl leans in. So when they popularly entertain together, the great room instantly fills.

Bertrand Oliphant is well regarded on the docks too. Though not exactly the quintessential rugged man's man, he is nonetheless a consummate sportsman. He's a crack shot in gunning for pheasants or quail and tells that he developed his shot gunning skill by jump shooting ducks in the Louisiana bayous of his youth. Bertrand is also a top-tier tournament fisherman. He's the unlisted owner of one of the finest sport fishing boats in the Keys, a 54-foot Cabo with a tuna tower that kowtows to no other in the area. You can see it there, the *Mercy*, sometimes tied at the A&B Marina where slender lines moor all makes and models of yachts and deep sea fishing boats. These render, define, and redefine the view out the second story prow-front windows of Oliphant's Blue Rendezvous.

There is this too about Bertrand Oliphant: he is every bit as congenial with the various dockworkers and crewmembers as he is with his ritzy pals, friendly competitors, and renowned boat captains. Another thing to admire is the fact that Bertrand is absolutely immune to seasickness. The most seasoned salt might be green to the gills in stormy weather while the diminutive Bertrand sits smiling in his fighting chair—big sunglasses, white slacks, and pink polo shirt, balancing yet another dry martini and vigorously gossiping above the winds of an approaching gale.

"Oh, and another thing," says Mercer Pendarvis, a disbarred attorney and known Oliphant associate (though sometimes retained by others for his *free advice* offered during *office hours* from his regular bar stool at the Blue), "it may seem that Bertrand is always drinking, but he's never drunk. He's always talking, yet he's always listening."

Chapter 2

This is so. Valued factoids tossed about in multiple conversations around Bertrand Oliphant never escape the audio antennae of his discerning ear.

Anyway, everyone sooner or later tells Bertrand their secrets. And of course they already know that sooner or later he will reveal them. Maybe they don't really care because Bertrand Oliphant has such a sophisticated way of telling things. He makes even the most tasteless of episodes somehow seem charming or adventurous or at least eccentric in some fascinating way. It's a gift the man possesses—an ability to illuminate the commonplace—so that the most mundane of secrets he tells in his silken Louisianan voice always seems to be, as he puts it, *"Summmethin' speeeeecial!"*

So then gossip is also Bertrand's Oliphant's stock and trade. It's a way of doing business. And a lot of business gets done in the Blue Rendezvous these days—not all of it his own. Some good music and literary deals have been inked there, right alongside clandestine contraband deals. Saltwater cowboys rub elbows with international tourists, book editors, high-end antique dealers, and art collectors. Bertrand knows or will come to know the details of each. He's mixed and mingled and made the introductions. It's his business to know everyone else's business as well as he knows his own.

Bertrand may talk in his slow, languorous style, but he is rapid each night to tally to the penny his daily receipts. Both for the Key West restaurant and his elegant antique emporium on Royal Street up in New Orleans, the sales data comes directly each night to his large, ancient, tiger-oak desk in the office upstairs. Moreover Bertrand will file a dozen or more profiles of new patrons he's met, though each of these is only in his head. He has perfect recall (or so it appears) by some system he's developed for himself. Whatever the method, Bertrand Oliphant demonstrates time and again his keen ability to catalog seemingly random contacts for any future, even if impromptu, business connections he might wish to make.

And Bertrand Oliphant is most certainly connected. But what virtually nobody yet connects to him is his own best-kept secret. You see, this genteel little fellow in the tailored seersucker suit and real tortoise shell sunglasses, the grandfatherly man adjusting his panama hat with a cockeyed brim, the one striding along Harbor

An Unfinished Sunset

Walk in his crocodile oxfords, is the anonymous kingpin of a highly sophisticated, illegal immigrant trade out of Cuba.

No petty crime that. If found out, Bertrand Oliphant and any coconspirators charged and convicted would face up to ten years in federal prison for each immigrant related to the conspiracy charge. Bringing illegal immigrants into the US currently yields a mandatory minimum of five years with a maximum term of fifteen years in federal prison. Violating a federal regulation that prohibits departing US waters with intent to enter Cuban waters without authorization alone can result in a maximum sentence of ten years in federal lockup.

That's not the end of it. The Feds also seek forfeiture judgments, going after the proceeds of the charged criminal. Those likely include any vessel or real property otherwise, which, in Bertrand Oliphant's case, would easily result in forfeited substitute assets amounting to millions of dollars.

So how does Rachel Perl connect? Well, as directly as Boca Chica, about three miles north on Highway 1, connects with Key West. At least once a month, usually on the darkest of nights, Mercer Pendarvis (in Oliphant's service) will stride by Rachel as she performs down by the Southern Cross. He will inconspicuously drop a fin—a five dollar bill—in her hat.

Oh, and almost always there is this: a rusty old pickup truck parked up the side street, its faded door signage advertising a long-defunct ice house. It doesn't escape Pendarvis's attention either that often obscured across the street in the zigzag shadows over a broad span of storefront steps sits the hulking figure of a roughneck in a sleeveless chambray shirt. Over there the man's massive hands rest on his bare knees, his large head sporting a raised curly forelock. The brute sits mesmerized by the music Rachel Perl makes.

Bertrand Oliphant of course possesses the advantage of this information. And sometimes, making his way from the Blue Rendezvous back over to his great house on Whitehead, he also observes the character there. Neither Pendarvis nor Bertrand exhibits any recognition of the man to whom the latter refers rather affectionately as the "Colossus Pavarotti" of the *Mercy*. But then neither shows any real recognition in passing of the gypsy girl singing boldly, scuffing the sand beneath her tatty Mary Janes. But in his observation of the two there is for Bertrand Oliphant the faint smile that forms in his sweet recollection of an old fairy tale, one his bayou-bred mother told of *La Belle et la Bête—Beauty and the Beast*.

Later, at the second story apartment off Caroline Street that Rachel shares with the Balassi brothers, she will transcribe a series of neatly printed numbers from the fin to a small note pad. When deciphered, the sequence of numbers reveals a GPS coordinate and estimated time of arrival to be anticipated off the coast of Cuba. These are numbers deciphered from the droning sequences broadcasted by shortwave radio from Cuba.

After midnight Rachel will drive her VW convertible over to Williams Street, switching off her lights as she pulls up the shrouded lane. When she stops, the slender form coming from the shadows of the banyan tree will slip into her passenger seat. There'll be no conversation until she is up on Highway 1 where she'll pull off for gas or a coffee—something to buy and pay for with the fin. When that bill is safely returned to anonymous circulation, their destination is a weathered, nondescript boathouse down a shell grade off Boca Chica Road. This is up around the Geiger Key Marina with its thatched, Seminole-style Chickee roof and the old RV park they pass by.

2.2

Surprisingly enough the Boca Chica boathouse, with its loft apartment, stands not far across the dark mangroves within sight of the moonlit white radar domes of the Boca Chica Naval Air Station. Electronic surveillances and hot pursuit interdictions are made from there, but a busy little cottage industry of private intelligence types set up shacks in the area to intercept radio traffic from the base. They have their own discreet (if disreputable) clientele. The quarters over the boathouse are outfitted in just such a way. They may serve as both a listening post and a workshop for the equipping and maintenance of the fast boat concealed below.

An Unfinished Sunset

Before Rachel Perl first persuaded Bly to let her in on the ride, she'd monitor from there and communicate any helpful intel in his race back across the Straits before dawn.

Sometimes, when there isn't a *flight* to make or inclement weather delays, they walk the sandy road in the dark back down to the marina's open-air restaurant and bar. Often the music comes over speakers mounted on the exposed beams beneath the palm thatch. On late Sunday afternoons there's frequently a rough little band called Randy and the Reefers. It's a boozy so-so group without extraordinary musical abilities or any false pretenses otherwise. As Irish Bly observes, they're simply crusty, barnacled chroniclers of true conch life in the Keys.

Irish and Rachel admire their authenticity over Bahamian beer, especially Danny's melodious storytelling that borders more on the traditions of troubadours than those of glitzy rock stars. The two blend in well at the bar with other locals and usually stay to the last set.

When they walk back to the boathouse, they listen toward the dawn for significant electronic information, noting patrol patterns or anything that may serve as reconnaissance before their next night flight. Increased activity in the Straits has become predictable over the years when the time is ripe for *tickets*. That's when the economic conditions are still more dismal or desperate. ("Watch for the news *not* coming out of Havana—this more telling that there is," Oliphant observes.)

In any case, if the Cuban economy worsens while the weather improves, that's when rafts and rustic boats are pushed out from unguarded harbors and beaches. When those two factors occur simultaneously and when the moon is right, the tides just might take rafters far enough out to catch the Stream, prayerfully undetected out across the Florida Straits.

"That's when they come—the *balseros*—by the dozens maybe," Bly quotes an experienced Coast Guard spotter he knows from the Blue Rendezvous. "They'll wade out with anything that floats, push off in a leaky, tar-patched dinghy or catch a mat of Sargassum weed if that's all they've got. Whatever. It's pitiful, man. But what can we do?"

Chapter 2

   As Irish and Rachel sit at their listening post this time, it's Cubans on a makeshift raft of Styrofoam sheets and old canvas lashed over six truck inner tubes. The spotter has them in focus, the circular frame of his binoculars likely holding upon the faces of hope and determination now fallen to dread or fear. Their buoyancy of spirit is diminished by the salt and sun to mere exhaustion in the spotlight and the dark wind. Now they are intercepted and will be taken back to Cuba.

   The air crew notifies the Key West sector and remains in the area until a patrolling ship arrives. The cutter comes around, and the hungry, dehydrated, forestalled émigrés are safely embarked. On board the Coast Guard cutter the *balseros* (rafters) receive water, food, and basic medical attention but not their freedom. They're to be returned to *Bahia de Cabañas*, the province of *La Habana*. There's been worse. Over the decades thousands have been lost beneath the deep and dangerously vast blue space in between.

   "You have to wonder," Bly says to Rachel while they listen to the radio activity, "what were they thinking? The ones who go under. In that last gasp, the unfortunates who don't make it. Drowning, did they really prefer death to repatriation? You take your chances, you know?"

   Rachel sits silently with big brown eyes glistening in the shadow of the shelf of electronics blinking automatically before her.

   Bertrand Oliphant's network offers an expensive, though less dangerous and risky alternative. Via his arrangement, some Cuban-American family, a wealthy patron, or a major league baseball scout could liberate someone from Cuba for $10,000 a pop. The *rescue* occurs when the unlit speedboat slides quietly away from the boathouse, a skillfully muffled run out the channel to open water. The racing craft then zooms out of the Keys to cross the Florida Straits in less time than it takes to commute from Jersey to New York City. To turn eighty to a hundred thousand dollars in a single dark night is routine. It's good money by any standards, and the consequences for getting caught are a lot less severe than other types of smuggling.

   The price of a *ticket* isn't all profit though. Bribes have to be paid on the other end. Handlers too. And then there's Bly. The barnacle man by day, come those dark nights when conditions are right, he remains astonishingly adept at handling fast boats at astounding speeds in weather tranquil or unexpectedly foul.

More to the point, Bly can flawlessly hone in on a small flotation beacon set somewhere in the pitch dark off the Cuban coast. There the well-financed political *refugees* will be swooped on board before an armed patrol boat can close in. The dark bow of the racer will rise, the boat will pivot on its propeller, and Bly will roar back across the straits to a Florida destination not signaled to him until his return. But he has the final call on that. Whether by intel or instinct, his job is to find a US beach—a place to land safely. With any luck it will be some unobserved misty stretch of beach along the Florida Keys.

2.3

A boy in a large pirate's hat boasting a snowy plume announced himself to be *Irish Bly*. The railing of the upstairs landing in the grand old house fronted the quarterdeck of his corsair. The circular stained glass window behind him made for a mysterious seascape out of which he could sail. There's a fading photograph of this scene.

As a boy, Irish (a name he insisted on) looked up to a particular friend of his grandmother. The man was a fastidious little fellow, a reader—*el lector*—at one of the cigar factories in the Ybor section of Tampa. He read aloud to offset the boredom of such a tedious task as rolling cigars for hours on end at the factory floor benches. His name was Victor Emmanuel. He would read in a deep, slightly raspy voice from newspapers, magazines, and books, especially sagas through which he captured and kept his listeners' attention (sometimes for weeks) with a single story.

Cervantes and Dickens were good for the long haul, but he also read from the sporting news. When he could get the reports on Cuban baseball games, they were prized by him personally, as well as by many others hard at work in the vast room with high red brick walls.

Chapter 2

Irish's grandmother took great pride in her eclectic coterie of delightful visitors on Saturday afternoons at their grand old house in a leafy, once prestigious Tampa neighborhood. With a hive of perpetually dyed red hair, buxom as the grand archetypal opera singer, Lydia Redmond stood on Saturday afternoons at the gaping front door, singing out "Come on in, boys! Join the saturnalia."

Many who darkened her door were from among the social and political elite. Others bossed the docks or streetcar lines. Some were cops and some ran rackets. A brick mason might sip a glass of *Miz* Lydia's "spiced tea" along with members of the burgeoning bohemian arts community in Tampa at the time. The majority—representative of virtually every walk—were regulars. One occasional itinerant guest in particular was always a welcome addition. This was the already iconic purveyor and factor, Henry of the Hive.

Despite his ever-rumpled linen jacket and weathered panama with its sweat-stained hatband, Henry was a favorite of the fastidious hostess, Lydia Marchant Redmond. Moreover Henry was particularly popular among many of the regular visitors, especially the elders and memoir aficionados who reveled in his jocular reveries of Old Florida.

A self-styled folk historian, many episodes Henry described frequently in vibrant detail, insisting that he must attribute the current version to one or another of his older relatives or else to some more recent acquaintance made by a daisy chain-like connection to his own relationships and experiences. Sometimes Henry would retell a certain tale on request but say, "Oh, that one! Well, that was Uncle Perdue's version I told last, but let me tell you how Aunt Lou Della told it. Look he'ah, *now* you'll see a cat of a different color!"

No matter the version, Henry was innately theatrical and gleeful enough to offer at least one good tale to Lydia and the appreciative gaggle of cigar-smoking men congenially gathered around him. Wedged in with his pirate's hat, festooned with its prominent plume, was the boy who called himself "Irish Bly."

"Tell about the turtles, Mr. Henry!" he was as apt to shout with his adolescent voice ascending like a fragrant smoke ring rising through the deep buzz to Henry's ear.

"Okay then, boy. Late one night Uncle Absalom and Nate—that was my Cousin Thelma's boy—and some other men was turtling out of Cedar Key. They was way down the coast he'ah, somewhere near Anclote Key. Anyway, their turtling boat was tied out from a campfire built high on that sandy shore. Around the fire they was campin' rough. It was a tough bunch that made a life on the sea back then. They'd had their supper and was tossing scraps of oily mullet skin with bits of fry bread to a little jip dog among their crew.

"Nate, he weren't more than a boy then—but I knowed him as an old man—he'd stoked the fire with knots of lightered pine and driftwood from along this low sand and seaweed berm that estranged the beach from a big saltwater lagoon back behind. Well, don't you know the flames cracked and popped cheerfully into the dark? Absalom said then they seen a silent web of lightning low on the dark Gulf's horizon. The men had seen that spidery light making the sky purple all around but paid it no never mind. They sweetened their cups with Aunt Vivian's all-purpose scuppernong wine from a masonry jug. 'All purpose' she'd say desolately, as she felt that her fermentation served purposes both good and bad.

"Be that as it may, what happened next old Nate said might have first been credited to the wine's potency. There certainly seemed some strange chicanery about. For suddenly a deafening, rumbling, and snorting sound arose from the still sea. These were sounds louder and stranger even than any circus clatter they'd ever heard as boys or men. Growing louder, shapes as large as river-smoothed boulders began to appear from where the boat was being banged about. In what appeared to be a single horrific instant those heavy shadows, making the most awful noises, was upon them. Like a great herd of buffalo stampeding up from the sea, a clashing of thick shells and scrambling of great flippers closed on that sandy camp. What it was, it was an enormous shoal of sea turtles in their laying season coming on fast out of the dark over the forsaken bed rolls. Frantic flippers scattered the campfire like a low-slung Fourth of July spectacle. The yelping jip dog raced off down the dark beach with all the men at his scampering little butt!

"Tell you what. I say you won't never see such a thing in this life again. It was some invading armada of huge sea turtles headed for that lagoon where they were accustomed to waiting out bad storms. And there was a bad storm a coming too! That looming spider web of lightning out on the bay weren't no idle rumor. Those big buffo-heifers scared the hell out of them boys but just might have saved their lives. That storm? Now boys, that's another story!"

Henry would be back around, always with another story, but Victor Emmanuel was a constant among the Saturday crowd spilling out into the walled brick patio in the back yard. Victor, ever the enchanting storyteller in his own right, also had his rapid-fire quips and quotes, his ready recitations recollected from his routine readings from the best of authors out of the ages. These certainly spiced his own entertaining conversations and didn't escape the interested ear of the boy who'd chosen for himself the curious appellation of *Irish Bly*.

The patio brick lay in a herringbone design beneath the giant roots of an ancient shady oak that made a sort of platform from which Victor Emmanuel would sometimes regale guests with heart-warming tales of dramatic events. Proclaimed with even more excitement than his pirates' battles at sea or chivalric rescue of some damsel in distress was Victor's histrionics about his beloved *Almendares* baseball team, a club of the Cuban League.

Known by their colors, the *Blues* was one of the oldest and most distinguished baseball teams in all of Cuba. They represented the Almendares district on the outskirts of the old city of Havana. In Victor's youth the *Blues* was among the most successful franchises in the Cuban League, its famous rivalry with the Habana baseball club legendary. Some of those games were all-time classics. Victor Emmanuel could list the rosters and heroes of virtually every championship game. His passionate (even if make-believe) play-by-play accounts included fantastic self-produced sound effects more comical than exact. Irish learned those too. Particularly the cork-like pop Victor substituted for the crack of a baseball bat striking the ball. Irish learned from Victor how to swiftly and expertly extract his pointing finger from inside his cheek to make the same sound.

So Irish Bly, the boy, got baseball into his blood. Playing baseball was a great enthusiasm, but it was no greater than his fierce passion for being a true buccaneer. Fortunately for the boy's personal

An Unfinished Sunset

pirate fantasy, it was also about this time that Tampa entered the golden era of its annual Gasparilla parade, an event originally set to coincide with the opening of the Florida State Fair and another popular haunt for Henry of the Hive.

The Gasparilla festivities celebrated the fictitious exploits of one José Gaspar, who (so far as is truly known) first sprang fullblown from a fanciful 1900 advertising brochure for the Charlotte Harbor and Northern Railroad Company. That was the nineteenth century financier Henry Plant's railroad with a terminus at Plant's Boca Grande Hotel on Gasparilla Island in Charlotte Harbor. As manufactured as the historical Gasparilla was the chance to play pirate openly in the Tampa streets—flush with colorful floats—intoxicated Irish. There was a sweetly sympathetic photograph of him in an elaborate costume his grandmother had made, replete with a broad scarlet sash. This was a photo, among the last perhaps, that the multitalented Victor Emmanuel took.

Yes, there was Emmanuel's photography too that would have an immense influence on Irish, the young boy whom the Cuban émigré knew first as "Jack" in the 1950s. Jack Redmond was, as Lydia Redmond introduced him, a name that had belonged to his father before him. Emmanuel already knew Jack the elder had been lost in the war when the plane he piloted went down in the icy seas off Britain's Shetland Islands.

So Victor Emmanuel was an amateur photographer when being an amateur was as expensive as photography was for a professional. His hundreds of sepia photographs chronicled the life and times of Tampa's historic immigrant neighborhood, Ybor City. Also in one of his collections (now archived at the University of Tampa) were photographs of the great house and the prominent gatherings off Bayshore. It was there, swinging wildly from the banisters, that the boy, Jack Redmond, first played the pirate he would inexplicably proclaim to be—Irish Bly. Some fifty years on, it would be as inexplicable as was his childhood reverie, but Irish Bly would be the name to which Redmond would return.

2.4

So it is on a night down on the Key West Bight, reclining on a dock locker over by the old turtle kraals, that Irish finally answers Rachel Perl's curiosity about his childhood. He speaks wistfully for the first time of his grandmother, saying pensively in a near whisper, "She was such a sweet liar."

He goes quiet then, and Rachel is quiet with him. Despite her immensely talented voice, Rachel Perl also has a talent for silence.

"There was a day I awoke," he says after a while, "to the rain ending abruptly. I remember the water pearling up in heavy beads along the eve of the upper story. It dripped drop by drop down from the peeling paint to banana leaves in this nook between the chimney and screened back porch below. I delighted in that sound—the drumming of the rain drops on the banana leaves. And I remember suddenly the drum thud over the leaves overcome by the click-it-ty-clack of the first streetcar out on the avenue that morning. It's funny how such an instant lodges and lingers in the mind. But I remember that instant more vividly than I do my first day at school."

"I know that sound," she says. "Not the streetcar but the sound of rain drops on banana leaves."

"That was the last year the streetcars would run in Tampa, at least for a very long time. I didn't know it then—didn't know that was ending too. My grandmother came to my room that morning festooned in the style of spring. The cut of her colorful dress and the broad hat she wore weren't the style of the day, but they were her style. She laid out for me a suit too small or nearly so. It was the best I had and would have to do, she said. The tie she liked—this one, not that one. That one had been my father's before the war."

"Where was your father?"

"He didn't come back. My mother either."

"She was in the war, Irish?"

"No. She just didn't ... come back."

Rachel looks away deep into the stars on the water on the bay but doesn't ask more.

Irish continues, "While I brushed my teeth, she reminded me again of the importance of shined shoes and exactness in the part of my hair. 'A young gentleman's attention to such detail,' she'd say, 'is as admirable as brave deeds.' She really believed that."

Rachel shifts more comfortably on the locker as Irish goes on.

"One's appearance, insofar as one was neat and orderly and made the best of what one had, was by her reckoning an outward manifestation of the soul within. That was how we lived then in the afterglow of this life her father had made. The house was pretty much as he had left things, even if it was crumbling at its foundation. I knotted my tie, thinking her ignorance—this refusal to acknowledge the decay about us—to be more her bliss than folly. She was happy about things as they were except as they pertained to me. She wanted more. Outside my window the dense shade of old oaks obscured the new cracks in our foundation, the faded paint, and the buckled roof shingles overhead. Yet we lived on in that great house as my grandmother fancied our lives ought to be. I suppose it was true, as she said, 'We must look our best with what we have, or lose all. We must be seen.'"

Irish, now earnestly transported back in time, adds, "There was a man we would see that day. Not the usual sort of man, but a poet."

"A famous poet?" Rachel asks with genuine interest.

"Not yet. This was a living poet, or at least he was at the time. I don't know that a poet is ever quite famous while he lives."

Rachel frowns softly and leans forward on the palms of her hands. She could see from the dock to a swarm of moths over a large fish swimming in a pool of light on the water.

"Grandmother said he would see my folio of photographs and that something may come of it. I had been taking photographs of my own by then. 'A very important prospect,' she kept saying. 'Very important indeed.'

"With the money I had saved lifeguarding at the city pool I'd bought a six-year-old Speed Graphic camera with a large flash attachment, a camera commonly prized by the press photographers at the time. Grandmother had already shown and sold a few of my photographs. These were of certain men, men with traction in the downtown business district like the chiefs of police and fire and various politicians. They were the men who made their money trafficking bootleg liquor and running rackets and the lawyers who represented both. Money and politics still mingled more by social habit in our parlor than any real gain. They spilled out onto the patio in the walled garden behind the house. Maybe sometimes deals got made over whiskey and cigars. But really it was a safe house in a strange sort of way, a type of twilight zone where no reprisals for whatever happened elsewhere would occur so long as each remained ... polite."

Some revelers in flip-flops pass by on the dock, going round the walk in artsy T-shirts toward Bertrand Oliphant's Blue Rendezvous.

Irish continues, "I had done their portraits, many of these men. I'd always been fascinated by Victor's camera, his photography. My grandmother would usher these guys in front of the dusty velvet drape we'd dragged down from an unused upstairs room. Some of the guests were or would become men of means far greater than ever my great-grandfather was. Some went to prison. Some managed both. The photographs I took reflected their best days, taken ironically in a place that had known its best days."

"*Amore* in ruin?"

"Yes," Irish says regretfully. "You might say that. Anyway, the man we would see that day *would* become famous. He wasn't yet but had come to town for a reading from his new book. My grandmother was much impressed and somehow managed a meeting through her position on the library board. Outside on the avenue we boarded the streetcar to Ybor City where a once-popular little restaurant served dark Cuban coffee and sweet rolls ladled with this sugary icing, sprinkled with crushed nuts."

"Sounds decadent," Rachel says.

"Delightfully. So we went in. She was a sweet liar, my grandmother," Bly repeats. "She didn't know this man nearly as well as she'd said. I could see *that* in his dark eyes as we approached. I think she sensed his skepticism as we came up but smiled her magical smile, raised her bosoms, and lifted her wonderful hive of red hair with that regal bearing of hers. It didn't matter if she was not all she might have implied of herself. I mean she wasn't *all that*, but she strutted who she was in refuge and revenge, the best revenge being to live well (Fitzgerald—according to Victor Emmanuel). She lived as well as she could."

"And you with her."

"She prided herself in me and pushed me forward."

"But she really was proud of you," Rachel insists with a lilt in her voice.

"I was proud of her," he says softly. "We came to where the poet was waiting at a table in a darkened corner, this thick-browed, rail-thin man in tweed. He stood, mustachioed and gaunt in his heavy, ill-fitting suit. He waited until her hand was extended before he offered his. We were introduced. 'Yes, yes,' was all he said, never quite looking at me. My grandmother talked incessantly even before we sat. Neither he nor I had any inclination or even opportunity to interject. She ordered coffee and the sweet rolls without slowing the pace of her promotions. Her effervescence was effortless. There was just no heavy lifting for her in this, nothing to unwrap or bind up. She laid out immediately her insistence that collaboration between this poet and me would be both prominent and profitable. I had brought with me all the landscapes, some of the shore, and a dozen more of the old homes draped in jasmine and wisteria along our streets. She'd said there would be a fortune in our collaboration. This man looked like death as he leafed lazily through my folio. I sensed immediately no prospects would come my way."

"How could you know?"

"Well," Bly begins and then sits in contemplation, as if cross-checking his thoughts before continuing, "when she let him talk at last, he said in that slow, elongated Mississippi drawl of his, 'Well ... yes. *Yes*.'" Irish repeats himself, saying, "Yes ... *yes, ah yes* ..." mimicking still more dramatically the poet's thick, lingering intonation.

"And that was all he said?" Rachel Perl asks plaintively. "Yes, yes?"

"As if nothing more need be said," Irish offers. "And of course, *yes* was nothing less than what Grandmother required. So after it had rained again for the last time that morning and we stood on the wet pavement, he said finally, '*Yes*. Thank you. *Yes*.' Then with a slight bow, he went back up the street, taking his long shadow with him."

Chapter 2

"Yes ..." Rachel repeats softly with an inquisitive smile.

Irish laughs easily. "On the streetcar the poet's *yesssssss* seemed to rise in the sprinklers coming on in sunlit showers over the lawns along the avenue. Grandmother sat with her purse on her knees, smiling with satisfaction at the certain publishing future she now imagined for me. I sat within the click-itty-clack of the car without a word while we returned to the past that was the great house in which we lived down the avenue."

They watch together as a boy rows a woman in a white dinghy to a sailboat moored out from the docks with a lantern lit at its aft.

"So, *yes* was *no*." Rachel says after a while. "That was the thing, wasn't it, Irish?"

Bly nods, "That morning, 'yes' meant everything my grandmother wanted to hear. It meant nothing, exactly as the poet meant to say. I already knew at seventeen that his yes was less substantive than the sugar disappearing in the slow stir of his cup of hot coffee."

"I know something about yeses like that," Rachel says. "They can be more cruel than a stone-cold no."

"Yes," Bly says and catches himself with a start, and they laugh aloud together in a way that was warm in the night breeze whispering through the riggings of boats moored close by.

"But Lydia Redmond, my grandmother, always invented her history as she went," Bly insists. "The more distant that day became over time the more insistent she was that this book she promoted was bound to happen. In her last years, my grandmother spoke of the proposed collaboration as if it had actually occurred. She would introduce me over again to her oldest friends and speak of *the book* like an object they could actually take up from some hallowed place in the house if only she could remember exactly where she'd last put it. Her clear implication was that, if not by then so very frail, she would go immediately to find the book, so beautiful and recognizable immediately by its handsome green suede binding and gold leaf. 'Surely you've seen it,' she'd say. 'Such exquisite photographs illustrating the now-celebrated verses of the once and future famous poet.'"

"But it wasn't there?"

"No. It never was."

An Unfinished Sunset

The boy in the white dinghy was rowing back alone on the silken swells of cobalt water.

"That's the way it was with her," he says. "I may have made it worse. I was, much to her disapproval, away at war myself by then. She was so aggrieved by what war had already taken from her that I think she must've dissolved more rapidly into her dementia."

Bly plunges deeper into his well of memory. "I was in the Navy on a riverine craft that day, photographing the dust-off ships—the choppers coming in low over the swaying grass across that brown river somewhere in Southeast Asia. My chief climbed on board and told me I was requested over at the Red Cross office. That was in a line of shacks up a muddy street from the river wharf. There was a nurse there, a pretty Swedish-type who told me my grandmother was dying. She had a sunny way about her, this nurse, having a grandmother herself, she said, in Minnesota. She was direct but kind in her manner. She helped me with my leave request, corrected my spelling, and then got me underway stateside, suggesting that an old congressman once familiar with our house had held some sway."

Taking a hard swallow, he continues, "That summer's eve of my return I remember there was a dazzling moon, its golden light gilding her window ledge. I had come home and set my sea bag down at the foot of those golden oak stairs. Lydia Marchant Redmond died in the gauzy dark between the jeweled shadows made by the massive posts of her bed. I could swear a *yes* was just then forming—fixed then, firm and crisp as starched lace upon her aged, lifeless lips. *Yes* was what she wanted. *Yes* ... was the way she went."

Rachel Perl sits quietly for a while and watches the white, wafer-shaped moon light the wispy pines of Wisteria Island beyond the harbor lights.

"Did you make her up, Irish?" Rachael asks plainly.

"No," he replies softly. "She made me up."

Chapter 3

A revolution is an idea which has found its bayonets.

—Napoleon Bonaparte (1769–1821)

THE SCREENED DOOR SCREECHED open from the back porch of the house. A young girl in overalls rolled to her knees came out after the dog—a lanky, big-pawed hound bred for hunting. His nose was soon to the ground. The girl called out to the woman in a voice mature for that of a child. Then she yelled to the dog, "Come here, Hobo! Come on back here!"

I knew the hound would find me. The bullet I'd taken had ripped through skin and flesh. How cleanly it had I couldn't be certain. But, as surely as the wound had attracted mosquitos and deer flies, it would now easily summon the dog. I knew I was bleeding again, this time from the exit wound. I could feel the hot trickle of blood traverse the shoulder blade and trace down my spine. I wasn't going to last much longer in the rising heat. The deer flies increased in number and intensity, soon taking over the gory bandage from the mosquitoes. The dog would come next, but there was no dread in this. Actually, I thought it just as well that he did.

The white sheets snapped and popped on the line in the shimmering heat. I listened to my irregular breaths in the muck and lay still to wait. There was the moist earthen scent like that of a rattlesnake lingering. The snake had come in with the rain—likely before I'd burrowed in—but it hadn't gotten too close. Still, I knew the wretched scent as keenly as the dog would know it the instant he turned into the breeze. I kept deathly still, and another snake writhed to recoil in a recollection from my boyhood.

One summer I worked shirtless in the watermelon fields east of Tampa. This jut-jawed man in a dark fedora, dribbling a stain of tobacco, was a watermelon broker. One afternoon a melon truck driver killed a big diamondback in the blackberry bushes where the broker had been carelessly picking berries along a fencerow. The summoned driver beat the snake lifeless with a hoe, chopped at its head, and finished the amputation with a big pocketknife from his greasy jeans.

But it was the broker who raised the rattler triumphantly by its long buttoned tail. Several of us who'd been loading melons came up to see. With a shrill war whoop, the broker swung the snake lasso-like above his head and then let her fly at me for fun. The length of the flaccid snake caught me at my neck just so and wound up around my mouth and turned my nose. The rancid musk of that rattler entered my splayed nostrils, never to be forgotten.

I tore the snake away from my face while the scales marred my scarlet cheeks. With the blood of the headless snake dripping down my chest, I fought the man fiercely. But he just taunted and held me off until the melon truck driver pulled me away. I would never see the man again, though the sweaty sot weed stench of him fares no better with me now than does that poisonous reptile's odious scent.

Something else there was about that afternoon and the diamondback, someone rumbling up behind me on the road I stomped toward town. I had not finished the day nor waited with the other boys for the ride in the bed of the farm truck. From deep within the shimming summer's heat over the asphalt came another familiar truck. This one had high sideboards supporting a sun-bleached tarpaulin. I waited on the roadside in the slender shade of a myrtle hedge for Henry of the Hive. Close by I could see Henry raise the brim of his hat, squint for clarity, and shout, "Lord, help! Boy, is that you, my fine young buccaneer?"

"Yes sir," I acknowledged, stepping up on the sideboard at his passenger's window.

Chapter 3

"What's that scuff and flush you got there all over your cheeks and down your neck?" Henry asked, leaning in for a closer inspection.

I told him about the broker, how he'd hit me with the snake, and how I went after him too and wouldn't load another melon on his trucks whatever the pay.

"Oh, don't fret on that," Henry said like a good uncle. "I imagine you'll have a lot worse tossed at-cha afore you're done. Hold on."

Henry pulled up and off the road and banged his shoulder against his door. Hitching up his suspenders, his sleeves rolled up, he got out of the truck to examine my injuries. I know now he kindly fathomed them to be more than skin deep.

"Let's see what you got he'ah. Maybe clean ya' up a bit," Henry said, coming around the burnt-orange hood of his truck.

I told him some of what he saw might have come from my scuffle with the snake thrower, but he said it didn't matter, adding, "You ain't got nothin' on ya that won't wash off," and said he had just the remedy for my abrasions.

Henry ignored my minor protest against any first aid and climbed into the back of his truck. He shuffled around beneath the tarpaulin a bit. When he climbed down, he came to where I stood with a small glass jar he'd extracted from his pants' pocket. The miniature jar was now displayed in the hollow of his outstretched hand.

"This is the just the stuff he'ah," he said with his wizened, possum-like grin.

The jar's bright yellow lid sported a red cross on it with one of Henry's trademark bees buzzing about. There was a gallon jug of water on the floorboard of the truck, and Henry took a clean handkerchief from his hip pocket to splash it with water. He dabbed at my face and cleaned me up with that and then began to apply a light application of salve from the jar.

I had to admit that there was an immediate relief from the rash-like sensation I'd felt on my face and neck. Even more gratefully no remnant remained of odor from the nauseating musty snake. Or at least it was mitigated in some manner by the contents of Henry's ointment. I wanted to know what was in it.

"I can't tell ya what all's in it, lad," Henry said earnestly, standing back to admire his handwork. "I mean I've seen her make it while I take my coffee at the kitchen table, this ole sister woman. She makes it up by the batch for me. Does it in a big white enamel pot. Powders up calendula and lavender, adds some coconut oil, and seems like maybe olive oil too. Mauls and muddles and stirs and stirs. It's a pinch of this and pinches of that. I don't know what all, but you can take this to the bank," Henry's voice began to soar with pride. "In every little dab of this unction there's a golden drop of Henry of the Hive's medicinal raw honey."

"Does seem like it feels better," I said more inquisitively than I meant to sound. I suppose I was also wondering what my face and neck might look like pasted over with Henry's curious ochre concoction.

"Yes 'sah, Henry of the Hive's Healing Ointment," he announced as he raised the small white jar to my eye level and reattached the yellow lid. "I got people all over that swear by it — whether for the baby's diaper rash or Paw Paw's sorry ole bedsores. They'll wave me down to get a jar. It's as fine a healing ointment as there is since Jesus walked, you he'ah me now?"

"Yes sir," I said. "Thank you."

Henry ambled back around the trunk and said, "Won't be so much as a mark in less 'an three days. Get in, boy. I'll drop you off in town."

Henry was still crowing about his mysterious healing ointment as we drove through farmland recently subdivided with billboard signs erected at faux Spanish gates announcing the lots for sale.

"Oh, it's ugly to look at, but it *dooooo makes ya purddy!*" he laughed out to me in the onrush of summer air as we rode with the windows down. "And that's all natural too, you know that? Or it can be," he assured warmly. "I got this ole gal I see from time to time," Henry declared with a wink. "She tells me the uglier she gets on the outside the prettier she intends to get on the inside. I was just thinkin' 'bout that."

Henry let me out a block from where I could jump a streetcar home out of Ybor.

Chapter 3

"Hey!" he shouted after me as I waved back. "You still the buccaneer boy! You still got a lot of livin' to do!"

~~~

Returning in my somewhat muddled mind from this youthful reverie, I never actually saw the snake in the palmettos. I never heard it stir in the rainy night. But I knew it lay close by, torpid and likely gorged on marsh rat. No matter. As I've said, I know the vile, revolting scent of a large diamondback rattlesnake. I knew too when it slithered away and writhed out over the sand toward the dense hammock behind me. Not long gone, a sudden gust of wind could draw the dog to the scent if my own wretchedness didn't. So I waited. Then the woman's voice soared again:

Glory to God, we gonna be with him ...

My thoughts trailed in a gauzy wisp of fog back to the fast boat I'd somehow gotten up the salt creek. *I must've rumbled past the long dock in the storm the night before. The boat was probably beached farther up,* I reasoned inwardly. The sheets on the line cracked in the wind again. Then I remembered the channel markers in a barrage of lightning strikes. The markers had been mere cypress poles hammered long ago into the shallow bottom. Most of these had reflectors tacked on them for night access. The lightning would illuminate their serpentine lines, and I'd steer by the next red flicker, fixed for an instant in the dark ahead.

I'd found the mouth of the creek and stayed between the high bluffs of needle grass after that. With no memory of beaching or getting out of the boat, I had no explanation for why or how I'd burrowed into the palmetto thicket behind the house. Maybe it was because I'd seen a light from that direction. I'd beached the boat farther up so as to come back around on the broad natural berm that formed the high ground. All I knew for sure was that the palmetto thicket was as far as I'd gotten or as far as I could get. I was wounded, and now the dog would come.

As the wind lifted to send its invisible waves through the marsh grass, it tossed the spiny, mop-like heads of cabbage palms in the outlying clumps of low cedars. The palmettos rattled, and I felt the shivering return. I tasted the metallic hint of gunpowder in my dry mouth. Though she seemed nearer now, I couldn't make out what the girl was saying. The dog was closer, barking away from the girl who was shouting at him playfully. Then sweet Morpheus returned to dowse my pain with a feverish sleep.

3.1

"Errol Flynn was dead, to begin with," Consuela Doge states confusingly, albeit no less so than she had on Mallory Square when she first spoke to Irish Bly of a mystical cave in the hills of Malinalco.

They are sitting now out on the black-and-white chessboard of large tiles that form the back terrace of their great house. Beyond that is the Atlantic Ocean for a backdrop. Irish listens while the Sisters put their Mirror tale into play. They talk loudly in the sea breeze. A low tabby wall boxes the terrace from their neighbors. Windswept cedars in huge ceramic pots punctuate its corners.

Doge and Moth sit together on an ornate cast-iron bench, a bushel basket of iced oysters between them. They wear matching rice straw hats, broad-brimmed with hatbands, one black and the other white. Ribbons bind down their brims and are tied in dainty bows beneath their bony chins. Each sports big movie star sunglasses, alternately black and white too. So they peer from their bonnets like ancient crustaceans, comically gloved for shucking oysters with a blue steel blade. Irish Bly sits athwart a chair of the same heavy set. Doge cracks a large oyster at its back joint in her thickly gloved hand.

Moth sighs, saying then, "As to the *Zaca*, Flynn's world-class schooner—once among the finest sailing yachts in the world—we believe it is now absent its masts and abandoned to the mudflats of a boatyard in the south of France. Some documentarian found it there. Soon afterward, more about Flynn pops up in a biographical

Chapter 3

piece published posthumously by the daughter of the notorious Hollywood correspondent and snippy little tattletale, Hap Hollister."

Wiping oyster juice from her chin, Doge says, "Oddly enough, it wasn't until Hollister's little chitchat that anything about our La Malinché—the Mirror—had appeared in the media."

"Indeed," Moth continues. "But we put that on Flynn. He was quite the talker, wasn't he?"

"Oh yes," Doge responds. "So you see we are speaking of the same boat, the *Zaca*, in which our fine swashbuckler sailed to exotic ports around the globe, prowling the Caribbean in more recent times."

"*That* was in the sunset years of his fame of course," Moth insists.

"Yes," Doge continues. "Flynn had made all the best ports down there, but Cuba was perfect for his sordid passions."

Opening an oyster, Moth elaborates, "Oh my, yes, the swank hotel casinos, the flesh-pot nightclubs—those were his favorite haunts. But hedonistic as the scoundrel was, Flynn did make pals with the once-Spartan rebel leaders and Fidel first! Oh, he won't own up to it now, but he and Flynn actually were once quite chummy. Flynn languished and frolicked about Havana in the early glory days of the victorious Revolution."

"So that's how Flynn came to learn of the treasure," Doge says.

"From Fidel Castro?" Bly asks.

"No, not Fidel!" Doge corrects. "It was Camilo Cienfuegos, one of Fidel's top *companeros*. It was by Camilo's entrée to us that Flynn came to know of the secret Cortés treasure, our Mirror of the Jaguar Night. Sad to say, *we* told Flynn!"

"Trusted him. Ghastly mistake," Moth admits with the cast of her eyes heavenward.

"That's *our* sobriquet, La Malinché, you know?" Doge explains.

"Hap Hollister got it from Flynn, and it stuck afterward. We're certain of that now."

So the Sisters reveal how the international celebrity and bon vivant, Errol Flynn, would see the crown jewel of this legendary Cortés treasure. They speak with abject horror about showing him the exquisite obsidian and gold Mirror, the same gifted to the

An Unfinished Sunset

conquistador in parting by the native woman known to Cortés as Doña Marina and to history as Malinché.

"This is the moniker now bestowed by the unseen rich collectors of ancient and priceless objets d'art," Doge reiterates, "the black mirror known today as La Malinché."

Moth offers Irish an oyster on a saltine. He takes it with a dash of Tabasco from the cast-iron lawn table completing the lawn set.

"Do you know what it means?" Moth asks of Bly, hot sauce in hand.

"Tabasco?"

"No, La Malinché: 'the captain's woman.' That's the meaning of it. It's argued of course. But that's the meaning we take for the woman so named. She was certainly that."

Doge plunges on, saying, "Camilo Cienfuegos was one of the titans of the Revolution, you know. We were friendly. Camilo was friendly. We often engaged him in casual conversation when he'd stop by our table at the Tropicana."

"We did so love the Tropicana," Moth reminisces, "as did Camilo, and he was our special friend there. He was the club's special friend."

"Indeed," Doge sniffs. "He was a lot more accessible after all the trooping about, the flag waving, and victory parades—much more so than Fidel."

This Camilo Cienfuegos was an abundantly bearded individual, the Sisters explain. He was a man of the people, a top-tier leader of the new regime who had been with Fidel from the birthing of his Revolution while still in exile in Mexico. In Moth's opinion he looked like a slender rock star of the next decade—Jim Morrison maybe, although he still dressed in the signature olive drab fatigues of the Revolution. A gregarious man of the *campo*, he was back-slapping congenial with an exceedingly high tolerance for *el ron*. The Sisters also confided that Camilo had a vigorous eye for the exotic dancers and models of the Tropicana.

"He had this buzzing interior energy. It was magnetic," Moth says. "And for a while Camilo was the rugged guardian angel of that glitzy, world-famous nightclub, though he always entered

Chapter 3

through the kitchen back door, ringed by an entourage of uniformed bodyguards."

Doge and Moth, as they were eager for Bly to know, also had their regularly reserved table at the Tropicana. So it was Camilo then who'd brought Flynn by one summer's eve. Ever the philanderer, Flynn made his own entreaties after that. In fact it was soon rumored that he was courting the old girls for their backing of a low-budget film he was planning.

"*Cuban Rebel Girls*," he called it," Doge groans. "It was a silly and exploitive idea, really. It was all about *the girls*."

"Yes, all about the girls," Moth agrees. "Particularly *his* girl. But we quite enjoyed it in a tacky sort of way after he finally got it made."

"What did Hap Hollister think? His review ... favorable?"

"Who knows?" Moth says drily. "He was an insignificant little twit, Hap Hollister. But for his blabbing about our Mirror of the Jaguar Night we'd have no interest in him at all. Frankly we wish now we'd never met that scamp, Errol Flynn, either! Or his tacky little trollop with her debut in *Rebel Girls*."

"And may I assure you," Doge says pointedly to Bly, "Flynn made that trashy bit of cinema entirely without *our* awareness. We were really quite taken in by him."

"Taken to the cleaners, you mean," Moth says with a smirk over her oyster on a half shell.

So it was there in Miramar, down a tree-lined avenue before their disenchantment, that Flynn made regular visits to the Sisters at their mysteriously retained manse. For, even as personal friends of the Revolution, it was indeed strange that this private property should be reserved to them at all.

"Well, it was *so far so good*," Moth sighs.

In a confidential tone Doge then introduces the tale of how a black Mercedes would occasionally park in their drive after midnight. The mysterious man being chauffeured would enter through an obscured side entrance. Two soldiers (one the driver) waited in the shadows outside, the orange flecks of light from their cigarillos swirling like fireflies in the dark.

Moth whispers behind her hand, "*El Comandante* himself would come sometimes very late at night."

"He'd smoke his awful cigars," Doge relays, "and he'd regale us with these random, encyclopedic machine gun bursts of intellectual thought well into the wee hours. We nodded off, often without his notice. It was incredible—his exhausting, ebullient, and boundless commentary on books and politics, completely inundating our salon with so much smoke and fury."

"He *was* brilliant," Moth observes wistfully.

"Well, of course we *thought* him brilliant," Doge huffs. "He had all the guns."

"But we didn't show him the treasure," Moth says spritely.

"No, we didn't, and I fear that it may have been poor Camilo's undoing," Doge sighs thoughtfully. "We wonder now if Camilo's impending demise harkened back to his secret, near-exclusive knowledge of the obscure La Malinché."

"We're almost but not quite certain of that," Moth says. "We do think Fidel found out that Errol Flynn was chatting with us about the Cortés treasure. There were whispers—we're sure of this now—that Flynn had been spiriting treasure coins out of Cuba on the *Zaca*."

"That wasn't our affair, the business about the treasure coins," Doge declares.

"No! Not our affair at all," Moth insists. "But we know who, and *that* is likely what turned Fidel and his henchmen against Flynn, you see."

"Well, it was certainly enough," Moth agrees. "And if Camilo was thought to be giving him cover, giving Errol cover we mean to say—as that braggart Flynn might well imply for safe passage—he'd have put Camilo squarely in Fidel's crosshairs, don't you think?"

Irish Bly knows nothing of all this and hasn't given it a thought before now. He'd been a boyhood fan of Flynn films of course: *Captain Blood* and *The Sea Hawk* among his favorites.

"But Errol Flynn and Fidel? I had no idea," Bly says, cracking another oyster for himself.

"Well, it certainly tightened the screws on us," Doge goes on. "We can tell you with absolute certainty that when Flynn became persona non grata with the Revolution, it happened overnight. And

Chapter 3

poor Camilo, he saw La Malinché with Flynn. It was that *same* night in our salon in Miramar that Camilo looked into the magic Mirror, and then *he* disappeared!"

"That instant?"

"No, but soon thereafter. His plane went down," Moth recalls sadly. "There was a mysterious explosion, you understand—this on a night flight and the plane was ... well, lost at sea."

"But by then Flynn had made Bimini in the *Zaca*," Doge supposes. "He was holed up at the Compleat Angler out there, his Cuba days at an end. And in yet another despondent vodka daze he dribbled on about the Cortés treasure at the bar table one night."

"Well, drunk or not, he certainly described the Mirror perfectly well," Moth confirms. "At least according to Hollister's notes."

"You have Hollister's notes?"

"We have the tawdry article his daughter wrote," Moth insists. "She refers to his stay at the Angler out on Bimini and references the notes her blabbermouth father had made."

"Yes," Doge adds. "Evidently it was Hollister's daughter who excavated the contents of his steamer trunk full of his prodigious notes, out of which she penned this most unfortunate biographical sketch of her father for the entertainment industry magazine *Variety*."

"It's clear. Certainly Hap Hollister was pushed up to Flynn's bar room table," Moth laments. "Had to be. His daughter provides a spot-on description of the time and place, a precise description of La Malinché, just as her nosey old dad got it from Flynn!"

"Exactly," Doge continues, "consisting of obsidian and mounted between golden jaguars with emerald eyes. The Mirror itself was made of black volcanic glass. Perfectly rounded, six inches in diameter (about the size of a saucer), with the slightly convex glass, hand-polished to a flawlessly smooth viewing surface."

Moth says, "The gold jaguars, each crafted with extraordinary detail, frame the Mirror. A male and female with eyes of cut emeralds, did I mention that? Who would know such detail had they not seen it? Their bodies, the jaguars angled out by the ancient craftsman, together form a rather triangular mount for the Mirror. Their thick hind legs and long entwined tails comprise the base on which it sits. That was it, wasn't it, Sister? The Mirror of the Jaguar Night."

"Indeed so," Doge avows. "Precisely as Flynn must have told it. Worse yet, *we* are referenced! Not by name but even so as *the Sisters*."

"As eccentrics!" Moth scoffs.

"Imagine that," Doge says drily, about to suck another oyster from its pearly shell.

"And so," continues Moth, "we, along with La Malinché, are now outed, as it were. Why, it's only a matter of time before we're hunted down."

"By whom?"

"By treasure hunters of course!" Doge answers assertively. "By Fidel's men too, for all we know. There's not a more valuable find in all the Americas than our La Malinché. Worse yet, we know of one who would kill for it."

"Yes, who *ha*s killed for it. The German!" Moth declares. "But we never got La Malinché out of Cuba, you see?"

"Who's the German?"

"We're not there yet," Doge says. "Or rather, we're past the German, though he comes back around. It's La Malinché, the Mirror of the Jaguar Night, that's our focus now."

"Yes," says Moth. "It's still in Havana. We've told you that, haven't we?"

"I can't be certain."

"Well, we're telling you now," Doge says sternly. "We had to make a run for it, Irish. Broke our hearts—that full-throttled getaway, a deep moonlit gash made across the dark sea."

"My, yes, the Comandante's gunboats were throwing spotlights after us in the night," Moth recalls. "His bearded men on deck slinging machine gun fire in our wake. Our captain, believe you me, was scalding the brine for Florida with that little yacht of ours."

"Indeed. Smarter to be lucky than lucky to be smart, we still had the property here," Doge adds.

"But La Malinché, horrors of horrors, we left her behind," Moth notes sadly.

Chapter 3

After a pause, a steely eyed Doge instructs, "We want you to rescue her, Irish."

Moth chimes in, "It's time, Irish. You must."

Doge continues, "Yes. You go down there often enough now, don't you? And you are rather resourceful, we understand … and, by golly, we trust you!"

"You do?"

"Yes," Doge replies jauntily. "We trust you because you are an admitted prevaricator, openly deceitful about this Cuba business you're in. And who knows what unlikely mischief before that? We've checked you out, you know. You deal in a good many subterfuges, each guarded by a multitude of half-truths. Fortunately for us, half is quite enough. Frankly, our good man, we believe your mendacities to be entirely conducive to the stratagem we have here."

Irish Bly sits expressionless and somewhat astonished. His face flushes a bit, though his eyes appear to be an even more vibrant blue.

"It's quite refreshing, really," Moth adds gleefully. "We need a good liar, Irish, and we think you're just our fellow. And as a man who travels under the radar, both figuratively and actually, you'll come to understand our trust."

Turning instantly then to inquire of Consuela Doge, Moth asks, "The Seven Dials. What is it of the Seven Dials that comes to mind?"

Doge descends deep in thought a moment and then issues a suddenly recollected literary quotation: "The stranger who finds himself in the Dials for the first time at the entrance of Seven obscure passages, uncertain which to take, will see enough around him to keep his curiosity awake for no inconsiderable time …"

"Yes," she adds, very pleased with herself. "I do think that is it precisely: Charles Dickens, his *Sketches by Boz*, I believe."

Moth replies pensively, "That may well be so. It may even be relevant if I'm lucky. In any event, I don't remember precisely now what it was I had in mind." As a distant light in her winter-gray eyes draws nearer, the flat of her hand begins to pat the beat to a tune on the bony knee beneath her long skirt. "Oh, but yes!" Moth exclaims. It was this little ditty—"

She warbles the first of *Tree Top Flyer*, Steven Stills' smuggler's anthem, her voice aloft at *seven dials*. Bly joins in with a broadening grin, and they do a shaky, if enthusiastic, duet, harmonizing easily by the song's *low and fast, hot aeroplane* end.

"You two certainly seem to have struck a common chord," Doge says stiffly. Then to Bly, "So, do you fly? Do you, sir?"

Bly meets Doge's eyes evenly, saying, "Not planes, though I might manage to land one if I had to. I'm pretty good at landing on my feet. But boats, yes. When it comes to boats, ma'am, I fly."

"Excellent," Doge acknowledges, offering Bly another oyster on the half shell.

"And there's one other thing," Consuela Doge announces with the lift of her regal head. "We pay well."

"Very well indeed," C. C. Moth chimes in with a dash of Tabasco on Bly's oyster.

And so there was that too. The money—an assurance Irish Bly receives with his trademark mischievous smile.

3.2

Why Bly, really? Oliphant's confounding referral of Irish Bly directly to the Sisters notwithstanding, Bly has his own story as *resumé*. This includes an earlier tale, one cloaked in military fatigues hitched up for the tropics. Even more deeply it harkens back to a boy in his pirate's cap, brandishing a wooden sword as he scales the banisters of a great house in a leafy old neighborhood of Tampa, Florida. He'd fashioned the sword from one of the fence pickets replaced in a neighbor's yard. This goes back well before Bly blew in to Key West from Miami where he'd already done a shadowy decade before *getting real*, which meant getting a real job.

This earlier paramilitary gig was back when Miami was labeled the "Casablanca of the Caribbean." Some young newspaper guy with a passion for the Bogart film no doubt came up with that catchy Casablanca thing later. Bly's version washed up and slid back in real time out of the sixties. There were lots of guys just out of the armed forces about then meandering down to the Sunshine

Chapter 3

State for rumored guerrilla ops—blood and treasure said to be in the offing.

"I was one of those guys," Bly says to a bartender at the Blue Rendezvous of his early Key West era. "That was before I wised up to the life, you know. But by the time I hit Miami I was still filled with piss and vinegar and too much tequila, I guess. All I know for sure, man," Bly ruminates, "was that civilian life bored me out of my gourd. I hated the regimental, regular, military masquerade of organized machismo on parade, but civilian life was like changing the same flat tire all day long, seven days a week. I made a best-efforts tour of southern universities but busted out of each one of those PDQ. I mean I could get through a history class okay, but I'd already seen too much to know I was just getting somebody's version of what happened. I like to read; just being told *what* to read by what date doesn't do it for me. And math—I don't do well with anything that's only got one right answer."

Bly pauses to sip his drink and continues, "So I drifted south. I was like a mongrel dog sniffing down the back alleys of the Third World. Not a clue, no idea, and didn't care what was up with the other two."

"The other two what?" the bartender asks while polishing a glass.

"Worlds, man. I'm on the Third World kick here. So then I woke up one morning in Puerto Rico with a beautiful woman screaming in my ear about me losing her pet monkey in a poker game the night before. She had my boots in her hand, and that was that. So I got on a mission to find a mission, you know. That's what it was."

"Yeah, you and how many other vets?" the bartender asks knowingly. "Veterans of lost causes commanded by the captains of industry playing both sides. Guys trained for jobs in ravaged, sweltering places that still smell like napalm," he adds with a satisfied nod to the polished glass.

The quiet in the bar is broken again by the crack of pool balls coming from the next room. Ducky Durban, the mustachioed bartender, had been Oliphant's first Key West hire. That was when Oliphant had bought out Ducky's bar located on the same prized spot on the bight. Oliphant also acquired the upscale fishing outfitter's shop next door. He completely renovated both together. And against all odds laid by island watchdogs on planning and zoning, Oliphant went up another story above the two to complete the Blue Rendezvous. A brand-new building, it looks like it's been there a hundred years.

So Ducky stayed on as his main man at Oliphant's bar. The old cuss still has the upper body of a powerful gymnast but no legs. He has crossed anchors tattooed on one shoulder and a duck coming up out of the water in a bold circle on the other. He's a veteran too.

"But from a better war, World War II," he puts it. "The South Pacific, Battle of the Coral Sea. I was in the water for twelve hours, but I didn't kick about it," Ducky quips with his typical self-deprecating dry wit, bravely absent of any self-pity.

After the war, he and his wife ran a bar back home in Ketchum, Idaho. There was one in Pensacola after that sans the Ketchum wife. ("She liked taller men," he'd say with a smirk.) Having worked at a busy bar in a military town, Ducky knew the tantalizing rumors of soldierly quests of the sixties, rife in the VFW halls and watering holes like his all around the country. They were the same rumors Irish Bly said he was picking up in Puerto Rico about that time. The buzz was that soldiers of fortune were getting good gigs in South Florida.

"Yeah," Ducky tells Bly, "I made a few referrals myself. Had my contact down in Miami too. I guess we all did."

"Hell," Bly says, "I went straight off the boat to the guys who are supposed to know everything, wanting to find out where the action was. Where to connect, you know? I go to the press. I find this reporter at the *Herald*, and he tells me I ought to check out this place, a boarding house over on SW 4th Street."

"That's like Little Havana, right?"

"Right, lots of talk about Cuba," Bly acknowledges. "That was the hot topic where I was hanging. Haiti was also up on the board. You know, self-anointed president for life, Papa Doc Duvalier, and all that hoodoo voodoo government going on down there."

"Angola, the Congo," Ducky adds, wiping down the bar. *El Ché*, he was in the Congo—Congo-Kinshasa? But I think they'd got him in Bolivia, stirring things up down there by then," Ducky says distantly.

Chapter 3

"Guevara?" Bly asks before answering his own question. "Yeah, Ché Guevara. He was captured by CIA operatives with Bolivian forces for cover and summarily executed in a dirty little hut somewhere up in the mountains. That's how I heard it. But I don't even know who he was fighting for."

"What about the CIA?" Ducky asks vaguely, pushing from behind the bar, his boxy stool rumbling like heavy roller skates over the tiles to the ice bin. "Who were they fighting for?"

"I don't know," Bly answers nonchalantly. "Us, them—whoever was paying the tab, like everybody else I guess. Fighting for justice and freedom."

"Sure," Ducky responds, holding an ice scoop aloft. "Justice as in *just-us*. Freedom as in *free-dumb*. Hey!" he lightens up. "Don't get me wrong. I was up for the adventure, the just cause, you know. I just didn't have the legs for it," Ducky jokes.

So then they talk about Miami. Miami, as Bly found it, rife with commandos training out in the Everglades and shady politicos plotting invasions in the bars and outdoor cafés of Little Havana. Bly reminisces how he (like many of the would-be mercenaries) found his way over to a boarding house, a scruffy vestige of old Miami.

He recalls, "It was run by this gray-haired lady named Nellie Hamilton. She had to be in her seventies by then, but brother, she was a pistol. Had that Granny Smith look, but she was a real spitfire."

According to Bly the place was jammed with testosterone-infused young men in camouflage and olive-drab military clothing equipped in snapped-back fashion for life in the tropics. Bly joked that guys sometimes slept three to a room at Nellie's, the last one in dragging a pallet stashed under one of the beds. He'd had his turn on the floor more than once, Bly tells, stumbling in before dawn from cockfights in an old warehouse down the street.

"It was crazy, man. We had weapons stashed everywhere: under the beds, in the overhead, in Mother Hubbard's storage shack out back."

Irish Bly is confessing to Ducky as anonymously as he had to the same reporter who first tipped him off about Nellie Hamilton's boarding house. He'd lived it. He tells Ducky the backstory, how he'd enlisted in the US Navy and gotten some frogman training on an underwater demolition team in the early days of the *conflict* in Vietnam.

"I got pitched out of UDT though. Didn't have the discipline for it," Bly comments, feigning an apologetic frown. "But I landed in Nam anyway, the brown-water navy, running riverine craft—PBRs. I can't explain it exactly, but I just had a feel for the boats. Driving boats, that was my thing. Did my second tour behind sunglasses with a .45 strapped over my UDT-issue swimsuit. Had a hell of a tan, dark as the dark-leaf cigars I smoked to discourage the flies when things got still. But we got in fast on some pretty good scrapes up the Mekong. Did some damage and got out faster than we went in, which made me a pretty popular guy with my crew, believe me. But I ended up busting out of the Navy altogether. Just another screwed, blued, and tattooed misfit son-of-a-bitch back in the US of A. 'Reckless for life,' my last CO said."

"Sounds like you were a problem child," Ducky observes, polishing a glass.

"Yep, was. I've been kicked out of some pretty good places since too. Hell, I even got kicked out of Puerto Rico. That woman with the monkey I told you about. Her father was a cop. Now how bad is that? Arrived in Miami with a buck sixty-eight in my pocket. I had this newspaper clipping, an article a kid reporter for the *Herald* had done on the Cuban thing. About all the training and maneuvers out in the Glades. So I looked him up, like I said. The air-conditioning in his office was nice, and I milked the conversation for all I could. He pretty much had the skinny on what was going down at the time on the mercenary scene, this newspaper guy did. He turned me on to Ma Hamilton's."

"The place to be for the rest of the story?" Ducky wisecracks.

"Well, let's just say I fit right in with the other misfits," Bly continues. He names names: "F. X. Casey, Ralph Edens, and Little Joe German. He was about six foot three, son of some Kentucky judge. There was a Canadian, William Dempsey, this Finish vet, a Green Beret, Edmund Kolby, and some other wacked-out guys. Some that just went by self-assigned code names: *Skinny* and *Fat Earl*. Jerry Patrick Hemming—he was for real. He was like top sergeant or something around there. Hemming was a big, dangerous cat."

Chapter 3

Bly takes a slow sip of beer, looks wistfully out over the marina, and says, "There never was any money, really. Just a lot of jacked-up training. Most of us couldn't pay the rent on time. So Nellie, she'd let us do yard or kitchen work instead. Mowing, trimming hedges, washing dishes, or whatever. But see, she had some good paying clientele too. They were people just released from mental institutions, their room and board paid for by the state. So it was like a really crazy place, man. I mean, really crazy! You had these senile loonies at the windows drooling in their cups while this hyped-up guy, Hemming, conducted commando drills in Nellie's side yard."

Ducky thought he'd heard of Hemming.

"Could be. Hemming, he got tagged by conspiracy theorists. Something obscure about the Kennedy assassination. They said Lee Harvey Oswald was involved in one of the training operations Hemming ginned up out on No Name Key."

"Was he?"

"Can't say. Wasn't there. I'm a nowhere man, you know. I have a theory that all conspiracy theories are based on perceived coincidences, and there are no real coincidences."

Bly is expert at chumming up sufficient detail to hold his listener's interest. It doesn't escape Ducky, however, that Bly runs a little short on specifics, although he readily recites all the paramilitary plots brewed and thickened in the Miami heat. Telling of his time there, Bly describes the anti-Castro training camps out in the Glades and down into the Keys.

"Somebody was always organizing a mission to Cuba," Bly recalls. "The Bay of Pigs invasion was in the works, but damned few Americans were really in on that. Not in the landing anyway. There were gun-running gigs down to Cuba. That was my first play. Some guys worked both sides like that, you know. But pretty soon Fidel was running the only game in town there. Later, getting guns down to South America, that was always hot. Man, word spread like lightning when somebody new in town was contracting for Africa or Haiti or wanting to toss some Willie Pete at Papa Doc."

Bly ratchets down on some detail regarding this one. He tells about the so-called "Deputies Invasion" when eight men (two Dade

County sheriff's deputies, three former Haitian army officers, and three other *Americans*) left Key West aboard the 55-foot *Molly C*.

"That was about as big a joke as the CBS Invasion up at Marathon. That never got off the ground either."

"Yeah, yeah," Ducky recollects. "Where CBS bought the exclusive rights? Bought themselves their own little war to report."

"Affirmative," Bly acknowledges. "Financed the whole operation so they could get out in front of the news. It was like the first documented episode of the news making the news."

"Some business, the news," Ducky gibes.

"Well, there was no paid *film at 6:00* in '69, believe me, when some of us went up in a Lockheed Constellation. We lifted right off the runway at Miami International and came around with a lean toward the South Caicos in the Bahamas. The plan was to pick up some Haitian commandos who were hopefully trained and waiting on us down there. From the Constellation we were supposed to firebomb the capital and then drop in the invasion forces, maybe fifty Haitians readied for the operation."

Ducky refills Bly's glass.

"But there'd been rumblings in their ranks, these commando cats, all kinds of resentments, bad blood, and talk of reprisals. We didn't know all that. Anyway, the warriors walked. They didn't show. So it was F. X. Casey, Edens, me, and a few more on board the Constellation. That was it. We just looked at each other and agreed with Casey. We weren't going back to Miami with our tails between our legs.

"Casey was the real deal, I'm telling you. Out of all those guys F. X. Casey was the man. That whole Miami scene was like one big machismo snafu. Kind of a world-class liar's contest, particularly the guys coming in gaming up some *top secret* operation. Guys claiming to be CIA who weren't, the real CIA guys saying they were working for somebody else; they weren't. But F. X. Casey, he was a man on a mission—a man among men, as they say. He wasn't the biggest or the baddest if you know what I mean. But he had a brave heart, brave and true."

In the pause following Bly's ongoing account a man and a woman walk in and sequester themselves at the other end of the

Chapter 3

bar. Ducky rolls down and sets them up with drinks. It's a very sophisticated looking woman in a slinky red dress and a biker dude with a shaved head. The biker asks Ducky if he'll turn the volume up on the music playing over the surround sound. It's a song the Righteous Brothers sang. A slow one: "You've Lost That Lovin' Feeling." The biker and the woman in the red dress begin dancing cheek to cheek out from their bar stools. Ducky rolls back to Bly who picks up where he left off.

"Mid-morning, June fourth, the Constellation came round that hilltop outside Port-au-Prince. We swooped down on Papa Doc's palace, but we were having problems with the plane's internal communications system. We kept waiting for the pilot's call, confirmation that we were correctly positioned over the target. I mean we *had* to be close and kept calling for confirmation. Then it came, or so we thought. The pilot was yelling, 'No, no, no!' Hell, we thought he was shouting, 'Go, go, go!' So we're rolling the fire bombs to the cargo door, these drums of gasoline with mini-marine flares strapped to the side for detonation. I'd rigged them all myself. We lit the fuses and kicked the drums out between four hundred and three hundred feet. Then we started hurling the Willie Pete—those white phosphorus bottles. We watched from that wide cargo door while a good pattern of drums exploded across the palace lawn. Then a couple of them lit up some of the shacks clustered around the palace walls. That phosphorus smoke screen made a wild scene with the Willie Pete billowing up in these huge boiling clouds! Brother, they'd have made really great cover for that advance team of commandos. But, like I said, they were back there in the Bahamas in a snit."

Irish Bly drinks deeply into his mug and says, "It must've been on our third run that the Haitian guard opened up on us. You could see helmeted army pouring onto the parapets and running out on the lawn firing up with their .45s. Man, it was pathetic. But then some army freaks with Thompson machine guns show up. And a 50mm suddenly opens fire from somewhere. That maniac laid into us big time. The Constellation was hit thirty-four times, but she kept flying."

Bly examines his beer mug, as if inspecting it for bullet holes, and then goes on, "We made it back to Cap Haitien on the north coast where we'd planned to roll out our commandos and get the guerrilla action going—lead 'em down from the mountains there. The runway was covered with troop transports and trucks mounted with machine guns. That changed our minds, so we headed north, thinking we'd find a good landing strip on some secluded island up there. Then the weather turned against us too. The Constellation was dinged up pretty bad, and she began to smoke and pop. We were running out of fuel. That's when we put down at this US missile-tracking station on the edge of Grand Bahamas Island. It was like crazy, man. This wide-eyed technician comes out and he's shook, seeing all the smoke and bullet holes in the plane. The cargo door is raised, and we jump out in combat uniforms. We've got a stash of weapons behind us sufficient to arm the entire revolution, brother. This science guy, he looks at us like *What-in-the-hell?*"

Bly pauses for effect and then adds, "'Just out for a spin,' Casey says. Cracked us all up, man. It was hilarious. But that's when the Bahamian police showed up. So now I've been kicked out of the Bahamas too. The Bahamians deported all nine of us. Casey, me, and five others from Nellie's along with the rest. Back in Miami we got convicted for violating the so-called Neutrality Act. Served a whole seventy-three days. But that was pretty much it for Miami and the soldier of fortune scene. At least it was for me."

Bly folds his hands on the bar and says, "In a small park down from the *Herald*'s offices I did a debriefing on a bench with my newspaper buddy. This guy was covering that whole Miami mercenary scene. He was a good writer actually, from the inside out. I was just another anonymous source. He was a decent guy who got me my first real job since I'd left the Navy. It was working in the bowels of the newspaper business, and soon I was writing ad copy. Well, selling ads. That's how I got started with this little newspaper of record, one of those old press mullet wrappers that mostly printed legal notices and governmental press releases, requests for bid proposals—that sort of thing. I guess I showed some talent around the water cooler for coming up with a good line or two, something catchy for the ad copy. I learned layout and design.

"So there began my benign years. Fourteen of them to be exact. I was soon stranded on the edge of a world I didn't really want to know. Penny loafers, starched khakis, a white short-sleeved shirt, and a dark tie five days a week for fourteen years. But I dropped the tie after the first seven—I was married by then—and she dropped me after the next seven."

"Been there, done that. Got the T-shirt," Ducky says matter-of-factly as he wipes the bar.

"It wasn't what I wanted either" Bly continues, staring down the beer in his mug. "I mean that I didn't want her to leave, but I didn't want to stay. I did stay a bit longer while I gathered myself back together and sold the house and a nice flats boat I disappeared with most weekends. Gave it all up and let my hair grow. I got my first tattoo since Nam on Key Largo. I took my time and worked my way down the Keys grinding chum, working the docks at first, and then captaining a few charters after that when I'd earned my stripes with these guys around Marathon."

"Things change," Ducky says, as if he doesn't really mean it.

"Yeah," Bly agrees with the same amount of conviction. "Nellie's was already a parking lot by then. My ex-wife, she still looked—I always thought—a lot like Sophia Loren. She was heavier by then and remarried to some guy making big bucks with a high-end used car lot. Jaguars, Mercedes, Porsches, even an occasional Lotus or Lamborghini. I don't know what he did with my rigged out '76 Trans Am. But she got her husband to buy it for twice what it was worth. Said that was the least she could do."

"The least she could do?" Ducky asks, restocking the beer cooler for the bottled brews beneath the bar.

"Yeah, well, I've just always had this idea, this feeling that something, *something* truly extraordinary was going to happen in my life. I mean, I played this notion out when I was just a kid. So that caused us problems, you know? Here I was just another bee in the hive. Just some ordinary working stiff, writing clichéd advertising copy for a paper that was going in somebody's stinking garbage can the next day as I was tapping out the next."

Irish glances around at the dancing couple and then continues, "So there I was. I came home each day to a pleasant neighborhood, a pretty wife, and a nice little stucco bungalow in the palms. The house was painted a soft turquoise with white trim and had gardenias blooming in the yard. And I was one miserable son-of-a-bitch. I just couldn't accept that *this,* you know, that *that* was all there was for me. So I made her a bitch. She was a good woman. Never missed mass on Sundays. Even when we were younger and partied hearty on Saturday nights and made love before dawn in our bed until the sheets were wet, she'd still be up early and off to Sunday mass. But my drinking and leaving towels and skivvies on the bathroom floor, drinking more, reading adventure novels too much, and saying too little except for my constant ranting about something I couldn't find—from car keys to cork screws—all that finally did me in. I'm telling you, I was one miserable bastard and worse than that to live with."

Ducky looks up at Irish Bly squarely and says, "Maybe you had something *extraordinary* there and didn't know it. Hell, you aware you've never even said her name?"

"Yeah, well, it's too sad to say. So I don't have a beautiful, loving wife now, one most guys would fight for. I don't own a house or even a car. Not even a dog. All I have or think I have is that outside chance, the gamble that's back on back. The notion that something, *something* truly extraordinary just might still happen in my life."

After a long silence Ducky asks, "You still handle a fast boat pretty well? Smart craft?"

The biker and the woman in the red dress walk out locking arms as they pass by Bly and Ducky.

"I can fly, brother. Low and fast."

"At night?"

"Like last night."

3.3

In a rosy dawn Bernard Oliphant walks his matched pair of white French bulldogs down Whitehead Street. Their huffing and puffing and snatching opposite of the other on the duel lead are all part of the daily routine. Sometimes Oliphant wears an Olympic style warm-up suit, blue with red piping, *USA* emblazoned on the jacket. With it he couples a *Saints* ball cap, New Orleans being his

Chapter 3

home town. Or if hurried, as he is on this morning, he walks "the girls" in his long luxurious bathrobe and the old panama with the cockeyed brim from a hat rack in his foyer. Either way he is faithful to the morning regimen, with the little dogs dancing about the crepe soles of his Italian-made walking shoes.

On this particular day Bertrand is impatient with his girls. Strolling with one of his cell phones in hand, he scans its vacant face several times for any indication of an incoming call. It wouldn't be unusual for Oliphant to receive a business call or two on these walks. The New Orleans manager of the high-end antique store Oliphant owns on Royal Street might call. There is considerable business on Royal Street with European clientele, several who insist they deal with Oliphant directly. He doesn't mind and rather appreciates their occasional requests. But on this morning Oliphant is clearly expecting a specific call.

Meanwhile the dogs are sniffing and fidgeting at a wrought-iron gate. Oliphant scolds in a sweet, syrupy voice laced with Old South idiom, "Now see he'ah, my sweets, your priss-butts are about to be food for the crows if you don't get along back to the house."

As if they instantly understand, the dogs are off again with Bertrand Oliphant leaning back in tow. They reach the latched gate before the grand old house Bertrand has been restoring for as many years as he's lived in Key West. The tall Victorian structure standing in a narrow yard crowded by tropical plants is already listed on the National Register of historic homes. His unapproved renovations have modernized its interior extravagantly. Even so the house is fully furnished with massive antiques equal to any in his Royal Street shop.

As he arrives at the front steps, the phone begins to buzz in his hand. Oliphant scurries the girls through the massive front door. They drag their
leash over the polished oak floor inside, and he answers, anchoring himself on the old brick of his scalloped front steps.

"Yes?"

A muffled voice speaks. "My friends need tickets."

There were commuter train noises in the background. The voice was known to Oliphant. The caller he knows as "Jonrón."

"Yes, of course."

"He is a very special friend and must have a private box."

"That's fine. It's expensive though, the entire box for one friend."

"There will be three, his mother and girlfriend also. That's it."

"Very well. You have always been most generous to your friends, Jonrón. Very thoughtful, sparing no expense."

"Don't jerk my chain," the voice says tersely into Bertrand's ear. "I know the number."

"Indeed you do." Bertrand replies softly. "When may I expect your instructions?"

There's a long pause. The train could be heard clacking along the cold track.

"Immediately," he says. The phone goes silent, and the call ends.

There is a red Jeep parked across the street. Bertrand looks up as a woman crosses toward him from the vehicle. Her long black hair is shiny as a raven's wing in the morning sun. She carries a brown bag of groceries, pineapple and celery stalks visible above the serrated top of the bag. Deep inside will be bundles of one hundred US hundred-dollar bills, these in bank straps of ten thousand dollars each wrapped in butcher's paper in the bottom of the bag. There will also be three names with contact information typed on an electric typewriter.

Obvious (though he intended it to be veiled) is Bertrand Oliphant's inquiring expression of surprise. The woman approaching is Asian in appearance and slender, rendering her taller in appearance, or so she looks to Oliphant. Her Mandarin eyes are iridescent, a shimmering green seen at arm's length. That close he takes the grocery bag, paying particular notice to the distinctive gold coin she wears on a gold chain around her neck.

While Bertrand Oliphant warily receives the groceries from the woman, further north Jonrón returns the cell phone to a pocket inside his stylish suit jacket. He sees his reflection in the grimy window of the train blinking past, a black cat perched there out on a long, insulated steam pipe beside a closed and shuttered Boston shoe factory.

The red Jeep pulls away from the curb. Oliphant looks back from his door, and the woman's not driving. A man is. Oliphant

Chapter 3

sees his not-quite-familiar face. He has a flat, pasty face with dark eyes. He's wearing a black leather jacket despite the early heat. Oliphant can't quite make the connection or place the guy or think where he's seen him before. But he's pretty sure he's a Russian.

Chapter 4

Words are soldiers of fortune hired by different ideas.

—Maxwell Bodenheim (1892–1954)

THE DOG'S BARKING WAS closer now. I lay deep within the swarm of mosquitoes beneath the camouflage of spiny frond and lattice-like shadow. My hand rested at guard over my grisly face.

Then the dog was upon me. Through mud-streaked fingers I saw his wet nose punching the palmetto fans. His red tongue writhed back over sharp teeth until his barking reached a deafening pitch. The barking seemed beyond the dog himself, as if the sound welled up from that same cavernous dimension where I'd first heard the woman singing. Out of the darkness behind my hand I shuddered as I saw in a feverish, elongated flash a highway bridge low over a dazzling span of water ahead. This was the bridge over the Vica Cut, down in the Keys where US 1 crosses below Marathon.

I saw the pale turquoise water cresting and churning around the pilings ahead, as it does in the tidal rush on that deep cut between the Atlantic and the Gulf of Mexico. I had made my drop and saw myself racing through, the bow rising slightly against the onslaught of a rapid tide. In the early light a red Jeep with a dark soft-top stopped on the bridge. A man in a black leather jacket at the railing positioned himself and fired on me with an automatic weapon, splintering the bow of my boat with a hard rain of gunfire. A sharp pain ripped through my shoulder as I sped under the bridge just a few feet below in the high tide.

Chapter 4

The automatic gunfire chased me into the Gulf while I ran an erratic zigzag course beyond its range. I crouched low at the helm, staying down until I bounced over the wake of a drift boat coming across. Then I turned out into the blustery whitecaps before the distant curtain of storm clouds rising on the horizon.

I'd thought for a while that I had a pursuer. An anonymous craft was coming fast out of the skeletal outline of the archipelago behind me. It trailed my slipstream for a considerable distance toward the storm, or so it seemed. Then there was nothing—not a speck of any color to indicate a suspicious vessel. There was only the silver sheen of the Gulf and a bobbing flock of shrimp boats moored off to the west.

These were shrimpers at anchor together, sleeping in their bunks by day before working their nets again at night. With no urgency-instigated pursuit, I'd managed to rummage through the console for a first-aid kit. I packed my shoulder wound and wrapped gauze tightly with the bandages in the fashion of a shoulder holster over my torn, bloody shirt. That had held me through the day but had given way in the scraping tangle of palmettos. So the bandages hung loose on my body as the hound found me in my nausea and worsening malaise. The dog was sure to bring the girl. Or there was no dog, and I was dreaming again.

4.1

From Bly's front porch swing the Sisters narrate or recite again, as if from an ancient text they've translated and titled *Mirror of the Jaguar Night*. On this late Friday afternoon they describe the brilliant conquistador, craftsman, and shipwright, Martín Lopez, as vital to the story's accurate unfolding. They say that Lopez was to the Cortés adventure what Daedalus was to young Theseus in the Minotaur mythology of the ancient Greeks—a clever and inventive artisan, a jack-of-all-trades, and master of many.

"But Cortés was for Lopez more Minotaur than maze," Doge explains haltingly, as if uncertain of her own analogy.

"He *was* most certainly his captain," Moth asserts. "Lopez could build no labyrinth to contain Cortés. Rather, he built ships that

An Unfinished Sunset

Cortés commissioned and outfitted each with weaponry to assault the watery world of the comely Montezuma."

"Then there were the mines and mints for coinage and a mirror-perfect phantom ship that held treasure for Cortés to sail secretly back to Spain," Doge plunges ahead confidently. "All this was necessary because Cortés had earlier torched and sunk those on which his troops had arrived. You see, they'd become near mutinous with all the horrors and hellishness of the Mexica. With the *flota* at the floor of the emerald bay, they had to fight on now or die among the cacti. So of course there would be blood."

"And treasure! Gold. I'm suddenly thinking of Bezalel," Moth says contemplatively. "Remember that he—also the gifted artisan—was selected to build the Ark of the Covenant? Now there's yet another *where is it now* mystery for you."

Ignoring Moth's biblical supplement, Doge explains that Cortés had successfully sequestered his army in the Aztec capital where they witnessed daily the horrors of the Mexica who bounced bloody bodies relieved of their still-pulsing hearts down the temple steps. The severed heads tumbled and rolled to their Spanish boots. Doge claims further that after the night of horrors, Cortés did more than command Lopez to build him two identical ships. He also had him construct a mint in a hillside above the obscured cove where Lopez melted down silver and gold objects looted from the Mexica. Much of this was the gold and silver booty carried out over the bloody causeway to be made covertly into ingots for his private trove—one he would horde away in a network of limestone caves guarded by his most trusted combatants.

Moth explains further with melancholy, "Many of the precious and jeweled items are described in what is known today as the *Lopez Codex*. That artfully penned listing provides finely drawn illustrations of the numerous items taken, most of which were destroyed for their gold. These were first transported by horse and crude wagon from Totocalco."

"The Palace of the Birds," Moth chirps.

"Ah yes," Doge continues, "the majestic aviary where Montezuma secreted his vast personal treasure. But Lopez and his captive drudges made fast work of most of that booty back at the bay. Laboring at his crude mint, they perched high on the dusty plateau—to be guarded more easily—until the treasure was largely transformed to coinage and rolled on wooden cart wheels down the rocky ramp to the stone quay where two new ships awaited."

"The Tototalco," Moth backtracks, "was actually a complete zoological garden attached to the royal palace. Cortés took command of it too after the fall of Tenochtitlan, the renowned Aztec city that appeared to Cortés and his minions from high above. They saw it first from the pinnacle of a mountain passage, led by the woman, Malinché. It must have been an astonishing spectacle."

"Indeed," says Doge. "They thought the great city, with its astonishing pyramidal architecture, appeared to levitate over the vast, glass-like lake far below."

Irish Bly sits cross-legged on the planking of his porch, his back to the old chifferobe. The throaty burst of a late horn from a cruise ship was sounding down at the docks by the old Custom House. The last refrain of the bell from the Conch Train sprinkled the silence from beyond the barricade of bamboo.

"I'm just curious," Irish inquires, as if seriously perplexed, "is it *Cortés*, as you say? Or *Cortez*, as my fifth grade teacher, Miss Lee, pronounced it? She was gorgeous, Miss Lee. Everything she said was poetry. I lean toward Cortez, myself."

"Well," Consuela Doge instructs abruptly, her elitist tone baring a tinge of accent that sounds to Bly vaguely French, "in English they have two different sounds for *s*, don't they? The voiced and unvoiced. The voiced pronounced with *z*. Perhaps that accounts for the confusion. In any case, we say *Cortés*, as it pleases us to be more authentic."

"Tomato/*tomahto*," Moth snickers.

"Don't be silly, C. C.," Doge scolds her. "Must I beg continually not to have us plummet into nonsense?"

4.2

The Sisters make an impromptu visit to Oliphant's office up in the Blue Rendezvous. They are eager to discuss politics, but it is the political landscape of Mexico in relation to Cuba in 1528 they

An Unfinished Sunset

have in mind. That, as the Sisters insist, must have been the year the mystery ship sailed with the Cortés treasure.

Oliphant sits at his desk before one of J. M. W. Turner's massive oil paintings of a smoky maritime battle between warships, tattered sails aflame. He asks casually by what degree of certainty the recovered treasure they announce is that of the Cortés mystery ship. Or might that ship have found safe harbor while still under sail from its concealed berth in the emerald cove below Vera Cruz?

"Not likely at all," Doge insists. "I'd say the danger of impoundment there by the governor, this Velázquez—Cortés's archenemy—was much too likely. The fact is that the Cortés galleon never intended Havana."

"She may have tried for safe harbor somewhere else on the north coast as the storm came on," Moth offers with a shrug.

"There were many ships like it that sailed," Doge instructs. "They all had names, registries, and manifests known to the House of Trade in Seville. They sailed for the kingdom of Spain. This one sailed for Cortés and for Cortés alone."

"It went down," Doge says. "La Malinché tells us so."

"According to his codex," Moth continues, "it was also Martin Lopez, the shipwright and author of this definitive folio, who designed and constructed the minting tools Cortés required."

"These were molds and stamps," Doge says. "So the Aztec gold and even other Spanish coins—some already stamped at other mints in Mexico—were melted down. The octagonal cobs could be cut and stamped then with their curious emblem: a cross on their face with a crude octopus opposite."

"Thus a phantom ship with newly minted gold," Oliphant sighs, sitting low in his high-backed chair. "Tons of bars and coins with the cross on their face and the octopus opposite."

That was exactly the same sand-washed coin he'd seen around the neck of the woman with the groceries. But Oliphant did not mention this observation.

"Yes," Doge responds. "That, with other treasure items guarded by select seamen and elite soldiers sworn to secrecy and bound by the riches in which they too would share."

Chapter 4

"Had they made it back to Spain," Moth interjects, "which they most certainly did not!"

"Well, Lopez received his reward," Doge huffs. "He stayed on in Mexico, and that is how his vast Mexican estate came to be. It was all inside the cracked and peeling leather-bound box the German found."

"But, yes, to answer directly," Moth adds with a nod, "before a breath of wind ever wafted her sails, before she plunged from the rolling logs to float in that secret jade cove near Vera Cruz, this was already a ghost ship."

They haven't yet spoken of her treasure exactly. Oliphant wants to hear more about that. It was meticulously inventoried, they said.

"Of course," Moth elaborates, "from what we know the treasure was in three chests nearly identical in size and weight. Their fill was coins, or more correctly, *cobscabo de barra*: from the end of a bar."

Moth explains how Lopez likely cut the gold from the end of the bar to make the coin: "Indeed, these were cut from distinctive bars, ones made in octagonal molds filled with the molten gold of Aztec idols, jewelry, and myriad other plundered items."

"My, yes, all the plunder melted down," Doge agrees, "save that of the Mirror of course, which we frankly think was more the salvage of Lopez's sentimentality rather than any Cortés felt."

"Yes, the Mirror," Oliphant wants to know more about that. Did they suppose the base to be solid gold? "I'm curious," he adds, "I've read that the Aztec idols were generally gold-plated or silver-plated, especially the larger ones."

"The jaguars of the mount are *solid* gold," Doge asserts firmly.

"We're not alone in that," Moth agrees eagerly. "Errol Flynn said he certainly thought so too."

"That settles it," Oliphant says with a smile—that smile familiar on the face of the cat that has tasted canary. "Ladies," he says, extending his arms in a long-sleeved guayabera shirt, "you persist in involving me in this little production of yours. Why be coy? I am at your service, but you must know I operate exclusively through my associates and assigns. You've already had considerable conversation with Mr. Bly, I believe."

"Yes," Consuela Doge says unswervingly. "That's why we're here. The coins—the Cortés coins—they've been showing up for years now. Quite naturally we have our suspicion about who's doing the dispensing, initially at least. Of course, we've picked up a few ourselves along the way."

"Oh my, yes, I'd think you'd have your share," says Oliphant. "Likely by the latched and locked chest load," he adds drily.

"But ye-gads," says Moth, "they're bought and sold on eBay these days!"

"And you expect our Mr. Bly to find the dragon who hordes this gold?"

"Not so," Doge says, quite taciturn. "We expect the dragon to find you, my dear Lord Oliphant."

"If he hasn't already," Moss asserts with a steely eye cocked in Oliphant's direction.

"Well, *he* has not," says Oliphant. "Trust me."

"We *don't* trust you!" the Sisters all but shout in unison. Doge continues their caution, saying, "But Bertrand, we know we must throw in with you, so to speak."

"We're running out of time, you see," says Moth. "We must trust someone, and we rather think it is Bly. That is, we trust him to be who he is. Irish Bly is a romantic."

Doge concludes, "You, sir, my dear Mr. Oliphant, are a man after our own fathers' hearts. You, sir, are *the man who owns the boat!* And so we're keen enough to know we should also be talking to *you*."

4.3

On a night within the same week of the Sisters' visit Oliphant puts a match to his cigar at the window of his office up in the Blue Rendezvous. The marina lights float like illuminated hyacinths on the water below. He shields the match from the staccato waft of a ceiling fan with a glass of Widow Jane bourbon in his hand. Pendarvis turns in Oliphant's high-backed desk chair to slide aside a hidden panel behind the desk. A shortwave radio sits on the shelf inside the well-crafted cabinetry. It is by late night transmission out

Chapter 4

of Cuba that Oliphant's next scheduled "rescue" is confirmed. The streaming audio cipher, set to loop continuously until stopped, will confirm the date and time for rendezvous at the exact coordinates provided for some desolate coastal location.

There are many broadcasts like this. These so-called numbers stations transmit from around the globe. No government or private agency ever acknowledges them—shortwave broadcasts in monotonous formats of seven digits said over and over again. The voice, such as the one to which Oliphant and Mercer Pendarvis now listen, is most often a female's. Her unchanging inflection and droning sameness sounds like a machine-made voice. It is similar to those computer-generated messages used by the telephone company except that nothing but the repetitive sequencing of numbers is ever broadcast.

Other numbers stations operate out of Cuba too. Some have been broadcasting for decades from who knows where because atmospheric reflections make direction finding exceedingly difficult. Maybe they're operated for communication with spies across the Florida Straits. Maybe other smugglers use them. Oliphant established this one through his key Cuban contact, Ramón. Only he knows the location from which these broadcasts are made and when that location is changed.

It was Ramón who first recorded his sister's reading of each number in a precise Spanish monotone. It is Ramón who now devises the coded messages to be sent. Each will have a definite beginning and end. They start with an indication of how many number groups the message will contain, repeating each group carefully to establish the matrix from which the sequence may be deciphered. Each sequence will be repeated seven times, each one in the private parlance Oliphant has devised and to which he refers as a *dial*. If the message is authentic, it will contain seven dials.

Somewhere on the coast of Cuba the transmitter broadcasts at certain times on certain nights. Oliphant knows when. He listens for the seven dials:

Uno. Tres. Dos. Diez. Cinco. Uno. Tres. Dos. Diez. Cinco. Uno. Tres. Dos. Diez. Cinco. Uno. Tres. Dos. Diez. Cinco.

Uno. Tres. Dos. Diez. Cinco... six times more.

An Unfinished Sunset

Or, as on this night:
Ocho. Seis. Cuatro. Nueve. Siete. Ocho. Seis. Cuatro. Nueve. Siete Ocho. Seis. Cuatro. Nueve. Siete Ocho. Seis. Cuatro. Nueve. Siete Ocho. Seis. Cuatro. Nueve. Siete ... until the seven dials are completed.

Pendarvis is now skilled in the use of Oliphant's matrix. He decodes the apparently random five-digit groups of numbers through which Ramón encrypts his messages. Pendarvis reads the message out with the aid of a numbered grid now spread upon the glass top of Oliphant's desk. It is a process similar to the intersection of vertical and horizontal coordinates on a road map. In fact, by all appearances it's a nautical map of the Bahamas Pendarvis consults, though the matrix for deciphering Oliphant's code has been skillfully embedded there.

"We're confirmed for the twelfth. ETA Saturday, 2:00 a.m.," Pendarvis says without looking up from his notepad.

"What's our location, Mercer?" Oliphant wants to know.

"It appears to be that north point off the preserve down there."

"Good. I prefer that location. We've been most fortunate in and out of there."

Oliphant takes a long draw on his cigar and exhales slowly. He has been studying the boats tied below, especially the *Mercy*.

"I have a little backup plan in mind, Mercer. We're doubling down on this one," he drawls. "I'm going to want Cobb in at the Marina Hemingway down there. I'm also thinking of a little change of plans for Irish. Those two old hags are too smart by half."

Pendarvis pours himself a drink at the small bar Oliphant keeps in his office before joining him at the window and says, "You do know that the girl handles the boat perfectly well."

"Oh yes," Bertrand Oliphant sighs. "Isn't she a delight? A big surprise in a small package of talent."

Chapter 5

The man who finds his homeland sweet is still a tender beginner; he to whom every soil is as his native one is already strong; but he is perfect to whom the entire world is as a foreign land.

—Hugh of Saint Victor (1096–1141)

THE GIRL WAS SHOUTING to the dog, "Come here, Hobo! What have you got on to now?"

The woman shouted to the girl, "Get that dog back from there, girl. He's got on a snake or somethin'."

The dog wheezed and whined while the girl wrestled him back by his collar. I could see the girl's honey-brown feet. And then, up through the green thatch, her eyes wide in a startled expression.

"Gram! There's a man in here!"

"What're you talkin' about, girl? Get yourself back from there right now!"

"No, for real, Gram! He's dead or somethin'."

"Get yourself back! Don't let that dog go in there," the woman commanded while she hurried toward the house where she kept an old shotgun.

The woman came out with the gun raised, as she would when approaching a rattlesnake or some rabid creature. These did sometimes come up out of the dark hammock ranging the coastal plain behind the house. She quickly walked to where the girl was standing. The dog barked angrily, squirming between the girl's knees and snatching at the double-fisted grip she had on his collar.

"I see him!" the woman shouted. "I see that sucker in there!" Then, in a steadied, commanding voice, she said, "You better come on out from there, right now! *Right now*, you hear?"

I saw the barrel of the shotgun raise a palmetto fan above me, but I could do no more than let the mud-encrusted hand fall from my ashen face.

"Lord, Lord," the woman said.

"What is it, Gram?"

"This ugly white man is shot. Shot bad."

I tried to lift myself to speak from the well of my delirium, but there was only the taste of salt and muck in my mouth. The woman with the long gun, the palmettos, and the girl astride the surging dog with his collar clamped firmly in her small hands—these paled in my queasy vision. All such images drained of color with my return to unconsciousness.

5.1

Much to his own consternation Oliphant is feeling himself oddly off balance with the old girls. He can't quite think why, but ever since they lassoed him into their story of the Mirror of the Jaguar Night, a sort of vertigo had set in. *Perhaps the way into this story was the way out*, he thought to himself. But such thoughts only confounded him further now that the queasiness had set in. More curious still, a specifically described vertigo would enter into the Sisters' lengthy telling of the Jaguar Night tale itself. This recounting would occur on the *Mercy* on a bright October day.

With her diesels rumbling the *Mercy* makes her way out of the marina, the wake of the tall sport fisher rippling over reflections of other sea-going boats with dinghies bobbing alongside. They are going out the main channel, out past the Pier House, the sunset decks, and the great white cruise ship at the Mallory Pier. Then out past the Old Customs House—a massive edifice of red brick crest with terracotta tiles. These are soon at the aft. Captain Asa Cobb lay forward on the throttle, and the *Mercy* cuts a fine spray in the turquoise water out toward the Marquesas.

Chapter 5

Up on the steering deck with the captain Irish Bly is holding his hand to his ball cap. The morning is clear and clean and sweet. Mercer Pendarvis is propped up in the fighting chair on the deck below. Consuela Doge and C. C. Moth are sitting side by side on sturdy deck chairs, watching aft behind the captain and Bly. Each is wearing big sunglasses and long-billed fishing caps—Doge's a bright white, Moth's black with the flap down over her slender neck.

The brawny mate, Estevar, is working his way along the low rail past the cabin to the bow. The *Mercy* gains speed in the open water as the red roof of the Customs House and the steeples and spires of the old town lay back, colorful as a fruit bowl submerging under the blue horizon.

Coming out the Key West Bight, Captain Cobb has his weather-beaten cap cocked against the sun. He is unshaven and has already chomped an unlit cigar down to its half. The *Mercy* crosses the wake of a dive boat striking out ahead. Bly tightens his grip on a handrail beside the console.

Cobb, a consummate storyteller and marina gossip himself, had all but washed out of the sport fishing scene only a few years before. That was when the cost of diesel had gone sky high. Then the fishing went bad, he'd said. Cobb lost the *Mercy* to the bank. So he was reduced to operating a scowling little cabin cruiser out of a rusty bucket of a marina over on Stock Island.

Then along came Estevar, a Cuban refugee, a *rafter* who appeared as a fishing mate on Cobb's boat. Estevar, Cobb always insisted, brought with him luck from the sea.

"You can have all the skill, the best boat and tackle in the world," Cobb would crow, "but me, I'll take Lady Luck any day."

So lucky was Cobb with Estevar aboard that there was some talk on the docks that the colossal Cuban practiced some sort of magic. Estevar might be a *babalawo*, a master of mysticism, some of the other Cubans whispered. He wasn't. That was just green-eyed bar talk among the deck hands in the dives over on Stock Island. But the talk got round to the Blue Rendezvous too.

Meanwhile, on the Key West docks, Estevar had taken on something of a celebrity status among the tournament fishermen. He shyly avoided the hype. According to Cobb, Estevar cared not a whit for all that fine talk. Estevar himself insisted that his gifts were uncertain. But what *was* certain was that the tides of good fortune seemed to be with Cobb now, and they were in full flood. Estevar had long been putting lower-ranked fishermen on the best fish. Cobb, with Oliphant's help, eventually got the *Mercy* back from the bank. Now he was running those giant fish down for top pay by top-tier competitors.

By Boca Grande Cobb's mysterious first mate is standing out on the bow, arms extended, lifting his face as if to a divine light out of which some heavenly aria was flowing from the sky. The huge Cuban is a bull of a man, his muscular torso and massive arms having long worn to tatters the faded chambray of his shirt. Yet, bestial and brutish as he is in appearance, Estevar might well have truly been an *angel unawares*.

He raises himself up on the toes of his bare feet. His mouth shapes something indecipherable, as though he is singing boldly. He brings his arms to cross at his wrists over his barreled chest. Then, bending slightly at his knees, he hauls his heels gradually back to the deck. His left hand over his heart, Estevar shows his rugged profile across his thick shoulder while he makes a broad sweeping gesture with his right like a matador. Then he is on his toes again, reaching sweetly to a gull that had appeared suddenly as if from a hole in the sky.

"Never mind all that," says Captain Cobb. "Maybe he's crazy, I don't know. But I can tell you this, sir. Estevar knows these waters better than I do. I don't know how but he does. He knows the Marquesas as well as he knows the coast over Havana way. He's a fine mate. He knows the fish and how they channel on the Stream. He knows what needs doing on a boat and does it good as any man. There's nothing on any deck he can't operate or repair. I've caught more fine fish with that crazy bastard there than any other man on any boat in the Keys—ever. That's a fact, sir!"

"It's in the record books," Bly affirms.

The record Mercer Pendarvis is after that day is a personal best: a sailfish caught on a fly rod. It had been done before of course, but it still remained one of the more difficult catches to make.

Chapter 5

"So what do you really know of him—Estevar?" Bly asks Cobb up on the bridge. "I mean, what's his story?"

Cobb leans to the helm and recalls, "I guess Fidel let the poor bastard out of a loony bin somewhere, and he got in with the raft people at Mariel in '80. That's what he did—Fidel. For a while there President Carter says, 'Let the people go.' So Fidel says, 'You want 'em? Well here you go.' Then he opens the prisons and asylum gates and chases the inmates like rats or *ratas*, he says, down to the docks at Mariel. There must have been several thousand of 'em mixed in with all the rest. Maybe it was 125,000 over time. Brother, we had Cubans calling charter captains from all over."

Cobb adjusts his course and adds, "Miami mostly, but I got calls from New York and New Jersey myself. The fishing was slow, my man, and the money good. They might go a thousand dollars a head. Did whatever they had to do to get their relatives back across the Straits. Anybody who had a decent boat was going over. Trucks and empty trailers were rammed up every side street and lane in Key West. Hell, you remember that, Irish? You were over on one of the Orbis boats, *Finnegan's Wake*, wasn't it?"

"Yeah man," Bly replies with his hair flagging. "Crazy days. There were some we made money on. Others we got out of the water just because it was the right thing to do."

Estevar was in the latter group according to Cobb. He says that maybe Estevar had spent so much time in the water coming out of Cuba that he had learned to *think* like a fish. The huge Cuban had held to the side of an overcrowded, slowly sinking raft for almost three days. His steel grip and a deliberate, steady scissors kick were all that kept his head and shoulders above the wash.

When the raft began to sink lower into the sea on the second day, a woman with a child in her arms began to shout for Estevar to let go. She was convinced in her panic that his massive body was a drag on the raft, and he would take them all under if he didn't let go. Others would say later that Estevar rolled away from her in the water only to take hold at the other side and kick harder. He held up his corner and perhaps the whole raft with little more than one eye visible—large and dark as that of a bull protruding through the

An Unfinished Sunset

mat of his long mane of hair. That was how Cobb first saw him, he said, on the day he'd pulled him from the sea.

"All I know is he's brought me luck ever since. And goodness me, I needed it! He was grateful and clung to me and my boat from the time I got hold of him. I helped him through the paperwork, and he got me back on the tournaments. Time of my life, sir," Cobb sings merrily. "Time of my life!"

About an hour and three-quarters out they come on the Gulf Stream. Cobb lets back on the throttle. Minutes later Estevar spots a nice school of bonito tailing out of the green-blue side of the stream.

Cobb removes his cigar and warns, "Oh, that's good. Better steady yourselves, lads."

The Sisters look back and see a hammerhead shark just inside the color, coming fast up the green edge. They call to Cobb, Cobb to Pendarvis: "Alrighty, this is when it happens—be ready, my man! This will be a day for the *Mercy*. I can feel it!"

The captain barely gets the words out when Estevar gives out another shout. Sure enough there are three sailfish tailing down sea, heading right for the *Mercy* about forty feet ahead and going under. Estevar is already grabbing the teaser rods from the gunwale and furiously winding in the bait. The captain spins the *Mercy* around and pulls back on the throttle to give chase.

The big fish are about thirty yards out from the sails, running alongside them in the ink-blue water of the Stream. The captain can see them perfectly from the tower, their blazing-fast fins knifing the dark water in the midday sun. Estevar nods up to the captain that he's ready. Cobb puts the *Mercy* forward, cutting in on the billfish so that Estevar can get a teaser out ahead of their sails again. Within seconds the larger sail is gaining speed and slashing at the bait. Estevar roars with delight.

This is what makes the sailfish such a good game for the fly fisher. The sailfish chases bait fearlessly, sometimes right up to the transom. It strikes fiercely again and again to take the bait, becoming angrier and more determined with each miss. Estevar is playing him now, teasing him with the bait to make it seem like a live bonito right before him swimming for its life.

Chapter 5

Suddenly Estevar nods to Pendarvis and lifts the bait from the fish. Mercer steps forward and casts a big white popper over the fish to its side. Cobb shouts down, "Bring it!"

Mercer is already stripping the line back toward the fish as Oliphant, clutching his panama hat, coaches. Pendarvis churns the popper in the water. His lean arms, dark and oiled, work furiously. The sailfish sees it then and whirls back on the popper with his dorsal fin ripping the salt spray. He closes instantly and in a single lunge takes the lure into his sharp, angular mouth and goes under.

Cobb yells, "Hit him! Hit him!"

Pendarvis sets the hooks, lets the line run, sets it again, and then another time with a firm pump of the rod just as the great fish makes its first towering leap—angry and magnificent as a bull in full charge. Everyone sees him now. He has to be more than six feet. Cobb gauges him to be well over eighty pounds and still running hard. Then the great fish slashes at the surface a few times, his head going back and forth dazed-like.

Cobb says hoarsely, "The good ones do that. They just really can't quite believe what's happening. They can't believe they've been taken. Then it hits them, you know, and *wham!*" Cobb slams his hands together. "The bastard comes unglued!"

This one is no exception. He comes up and up and up out of the water, going completely airborne. He shakes from side to side to throw the tandem hooks.

Mercer calls above the fray, "Walllkin' tall, Cap! Woohoo, she's rockin' and rollin', Bertrand!" And then the fish is under again.

"There he goes!" Oliphant calls out. "Boys, he's runnin' for his mama now!"

The fish is a great silver bird taking flight for what seems like a hundred yards, racing on and coming up again with that magnificent dorsal arced against the sky. Then he turns. The fish has pivoted completely and is coming on fast and lunges up again.

"Get that line in now!" Oliphant bawls.

Mercer is reeling like a wild man. The heavy gold watch he's wearing is blazing in the sun, flashing with each furious crank of the reel. And the fish keeps coming on and up again, dancing above the sparkling sheen over the water like he was mad—crazy

An Unfinished Sunset

mad—and he means to put that long bill of his right through the *Mercy* into Mercer's chest.

Then engine smoke appears everywhere when Captain Cobb powers up to keep that giant billfish out of the boat. Suddenly he is bringing her back down, backing down hard because the fish has turned again.

"He's away runnin'!" Oliphant yells excitedly, raising his tumbler of rum. "He's runnin' like a scalded dog now, brother!"

The sailfish spools more than a hundred yards of line out this time. Then, inexplicably, it goes completely slack. The fish is off and running away from the boat, making a final victory leap into the shining path of sun on the water.

Estevar says in his rich baritone, as much to the fish as to anyone on the boat, "Le'em ron. 'Es a beauty, this one. Un beautiful fish. Le'em ron. Le'em ron!"

5.2

Cobb puts the *Mercy* into Garden Key. It's there in the shadow of Fort Jefferson (that colossal island fortress on the Florida Straits), down in the *Mercy's* renovated salon, that their meeting comes to order.

Oliphant has already promised dinner on the afterdeck, but first it must be prepared. Braced comfortably in the cabinet-lined galley, he says, "My dear ladies, you have suggested that there are certain services, such as Irish he'ah may require, in some business you have to do. Services I may provide. So tell us, my sweets, what we must do?"

Consuelo Doge begins boldly, "Well, you know full well it's about treasure, Bertrand. It is about a treasure that has been ours to secure and protect and that ought now to be conveyed to its proper place."

"Oh dear, sounds to be a noble cause," Oliphant moans. "Those are always so expensive."

"Very expensive," Pendarvis agrees. "Always more expensive than simple avarice or greed."

Chapter 5

"Well," Moth sniffs, "the treasure has been quite expensive as it is."

"But of course, but then there's quite a bit of history in all of this," Doge begins to lecture. "Quite a bit of history, yet perhaps no future really, though we are speaking of one of the most exquisite works of art found in the Americas."

"Except that it *is* lost," Moth exclaims. "It *was* found, but now it's lost again."

"Oh my," Oliphant gasps. "I'm listening intently, ladies, as I prepare your dinner."

"Well, it's quite complicated," Moth insists. "No doubt you have read of *La Noche Triste?*"

"The Night of Sorrows?" Doge translates.

"We've all had such a night," Irish Bly grins.

Pendarvis asks Moth, "Exactly to which night do you refer, madam?"

Oliphant turns back with an eyebrow cocked while opening a chilled bottle of wine.

As if aghast at such ignorance, Consuela answers impatiently, "But you must know that when Cortés had conquered the Mexica-Aztec capital, there was a night of depraved slaughter there!"

"A night of horrors," Moth laments, "this night of sorrows. When the Spaniards first saw from on high the vast lake with its island city of Tenochtitlan, they asked each other if they were dreaming. Surely this was the most magnificent city in the world! So tranquil there—the majestic city floating upon the lake beneath that jagged ring of volcanoes. And, for goodness sake, Cortés and his conquistadors had arrived as exalted guests. Yet they impertinently asked among themselves how God could allow *heathens* such splendor."

Oliphant tastes and approves the chardonnay. He then serves each of the others a glass while the Sisters continue.

"Ah yes," says Doge. "Some described the Aztec city as the Venice of the West, insisting that it was surely the largest city on earth. After 40,000 years of fortunate isolation, *this* was the true discovery of the New World."

The Sisters go on to tell how Montezuma welcomed Cortés into his great city:

An Unfinished Sunset

"As if he were a god."

"Which indeed they thought him to be. How lucky for Cortés to arrive in precisely the One-Reed year of 1519, as the Quetzalcoatl legend foretold," Moth adds.

Pendarvis retorts drily, "The old Quetzalcoatl legend, yes."

Oliphant sets aside an ounce or so of the chardonnay in a measuring cup.

Raising a finger, Moth says, "Ah, but aided by the sage advice of his lovely translator and paramour, Malinché, Cortés took *full* advantage of the myth."

"The woman and the legend," Pendarvis playfully acknowledges.

"But what was it, Sister, that our dear poet friend Octavio Paz called the condition in which the Mexica had been put?" Moth asks Doge.

"Sacred vertigo," Doge answers stridently.

"Yes, precisely. The Mexica-Aztec natives were thrust into exactly that: a sacred vertigo," Moth says, looking at Pendarvis.

"Fascinating diagnosis," Oliphant notes while slicing a lemon and lime to juice.

In tones not unlike the salacious delivery of Hollywood gossip Hap Hollister himself the Sisters alternately advance their version of Cortés's La Malinché story. They tell how Cortés, a vassal of King Charles I of Spain (aka Charles V, Holy Roman Emperor), demanded ever more gold. He also insisted that the two large idols be removed from the main temple pyramid in the city. He ordered the human blood scrubbed from the towering steps. Shrines to the Virgin Mary and Saint Christopher were set up in place of the Aztec idols.

"Beautiful Aztec maidens were delivered to his army, although they were required to be baptized before being *of service* to his men," Moth sniffs.

Doge says sternly then, "So all Cortés's demands were met by Montezuma, much to the increasing consternation of his own people."

By now Oliphant is whisking the citrus juice slowly in a saucepan of heavy cream, butter, and wine. He and Pendarvis are casting weary glances between themselves, though the Sisters'

Chapter 5

story has only begun. But neither has his secret citrus beurre blanc begun to thicken.

Doge, oblivious or obsessed, continues, "Well, astonishingly enough, Cortés then made Montezuma his prisoner!"

Moth gasps, "A prisoner in his own palace, mind you. So Cortés—rogue that he was—demanded an enormous ransom of gold."

"Duly delivered!" Doge says with verve and a loud snap of her fingers.

The hatch to the upper deck opens, and Estevar passes down to Pendarvis a tray of snapper filets on crusted ice. C. C. Moth then delivers a soliloquy on other troubles surrounding Cortés. Speaking authoritatively on colonial politics of the Spanish realm, she explains the ongoing feud between Cortés and this man, Velázquez, the governor of Cuba. About the time things were boiling over for Cortés in the temples of the Aztecs she says he learned that a large party of Spaniards had been sent by an envious Velázquez to arrest him for insubordination.

"Cortés marched with his Doña Marina and his best fighters over the causeways to Tenochtitlan and took care of business back on the coast, mind you," Doge reports. "He defeated Narváez, Velázquez's man, and tantalized the survivors of battle with tales of gold in the mesmerizing Aztec capital where he had taken up residence with Doña Marina, his Malinché."

"So *now* his attackers are turned into allies stricken with gold lust," Moth says.

"A sweet bit of business," Oliphant observes over a pot of rice, gauging the crispness of the asparagus in the steamer on the other burner.

"Oh yes," Moth agrees. "Señor Cortés could be quite convincing, as is the nature of men obsessed. So there was the arduous trek back over the *Sierra Madre Oriental* only to find on his return that those he'd left in charge—Alvarado and his captains—had massacred a goodly number of obstinate Aztecs in his absence!"

"There was trouble then?" Pendarvis asks.

Ignoring his jaunty tone, Moth continues on. She relates how the survivors had elected a new emperor, this fierce fellow,

Cuitláhuac, who had ordered his warriors to besiege the palace housing the Spaniards and Montezuma.

"The *Caudillo*," as Doge now refers to Cortés, "ordered Montezuma to speak to his people from a palace balcony, insisting he persuade them to let the conquistadors return to the coast in peace."

"But Montezuma was jeered and heckled. His own people stoned him, injuring him badly," Moth exclaims, nearly rising from the couch.

"It was the end of Montezuma, really," Doge says, "this beautiful, cruel man coming alas to wisdom and enlightenment only to be shaken down by that Spanish gangster, Cortés!"

Oliphant has dipped the filets in egg whites, salted, peppered, and dusted them lightly with flour. He begins to sauté these in a larger pan.

All the while, Irish Bly is drifting off deeply into an imagining about some things Moth had flung his way in an earlier recounting. He wonders through peculiar popup images arising out of her description of Montezuma's private chambers. These are so vivid as to evoke the charred scent of a light ochre dust over the fan-like headdresses and flowing feathered cloaks of *quetzal* and other flamboyant birds. Pots and ampules of exotic oils, potions for love, and pasty remedies for wounds would have perfumed the air. There are gold miniatures of ducks, jaguars, deer, and monkeys. The stone and leather scent of these small, truffle-like cacti, *peyotl*, had flared the nostrils and made wide the eyes of Montezuma, his hand knotted into the hair of his favorite wife in the Mirror, beyond which the Gate of the Eagle lay in ruins.

Doge, getting there, says, "This was the Mirror of the Jaguar Night. Malinché entered the chamber on the Night of Sorrows, and she took it. Anything else that was gold or bejeweled the soldiers and their concubines plundered after she had quit the palace."

"And the stone altar upon which the jaguar sun once stood," Moth adds in little more than a whisper, "lay in jagged pieces on the stones of the square some fifty feet below."

"This," Doge proclaims, "brings us then to La Noche Triste—The Night of Sorrows."

Chapter 5

"The Jaguar Night?" Irish Bly asks thoughtfully and more loudly than he'd intended. Bly thought that Oliphant and Pendarvis might break into applause, but they only nod politely with pursed lips, Oliphant returning immediately to his cuisine.

Doge marches bravely on, saying, "Determined to break out that fateful night, Cortés had the horses' hooves muffled. His underlings shouldered planks to fill in the causeways that had been breached by the Aztecs to prevent their escape."

"But a hag saw this strangely silent procession in silhouette against the carved stones and alerted the city," Moth relays.

The fighting was ferocious, the Sisters say. Many of the Spaniards were mired in the breached passageway, having laden themselves with as much gold as they could possibly carry.

"Oh," says Moth, "but the more treasure they concealed and carried the more vulnerable they became."

"Isn't that the way?" Pendarvis comments rather pensively, absent his earlier unctuousness.

"Well," Doge continues in a cautioning voice, "the Caudillo himself might *not* have survived except that the Aztecs wanted him alive."

"Surely the offering of the heart of such a warrior would win back favor from Huitzilopochtli, their god of war!" Moth exclaims.

According to the Sisters the gap in the causeway (removed to prevent their escape) was soon filled with bodies. The fugitive Spanish and their Indian allies swarmed across, over the slain Spaniards in the hundreds, their native allies, and the Aztec warriors in the thousands filling chockfull the breach.

"But Cortés and his co-conspirator lover—she was still in secret possession of the jeweled obsidian Mirror from Montezuma's chambers—managed to fight their way out of Tenochtitlan," Moth asserts. "They made their exit behind their vanguard and escaped the bloody causeway into the hellacious fiery night."

With grandiloquence Doge says, "This was the great Aztec victory remembered to this very day as La Noche Triste, the Night of Sorrows."

Oliphant then makes an announcement of his own: "Dinner is ready. Captain Cobb has a table set on the afterdeck. Let's dine while we marvel at the massive bulwarks of Fort Jefferson on the sea," and he takes Doge's arm in his.

Like an impresario Pendarvis says, "It's the largest brick structure standing this side of the Atlantic." Adding more quietly to Bly, "Now *there's* a bit of historical trivia for you."

When each one is seated, the white table cloth flutters at their knees in the evening breeze. The great fortress is set out before them like a colossal chess piece upon a board of dusky purple and deep turquoise.

Oliphant asks Doge, "My dear Consuela, is there some particular reason this history you both so brilliantly dramatized need be known by us? I mean, generally speaking or in any particular part if you wish, is what we've been told vital in locating and securing the Mirror now?"

"No, of course not," Doge retorts. "Merely that it's important to tell so that you have some estimable sense of value about what we intend to do about it. We've consulted extensively and at considerable expense with our protégé in Florence, Castellan, on these matters. He's quite the expert, you know?"

"Yes," says Oliphant. "Interestingly enough, I do know him by reputation. Castellan is indeed a foremost authority on the Spanish treasure fleets."

"Well, he has his facts together," Moth adds, "but we have our story. And it's always interesting to revisit the story to see if anything has changed. Things do, you know, over time. Even that which is past—long past—may change in relation to new points of view. Time has a rather kaleidoscopic way of turning things, doesn't it?"

"True," Doge agrees. "You see, we're telling the story, *this* story, and you are now in the story we're telling. And we don't know the end of the story yet, do we?"

"So, to that extent," Moth adds hastily, "it is important that you know what we now know, Mr. Oliphant. Otherwise you won't know later how our plot changes or not. It's important," Moth reiterates. "Besides, Sister and I believe that without a good and proper start expectations are decidedly diminished for a good and proper end."

Chapter 5

"Oh, I do agree," Oliphant drawls over his best vintage bourbon. Out below, a Coast Guard cutter coming in makes for its berth across the ink-like brine of the bay.

5.3

The Sisters' file on Diebolt Krym is tattered and frayed at its edges. Cryptic notations, sketches, and ciphers are scattered like passport stamps over its smudged manila face. In this spacious second story reading room up in the Doge manse Irish Bly scuffs in well-worn leather slides over the polished black marble floors with spidery white veins. Consuela Doge waits behind a large map table at the center of the room.

This is the library, as the Sisters call it. Its walls are indeed lined with bookshelves, each supporting a heavy versicolor of leather tomes and numbered volumes except for the southerly one. That wall is largely glass, transparent, and open to the sea. From ceiling to floor, panels of white-framed windows stretch to the ceiling with an indistinguishable door at the center. It leads to a center balcony, balanced in the recess between the east and west wings of the great house. Outside, beyond the ornamental balustrade of the balcony and the choppy water, is the usual confusion of gulls found about the place.

The Sisters are each dressed in long-sleeved nautical blouses they call *camisaccios*.

"As did the quiet, elegant woman who displayed them in her little shop on the isle of Capri," Consuela informs Bly after his compliments.

Consuela's is black with white bands on the rolled cuffs and sailor's collar. In an overstuffed leather chair nearby C. C. Moth predictably wears a white camisaccio sporting black bands, though the Sisters' long white skirts are precisely the same.

Consuela Doge tosses the Krym file with a flat smack to the glossy top of the claw-footed table and says to Irish Bly, "This is our file on Krym. Diebolt Krym."

"It's time you know about Krym," C. C. Moth adds emphatically. "It's for your own good."

An Unfinished Sunset

Bly acknowledges Moth's caution with a soft frown and shoves his hands deeper into the pockets of the timeworn white dinner jacket he wears over a T-shirt and faded jeans.

"It's known of course," Doge continues, "that German Nazi agents from both the Gestapo and the *Abwehr* or German intelligence agency were operating in Mexico well before World War II. Diebolt Krym's diabolical father and treasure flota fanantic, Helmut Krym, was one of those. He was there. We're certain of that."

"We know this from various sources," Moth insists, "not the least of which is the world-renowned Mexican muralist, Diego Rivera, and Frida Kahlo, one of our favorite artists and a particular friend."

"She—Diego's Rivera's wife, unfortunately," Doge surges ahead.

"Unfortunately?"

"Oh yes," Moth says. "Diego Rivera was a pig. Brilliant and amazingly talented, but a pig. Not as soulless as that monkey with a brush, Picasso, but a pig all the same. Frida was—"

"I'm not an art critic, but I thought he was a genius—Picasso," Bly says in a genuinely perplexed tone.

"Picasso was a genius at being Picasso," Doge plows on haughtily, Moth nodding affirmatively in her wake.

"But Frida, she could be, shall we say ... difficult," Doge continued. "Beautiful in a most exotic way and amazing with color. Surreal, yet evocative of all the great traditions of her ancestors, even to the time of the Aztec Mexica. That's her work there," she says gesturing reverently toward the wall across from Moth. "There, you see it, don't you? Next to the exquisite, passionately mauve landscape entitled *Provence-Alpes-Côte d'Azur* by Dora Marr, another goddess."

"Yet it is Frida. Her *Retrato en Azul*," Moth chimes, her bony finger jabbing the air toward that paintings above the bookcases, "is an antecedent of her piece, *The Frame*, purchased by the Louvre in Paris, you know? But we bought *Retrato en Azul* long before her Paris show, the one that made her famous. We were there too of course, but this was purchased at her studio in Coyocoán. Ah yes," Moth recollects suddenly, as if this is just coming to her, "we acquired ours there where we found Frida first in her *Casa Azul*, the *Colonia del Carmen* neighborhood of Coyoacán in Mexico."

"Such a sensually rousing suburb of Mexico City. But there was nasty business going down with the Nazis in Mexico about then," Doge says abruptly, putting back on track the political topic. "Certain recent disclosures show that Nazi operatives circulated quite freely there and throughout Mexico at that time. Concealed by their various associations in the corridors of wealth and influence, they set about their diabolical espionage against any US interests."

"There was *also* the German pharmaceutical company, I. G. Farben," Moth interjects sharply. "They made the gases, Farben did."

"The gases?"

"For the Nazi death chambers!" C. C. Moth declares in a hissing whisper through her cupped hand.

"Quite so," Doge continues. "Farben had offices in Mexico City. These certainly served as a cover for agents of the Nazi Third Reich. One of those—"

"Helmut Krym!" Moth preempts, half rising from her chair.

"Yes. Krym the elder was also an amateur archeologist, self-styled because he was not university-educated or credentialed or associated with any prestigious institution of any sort, so far as we know. Really," Doge adds stiffly, "he was an opportunist. Nothing more than a treasure hunter at best, a treasure hunter at his worst. And don't think he didn't use his information and rank to raid for treasured artifacts during the war. Especially anything associated with the Spanish treasure fleets."

"Meanwhile," Moth elucidates, "his all but paternally abandoned son, young Diebolt, struggled to keep up appearances in the zealous Hitler Youth movement of the time. He was a boy more given to *Schadenfreude* than any strident success of his own."

"Schadenfreude?"

"Pleasure in seeing others fail," Doge narrows her eyes to explain. "Even as a boy Diebolt would rather trip a fellow in finishing the race than win it outright by his own athleticism and training. Here, have a look at this," Doge proffers, producing a creased, yellowed photograph from the file. "This is Diebolt Krym at fourteen. Notice the icy eyes of a psychotic child, uniformed in black lederhosen and that standard-issue brown shirt, sporting those alarming decorations and badges of the *Deutsche Jugend*."

"Diebolt soldiered on as best he could," Moth observes analytically, "a loner, a sniveling squealer of a cadet with a habit of dwelling enthusiastically on his evil thoughts. But, despite his achievements in the Führer's youth corps, Diebolt could never live up to his stern father's idealistic expectations. No more than Helmut could live up to the fierce expectations he had for himself."

Doge continues their history: "After the war, holding on to the family's much-diminished estate, Helmut was increasingly, impossibly discriminating and entirely unreasonable in his mustachioed egomania. He was a menacing enigma. He held fiercely to his avowed love of home and country, but he was rarely there. Never mind the vanity of his uncorroborated claims to ancient nobility. Helmut Krym was little more than a bully and an obscene grave robber. He was a Bavarian brute who would've been a war criminal had he actually been more than a desk-bound bureaucrat, networking through armed collaborators in the field. And he surely had connections with shady art dealers, coin collectors, and swank pawnbrokers behind bulletproof glass in Berlin. This is shameful stuff," Doge pauses briefly, "the netherworld of art and collectables of true historical significance—an underworld in which the priceless is defiled with a price."

"So!" Moth exclaims with a tone of finality in her voice. "He, Helmut Krym, came home from the war—even if briefly—with a driver on the muddy roads of a shattered world. He returned to his huge timber-framed brick house with its mossy roof and disgusting wild animal carcasses tacked to the walls. All those fantastic skeletal antlers on display in the smoky den of Helmut's deteriorating family estate coming apart despite the best efforts of his subservient wife, Yseult."

"And bitter young son, Diebolt," Doge adds. "The wife didn't matter to Helmut so long as she kept something brewing in those copper pots in the kitchen."

"Frankly, you see," Moth clarifies, "the boy, Diebolt, simply was in the way of Helmut's extended travels to philander and pilfer."

Chapter 5

"Of course," Doge advances immediately, "Helmut always claimed his undertakings and escapades were necessary to reestablish the greater glory of the house of Krym."

"Yeah, I get that—the greed of Helmut Krym," Bly acknowledges with a shrug. "But how does Diebolt link to this business of the Mirror of the Jaguar Night?"

"Oh my, it's a matter of the bad seed, don't you see?" Doge yowls. "Helmut Krym had a thorough knowledge of the sixteenth century Spanish treasure fleets. After all, he was in Spain *before* Mexico. Krym recruited and trained Spanish volunteers there for the Nazi forces."

"In complete liberty Krym explored fully the archives of the *Casa de Contratación*," Moth explains. "The House of the Sixteenth Century that collected all colonial taxes and duties, approved all voyages of exploration and trade, maintained secret information on trade routes, new discoveries, and licensed captains, and administered commercial and maritime law. It remains the principal archival authority on the treasure fleets."

"No Spaniard could sail anywhere without the approval of the Casa," Doge sniffs. "Smuggling, however, often took place in different parts of the vast Spanish empire, with all attempts to evade the *Quinto Real* of course."

"The King's Fifth!" Moth proclaims.

"The *Quinto del Rey*?" Irish gets it right.

"Yes. Precisely," Doge confirms. "Helmut Krym was a serious student of the Casa de Contratación. It's quite possible that he knew before Mexico that there was one or more of the Cortés treasure ships unaccounted for."

"*Known* but unaccounted for," Moth qualifies. "Something there in the archives may have tipped him off, someone or something that advocated he look further in Veracruz, Mexico. We don't know for sure."

"But *something* certainly prompted him," Doge agrees. "Although about that time he was up to his sallow eyeballs equipping Spanish recruits with uniforms for the Russian front."

"You'll remember," Doge maintains with a nod to Bly, "that Franco, dictator then, was sympathetic to the Axis cause. But

Franco had resisted Hitler's advances to bring Spain *formally* into the war."

"So never mind that he *did* allow Spanish volunteers to serve under German arms on the Eastern front," Moth says snidely. "He thus cleverly maintained the *appearance* of Spain's neutrality. All the while he repaid the help Germany provided him during the bloody Spanish Civil War and—"

"And he continued his fight against Bolshevism," Doge finishes Moth's sentence.

"That's how the Spanish 'Blue Division' got formed," Moth says sharply. "And Helmut Krym, the bloody bastard, was in the thick of it."

"Sister," Doge admonishes, "your language!"

Unfazed, Moth rallies on. "But Krym wasn't marched off with the Blue Division to fight Bolsheviks on the Eastern front in their blue shirts of the Falangist movement. That's where the division received its name, you know? Those blue shirts tucked neatly into the khaki trousers favored by the Spanish Foreign Legion."

"Krym—the German officer and insurgent—he shows up in Mexico next, and this is before Frida Kahlo, right?" Bly asks.

"Well no, this was after Frida's show in Paris, but then, yes, she may well have been back in Mexico by the time Krym arrived," Doge assures.

"Anyway, it doesn't matter about Frida at this point. The point is that it would've been *after* he'd pilfered certain properties of the Archive of the Indies in Seville, the archives of the Casa de Contratación, as they're known today," Moth contemplates further. "But you see then, interestingly enough, Helmut is dispatched to Mexico. *Brer Rabbit* to the briar patch!"

Doge picks it up from there and says, "Yes, he'd been quite successful in Spain despite his private obsession with Spanish treasure," patting the file on the table with her thick hand. "So Helmut Krym, loyal to the Führer and adept in his duties, plays the Reich and gets a cushy post in Old Mexico. It's not so surprising that he'd be selected as a special agent to Mexico to work in its Nazi network. Now there's evidence that he quickly became one of the Führer's

Chapter 5

most important operatives in that country. His principal mission: to expand the German espionage network of course."

"But it wasn't Krym who recruited Errol Flynn as a Nazi agent," Moth sings out.

"Errol Flynn!"

"Well, we don't think that's actually so," Doge explains. "Hap Hollister did, but his suspicions were based principally on the coincidence that Flynn and the Nazi spymaster, Hermann Erben, met by happenstance aboard a sailing vessel on its way from Rabaul in the South Seas to Marseilles in France."

"There was more—" Moth insists.

"Even so," Doge interrupts, "it was Flynn's drunken gibberish, some tirade about Jews that more than any documentation or rock-solid evidence implicated him as someone who really did anything for the Reich. As far as Robin Hood being a Nazi goes, I'd say he was doing the same thing with those *volk* as he would later do with Fidel. Simply *in like Flynn*. Always looking for a good time. A real player, as they say these days."

"Most likely," Moth agrees.

"It's a fact though," Doge continues, "that Hermann Erben did come to head German intelligence in Mexico during the war. It was Erben who tasked Krym in Mexico. No real Flynn connection there that we know of, but the Trotsky thing—that gets weird."

"Trotsky?" Irish asks.

"Yes, when the going gets weird, the weird turn pro!" Moth declares, after the gonzo journalist, Hunter S. Thompson, who had once been a Key West neighbor.

"Trotsky, the Russian revolutionary in exile, he was living in Mexico then?"

"Here's the twist, Irish," Doge says in a lower tone. "Recent files released show that Erben and Krym collaborated with Moscow agents in Mexico to kill Trotsky!"

"Hermann Errrrben supervised his assassination," Moth hums.

"Krym," Doge croons, "likely had something to do with the preparations for the murder, taking photographs of the Vienna Street house with its barriers and bodyguards."

An Unfinished Sunset

Doge makes a sound similar to the click of a photo shot: "Click: Trotsky stroking his dog. Click: Trotsky watering his plants. Click: Trotsky drinking coffee, sometimes sipping the fruit of the vine at the garden table with his friends Diego Riviera and Frida Kahlo. Click, click, and click: those were Helmut Krym's photos according to our file. But what Krym was really interested in wasn't a philosophically exhausted Russian politico. It was the Spanish gold—the lost Cortés gold."

"Albeit he didn't know about La Malinché yet," Moth supposes, "our Mirror of the Jaguar Night."

"No, not until Veracruz," Doge agrees.

"Veracruz?"

"Correct," Moth says, rising from her chair and walking to the wall of windows on the sea as if to peer out toward Mexico. "The crumbling old mission there, that's where Krym located a dusty peeling leather box with the ship's manifest inside," she says dreamily.

"What he didn't find was the Codex!" Doge proclaims.

"What codex?"

"The Lopez Codex," Moth says over her shoulder, apparently annoyed that Bly ought to know which, "that was bound up in the Martin Lopez estate and later sold by his heirs for a bundle to a private bidder. It drifted about afterward for a while but landed some years ago in the collection of Sergio Castellan."

"Okay. Who's Castellan?"

"We'll get to Castellan, a former Formula One racing champion, though an invalid after a horrific crash. Yet he is, or was, also a world-renowned authority on the coinage and relics from the sixteenth century treasure fleets. But it's more important to know first about Krym," Doge insists. "We are coming soon to Diebolt."

Moth turns, comes back to the map table, and says, "So Trotsky is dead, and there's nothing to be done about that."

"Politically speaking," Doge goes on, "Diego Rivera was never taken seriously by his comrades. Dear Frida, she was racked with pain by then. A bus crash, wasn't it?"

"But here's the rub," Moth interjects. "There's this connection now, you know, between Mexico and Krym and Cuba. This is after

Chapter 5

the Cortés treasure and our La Malinché. Alas, the Mirror has been found. So it's afterward that Cuban strongman, Fulgencio Batista and his lovely wife, Marta, have possession of most of the treasure along with much of the rest of all Cuban art and historical relics. Fidel routs Batista and, still later—immediately after Camilo crashes—Flynn sets sail for Bimini. So you see the treasure *has* already been found, and shenanigans abound. And who shows up next in Cuba?"

"Helmut Krym, that's who!" Moth proclaims.

"Righto," Doge says. "*Now* the president of Cuba, Fidel Castro, is recruiting former Nazi SS types who worked for the Führer. These thugs are rounded up to help train Fidel's rogue-gone-vogue military and intelligence forces. And here we are at the very height of the Cuban missile crisis set off by Russians—bulls in a china shop if ever there were. Anyway, this is fact: Fidel had already recruited the SS officers according to declassified documents recently released by Germany's secret intelligence agency, the *BND*."

"The *Bundesnachrichtendienst*," Moth clarifies, bracing herself with both bony hands upon the map table. "Might as well have been the B.A.D."

"Indeed. Now Castro invites certain former SS officers to Havana where he's paying them quadruple the salary any had made under the Reich in exchange for their expertise," Doge says. "One of those hastily accepting his offer—"

"Helllmut Krrrym!" Moth announces, as if introducing a professional wrestler to the ring.

"Yes, now Krym is on Castro's payroll as a consultant, and all the while he's after the Cortés treasure. He's knows about the Batista New Year's Eve fiasco. He knows by the time the Revolution rolled into Havana that the city was turned as upside down as it appears in the Camera Obscura."

"Politically speaking of course," Moth says.

"Anyway, we were long gone," Doge adds. "Long before Krym came knocking."

"Yes, Helmut Krym came one night to our door at the house in Miramar, but we were out of Cuba by then," Moth says with a sigh. "That must've done him in, poor Helmut, to have been *so* close to

An Unfinished Sunset

the Mirror. Horrors of horrors, he was later found deceased in his car in *our* driveway, the remains of a crushed glass capsules in his mouth! Gan, the housemaid to whom we entrusted the place, found Helmut. The sharp odor of bitter almonds remained redolent inside the black Benz. We could conclude that his death was suicide by cyanide poisoning!" Moth says aghast.

"But," Doge goes on stalwartly, "according to Gan the driver's side window was down unevenly. Krym's tie was askew, and there were heavy scuff marks on the drive. These together might indicate some kind of struggle. So maybe it was *not* a suicide after all. Who knows?"

"What we do know," Moth says sweetly, "is that Helmut Krym's berated and discounted son, the diabolical Diebolt Krym, will take up where his belligerent father left off."

"It's the one thing he can do to avenge himself against his father," Doge says in the erudite manner of a psychotherapist. "It's just unfinished business, you see? Diebolt Krym can finish what his abusive father, Helmut, could not."

"How ... how do you know all this?" Bly asks haltingly. "Helmut Krym coming to your door? The cyanide? Diebolt the avenger?"

"Lim told us," the Sisters say in unison, each with a reverent cast of their eyes up upon a luminous surreal painting hanging exactly opposite Kahlo's *Retrato en Azul*.

Chapter 6

> Mysterious love, uncertain treasure, has thou more
> of pain or pleasure! Endless torments dwell about thee:
> Yet who would live and live without thee?
>
> —Joseph Addison (1672–1719)

IT HAD TAKEN EVERYTHING the woman and the girl could do to carry me into the house. The girl tied the dog and got into the palmettos with her grandmother to wedge a small shoulder up against my other side.

"You must be least two hundred pounds of full-grown man, I'm tellin' you what," the woman said beneath her breath.

I'd tried to help, though now I found my left knee was injured too. The woman and I grunted and groaned our way by straining, resting, and limping across the yard. The girl helped to steady and guide our awkward formation through the sand and prickly pears before collapsing on the heavy cypress planks of the front steps. We'd rested then, all three together on the steps, as if the travail of those thirty yards from the palmetto thicket had made us a crew.

A shadow from puffy white clouds drifted out of the southeast over the vast expanse of salt grasses before us. I listened to my own heavy breathing and marveled dizzily at the movement of my bloody hand.

"Ooh my days," the woman sighed, shaking her head slowly.

The girl looked up at each of us from the bottom step. I was amazed in my nausea that she seemed not frightened of this gory, rough man sprawled above her.

An Unfinished Sunset

"I'd take some water," I said weakly.

The woman nodded approval to the girl. When the child returned from within the cool darkness of the house, she'd brought two large cups of water. I took one with my good hand. She sat on the top step with her grandmother and shared the other.

"That shot hole in your shoulder has to be tended," the woman declared. "You reckon it caught bone?"

"No," I replied raspingly.

"You a bad man?" the girl asked.

"Hesh-up," the woman said to the girl. "If he is one, he's not gonna say such a thing!"

The woman studied me again. Her cautious eye went the full length of me slumped forward on the step below.

"But look here, Mr. *What-cher-name-is*," she warned, "you don't have us courtin' trouble by gettin' you outta them bushes. We are plain folk doin' what Jesus say do. That's all."

I tried to speak, my voice holding in my throat, and finally gasped, "I don't mean you any harm." I swallowed from the cup again and continued, "I was raised by a Christian woman."

I tried to lift my head but lost consciousness again, my mind's eye opening slowly beyond the field of time to an ancient city in winter.

6.1

Florence, Italy

Castellan looks out of the vaulted bank of windows down to the slate-gray Arno River sluggish with cold. While the city pales in the overcast to a powdery blue, he fixes a panoramic view, zooming sometimes to an errant flurry wresting snow from a distant spire or turret. So skilled is he now with his electronics that he can follow the tumble and chase of a single snowflake into the fragile plume of wood smoke swirling low over the shops along the Ponte Vecchio.

The darkened room where he waits holds warmth that is dense with the fragrance of coffee and overripe fruit. Sitting by the frosted windows, a single gooseneck lamp is lit, adjusted by remote control to focus on freshly cut flowers in a crystal vase beside a glass box

Chapter 6

on the table. The light concentrates around the flowers and yet diffuses throughout the room like a mist over the burnished wood of heavy furniture, objects of art, and bronze statuary. Wisps of light reach the gold leaf of ancient books neatly shelved.

Now again, with the precise twitch of a single set of facial muscles, he changes intention into action. A dot—this small wafer of digital electrodes placed on his forehead—responds instantly as a sturdy aluminum construction rises from the back of his motorized chair. When this gantry locks upright with a soft wheeze, a set of pincers extend up from the metal neck and level horizontally to protrude like the beak of a great water bird into the pond of light.

He twitches again differently, and the length bent back rotates as it lowers and draws down upon itself to clasp the catch of his gold wrist watch. The most meticulous movement is possible for him in this way. The pincers loosen and roll the clasp next so that the latch of the watch bracelet lay open against the black cashmere of his sweater. In his mind the watch would rise from his wrist out over the milky, translucent skin of his now-withered hand. He wills it so with a twitch above his right eye. His intentions are made complete then by the whole motion of the apparatus that brings the watch to a glass box beside the vase of fresh flowers on the carved table. A cushioned cylinder is mounted within the etched glass. It turns in precise motion by a micro-motor mounted within ball bearing rollers. The pincers extend and position to secure the gold wristwatch on the black rubberized fabric over the cylinder. This is how Castellan winds his watch.

A computer screen rises in a single motion from the mahogany desk and locks in place before the row of windows. There is a familiar chime signaling a new e-mail. Castellan secures his motorized chair before the screen. He opens the new message, skillfully maneuvering the remote mouse with a flinch or wince.

An antique Persian rug in excellent condition lay on the oak floor behind him. It comes from his family's estate on the coast road south of Naples, a palatial home accessible only by a bridge to the great rock on which it stands. Many of the priceless marvelously bound books, folios, and ancient artifacts are an inheritance from his mother's Spanish line, dating back to aristocracies

An Unfinished Sunset

of Cortés's era. Castellan keeps these treasures in hermetically sealed museum cabinets, their special glass doors lining the walls behind him. Each cabinet is environmentally controlled. His computer continuously posts real-time readings, including levels for gaseous contaminants, temperature, relative humidity, particulates, and air flow display case by case.

In designed open spaces more modern art pieces hang beneath tracts of gallery lighting. Some are by Zhou Chunya, Miguel Barcelo, and Peter Doig. And one other: a fantastic painting by the Chinese-Cuban artist, Yohan Lim. This, however, is an exquisite copy, made without mechanical devices or a screen. The strange and enchanting image has virtually the textures, tonalities, and hues of the original painting, but it's a copy of the one hanging in the Sisters' manse in Key West.

Among the most valued of Castellan's books and folios are seven codices from the time of the Aztecs. One of these is the so-called Lopez Codex that Cortés himself spirited back to Spain as an illustrated manifest of sorts for the treasures his secret ship contained. Castellan had (as with each of the originals in their vault) made careful electronic copies of each page. The request received for an actual copy of the Lopez drawing of La Malinché, the Mirror of the Jaguar Night, could easily be extracted by Castellan.

With the autumnal hues of the Florentine cityscape across the Arno shimmering in his window glass Castellan makes his congenial response by electronic mail to the Sisters in Key West. He is attaching a copy of a precise drawing, a graphic interpretation of the secret instructions embedded in Lim's final painting. Castellan certifies to the Sisters the exact time and method by which the true location of La Malinché is to be revealed. With a twitch of his nose the e-mail is sent.

6.2

As if it were a wisp of sea foam high upon the indigo sky, the crescent moon remains visible in the early afternoon. Now the shade of a flowering Poinciana tree down on Caroline canopies the spacious balcony where Rachel Perl stands brushing the thick curls

Chapter 6

of her long dark hair. This is the garage apartment she rents adjacent to a shabby Victorian. Her cell phone vibrates with a clipped staccato buzz on the glass top of a weathered wicker table close by. Undisturbed, a large rooster occupies one — a spangled Claret of which dozens were crossbred down through generations from some escaped fighting cock on the island. The rooster is sometimes Rachel's pet. He decides when. Her speaking voice is soft and husky in the absence of any earlier conversation.

"Hello?"

"Ciao, Rachel! Consuela Doge here."

"Good morning," she answers, mystified that Doge should call and that she even has her cell phone number, though she knows the older woman from parties at Bertrand Oliphant's home. She also sees the Sisters around often enough, especially on Sundays, when she performs with the Balassi brothers out on Mallory Square.

"Rachel," Doge plunges on, "Sister and I were just talking about the grape harvest bullfights we watched in Arles when we lived in France. And about how we made our way through that rowdy crowd — the vendors hawking peanuts, ice cream, delightful beignets — all sorts of things. There was a peculiar little fellow who sold seat cushions in all the bright colors. But we always brought our own, don't you know, to sit upon the stone steps of the old Roman amphitheater. That's where the blood lust would occur. We disapproved of the killing and bloodcurdling cheers but were aficionados of the matador's silent opera, acted out on those sunlit ochre sands below."

"I see?" Rachel says, the tone of her voice shaping a question as to relevance. The rooster crows without warning.

"Well, the point of it is … *that* is," Consuela surges on, "we've witnessed a good many things over our years, Sister and I. Not all pleasant either. Not at all. Sometimes the most beautiful to be damned."

"Yes, indeed," Rachel hears C. C. Moth agree in the background. "Not all pleasant, to be sure."

"In fact," Doge states emphatically into the phone, "some were downright bloody. We saw *all* the gruesome newsreels featuring the Battle of Stalingrad in a dingy little theater in London, didn't we?

And, my God, we walked those narrow paths along the towering precipice above Omaha Beach, our Memorial Day corsages beaten down unmercifully by lofting winds. That's where our boys—the gallant 2nd Rangers—were thrashed horridly while they so bravely scaled the bloody cliffs of Normandy. And then there was the Ali/Cooper fight out in Wembley. We were there too, you know? The old stadium at Wembley. Not that modern monstrosity of today but the stately, sophisticated Wembley. We were there when Ali fought Henry Cooper. *Enry's 'Ammer*, they called it, Cooper's famous left hook. How marvelous to see it come down. But beautiful Ali was a dancer masquerading as a boxer, wasn't he?"

"*Cassius Clay* then, Sister," Moth corrects from nearby. "He wasn't Mohammed Ali *yet*."

"Well, even so, it was bloody, bloody, that fight. That's *my* point," Doge huffs. "Simply horrid! Cooper, you see, was a bleeder. Tough as a rail spike but a bleeder."

Rachel waits silently.

"Are you there?" Doge wants to know.

"Yes. Just listening," Rachel Perl answers, waiting for some nexus Doge might eventually make to her and the balcony where she now stood gazing over the rooftops to the tall masts and boat antennae bobbing gently in the marinas.

Doge delivers then. "You see, we know keenly, dear Rachel, the danger to which you now submit yourself. We do know, Rachel. And we also know that, like Cooper, you're a bleeder too, dear," Doge says compassionately. "We know your heart, Rachel. And we want you to know that *we* do *know* and yet trust you in your zeal, as we would the real Joan of Arc or Buffy the Vampire Slayer. Strong, spirited women whose transcendental lives and legendary stories have elevated humankind with their mystique, ethereal beauty, wisdom, virtue, grace, and kindness. Their exceptional courage, really."

"Thank you ... I think," Rachel replies amidst her confusion over what the call from Doge is actually about.

"Not to be mentioned," Doge answers stiffly at the other end of the line. "Not to be mentioned, dear. This call never happened."

Chapter 6

The abrupt clank of Doge slamming her telephone receiver to its cradle ends the conversation such as it was. Back at their manse by the sea a pensive Consuela Doge's hand still rests on the heavy telephone on the massive library table. Its shiny mahogany top is rimmed an inch in with a checkered stripe of ivory and jet. C. C. Moth is occupied at her telescope before the high arching library window on the sea.

"Speaking of auguries," she says vaguely to Doge, "I wonder exactly what signs Mars and Pluto—the planets of war and transformation—were transiting when Cortés descended on the Aztecs? Just what was that juxtaposition when La Malinché was pinched from Montezuma's bed chambers? And, more pertinent to the present, I'm curious as to our friend Irish Bly's astrological sign. Do we know his birth date?"

"Auguries? Who is speaking of auguries anyway?" Doge asks indignantly, though she doesn't intend exactly that tone. "Just what divinations do you have in mind?"

Moth remains occupied at her telescope. Doge says more melodiously then, "And do you *really* think it's relevant, Sister?"

"Relevant-shmelevant," Moth replies, looking far out to sea where a sailboat regatta of multicolored sails is cutting an expansive course through the turquoise water. "To quote Jung, our preferred psychologist, 'Astrology represents the summation of all the psychological knowledge of antiquity.' Yohan Lim knew astrology. He was a surreptitious, clandestine master of it in his art."

"There's something to that," Doge agrees, coming closer.

"I do so miss his brilliant knowledge of the stars," Moth laments, keeping her eye on a purple sail by the number-nine buoy. "He had an uncanny knack—something innate, I should think—for interpreting the heavenly bodies in their courses. It's as easy to miss as it is plain to see everywhere in his art."

"I quite agree," Doge says sadly. "It was as if he could read God's own handwriting across the heavens."

"Well, yes, as I think about it ... layer upon mysterious layer of meaning juxtaposed with perfect nonsense in his paintings," Moth remarks through momentary distraction by the purple sail overtaking a green one beyond the buoy. Then she adds spritely, "It

An Unfinished Sunset

simply occurs to me that if Irish Bly is going to journey truly for the recovery of the Mirror, we should know something deeper and more insightful about his character."

"Yes," Doge agrees. "Rachel Perl, we know."

"Well, I'd put money on him being a restless Sagittarian," Moth asserts as she stands erect. "He has all of that old bachelor nonconformity and gypsy wanderlust. Probably a moon in Aries, don't you think, giving him a childlike impulsiveness with faith in his own instincts?"

"Yes," Doge acknowledges, taking a turn at the telescope herself. "Confident even to the exclusion of everyone else's ideas and abilities. That just may be Bly."

"Aries *is* ruled by Mars," Moth says, as if connecting dots.

"Mars—the god of war!" Doge announces bravely while she adjusts her focus on the regatta.

"So that connects Bly to this mysterious mercenary background of his," C. C. Moth says.

"Well, if you insist on analyzing him in this way," Doge declares, "then we'll have to find out his exact birth time so as to generate a proper chart revealing his ascendant and other important aspects. No use prattling about it is there, Sister? If we're to do a deep background on him, we must do it with a cosmic thoroughness."

"Certainly," assures C. C. Moth, standing even more erect and pleased to have brought Doge around to her idea rather than the routine other way around (though they always ended up in the same place).

The two stand silently before the colossal arch of the window when Moth says, "We must see what we can wheedle out of our friend Irish at our Friday afternoon mélanges."

"We'll do it subtly from his porch swing, chalice in hand, I should think," Doge muses. "But make no mistake about it, Sister. The pure light of Rachel Perl is ascending in Irish Bly's tawdry universe. It blazes powerfully as any actual star we may astrologically chart."

6.3

Suspended above the cascade of yacht shadow in the aqua marina all is silent below the surface while no screw turns. Then the sound of the diver's regulator breathes in *oooooh* and breathes out *paaaah*. The bubbles he casts off gurgle up to the surface sheen over the Key West Bight. With a series of slight kicks the diver ascends above his long supple fins, surfacing slowly now with the yellow compressor hose trailing serpentine in the effervescence.

Irish Bly pulls himself up on the dock at the A&B Marina. He spits out his regulator with water beading from his wet suit. The noisy compressor is switched off by an unseen hand behind him. Bly removes his mask and sits with his fins dangling while he rakes back his neoprene dive hood, letting loose, long, champagne-colored rivulets of hair fall to his burnished shoulders.

"Whew!" he gasps without looking back at Rachel Perl sitting cross-legged behind him on the white sea locker.

"You've been down a long time," she says, and Bly nods in acknowledgment.

Bly has that day scraped and scrubbed the bottoms of a fifty-six-foot sport fisher and a thirty-five-foot sailboat, feeling his way around below in the aquatic shadows that cascade the line of world-class boats back to their berths. Using a trowel-like tool of his own design, he breathes steadily as he works with the yellow hose that's streaming.

"These boats," Bly says matter-of-factly, "they don't stay clean long. Barnacles are good for business though. The paint collects this thin algae film within weeks. A few months down here and the hull will be flush with a full beard. So then she's slower, takes on damage to the hull."

"It's important?"

"Three dollars a foot important to me," Bly replies.

After a pause—one long enough to cause Bly to look back—Rachel says finally, "I had a strange call today, Irish."

"Yeah?"

"Yeah. Consuela Doge, you know her? And C. C. Moth?"

"Sure, I've seen them around. Here and there, you know. Sometimes at Oliphant's parties."

"Irish, what do they know about ... about Cuba?"

"They know everything about Cuba."

"*Everything* what?"

"Well, for starters, they lived in Cuba back in the day. Fidel propped his boots up in their salon and smoked his cigars and talked politics and the literature of the barrios and the bodegas with them till all hours of the night. That's how they tell it, though they say they somehow got on the wrong side of the aisle with him."

"That's not what I mean."

"Okay. They know I go down to Cuba now if that's what you're asking. I didn't know they knew that *you* go too. But then that's not surprising, not really, that they know—or that they know anything at all."

"Everything, you mean?"

"Yes, anything and everything. They're quite resourceful, the Sisters."

"I sense that. I saw them deep in conversation with Oliphant at one of his parties. He was waving his whiskey glass about, as if gesturing toward the tall paintings on his wall. But I had a curious feeling they weren't talking about art at all."

"No, likely not, and that may have been the night he gave me the nod and sent the old girls in my direction with their crazy tale of this Mirror of the Jaguar Night."

"Sounds like something out of some forties-era action hero serial: *Mirror of the Jaguar Night!*" Rachel intones in her best movie trailer announcer voice.

"No, it's the real deal. I'm pretty sure now, but who knows?"

"So, dude, what *is* it?"

"It's the Aztec Mirror we are to retrieve from its hiding place down in Cuba. Somewhere in Havana, as they tell it."

"You're not serious. I hate it when you try to play me."

As if he'd been hiding in plain sight, Irish begins openly to fill Rachel in on the story of La Malinché, the Mirror, and its convoluted history from the mystical cave in the hills of Malinalco in Mexico to the lakeside temple mount of Montezuma. He speaks

Chapter 6

of Cortés and the conquistador's native guide and lover (whom he would call Doña Marina, also known as Malinché). Bly stops just short of the wind that fills the sails of the mystery ship to be lost at sea.

Though briefly interrupted by his short intermission to rinse and change in the marina's shower room, Bly carries his tale seamlessly to the outdoor café where they now sit at a table in sight of the harbor. There, into the remains of the day, they talk in the evening shade of bougainvillea twined in trellises above. He recounts the provenance of the Mirror up to the time of Yohan Lim. Bly wipes away the table-top map he's made of the Cuban coastline, a sketch he completed with condensation from his beer bottle on the laminated surface. Rachel sits back and slides her fingers through the thick curls of her hair, her dark eyes gleaming like freshly washed grapes.

Almost bemused, she says, "You've made this whole thing up, Irish."

"No. It's all true. I really think so now."

"Why do I listen to you? Why, no, wait! I *do* know why," Rachel exclaims with ersatz glee. "It's the insane stories you tell, that's why. True or not. I never know anyway, but I love the ones you recount about your childhood and your grandmother. Not to mention that you gave yourself a nickname, some sobriquet that includes names both first and last. And if that's not crazy enough, you carry this name into adulthood to wave about like a pirate's flag. And then you come roaring around in a Navy patrol boat on some muddy river in Viet Nam with all your bizarre soldier of fortune stories about launching wacko wars in the Caribbean from Mother Hubbard's boarding house up in Miami no less. My God! Who in their right mind would believe such fantastical things?"

"I believe them."

"Well, this one, Irish, really? A lost Aztec treasure in the form of a mirror of onyx and gold?"

"Obsidian. The Mirror is mounted between golden jaguars with emerald eyes. A male and female that meet and nuzzle at the top. Their bodies angle out to form a triangular mount for the Mirror,

An Unfinished Sunset

and their hind legs and long entwined tails create its base. That's La Malinché, the Sisters' Mirror of the Jaguar Night."

"And you know where it is?"

"I know where to look. Where to begin to look, that is."

"Because the Sisters told you, these *über* eccentrics out of the nineteenth century who dart around Key West in their flamingo pink Citroën convertible? Please. You are made for each other, Irish—you and your Sisters—you know that?"

Bly sits up straight and says with a confident smile, "Yes. Yes, I do."

"Brother," she huffs incredulously while tapping her sandal on the limestone floor. "You really do believe this story."

"Yes."

"Well, if any of it is true and you expect me to follow you down to Cuba like some giddy Alice down the rabbit warren—"

"It's all quite possible, you know. But true or not, I've come quite a long way in my life for this."

Rachel pushes back her dark hair, shields her eyes against the late sun over the swollen harbor, and says softly, "Same old Irish. Same old paradise."

Chapter 7

> I give it to you not that you may remember time, but that you might forget it now and then for a moment and not spend all of your breath trying to conquer it.
>
> — from *The Sound and the Fury*, William Faulkner (1897–1962)

Lying up in the high bed, I was supported by an abundance of pillows stuffed behind my shoulders. I put a sore hand to my disheveled head and felt a warm breeze entering through the gauzy curtains flapping at the screened window. It ruffled the clean white bed sheet, rolled down to air the claw-like palmetto scratches roiling red beneath the greasy ointment smeared across my torso. That ointment bore a vaguely familiar, comforting scent. The thick bandage on my shoulder had been changed again. The girl said my name. Then she said my name again, or so it seemed in coming to.

Opening my eyes slowly with a deliberate blink, I brought her into focus at the foot of the bed. I pondered drowsily how she'd know the surname to which I was born. I didn't ask yet. Another sluggish quandary interceded as I was correspondingly curious to find myself in this strange bed, not remembering how I'd gotten there. Moreover I didn't know how to map my rough landing— neither the day nor the sand through the hourglass. Despite some discordant earlier acquaintance with her voice, I did not know the girl waiting now for me to speak.

Yet there she stood, smartly erect, with loosely brushed tangles of Bahamian-like tresses framing her bright face, the polished ebony of her deeply piercing eyes tempered by an inquisitive smile.

An Unfinished Sunset

Something about her demeanor conveyed plainly that she'd waited at the foot of the bed for some time, waiting with intrigue and mild amusement until some secret of mine might be revealed. In my fevered murmurings she must have prompted certain unintended information.

I looked around the small scrubbed room. My torn, blood-speckled shirt had been washed, mended, and folded on a bedside chair. Alongside were my grimy khakis, now clean and neatly draped on a chair arm. From the window by the chair I could see the long narrow boardwalk out to the tidal creek with glimpses of its mirror-like surface in a slow drift through the salt grasses.

"I'm thirsty," I rasped, looking back to the girl.

She pointed to a small jelly glass beside a crockery pitcher on the bedside table. I pushed myself up higher on the pillows. There was water in the glass, but I took up the pitcher, turned it in my hand, and drank gratefully. I lay back looking at the girl, resting the pitcher on my belly, and drinking small gulps after that without averting my eyes from hers.

"I ain't scared of you," she said, raising herself.

"You don't have to be."

"Gram says you're not hurt bad as she first thought. That bullet cut clean through, more like it dug a ditch in your shoulder. She say you lost a lot of blood though."

I looked out the window again. A flotilla of puffy white clouds was coming up like the great billowing sails of sailing ships on the horizon.

"Do you know Cedar Key?" I asked.

"Yeah. Course I do. It's out over yonder," she gestured with a bob of her head toward the open window.

I drank from the pitcher again.

"How far?"

"Why is that?"

"That?"

"That where you's going, Cedar Key?"

"I'm just getting my bearings. I don't know where I'm going right now."

"You not going anywhere, Gram said. You's still hurt pretty bad."

Chapter 7

"How'd you know my name?" I asked her then.

"You told me."

"I told you?"

"Yeah, I ask you while you was still out and mumblin' some mumbo jumbo. And you said, 'Red Man.'"

My eyes narrowed with prying amusement. Red man. *Redmond*, I deciphered without saying so aloud. How long had it been since I'd said my own true name or even acknowledged it at all? I lay back deeper into the pillows with a perplexed smile. *Red Man*, Redmond. I'd evidently answered earlier from some dank chamber of my unconsciousness while she stood by.

"Yes sir," the girl assured me, crossing her arms over her chest. "You say your name is Red Man."

My eyes were closed by then. I was already adrift, letting go again in the outgoing tide of a restorative sleep. Entwined in my dozing, vestiges of authentic events sprouted iridescently and blossomed fantastically while the girl went outside to tempt blue crabs to a chicken's neck bone she'd tied to a hand line out on the sun-scoured dock.

7.1

Havana, Cuba

A vintage red automobile careens onto the Malecón after the pink Vespa, the scooter coming upright in the metallic streaming of cars around the seafront boulevard with its famed esplanade and seawall shaping the coastline beneath the crumbling pastel facade of the old city. The cinnamon-colored '58 Buick is blasting salsa-fused hip hop from its opened windows. The driver is drumming his thick fingers on the steering wheel and slapping the dash intermittently, as if smacking the ride cymbal on a drum set.

His passenger, a German who just flew in from Argentina, sits up front. He's wearing dark sunglasses that appear still darker against his taut milky skin and closely cut platinum hair brushed forward.

"Este soy yo!" the driver shouts over the music to his passenger.

The German nods and smiles quizzically, uncertain of his translation. Something about the music, he thinks. The driver's shaved head bobs rhythmically above his massive shoulders, bouncing like a big brown balloon—*boom bompa boom*—against the threadbare headboard. Then he reaches out and slaps the dashboard again. The music gets louder. So does the driver.

"*Este soy yo!*"

"*Si, es bueno!*" the German ventures to shout back.

The driver throws back his head and laughs incredulously. The pink Vespa darts for an outside lane. The driver's size 16 high-top basketball shoe hammers the accelerator to the floor. The Buick leaps playfully after the flamingo-colored scooter.

Arielle Vega, the oldest woman to have performed regularly with the national dance troupe, *Danza Contemporánea de Cuba*, is wringing the Vespa's handlebar for speed. In her early sixties now, she has choreographed and taught with such vigor that she maintains an athletic (if aging) dancer's physique. From the German's vantage point on the Malecón this woman, darting about on the pink scooter ahead, might have been thirty or so, albeit she is driving more recklessly than an audacious teenager.

Vega races in a high-pitched whine past an olive drab military truck with soldiers riding beneath a canvas tarp with the Buick tailing. The German looks up at the soldiers as they pass. They are each clean shaven, not rough bearded like the revolutionaries in similar uniforms who had come out of the Sierra Madres with Fidel more than half a century earlier. One of the soldiers looks down through the sideboards. He seems puzzled to notice the old German's nearly translucent profile flick by in the blue smudge of the Buick banging out hip hop as it passes.

Vega leans inward on the curve and accelerates again to right herself, zipping through the cavernous shadow of the tunnel before the *Vedado*. Then the sun is shining brightly in the straightaway. For a cloudless day the sea is lively, churning over the outcroppings of mossy stone. It tosses chalky green water in silvery bursts, the breakers lunging up as dazzling specters of great silver fish rising and then arching back to swallow their own tails in the surf along the wall.

Long trails of a colorful scarf knotted at the nape of Arielle Vega's neck pop in the wind behind her. Her shoulders are firm,

Chapter 7

her carriage taut, yet she is entirely agile as she maneuvers through the heavy traffic.

Despite having received a rather detailed physical description, the German did not immediately recognize Arielle Vega when she'd sought him out on his arrival. He had already cleared Cuban Customs and was waiting at the baggage claim while one of the many police officers had his sniff dog, a Spaniel, working the luggage circulating on the carousel. There had been a fierce tapping on the glass behind him. A throng of habaneras, friends, and family members of passengers with taxi drivers (and no doubt a few grifters) were pressing against the Plexiglas for eager observations of the newly arrived. Then he saw the woman in the bright headscarf pecking at the window with fingernails as red as her lips.

Arielle, the woman in the arabesque headscarf, observes that the German has spotted her. Her own eyes widen. She vigorously jabs her pointing finger at him, invoking in his mind some gypsy clairvoyant accusing him of a dark crime. The German points back at himself as if to ask, *Do you mean ... me?*

Arielle Vega nods enthusiastically. She gestures repeatedly at the German and then back at herself, as if to say "You/me! You/me! You are *with me!*"

A blue uniformed policeman comes up and directs the onlookers back behind a red barrier. The German is confident that the woman still signaling to him is indeed Arielle Vega—the one with whom his lodging had been arranged by email.

When he comes out of the terminal, she is waiting straight ahead. Arielle's intensely dark eyes and lustrous complexion strike him first. She's wearing running shoes, a white knee-length spandex leotard, and a pink bandeau under her turquoise tank top. Arielle Vega is indeed an exotic sort. Her edgy manner suggests a woman more highly strung than he may have anticipated, though he knows from his dossier that Vega had earlier been a dancer of extraordinary grace and considerable renown. This was before "some trouble."

Outside the terminal she approaches the German as a dancer still, her practiced composure erect and poised. Arielle Vega does

An Unfinished Sunset

not ask but rather announces in English (as each knew the other to speak), "You are Colonel Diebolt Krym."

"Yes," he says, "And you are Arielle Vega," he announces as directly in a distinctly *Bühnendeutsch* accent, altering his parochial dialect, one more likely to be associated with Nazis dispersed after the war.

"*Si, si!*" Arielle answers busily. "Of course, of course!" she adds, already gesturing toward the gigantic young man in baggy shorts to pick up Krym's large leather valise. "Your driver. Your driver," she repeats herself twice, as Krym soon learns it is her custom to do. "Hermanito. Okay? Hermanito!"

"Yes, I understand."

"Do you? You do." Arielle Vega whirls off abruptly out into the temporary parking area where elastic gaggles of the newly arrived are expanding and contracting around parked and departing vehicles of every vintage, shape, and color.

Krym, a tall man and slender enough to wear his clothes well, appears dwarfed by the massive Hermanito, who packs his XXL T-shirt with bulging arms and wears immense basketball shoes without socks. Hermanito's head and face are shaved as smooth as a Spanish onion. It occurs to Krym that in an earlier era he might have been a gigantic Basque strongman in some nomadic multinational traveling circus. Like the ones he'd seen as a boy in Bavaria.

Hermanito picks up Krym's leather valise as Arielle sharply instructs in Spanish. The bag, well-packed for several weeks of travel, looks no larger than a small sack of bread in Hermanito's hand. The giant effortlessly motions with the valise for Krym to follow.

They pass by all manner of vintage American cars, as well as boxy Russian Ladas and Moskviches in the drab colors of the more recent political era. At a considerable distance they come to the Buick, waiting with its polished chrome bumper and grill forming a toothy grin.

Hermanito's music explodes from the dashboard on ignition. The car vibrates with *rap Cubano* as they dart forward to become immediately immersed in the tangled snail's pace traffic, jammed and unruly in its unscrambling and emptying upon the Malecón.

Chapter 7

Hitchhikers—older mustachioed men wearing the straw hats of the *campo* and the cane fields—hold out their hands. So do young girls in tights, women in doctor's coats, and men with briefcases wearing guayaberas or jeans and T-shirts with rock bands and tractor advertising.

"*Esta es Cuba,*" Hermanito shouts above his music. "*Esta es Cuba.*"

They no sooner veer from their chase on the Malecón than Arielle races up a low-slung curb into a blind alley. She goes perhaps a hundred feet up the cobbled incline, braking instantly before a huge set of ancient wooden doors above a high, worn, stone step. The Buick comes to a squeaking stop abreast of her. Hermanito nods affirmatively to Krym and rolls out with hip hop still reverberating in the canyon-like confines of their destination.

While Arielle wrestles a large key in the door's ornate lock, Krym examines the alley, as if considering all prospects of escape in the dense blue shade between tall buildings facing opposite on the parallel boulevards. This is a space between, above which tiny birds flit noisily high upon the drain tiles exposed to a sky now softening with the twilight.

Arielle waves Krym in. A service elevator in the dank hallway leads from the rear door to a vacant lobby. The plate-glass windows on the street are waxen with street grime from the busy boulevard. The two elevators don't work and haven't for a long time.

"*Es Cuba, Es Cuba,*" Arielle mutters nonchalantly, gesturing toward the mangled wiring exposed in the elevator's dismantled control panel.

They enter a lobby of marble tiles, barren but for a dusty green velvet sofa stacked with dog-eared ledgers. A broad marble staircase ascends from the center of the room to an upper mezzanine level. As they climb up the steps, Krym looks back from the swerve of the railing to see down to the traffic moving in darkened blotches and smudges along the boulevard.

At the back of the mezzanine the dimly lit stairs continue against the back wall with wooden handrails on decorative wrought iron palings visible up four flights more. Krym follows Arielle to the fourth floor landing easily enough, especially for a man of his

An Unfinished Sunset

advanced years. Arielle peers down to find Hermanito struggling up with the valise. The youthful giant puffs into her view, and she begins to scold him.

"*Es fumar cigarillos! No cigarillos! Basta!*"

Her distinctively raspy voice reverberates within the stairwell while Hermanito's heavy shoes scuff the marble stone steps more rapidly in annoyed response. The third floor room she shows Krym is actually more of a studio apartment in this building Arielle Vega manages now as a *casa particular*, a private house licensed for guest accommodations in the city. It is spacious and seems perhaps more so because of the sparse furnishings situated unevenly across its magnificent oak floor. There is a private tiled bathroom. Arielle points to a bucket under the lavatory that could be filled with heated water for a soak in the tub if he prefers. The water in the shower runs cold. This is not a tourist's hotel.

"*Esta es Cuba,*" she says again. "*Esta es Cuba.*"

Arielle opens the tall louvered windows and narrow doors to a balcony large enough for a small table and chairs. There is an excellent view of the city from there. The balcony looks down upon the Paseo de Marti and the Prado—another famous promenade—this succession of parks cascading down the tree-lined median of the boulevard to the Malecón.

Hermanito sets down the valise and waits until Arielle and Krym return from the balcony. Krym goes over to pay him, but Arielle shoos the man-child out the door, not allowing payment or a single courtesy from Krym. This has already been taken care of, she insists. Just as abruptly she makes for the door herself, offering a quick curtsy before saying, "Tonight will be dinner. This is important. You will come down to number two, *dose*, yes? *Dose?* When you are bathed and rested if you wish. Now you *should* rest. Good-bye."

The door closes loudly behind her. The apartment has a freshly scrubbed appearance. It is exceedingly clean, even if the paint is flecked and the plaster chipped from the brick here and there. The wood floor hasn't been polished recently, but it is burnished by time and well swabbed with a damp mop. The heavy oak furniture in the rooms has the obvious appearance of office furniture except for the

Chapter 7

bed and the dresser that stand in a broad alcove opposite the terrace doors. Both are of simple, fine construction. Across from the bathroom a painting in a chipped frame hangs on the back wall. It appears to Krym to be skillfully done, even if it is a rather hideous depiction of native women dancing in a fire-lit pagan ceremony of some sort.

Krym decides in favor of a shower after his long flight and somewhat perilous drive in from the airport. He lays out a clean shirt and underwear. Then he sits on the bed with his shaving kit in his lap. From it he extracts the various parts of an improvised firearm designed to fire 22-caliber ammunition. This easily assembled instrument is made from apparently innocuous items sometimes preferred by hit men and assassins. It is a handgun, simple to construct because it requires a minimum of precision parts. The barrel is a large ink pen's metal sheath that fits to a repurposed Zippo lighter that becomes the chamber. What appears to be a small mahogany cufflink box forms the grip. The cufflinks themselves provide the hammer and firing pin. Everything necessary to make a lethal weapon is located in that leather shaving kit. Krym takes it with him into the bathroom.

He has showered, having welcomed the cold water after the initial jolt without curse or complaint. While he dresses, Krym's nostrils detect a waft of tobacco smoke stirred in his direction by the ceiling fan. Curious about the source, he crosses the room cautiously and finishes buttoning his shirt. He stands before the balcony doors. The sound of the traffic below is more distinct there. Then a voice says pleasantly from the balcony, "Good evening, Señor Krym. Welcome to Cuba. Welcome to *Habana*."

A small, well-groomed man of about Krym's age sits at the wrought iron table. His thinning silver hair is combed straight back over the bronzed skin of a noble head. His eyes have an Asian cast. The gentleman's hands rest on the table top, one folded over the other, with a lit cigarette protruding from between the fingers on top.

Krym addresses him in Spanish with surprise, *"Buenas tarde."*

"Yes, I hope you don't mind; I let myself in. The door was open. You were ... occupied," the man says with a shrug. "Anyway, it's important we speak. English is okay?"

"The door may have been unlocked," Krym replies drily. "It certainly wasn't open."

"Oh yes, so then you may be more correct. I did attempt the door myself. You were engaged. And, as the door did open, I let myself in. Exactly that." Extending his hand to the opposite chair, he adds, "But as I have said, it's important we speak. Please—"

Krym moves to the parapet. There is a lull in the traffic noise from the boulevard below. He responds, "You must first tell me who you are. What is your business with me?"

"Forgive me. I should introduce myself, I know. It is better just now that you do not know my name. That may be telling you too much for your own good." He pauses, thinking, and then says, "I do not ask that you trust me. Simply that you listen to me. You may decide later if I am a friend or at least useful to you or not. You see, I know why you are here, Colonel Krym. This is very dangerous business—your business here. You must know this. No?"

"Is it? I'm told the island is very safe for *touristas*," Krym replies, raking his slender fingers back through his short-cropped hair.

The visitor takes a long, pensive draw on his cigarette and then exhales slowly, saying, "But you are not truly a tourist, Herr Krym." He cautions with an almost comical scowl, "You have come as a *bandito* at best."

Krym laughs snidely and responds, "Do you see me armed and dangerous, my anonymous amigo?"

"You are a comrade in arms with dangerous associates who wish to possess certain treasures that belong to the people of Cuba. You know this. You are familiar with danger, am I not correct?"

"I have known danger of course," Krym shrugs.

The visitor shakes his head solemnly and continues, "Herr Krym, since 1959 thousands of works of art and historical treasures of Cuban patrimony—many of them from private residences of Cuban families that fled this country—have been disposed of by prominent members of the party elite. I myself witnessed many of these taken to large warehouses in *Avenida del Puerto*. They were later sold through *Cubartimpex*, a foreign trade enterprise, for a considerable profit all around the world—even in the US—under various auspices. I know this to be true."

Chapter 7

"Yes, and ..."

"Only a few years ago Sotheby's of London held an auction of a multimillion-dollar collection of Cuban art, previously in the care of the Museum of Havana. Christie's of London had already auctioned off Cuban works. They were said to be salvaged from abandoned homes of departed diplomats, even if I admit many to be from the estates of those fleeing for their lives when the Revolution came. They were not all from these homes or estates. *Ansorena*, a Spanish gallery in Madrid, hosted a sale paid for by the Cuban government. I know this personally. Items from the Museum of Decorative Arts, the *Museo Bacardí*, have found their way to international galleries, their auction houses, and into the hands of re-sellers like you. Similarly, though by a far more clandestine route, Bertrand Oliphant of New Orleans and Key West—your benefactor, I believe—recently held a private sale in New Orleans. Buyers or their representatives flew in from around the globe to attend. Art pieces and artifacts sold that very night were from the priceless collections of the Napoleonic Museum, right here in the Vedado. You were there, Herr Krym."

Krym sits expressionless, though a hint of surprise registers in his ice-blue eyes.

"Your Mr. Oliphant," the gentleman intruder continues as he smokes, "he has also acquired and resold items from the Montané Archeological Museum at the University of Havana. You spoke with Mr. Oliphant about them at his party in New Orleans. There are perhaps other encounters of which I am unaware. But of these I know."

"Do you?" Krym asks dryly. "Do you *really* know? I am *not* to be associated with this man, Oliphant," Krym says tersely, his eyes narrowing. "I am *not* Oliphant's man. Do *you* understand?"

"I understand that hundreds of lots sold have been described as decorations and objects from diplomatic residences in Havana. Yes! The 'diplomatic residences' were in reality the private homes of Cuban families whose properties had been confiscated by the Revolution. My family was one of them, except that I stayed, Herr Krym. I played the game and made a life in the ruins or rather kept my life here. Cuba is my home. And so eventually I have become both a victim and a conspirator in the sale of 138 paintings valued

An Unfinished Sunset

now at more than $18 million dollars. This event occurred in Milan, Italy, at the *Casa Della Aste*, Milan's *Instituto Italiano Realize*. I was present when these pieces were sold at auction after approval for export from the Cuban Ministry of Culture. That was on March 12, 1994. It is a day of dishonor marked in my memory."

Krym shrugs.

The anonymous guest continues, "Perhaps $40 million dollars in valuable books too. These have been sold from once-private libraries but also from the Cuban National Library and institutions, most to Western Europeans through East Berlin. I know this. But there are also dealers—like this Mr. Oliphant you disavow—located in Montreal, Buenos Aires, Mexico City, Madrid, Barcelona, and London. They pay dearly for a single page, a hand-painted map ripped from a leather-bound book somewhere in my country. Who knows where? There are so many."

The Asian gentleman pauses to light another cigarette, adding, "I have not yet spoken of important government documents stolen from Cuban archives. Thousands from the National Archives and the National Library have been systematically sold to dealers worldwide. The stamps and seals of these institutions are easily identifiable on books and documents. They clearly indicate their place of origin, but these are no obstacle to the greedy."

He is momentarily silent. Krym looks at him blankly, and then the man with almond-shaped eyes and silver hair continues calmly, "This is no secret elsewhere. Many of our most valuable rare books, illustrated with period maps and engravings, have disappeared from archives and libraries. What of the two copies of the *Libro de los Ingenious* illustrated by Laplante? They mysteriously disappeared from the *Palacio del Junco*, the Matanzas Museum. Similar works, such as a rare edition of Miahle engravings, have disappeared from the library of the *Sociedad Económica de Amigos del Pais*. I can list even more."

Stubbing out his cigarette, the man adds with resignation, "But, to be fair, these despicable things also occurred before Fidel. You know this. Batista, he did as much, more's the pity, because his lovely wife, Marta, was a darling of the art world here. This is what I think. But you must know that Batista removed art and artifacts by the freight box load to his private little museum in Daytona in Florida, the US. Art treasures by artists and craftsmen of such magnificent and historic proportions that they are priceless and irreplaceable. So there they are to this day. On that fateful New Year's Eve when he fled the revolution, Batista—and over one hundred of his family and friends—flew to *Ciudad Trujillo*, the Dominican Republic. He took into exile, with all his entourage, a fortune estimated at more than $300 million, perhaps $700 million in fine art and cash."

Krym shifts his weight and casts his eyes uneasily down to the Prado.

"I am getting closer, am I not, Herr Krym, to the purpose of your coming to this, the Pearl of the Caribbean? It was thought for many years that the Mirror, which is called La Malinché, was surely aboard Batista's plane that night of the New Year's flight. Am I not *correcto*—right?"

Krym makes no response, his icy eyes latch firmly as pincers onto the stranger's face. The visitor stands and straightens his suit jacket smartly.

"Well," the gentleman says finally, "it wasn't. La Malinché wasn't on the plane. Marta had made it a gift to her husband, just as Malinché, the Dõna Marina of Cortés, had made it a gift to her conquistador lover. Marta also loved Batista, and he—Batista—was fascinated by the Mirror. But it wasn't on the plane on the night of their final exile, my friend."

"Your little history lesson holds no interest for me, señor," Krym responds snidely.

The impeccable *Cubano* massages the antique cigarette case between his brown hands. He sits pensively a moment longer with his hands folded on the table. Krym watches without compassion as the diminutive, dignified man nods in acquiescence with a shrug. He knows Krym's repulsed reaction full well without looking up. He stands and goes immediately to the balcony door.

"La Malinché, the Mirror, is still here in Cuba, and you know it now for certain, Herr Krym," he says with a nod. "And I know this. You have come back for her."

The gentleman returns the cigarette case to a pocket inside his jacket. Krym's hand begins to lift within his trousers pocket. The man's hand returns empty from inside his jacket. He merely shrugs solemnly and disappears from the balcony. The heavy apartment door shuts after him with a hollow clank over the tiles.

Krym remains at the table on the balcony with the zip gun in his pocket. He gazes into the last of the twilight while a deep purple storm front moves in over the bay. Down below, the usual evening chatter and sounds of traffic waft up while headlights stir on the pale facades of the once-grand architecture down the Paseo Prado.

To himself, beneath his sour breath through stained teeth, he calls after the departed visitor, *"Heuchler!"* Hypocrite!

7.2

A page of the *Kong Wah Po* newspaper tumbles in the windy street in Havana's Chinatown. It lodges against the tire of a cream-colored boxy van parked on the cobblestone curb. A slender woman in black jeans stuffed into her high boots steps out. She's wearing a tailored military-style jacket absent of any insignia. Her raven hair flags in the wind, and the newspaper tumbles again, as if pouncing after her until she crosses through an alleyway to the *Calle Cuchillo*. This is a street reserved for pedestrian traffic now. It is where the restaurants and the Chinese social clubs are—the Calle Cuchillo—Knife Street.

Oriental music, bamboo-fluted and melodic, descends leaf-like from small speaker boxes in an upper-story window. Pale orange curtains flutter around an old woman there, her Cantonese eyes gazing wearily upon the narrow street where now the woman in high boots avoids a lengthy configuration of adults in T-shirts practicing Tai Chi.

The barrio is a labyrinth of Spanish colonial architecture festooned with colorful paper lanterns and bright storefront signage in Chinese characters. Now that the state is friendly with China again, the *Barrio Chino* is included in its travel promotions. The Calle Cuchillo in particular is busy with tourists, many of them Asian. Yet more of these are there than the diminishing numbers of

Chapter 7

Chinese-Cuban restaurateurs, shopkeepers, customers, hucksters, bystanders, and other passersby of that descent.

The woman from the van disappears from the crowded street down from the Fan-Tan restaurant. A heavy door, slid open for decades against the cracked and peeling stucco wall, gives entry to ornate floor tiles of an antechamber. A security guard once sat behind a small desk there, the weather stripping its veneer over time. The woman opens a smaller door inside one larger to subtle shafts of sunlight, blue through the hoary dust and grime over high windows on either side. The warehouse interior is vast and cavernous. Formerly a busy facility processing mangoes and guava for shipment, the cement floor sprawls shabbily across the long-disused space.

The hollow wooden sound of the woman's boots echoes in the emptiness. Pigeons stir from the high rafters. Their silvery wings rouse a shushing sound and quiver the narrow columns of light.

This was once the property of a wealthy Chinese-Cuban family descended from their émigré ancestor, Guan Po Lim. He had been among the first desperate Chinese to arrive on the island, fleeing from famine in the mid-1800s, when thousands of Chinese contract workers were brought to labor in the sugar fields. Their conditions would be little better than those of the African slaves they toiled alongside except that, according to the term of their contracts, repatriation to their homeland would be possible after eight years of chastening servitude. At least they had a choice, given that they were able to raise the return passage. Most did.

But, like Guan Po, many chose to stay and settle permanently in Cuba. Virtually all were male coolies from the Cantonese countryside. Their practice of buying slave women and freeing them expressly for marriage built families. Later waves of immigration brought Chinese women too, but few purely Chinese families (like the Lim line) would remain into contemporary times.

Despite their tendency to form tightknit communities, sharp class divisions also developed among Chinese Cubans. A large number remained as coolies in the fields or became domestic workers or small shopkeepers who barely scraped by. But a few became wealthy business owners. Some, like the grandson of Guan

An Unfinished Sunset

Po, established vast business interests with extensive international connections.

The Lim trade was in mango and guava exports. That ended, however, with the Revolution in 1959. The warehouse and port properties, the farmland and orchards, the luxurious colonial house in the Barrio Chino, along with the comfortable ranch house in the *campo*, were all lost to the new order. Oscar Lim, who by then managed the family holdings, escaped with as many relatives and as much Lim wealth as he could manage. He boarded a company plane to rebuild the collective business in Miami.

His two brothers remained though—each for his own reason. Luis Lim was the youngest of these. Despite his direct ties to the Batista regime, Luis had shrewdly doubled down sufficiently to covertly establish his credentials as a Batista insider friendly with the "spirit and soul" of the Revolution. Luis (who secretly despised Batista) had served as a cultural attaché in the dictator's regime. It was in this capacity that he became a close advisor to Marta Batista, Cuba's First Lady. She was an ardent admirer and faithful supporter of Cuba's museums and art collections. Luis would unhappily lose his ties with Marta Batista and yet survive Castro in Cuba quite well.

By the time of Marta's desperate, now historic New Year's night flight from Cuba with her husband, Luis was essentially the First Lady's personal assistant. Be that as it may, in the last flight out Batista himself made sure Luis Lim was left quite literally waiting in the wings. Luis's admiration (even if unspoken) for Batista's wife had not escaped the sharply instinctive sense of mistrust the Cuban strongman possessed. He craftily and deliberately left Luis behind. Fulgencio Batista knew what his wife did not: Luis Lim was silently and painfully in love with Marta Batista. In the last-minute panic, Luis was sent back to the palatial bedroom by Batista for the Mirror, La Malinché. He was thereby conspiratorially detained until the dictator's plane was in the air.

The oldest brother, though listed as a business partner (even if in name and monthly stipend only), also remained in Cuba. This was not a conscious choice he made between regimes. It was out of obliviousness and self-prescribed obscurity that he stayed behind.

Chapter 7

An eccentric artist of increasing reputation, his name — as he signed his strangely dreamlike paintings — was Yohan Lim.

The last painting to be "signed" by Yohan Lim (though not with his name) was the cryptic masterwork now hanging high opposite the Kahlo in the Sisters' Key West library. More recently others had been on the market. Occasionally a collector might sell. And there were the fractured pieces later recovered from Lim's rubbish bin. Also the pilfered pieces — incomplete castoffs scavenged long ago from his abandoned studio and sold. Occasional forgeries and fakes too. One of the most famous art auction houses had recently been embarrassed and scandalized by one of those. Unknown to but a few, however, was this one — the last authentic work of Yohan Lim, smuggled out of Cuba into the care of Consuela Doge and C. C. Moth.

Of this one they had made a single fine print for Sergio Castellan in Florence so that he could accurately advise them or confirm, as it were, about the symbolism in the painting according to his expertise and keen ability to decipher treasure maps. They were certain that Lim's last painting represented (or at least contained) an important secret about La Malinché.

Now, a quarter century on, the hard, chambered sound of the woman's boots are rising from the cement floor to a dull staccato ring, echoing then upon metal stairs riveted against the back wall. Deep inside the old Lim warehouse they ascend abruptly along iron railings. The steps extend in the dusky heights over a platform to an upper office.

Lourdes Lim, Yohan Lim's niece, lets herself in. She flips an antiquated light switch inside the door. The long rectangular-windowed office is illuminated with a yellowish light. From the floor it looks as if a railway passenger car suspended in the dark had suddenly been lit from within. At the last this space was Yohan Lim's studio. In later years his most important work had been executed beneath the skylight there in *el viejo Almacén*, in the old warehouse where Lim lived and worked as a recluse without permission or persecution.

Though small and bald, Yohan Lim was a sturdily built man, his head statuesque, with startlingly bright, jet-black eyes. His was a workman's body even though he had always carried himself in a most regal manner.

By the time his paintings were endorsed by all the best galleries, Lim's art was characterized by a strange polymorphism comprised of a curious juxtaposition of aspects of humans, animals, and plants, creating outrageous hybrid creatures. His works were dense compositions inspired by the primitive origins and lush tropical landscapes of his island *patria*. Influences of the native Taino people, the early Spanish, the Africans, and the Chinese all appear in vivid, complex portraits of contemporized Cuban culture. As grotesque as many of his figures seem, they also evoke a lustrous, shimmering quality, enhanced by each painting's steamy mood and unmistakably the pane of glass that is both canvas and translucent varnish for his work.

Yohan Lim's greatest creations (those proclaimed to be masterpieces in the highest echelons of the art world) were achieved by a mysterious, eccentric technique. He would arrange a collection of objects before a slightly convex dark mirror. Their mirror image he would then capture on a glass surface, meticulously tracing their outlines with brush and paint. The pane of glass was his canvas, and the mirror's amalgamated, synthesized reflections were his subjects. In this way the images were *carried through* on the glass.

To accomplish this extraordinary effect Lim painted backward from the traditional method. His working image was painted on the back of the glass. So, to be correct, when viewed from the front, the painting must be completed as a reversal. Lim's astonishing technique required details and accents that would ordinarily be painted last to be painted first.

"Yes, 'the first shall be last,'" Doge had once observed to Bly in a gentle reflection, some offhand reference to a Bible verse learned in early studies at her Episcopalian grade school. It's a reference, Doge thinks, appropriate to Yohan Lim in other ways too. But she confuses herself by quibbling inwardly with her own correlations and parallels before getting them said.

In any case, Lim's was excruciatingly painstaking work that he accomplished with the help of a pair of watchmaker's spectacles, the lenses of which were mounted with a series of adjustable loupes for magnifications of increasing intensity. The spectacle loupes were important to both Lim's artistic skill and optical acuity in the proper placement of his fine brush. For it would not be possible to make corrections afterward, not without destroying the underlying work. So it was, with a deft concentration akin to one-pointed meditation, that Yohan Lim applied individual brushstrokes correctly, with each action optically and sequentially in reverse.

There is something more to be observed about Lim's work, particularly as achieved through the dark glass. Halations, curiously similar to the so-called *disks of confusion*, were produced in the focus of an optical lens. These confusions appear as artistic technique in Lim's paintings. Each is precisely proportioned to distortions made by the Mirror. Yohan Lim translated these as spherical spots of time using high-toned paints. They are like small globes of light functioning as a sort of time capsule within each of his greatest paintings. Some objects within are barely recognizable; others, in part or whole, are easily recognizable.

For example, the spot of light we see in the ivory eye of a dark-skinned woman might be seen on closer examination as an elaborate orb, like one might observe in the diffused lighting from a street lamp along the Prado. Within each orb objects appear. Some are abstract while others stand out in brilliant clarity. Each of these carefully selected *objetos cubano*—be they of bird or banana leaf, a rolled cigar, or the sensual shape of a woman's supple breast—all integrate (however obscurely) to form an optical reality entirely unique to Yohan Lim.

According to art critics today the spheres of light and imagery suspended within his orbs are Lim's virtual signature. These are each more fascinating as they occur in direct relation to certain infinitesimal, crystalline anomalies over the polished surface of the dark Mirror that Lim used to create his masterworks. The Mirror is a map to his work, even as his final work becomes a map to the Mirror itself. In any case, it is these exquisite disks of confusion that eventually won Yohan Lim an unexpected critical acclaim and worldwide fame. But he was almost dead by then.

Lim knew his end was at hand. So that is why, months before his death, he abandoned his work with the special Mirror, the same one the Sisters had entrusted to him those many years ago. It was that which he referred to as *El Espejo de la Noche Jaguar*, the Mirror of the Jaguar Night. Lim made his careful plan then to hide the Mirror so that it could be found later, when and by whom he intended. The intricate instructions for that plan were contained within the luminous disks suspended in his last painting, *Number 111*. That is the painting he sent secretly to Consuela Doge and C. C. Moth.

The mirror of course is the Mirror of the Cortés treasure: La Malinché. It is the Sisters who had entrusted it to Yohan Lim and the one by which he had established his fame. When Yohan Lim first marveled at the object in the salon of their Miramar house, he had no idea what it would ultimately mean to him. The Sisters trusted Yohan Lim above all others, just as they trusted art over science, politics, personal position, or profits—especially those made by the backs and sweat of others. It is why they trusted Yohan over his brother, Luis.

"We knew Luis could not trust himself," Moth explained more than once. "So why should we?"

Now Yohan wanted La Malinché back in the Sisters' safe-keeping, thereby reversing its historical circumstances in a manner not unlike a dramatization of one of his disks of confusion. It was all quite clearly contained within one of the orbs found in piece *Number 111*. Lim urged that the Mirror be ultimately returned by the Sisters to its very place of origin, deep in the historic lands of the Mexica.

The Sisters agreed. They'd said so to Irish Bly over mojitos made without scant sugar (but with extra mint). Their mutual intention was to *put things right*. The Mirror ought to be returned, they said, to that cave of ancient sorcerers in the Mexican hills of Malinalco—its mystical stairway entrance flanked to this very day by two great jaguars.

7.3

Crossing in the night, the *Mercy* is coming out the Hawks Channel off Key West, loping gently in the light chop against a

Chapter 7

darkening sky. Mercer Pendarvis stands alongside Asa Cobb, the crusty crab boat captain steering from the fly bridge. Cobb had put the *Mercy* on a familiar course of 203°T, the winds being favorable. Out on the bow, sitting cross-legged with his long hair flagging, is Irish Bly.

A cold front had passed through the day before, so Cobb is making good time in the crossing. Seasoned mariners know not to cross the Gulf Stream during a cold front. That's when the north wind strikes, making the wind-over-tide effect trouble for smaller boats.

"The churning she takes fore and aft the axis of the Stream out there, it's like riding the thrashing tail of a sea monster," Cobb growls, his smelly cigar stub wedged at the whiskered corner of his mouth.

So the seas have settled ahead of their crossing, the prevailing easterlies returning to the Straits barely making a ripple over the cobalt-blue water in moonlight. This is the way Cobb prefers to go down to Cuba, waiting on the docks a week or so before a cold front to draft in order to cross at night when the winds tend to be light.

Cobb had received his orders for this Cuba trip from Oliphant via Pendarvis. Oliphant had his instructions from the Sisters mere days after the existence of the Mirror of the Jaguar Night had been revealed to him. That was at a meeting in his office above the Blue Rendezvous, a confession to him before anyone (at least insofar as the Sisters were aware) could have possibly known Lim's hiding place of the Mirror.

True that Lim's painting *Number 111* had already been deciphered by them with Castellan's help, but Oliphant knew the story only to the extent the Sisters had taken him into their confidence. They'd debated and strategized between themselves thoroughly, determining the degree to which they should tell Oliphant anything at all. Doge's point was that ultimately Oliphant would not engage his necessary resources unless and until he knew what was up. Otherwise he would cast about for himself and learn one version or the other, only to deepen his mistrust of the Sisters as they had mistrusted him.

Oliphant, they decided, should know about Montezuma's solid gold, mounted black Mirror hidden away in Havana. Though hopefully Oliphant would have just enough information to take the tease—sufficient to occupy his imagination rather than launch some intensive reconnaissance of his own.

"I agree, Sister. Bertrand Oliphant is the ultimate insider, and he wants to be treated as such," C. C. Moth had said. "We'll tell him a little while leaving out the lot. A fertile greed is magnificent for the manufacture of one's own facts."

"Yes, we'll let him think how easily he'll get his greasy little paws on La Malinché," Doge added.

~~~

Thanks largely to their Fridays on Bly's porch swing and the wine's handiwork, Bly was party to what the Sisters knew or at least what they had in their minds regarding where and when the Mirror would be located. That was about the extent of it. He'd been instructed on the specific day to be in Havana, though not the precise time of day or the exact location.

Thinking back, there have been clues about the escapade, enough breadcrumbs dropped by the old girls to take his suspicions (if not expectations) toward the Camera Obscura. But, as an emerald line of light spreads and contracts over the horizon behind him, Bly senses the time for actually knowing is drawing nigh.

Per his instructions Bly signs on as a sport fisherman going out, though Cobb knows to list him as crew going in to Cuba. Bly is Cobb's only crew, so far as he will declare. Cobb won't chance Estevar being detected aboard by the authorities down there. Besides, Estevar has an assignment of his own, one that could not have delighted him more.

During the night Irish Bly offers to take a turn at the helm. Pendarvis has retired to a bunk below. Cobb is obliged but remains in the cockpit close by, gesturing freely with the coffee cup that rarely leaves his hand. It is one o'clock in the morning, and Cobb launches a brief tirade against navigating the Florida Straits. But he concludes with his compliments for the weather and the seas as

Chapter 7

they are by saying, "And we ain't concerned about compensating none for the current here tonight either. Yes sir, looks an easy go of it this time down. Not to make much about it though. Don't want to jinx us if you know what I mean."

"I do know what you mean, Cap," Bly responds, his eyes forward on the ink-dark line that is the horizon in the airglow before sunrise. "No sign of the Coast Guard either. Not another boat light in sight except for that freighter off to the east about an hour ago."

"*Nada,*" Cobb agrees. "But then we don't have to worry much about the Coasties going down. It's coming back that you better have your keister covered."

Bly nods solemnly. Back in his Miami days he'd listened over a hundred beers to anguished exiles revive, rehash, and revise with gut-felt malice their hatred for the Castro regime and the homes, businesses, hopes, and dreams (each gilded now with golden memories) that the Revolution had ripped from their hands and hearts.

"Anyway, we're clean this time down, amigo. Embargo law only says we can't spend any money in Cuba. Hell, we ain't even got there yet. So what'll they do now? Run us down and take away our birthdays? The bastards! It's no business of theirs where we put in but our own. That's what I say. You think ole Fidel is missing any beans or fried plantains 'cause there's a hold on Yankee dollars down there? Not bean nor banana one."

Bly smiles and rakes his slender fingers back through his sun-bleached hair. He watches the *Mercy* track on a screen in the console before him. Cobb corrects the course slightly at the wheel.

By first light Cobb is back at the helm, heading westerly on that clear morning as the skyline of Havana comes into view. He gets on the radio and tries to raise the Marina Hemingway nine miles out of the port at Havana. Marina Hemingway is where foreign yachts (even if Havana-bound) go in. The narrow, oily, cluttered harbor at Havana lay in the nook Moro Castle makes and reserves routinely for larger commercial vessels. That's not to say a boat couldn't put in there, but the slip fees would be exorbitant, same as those imposed on cargo vessels or cruise ships. A sport fisher there would appear too obvious, too pretentious, and the expense ordinarily prohibitive. So Cobb is steering for the sheltered harbor of the Marina Hemingway at the mouth of the river *Jaimanitas*.

Cobb checks his setting and tries the marina again on channel 16: "Marina Hemingway," he barks into the mic. "This is the Key West *Mercy—Estados Unidos—*requesting clearance."

When he gets no answer, Cobb switches to channel 72. The marina usually monitors that channel too. No response there either.

This has happened before. Cobb, with his thumb away from the push-to-talk button, leaves a slipstream of curse words in his wake. Occasionally other boat captains relayed the same phenomenon, particularly at less traveled ports of call. More typically his radio would crackle a cheery welcome in broken English with an offer of correct coordinates to steer to the harbor's entrance. Pendarvis wants to know if there is a problem, although he's been through this drill before.

"No," Cobb croaks. "Maybe whoever's at the radio knows the *Mercy*, knows she knows her way in, and doesn't want to disturb his damned dominoes game. Whatever. We're going in."

Cobb has Pendarvis raise his Cuban courtesy flag. Bly runs up the requisite yellow quarantine flag. Cobb expects these together to have him signaled unfettered into the marina.

Soon the lofty flying saucer-shaped water tower and boxy gray marina building with its hedge of high antennae come into view. Distant from the irregular and decaying breakwater before the marina basin, the white and red-trimmed hotel pops up too. Now they see distinctly the masts of boats already moored inside the marina's grid of concrete-enclosed canals. Between the canals stretch sandy spits, tawny with brittle grass beneath a hither and thither planting of palms.

A red-and-white buoy ahead marks the treacherous reef lurking like dragon scales within the harbor's entrance. By the time Cobb brings the *Mercy* inbound between the lines of opposite red and green markers, a nonchalant guardsman is out on the cement quay. He unhurriedly flags them in.

The handsome young guard preens his blue uniform in the morning sun. He looks up at intervals as the *Mercy* rumbles slowly in. Now that Cobb is close enough the guard signals him around by

Chapter 7

a *Guardia* post to tie up for processing. Bly tosses ropes to waiting attendants.

That is no small thing, the processing. At least it never has been according to Cobb. He'd gotten through a time or two in an hour or so. But then again the *Mercy* might be tied there for the better part of a day. He couldn't say what made the difference other than the fact that any firearm on board made the processing more martial and thorny. Otherwise it was simply some luck of the draw as to which official was on duty, his or her mood, and the proximity to the marina that time of day. In any case the handwritten paperwork was quite as prodigious as the number of carbon duplicates that must be made.

On this particular morning a colorful cast of officials and officers assembles rather rapidly, boarding in turn according to their assigned powers and duties. The medical officer wearing a surgical mask is first. She's friendly enough. Still, her palm must be greased so that she might continue to be well pleased with the health of all crew and conditions aboard.

Pendarvis, being the most gregarious, is skilled in transactions such as these. Cobb despises them, the "courtesies," as the lawyer refers to such bribes. Be that as it may, and however begrudgingly, Cobb had certainly managed to finagle his way into the marina over the years. But with Pendarvis aboard (an envelope from Oliphant chocked full of Cuban convertible pesos tucked in his snapped pocket), Cobb is only too eager to turn his attention to some other matter of importance, say, the reshaping of his cap or retying the laces on his well-weathered deck shoes. As for Bly, his instructions are clear because Pendarvis has formally issued them according to Oliphant's decree.

Essentially, before and after any required presentation of (expertly forged) papers of his own, Irish Bly was to lounge about the boat as a lowly, inconspicuous deck hand. Just a salty scut, napping out of the way, preferably with a ball cap over his face.

The medical officer is satisfied. She removes her mask and has a Coke and cheese crackers. She suddenly demonstrates an astounding fluency in English. She and Pendarvis converse in leisurely fashion about nothing that matters very much. When

An Unfinished Sunset

Pendarvis escorts her dockside, the white doctor's jacket she'd been wearing clings loosely to her shoulders. She is attractive, possessing that regal Spanish manner, striking Castilian features, and bright, inquiring eyes. She is intelligent and corrupt, corrupted by the inherent skullduggery of a scavenger nation where the taking of bribes is as commonplace as the exchange of currency. But when Pendarvis offers his business card bearing his cell number, she declines. She smiles and waves the card away with a hand that sports a wedding ring. One of the Guardia standing nearby sneers to see Pendarvis's enticing offer declined. He doesn't notice though, as does the doctor, that a persistent Pendarvis has dropped the card in a gaping pocket of her medical jacket.

Then the equally cautious medical-masked Customs officials—a veterinary officer and agricultural inspector—take their turn. They are soon dipping into the variety basket of crackers and popping open cans of Cokes. Pendarvis slips each a Cuban fin for their "kind" assistance with all the forms more rapidly completed in duplicates on their clipboards.

There is some other person, an official without a clear distinction or rank. He doesn't wear a mask. His purpose and authority are apparently ceremonial, but that isn't clear either. His jovial cameo appearance is so comic that even Cobb is amused. His ambassadorial enthusiasm seems to warrant no particular interest other than that of being paid to disembark, which he does at his leisure. His rumpled linen coat pockets are stuffed with cash and crackers and a can of Coke, both right and left.

Finally the uniformed officers of the Guardia come on board, an older gallant man with his young, eager attaché. The attaché has a contentious sniff dog on a lead at his heels. Their military bearing is overt (including that of the dog). They are nevertheless quite courteous, clipping their English precisely to be plainly understood. The officers are less formal after crackers and a Coke. But they still unceremoniously confiscate Cobb's flare gun kit and tape down the *Mercy's* radio with stern instructions prohibiting any radio communications while in port.

Cobb and Bly have been through this charade before. The officers are politely plied and accept the cash as nonchalantly as they

Chapter 7

might inspect one's passport. Pendarvis is accustomed to this form of exchange. He is discreet and gracious. The officers are well pleased, but that is to be seen only in their eyes. The *Mercy* is cleared to take down its quarantine flag and motors to the slip in the second canal where several other American boats are moored.

One of the boys eager to help with the *Mercy*'s lines is the one Ramón had arranged to deliver the Chinese motorcycle for Bly's use. The boy's little brother sits on the curb just outside the marina's security gate, keeping watch over the Chinese motorcycle parked close by. He expertly spins a five-peso coin bearing the face of revolutionary icon, Ernesto "Che" Guevara, between his nimble fingers.

CHAPTER 8

The job of the artist is always to deepen the mystery.

—Francis Bacon (1561–1626)

THE GIRL WAS NOT in the room when I woke up again. While I fumbled for the water pitcher and it teetered between my briar-scratched hands, the woman came to the bedroom door. I didn't see her until I'd gotten myself awkwardly positioned back into the pillows, the sloshing pitcher resting against the side of my belly. That's when I saw her leaning against the doorjamb, slowly shaking her head in a solemn gesture of disbelief. She came and put the pitcher back on the bedside table.

"Let's make some sense outta you," she said.

She was large but agile and able to position herself so as to right me on the pillows and sit higher in the bed. She worked with an effortlessness that was nearly dismissive except for the low groans she made with each movement. The woman's skin was soft as satin against mine. She buoyed my back and stuffed the pillows. Satisfied that they were suitably arranged, she returned the pitcher to my hands and went wordlessly to fold a blanket neatly across the foot of the bed.

I drank slowly again and watched as she made easy work of the blanket. The woman was older, though decidedly some years younger than I. She'd aged better, the healthy mahogany glow of her skin boasting both a full and well-toned body, making her appearance more youthful.

Chapter 8

"Look here," she said when she was done with the blanket. "I don't know by which way you've come to this place, but with God's help you're still among the livin'. So, soon as you're able, you'll be gettin' on from here. Sooner the better," she added, looking me squarely in the eyes. "We're not studyin' on you all that much, you understand? We won't see after you when you go, and you don't need to look back. We're just gonna send you right along, mister man." She paused and seemed to be looking far out the window, adding then, "Send you better than we found you. That's what we gonna do."

"I am that—better already, ma'am. And I thank you," I said softly. "Miz ...?"

"Mazie Day is my name," she answered, standing back with her hands on her hips. "I don't expect I ought to know your name."

"No, I expect not," I said, turning my gaze to the thin blue horizon. A flotilla of cotton-like clouds seemed suspended there in both time and place.

"Well, that's just fine," she affirmed solemnly. "When you live on the water like we does, you get used to blow-ins. How'd King James put it? 'The same sea that brings a sailor safely to port may also thrash him against the rocks?' Somethin' like that."

"King James? That's a Bible verse?"

"No, child, please!" Mazie Day laughed. "King James was my husband, James Day. Least that's what most folks called him. But he was sometimes a preacher his own self and a powerful one too when he'd had his prayer wine. He was a big man and drove a rock truck for the lime rock mine mostly. But how he carried hisself and talked proud with such dignity and weight had people come to call him 'King James.' That was just the way of it. His way. I don't know where he come up with that sayin' about the sea, but it's right to say."

"Yes," I said. "I know it to be so. I've made my way on and around the sea for a good long time now."

"You look to be such a man," she said with a disapproving nod. "But I don't reckon you can blame the sea for your problems, mister."

An Unfinished Sunset

"No," I said. "The sea is not my problem. But it has sometimes been an answer to my problems."

Mazie Day smiled softly and said, "It was 'bout the first thing God created. You know that? I wonder sometimes if the sea is not made as much in God's own image as the Good Book say man is." She looked upon Bly disapprovingly again and left the room with, "We don't need to be doing all this talkin'. You sleep some."

I did sleep. And I dreamed about the sea again and the way it washed up against the wall on the Malecón, turning back on itself. This time it was as I had seen it in the night, the lights of Havana in the pitch and froth of the surf washing up and turning back on itself again.

8.1

This is not Lourdes Lim's first time to rifle through her uncle's studio. In the spot of light afforded by the skylight she again searches cluttered drawers and cabinets and pots of brushes and sponges for some clue as to what he had done with the Mirror.

Lourdes has a cell phone in her jacket pocket and pauses to check it for the time and to see if she somehow missed a call. It is now six o'clock in the evening, and she hasn't missed one. There have been no calls to her cell since she arrived from Miami around noon at *Jose Marti*, the Havana airport. The plane had been loaded with cheerful Cuban-American passengers disembarking for routine visits with family members, as she herself was supposedly doing.

But Lourdes Lim's travel to Cuba is about more than that. Her clandestine purposes are linked directly to the Machiavellian sports agent known as Jonrón. He is the same man who'd made cryptic cell contact with Oliphant while Oliphant walked "the girls." And more closely still, it is she, Lourdes, who delivered the groceries. Jonrón could not have said more clearly to Oliphant: *I know exactly who and where you are*.

Jonrón had his reasons which Lourdes Lim knew. For these two wheeled together in a scheme Lourdes cogged with that of her Uncle Luis. It turned without transparency to other schemes and operated in relation to still others as they popped up across the Havana cityscape like some fantastic Renaissance puzzle machine. It was a tight act, this business about the Mirror of the Jaguar Night. A tighter act than any one of the actors realized, for everyone operated within a clockwork of narrative cogs and gears the Sisters had unwittingly set in motion a half century earlier.

Among the more curious and perhaps promising of Yohan Lim's abandoned possessions are carefully made bound stacks of paper, ranging from scraps of fine linen paper to newsprint torn or cut and bound up to a size approximating a deck of playing cards. On these cutouts and remainders the artist had made notations and preliminary drawings with bits of poetry and incomprehensible mathematical computations—front and back—in his minute, precise hand. Some of these ciphers were mono-mythic symbols (hieroglyphic codes perhaps), archetypal images, or highly personal cryptographs of some sort. And of particular importance was a later find: a box of correspondence, most of which was written in the distinctive hand of Consuela Doge. These letters are essentially about art and the collection of art, though a few passages offer a clear indication that the Sisters are both caringly fond of Yohan Lim. Equally evident is their mistrust of Luis Lim. But most curious is a quotation included in one of Doge's letters that Yohan had circled with his pen and adorned with stars:

> This spherical aberration produces an indistinctness of vision, by spreading out every mathematical point of the object into a small spot in its picture; which spots, by mixing with each other, confuse the whole. This circle is called the aberration of latitude.
> —Society for the Diffusion of Useful Knowledge (1832)

This quotation made more interesting still those decks of astrological images drawn in pen and ink, tinted with spots or broad swaths of watercolor. But there was nothing, at least as far as Lourdes or her Uncle Luis had been able to tell, that indicated the actual location of the missing Mirror.

An Unfinished Sunset

Now there are footsteps on the metal stairs below—gritty leather soles Lourdes could not see, though she connects the sound of them with her expectation of Luis Lim's always spit-polished oxfords. The door opens slowly, and Luis, carrying a cardboard box, steps in. Lourdes comes forward with a faint smile. She is taller than he. Luis sets the box aside. Without a word between them, he lifts his carriage upward for the customary kiss on either cheek.

"The German is here," Luis says soberly as his niece backs away.

"So you are right about the time," Lourdes says.

"Yes, of course," Luis insists. "Absolutely certain, although I don't know what Krym knows about the time really."

"You spoke with him?"

"Yes. He is a guest at Arielle's *la casa particular*. I waited for him on the balcony there, but he revealed nothing to me. He has no conscience. No morality. No sense of history. Only greed."

"What do we have?" Lourdes asks without emotion.

After a long pause, Luis Lim gazes at his niece and says, "Memories."

Lourdes looks away and rests her pretty head on her forearm on the tall filing cabinet. She glances over at her uncle, who seems to be aging before her very eyes, and says drily, "But anyway, he is here in Havana—the German. All of a sudden he is here now, three days before the eleventh."

"*Exactamente!*" Luis exclaims. "November 11, 2011. 11–11–11. Once – Once– Once," Luis recites the numbers as if they are some ancient incantation while he removes a black light fixture from the box he'd brought with him.

A year earlier it had been Luis Lim who'd first shown his resourceful niece the studio. She already knew the history of the old warehouse from her father, Oscar. But it was Uncle Luis who was informed about the details of his brother Yohan's eccentric technique. It was Luis who had knowledge of the Mirror because it was he who had stuffed it in his briefcase while crowded around those intimates who helped the First Lady pack away her most prized possessions during the frantic New Year's departure in 1959. The Mirror had been placed on a marble pedestal in the palatial bedroom Fulgencio and Marta Batista shared. It would be rumored

Chapter 8

that the couple and their entourage had taken millions in cash and jewels and artworks aboard their plane that night. The situation was hysterical with so much tossing around of things that Marta may have thought the Mirror was packed away among her myriad other possessions.

Luis Lim couldn't say for sure, though he surmised Marta knew it remained with him. He imagined that just before being whisked away, her wistful smile back at him from the black limousine contained an acknowledgment that there was at least this secret between them. Luis Lim let himself believe that Marta Batista wanted him to have the holy grail of the secret Cortés treasure, the Mirror she also referred to as La Malinché. The coins—they didn't interest her at all. He had one of the better preserved ones made into a pendant. Luis himself had worked with a very fine jeweler in the city to have it mounted in the arms of a golden octopus with emerald eyes, like those of the jaguars that embraced the Mirror. She didn't really like it. Probably it was no coincidence she left it behind, a fact that Luis hopefully fantasized was a loving gesture toward him.

Regarding another observation, Luis Lim was confident that the curious paint splatter he'd noticed around Yohan's studio was not random. Rather, as he insisted to Lourdes again, the scattering of paint dots was identifiable as starry night constellations over the floor, walls, and ceiling. He would demonstrate that premise now with a black light he'd borrowed earlier in the afternoon from a nightclub on Playa Miramar.

"I had suspected a phosphorus composition in certain of Yohan's apparent splatter all along," Luis announces. "That is why I have brought the black light, Lourdes, so now you see how certain of the date I must be."

Luis Lim kills the overhead lights and snaps on the toggle for the ultraviolet lamp. In that instant the spectacle in Yohan Lim's darkened studio is revealed in a meticulous shattering of the black light made blue by countless specks of versicolor. The effect upon Lourdes and Luis Lim is as if they are levitating in a universe frozen in time. Stars and galaxies in multidimensional array appear in the sky beneath their feet. A perfect alignment of the cloud of

Elenin with Earth, Mercury, and Venus is made evident by chart lines directed through these to a larger illusory image of Earth inset on the back wall. The chart lines clearly target in on Cuba, on Havana.

Superimposed in a circumference of five feet or more is a sort of astrological chart. The position of the sun, moon, and planets of Earth's solar system had been plotted and illustrated by the luminous dial, serving as a sort of orbital calendar opened to a specific date: 11 November 2011. The sun's position is taken as the ascendant of the chart and tracked to precisely 11:00 a.m., the place of the eleventh hour being portrayed on a sundial face that Yohan Lim had rendered in a bold Aztec motif.

"He has gone to a lot of trouble," Luis Lim says from the dark. "It was his way, I'm afraid, always to make the obvious obscure. These planets are fixed in their orbits, their stars still within stationary galaxies, all orbits immobile, and comets locked down in their trajectories. The sun—there it is—frozen at an appointed hour."

"Eleven—*por la mañana*," Lourdes responds quietly.

"You see it all here ..." a suddenly agitated Luis adds, extending his opened palm to the florescent universe lit about him. "He shows us exactly this day and time."

"Yes," Lourdes says thoughtfully. "Dear Tio Yohan has apparently made an appointment. He tells us the day and time but not what time this *is*."

8.2

In his room with the balcony over the Prado Diebolt Krym removes the Yohan Lim *Number111* painting from the sateen lining of his suitcase. He flattens out the print on the made bed and holds it tautly over the chenille spread with heavy leather-bound books from a nearby shelf. He adjusts his reading glasses and examines it again. There, within a large cysteine bubble of light, impressionistic cigar boxes are arranged in a geometric representation plainly depicting the Havana cityscape. The date 11.11.11 appears on the surface of the bubble that permits a fisheye view similar in form to the image projected by the Camera Obscura.

Chapter 8

Krym knows that the painting is a treasure map of sorts. He knows Havana, and the spectrum of light portrayed soon indicates that his first impression of its significance was correct. The location of La Malinché, the crown jewel of the secret Cortés treasure ship, would be revealed by Havana's Camera Obscura at 11:00 a.m. on the eleventh day of November 2011. He knows someone else would also be certain or at least expectant of that time and place.

It had been rumored for a while among serious collectors that Castellan harbored some visual clue as to the whereabouts of the object. This was a print, however exquisitely made. The owner of the original painting, surely that collector must know by now the secret of the secret that leads to the thing itself.

Krym goes out on the balcony and looks below to the Prado. He can see down its avenue to the Malecón and the harbor of the ancient city. It pleases him to know that Cortés himself had once stood akimbo nearby and perhaps surveyed the city in much the same way.

Chapter 9

It is a riddle, wrapped in a mystery, inside an enigma;
but perhaps there is a key.

—Winston Churchill (1874–1965)

Out in the yard with her dog, Hobo, a sudden glint of light caught Alifair's eye. The transitory reflection came bright at midday, approaching in a rough sequence of flashes abruptly clipped where the forested canopy broke over brimmed ground. These were narrow berms of limestone and swamp pushed up in the last century, the earliest by great machines powered by steam. The woods' roads made a loose grid over Gulf Hammock, with this one extending for miles to the coast from the old road before it had become a highway.

The shiny red pickup truck bucked and bounded out beyond the tree line on the rutted sand road through the dry grass. Alifair's Uncle Linton—Pastor Linton Day—parked close by. He lowered the driver's side power window to the shoulder of his starched shirt.

"You hold on to that sorry hound of yours now, do you hear me, Alifair?" he called out to the girl. "I don't want no dog slobber and paw prints all over my pressed britches. I mean it now!"

"I got him," the girl called back, the dog's collar firmly in her grasp.

"Alright," Linton Day shouted back, "I'm coming with groceries. You hold him!"

Day got out then, impeccably dressed as usual. He adjusted his wire-rimmed glasses and walked around to the passenger side

Chapter 9

of his truck. From there he produced two paper bags of groceries, stuffed with the usual list of provisions he brought from the store in Bronson most Thursdays. As Alifair was staying with her grandmother in the summer, there were a few extra items not ordinarily on Mazie's shopping list. *Red Hot* candies were among the special additions.

"You got them Red Hots, Uncle Lint?" the girl called while she struggled with the dog.

"I got 'em," Linton said above the groceries. "You just hold on to that nasty dog."

"He ain't nasty!"

"Hold him!" Linton's pace quickened as he arched his back and stepped out like a drum major approaching the back porch of the house. "Hold him now!"

Linton was at the foot of the steps when the hound broke free, or the girl playfully let go. He couldn't know which.

"Run, Uncle Lint!" Alifair screeched.

But Linton Day was already bounding up the plank steps and acrobatically hiked a knee to balance one bag while he grasped the screened door handle and twirled his way inside without losing a single item from the bulging bags. Hobo's massive paws slammed the door shut behind him like the crack of a lightning bolt.

"Alifair!" Linton's tremulous voice reverberated with caution from with the board and batten of the house. Then more cheerfully, "Mama? Where—?"

9.1

Florence, Italy

The bells are ringing up in Giotto's Campanile, the gothic tower that's part of the complex of cathedral buildings on the Piazza del Duomo. Taking the staircase she prefers over the building's unreliable birdcage elevator, the old woman's soft shoes shuffle across the stone steps hollowed at their centers by centuries of wear. It is cold, colder still in the faintly lit corridor of her climb. She wears a heavy coat and a scarf tied around her ashen head.

An Unfinished Sunset

This is the apartment building on the Ponte Vecchio over the Arno River in which Castellan watches each day from his lofty penthouse perch. Every morning Castellan looks out of the vaulted bank of windows down to the slate-gray Arno River sluggish with autumn frost. He'd never spoken of this, but it is known now that he'd developed over the past year an acquaintance of sorts with a young woman whom he regularly spotted on the bridge just after the noon bells each weekday.

She would position herself to feel the sun on her face. Castellan supposed by her smock that she must work in the chocolate shop nearby. Day after day he waited within himself for her, thinking inwardly, *She is beautiful—beautiful without quite knowing or intending to make herself so.*

When Castellan had been a Formula One race car driver, he had known many beautiful women all along the celebrated Grand Prix. Being himself a darling of the *Fédération Internationale de l'Automobile* and European media, Castellan's movie star good looks, wealth, and celebrity virtually assured him of his pick among the glamorous set.

The women and the wine of the Grand Prix circuit were pleasant memories, but pain was his most faithful companion now. Sometimes, out of the drone of a plane overhead or perhaps the soft whine of his apparatus, a ferocious sound would rise within his ears. So deft was his memory of speed that it would be like a swarm of angry bees hollowing his ears to rattle his skull. In that instant the dark wing came over him again with an aerodynamic down force, pushing the screaming racing tires off the road as he cornered and the wing inexplicably failed. He would remember his acceleration then as an out-of-body experience, a sort of slow motion dreaming in the releasing drag of turbulence on the turn. And suddenly, inexplicably, he was airborne off a curve above the harbor at Monte Carlo.

That was long ago, and the styles have changed in both race cars and the hemlines of skirts. But Castellan, despite his infirmities, had not lost his appreciation of either. Each day in that late spring (in an impulse that both frightened and delighted him) he lifted with a twitch of his brow a flower from that crystal vase on

Chapter 9

the table. He let it fall from the opened window to the river below. And, as astonishing as it must seem, from his computer screen Castellan could see that she saw the flower falling.

At first the girl must have wondered exactly what it was that fell and floated toward her—this flower. She watched it come closer and saw more clearly then a delicate patch of colors against the sheen of the Arno, wafting beneath the center arch of the old bridge shedding the April sun.

It was not on the first but on the second occurrence that she raised her pretty head again, recognizing that the flower cascading down was indeed for her. He saw her face fully then, her inquisitive smile full of an innocence exceeding any expectation. It startled him when the exhilarating sound of racing suddenly returned in the same instant. Yet, surprisingly, the ferocious swarm fell away to a heavy purr like that of lions resting on rocks above a plain. The weight of the dark wing did not come over him this time. Nor was he sent spiraling away amidst the deafening scream of auto bodies scraping the stone wall where finally he lay still and broken.

Bernouill's Principle. The designers had demonstrated to him how pressure seeks balance, how the wing moves in the direction of the low pressure. Planes use their wings to create lift, but race cars use theirs to create down force. With wings a Formula One car like his would be capable of cornering, as if it had three and a half times its own weight. One of the designers had laughingly noted with a shrug that at a high enough speed he could drive upside down. "Theoretically of course."

Into the late summer the girl was still coming to the bridge. Sometimes Castellan only watched her reflection in the water, the gentle waves of sun highlighting dark curls as her head lifted with unremitting surprise at seeing another flower fall. He would watch on his monitor as she leaned out to observe each turn and spread of the blossom on the river beneath. He saw this too. He followed the flower and then tilted up to tighten his frame, watching her gazing up with such delight, up to the bank of windows, as if to ask yet again, "For me? Truly, the flower is for me?"

Violent visions would sometimes come in the night, and Castellan would race to recollect her inquisitive smile exactly as he'd first seen it. In his dreaming would be the turn again before the harbor at Monte Carlo where he'd gone upside down over the stone wall into a copse of trees on the rocks below. For more powerful than the violent suffering now was her smile—a beatific mystery greater for him than that of the *Mona Lisa*—the smile of this woman he wished only to behold, never to possess.

But one late November day she did not come to the bridge. Nor did she come in the days immediately following. There had been no indication to him that she would not come again, nothing about her to portend change, though perhaps her face had seemed fuller and more flushed. He had noticed that. Nothing else was visible to signal change except for a red coat over her loose smock in the autumn breeze. Still, Castellan continued to look for her patiently, scanning the passersby on the bridge around noon, but he had not seen her again.

Seven months passed. He was not sure at first, but then he was certain that the woman on the bridge waiting in his monitor was she. He examined the scarf on her head and the red coat—surely hers. Yes, it was definitely she. Within her arms a bundle was situated just so. She turned slowly then to show a rosy-faced child kicking against his blankets, waking with wonderment.

This is what he saw on the monitor's screen as he brought into tighter frame the young mother: her inquisitive smile and the vibrant child. And this is how he wound his watch. This is how snow flurries were made blue that day on the Ponte Vecchio and how two freshly cut flowers fell that noon to the Arno below, exquisite with cold.

That was a day months before this one, when the bells up in the tower with its marble encrustations rang the Angelus. The old woman, Castellan's housekeeper, came finally to his door. She fitted a heavy key into the lock, though the door opened on its own with no latch or lock holding it fast. In tragic irony the ringing of the cathedral bells invited the Credo for the dying, and death is what the housekeeper found.

Castellan's magnificent penthouse apartment had been ransacked. That much was immediately apparent and horrifying. The electronically sealed glass door to the case in which the Lopez

Chapter 9

Codex was kept had been shattered. The ancient folio was gone. On the wall nearby the Yohan Lim painting had been taken, the canvas unceremoniously carved from its ornate frame. By the vaulted greenhouse-like windows Castellan's pale, lifeless hand lay unnaturally protracted over the dark mahogany desk.

The housekeeper saw this first from behind the high back of his motorized chair. She saw then only Castellan's marbled hand extending from the black cashmere of his sweater. Inching a step closer in her squishy shoes, the hand became startlingly vivid in a color and configuration such as Leonardo da Vinci had famously painted on a chapel ceiling she'd seen as a girl. In shocking focus was Castellan's stilled yet reaching hand, which was now the color of the Arno River beneath a grim sky leaden with cold.

9.2

In Havana, the white cat walks out on the white parapet with the blue of the bay behind her.

"Is that your cat?" Lourdes Lim asks Ernesto, the afternoon bartender at the hotel's rooftop bar.

Ernesto doesn't look up from the glass he is polishing behind the bar in the shade of the cabana but replies, "No."

Lourdes has come for the mojitos, the breeze, and the spectacle of the sun—a soft golden light over the old city in the late afternoon. She drinks her cocktail slowly and talks to Ernesto about baseball mostly. This is an ongoing conversation of several years in duration, chiefly an exchange of observations and opinions about the sport. So sometimes their banter becomes loud and lively with dramatic gestures. It is a conversation that Lourdes easily manipulates toward Ernesto's grandson, Seve Acosta, who's maybe the best baseball pitcher in all of Cuba.

"Maybe the best in the entire world!" Ernesto would correct her, raising his right hand, as if this was said on his solemn oath.

But Ernesto is cautious. He is especially careful when speaking with Americans about his grandson. No matter that Lourdes is beautiful and not quite the *typical* American in stereotypes made familiar by the Cuban media. Nonetheless Ernesto is eager to talk about baseball if he chooses to talk at all.

Baseball is more than a sport in Cuba. It is a national passion. And, as passionate as politics are on the island, so is baseball. Perhaps everything in Cuba is political. Ernesto thinks so. And both Ernesto and Lourdes are acutely aware that one can go to prison in Cuba for far less than facilitating a national sports hero's defection.

On the other side of the Straits American teams were barred (since the US trade embargo of 1962) from spending money to sign Cuban players. To get around that obstacle, players obtained citizenship in another country, somewhere in the Bahamas or the Dominican Republic. Then they entered the major leagues as free agents. There's good money to be made in one of these signings, including a cut of the agent fee.

That's not Lourdes Lim's piece though. She's a *shooter*—a scout—secreted in the swarm of the stadium crowd, operating a small handheld video camera with consummate skill. So Lourdes Lim is not down in Cuba with *an envelope* of say twenty thousand, smuggled in with a previously signed, multimillion-dollar bonus as evidence of the possible if the player is up for a planned defection. There are others (she didn't know their identities) who carve that piece of the pie.

Video might be confiscated or snatched away or the media card ejected and crushed underfoot by a police or military boot. Maybe the card would be crushed like a cigarette by a plainclothes security guard impersonating an irate fan. There's risk enough getting the video out. But if someone is arrested for inciting a defection, that's going to be hard time for a long time. It's no better for a woman with Chinese-Cuban ancestry than it is for anyone else. And Lourdes is more than a scout showing up at the ball parks. She is good at the games, mixing in with the crowd, watching the action intently—a serious fan, a player's sister or cousin maybe. Cupped in her palm is the small video camera she covertly employs to film talented prospects. She gets in; she gets out. She edits in her Miami apartment on Bayshore. The video is posted online at a secure site, and the bidding war is on. That's what she knows. Nothing more.

Chapter 9

But Lourdes knows what she does know exceedingly well. She knows her way around Cuba and the ball parks. She knows her miniature camera and how to use it without drawing attention. She knows the prospects the backroom guys in pro ball back in the States want to see. She knows when to *shoot*. And there's more to know than how a guy throws the ball or swings his bat. The unnamed—the guys who sit deep in the glassed stadium suites high above the best baseball diamonds in the sport—they want to know the Cuban's habits too.

That's how Jonrón once put it to Lourdes: "Observe their habits. Before somebody spends good money getting this guy out, before some club spends around $3.5 million signing the guy, they want to know his habits. Maybe he has good habits. Or maybe his habits, they might not be so good for a long-term relationship, you see? Anyway, it is what we must know—his habits. You get me?"

Lourdes gets it. So she's also become an expert in what's talked about in the neighborhood, in the barrio, in what she can see at the nightclub, or even in the back alley. Maybe a guy's grandfather isn't the best source, but he's accessible, this one, and who knows what he knows? So Lourdes is his new friend.

Ernesto feels more comfortable with her now that she has returned so many times to the bar, but he's still thinking to himself, *What does this woman know about big league contracts in the States? She looks like a fashionista. So what does she know really about million dollar contracts or secret bank accounts in The Bahamas?* The "lies," that's what Fidel calls such promises as get made. Maybe the Comandante is right. Better to be careful, Ernesto keeps telling himself, but still, she does know baseball. She knows as much about his grandson as any fan. So they talk baseball. And sometimes, just sometimes, they talk about his grandson, Seve Acosta, "... the best baseball pitcher in the world."

Lourdes can read the caution light flashing in Ernesto's eyes, especially when she speaks of his grandson. He doesn't have to spell it out to her. In her position she knows the games that get played about baseball in Cuba by players and family members alike.

An Unfinished Sunset

Now, with evening coming on, there are only Americans on the rooftop. A rich couple is sitting out in the white chairs at one of the tables on the terracotta tiles beneath the cloudless sky.

Maybe it's true — the life, Ernesto keeps thinking while polishing glasses behind the bar. The life in the States. Maybe he does want to talk about his grandson, about all the possibilities that might await him across the Straits. Maybe he will see what this mysterious *baseball woman* with such fine shoulders, sitting with her back to his bar, actually knows about such things. But just now Ernesto must serve the rich Americans: the scotch for him, the daiquiri for her.

The woman says she wants to hold the cat. Her husband says to leave the cat alone. He is imposing, a big, athletic man, though soft around the belly. He wears shorts with all the pockets like tournament fishermen wear. A pale scar bends up his knee where a vicious football tackle had ripped tendon from bone. He is almost drunk and already too loud and obnoxious about the salsa playing from behind the bar.

"First it was the music," his wife tells him, "and now it's the cat."

He laughs loudly, accustomed to others laughing because he is laughing.

Lourdes looks up from the baseball scores in the newspaper folded in her hand. The woman seated nearby has cradled the cat in her arms. She looks down to the Malecón where Fidel and Raul Castro and the other heroes of the Revolution had paraded with their guerilla fighters years ago. It was where the parades of *Carnavale* now passed, wave after wave of fantastic costumes illumined by fireworks arching into the night sky.

Lourdes has taken her usual room at the hotel. It is expensive, the daily rate amounting to more than a Cuban doctor makes in a year. She has casually mentioned that to Ernesto. Ernesto reminds her about the informants, whom he is quite certain observe all who come and go from the hotel.

Lourdes knows this might be so. There are times when she's quite sure she sees the same man following her when she walks on the Malecón, and he seems to be keeping an eye on her at the baseball stadium as well. But she's equally certain this is not always so,

Chapter 9

for there are times she could casually give the best of surveillance operatives the slip.

The American woman comes back to the table with the cat.

"You know I don't like cats," her husband complains.

Lourdes resumes her thought that there are other times like this when, quite simply, no one else is near, though Ernesto could be recording. Therefore everything she says is playful, cryptic, and laced with some double entendre. But just now Lourdes and Ernesto aren't talking at all as she reads the baseball scores from the newspaper he's folded on the bar.

Ernesto, in his white server's jacket, approaches the table in the sun and asks if either American wants another drink. The woman says no. She thanks him while she smooths the cat's fur.

Her husband bellows, "In Cuba I should be drinking rum, but I don't like rum. To hell with rum! Bring me another scotch!"

Ernesto bows slightly and returns to the bar at the cabana. The loud American at the table calls to Lourdes, whom he's noticed has paid him no attention at all: "What's that you're drinking over there?"

She doesn't answer immediately. Then she answers, "Mojito," lifting her glass, her eyes still fixed on the folded newspaper in her hand.

"What the hell is that?"

"Rum, crushed mint, soda, lime," Lourdes says, looking back at Ernesto pouring scotch. "What else?"

"Say, good to hear American! Where ya from?"

"You called it."

The big guy laughs loudly. "That figures. Three people up at this godforsaken Cuban bar, all Americans. And we're not even supposed to be here!"

"I'm not here," Lourdes says.

The man laughs again, "Me neither."

He speaks more quietly to the woman, his wife. She looks over at Lourdes, smiling a faintly quizzical smile. Ernesto brings the scotch.

The loud American invites Lourdes over, telling Ernesto with a heavy pat on the table top, "Bring her another of those things she's drinking."

The wife puts the cat down and smiles back at Lourdes as if to say, *Don't worry about him. He's just a blowhard.*

Lourdes pays Ernesto for her mojito with Cuban convertible pesos and leaves him her usual generous tip in dollars. "You understand," she says quietly.

"*Entiendo. Gracias,*" Ernesto replies.

Lourdes goes over to the American's table, though not to stay. She has to be going, she says. The loud guy introduces himself, extending a thick hand with an expensive gold diver's watch latched to his wrist. He says his wife's name, gesturing toward her. She looks up from the cat and smiles at Lourdes vacantly.

The man's name is familiar to Lourdes. Then she remembers the injury, the championship game, the crushing defeat of the Vikings that year. There are car dealerships that bear his name now, big ones that advertise on cable TV in Minnesota and Florida. The Viking insists again that she join them.

"Hell, you can have one drink with us. We'd be offended if you didn't."

His wife says that she is sure Lourdes has better things to do in Havana than sit and listen to them.

The Viking says, "Listen to *me*, you mean!"

The Viking's wife goes into this singsong, still preening the cat, "Ohhkaay, he fishes and wins all the tournaments except here, never in Cuba before. But now he's going to fish here, so he'll have won everywhere and been the *Marlin King*, and *that's* what this is all about."

The Viking's face reddens.

"And so you will be the *Marlin Queen* then?" Lourdes asks, not quite smiling.

The Viking looks away, swallowing wrath, or else he is frustratingly bored. Lourdes isn't sure which.

"No," the wife answers. "I'm here for the music, the dance."

"Oh really?" Lourdes replies, as if her interest has been raised. "You have been to *El Túnel, Tikoa*—those are good. *Callejón de Hamel* too, but *La Tropical*, you know, that is the real place. *Avenida 41 entre 46 y 44, Municipio Playa*," she adds in Spanish.

"Wow! Sounds fun. But I'm just the cheerleader here and—"

Chapter 9

"So," the Viking interrupts, "you know Havana? I mean you have our story. What's yours?"

Lourdes matches his insolent gaze. "I'm a pirate," she replies brazenly.

The woman giggles, cautioning the cat that a pirate is in their midst. "Arrrhhh," she growls, but the cat merely cracks a golden eye and closes it again.

The Viking grins impulsively and says, "Captain, have a damned drink with us."

Lourdes relents with purpose. Ernesto brings rum. Lourdes wants to know all about the Viking's boat, especially the speed. Not surprisingly, the boat was built by Viking, a 54-footer tied up at the Marina Hemingway. The Viking—the former All Pro and currently prosperous automobile dealer and tournament fisherman—offers abundant details about his sleek craft, built, he says, "to chase the finest fish in the world."

His pretty wife goes with the cat back to the parapet. Across the oil-streaked water, a rusty tanker sails beneath the cliff top fortress, *El Moro*. Vintage cars pass on the Malecón. Lovers promenade; sunbathers and charlatans line the sea wall. Two shirtless boys come out of a pale pink ruin and bend away the orange barrier wire before the street. They cross the Malecón with lines for fishing in their small brown hands.

"You fish?" the Viking asks abruptly.

"If I'm hungry enough," Lourdes says, taking a sip of the rum.

"Ah, a meat fisherman. Not a trophy fisherman."

"No offense."

"None taken," the Viking says. "Damned expensive hobby." He looks out toward his wife at the parapet, adding, "I get bored easily except out on the boat. Too much too fast to get bored out there. It just breaks you in other ways."

"You seem to be holding up quite well," Lourdes observes absently.

"Things aren't always as they seem," he says, looking back at Lourdes.

"No."

The Viking continues, "So what's really your story? You're no damned pirate."

Lourdes decides to bait him. "Baseball," she says. "That's my game."

The Viking throws back his big burr head and laughs loudly. "Let me guess!" He pretends to think, saying hurriedly then, "Pittsburgh! The Pirates! But you don't look like a player to me," he adds, lowering his voice and warming his expression.

"There are many ways to play the game," Lourdes says with a deceptive smile.

"Got it," the Viking responds, as if he knows exactly what she means.

But it isn't Pittsburg of course. It isn't any team in particular. She lets the Viking think what he wants to think himself clever enough to suss out. That's what his wife does. That's what everybody around him does, she decides. Dispassionately, Lourdes thinks him also one of the loneliest men she's ever met. She stands.

"Thanks for the drink," she says, turning to the pretty wife, her thick hair wafting in the evening breeze.

"Yeah, anytime," the Viking says. "Maybe you—"

"You should take your wife dancing," Lourdes cuts in cattily and goes out through the door to the elevator across the elaborate pattern of the tiled floor.

9.3

At this time Cuban-American families are permitted to visit relatives remaining in Cuba. Four charter flights take off from Miami daily. Forty minutes later they're in Havana. The excited passengers applaud on landing and eagerly gather up their bundles of gifts that range from perfumes to toilet seats, brake pads to boxes of chocolates. Many bring cash. The US Treasury Department estimates that millions of dollars a year make it into Cuba from the United States. About half of that is being carried by couriers or mules—*mulas*—as they are called.

Bertrand Oliphant has been using the same mula for seven years to ferry his cash and encrypted information to the island. Everyone calls her *Abuelita*—little grandmother. She is just that: a petite, apparently fragile woman bent and stooped by her years.

Chapter 9

Her caramel-colored skin has wrinkled darkly, yet she is spry and has eyes as innocent as those of a sympathetic child. Moreover she is absolutely expert at her craft as a courier and so disarming as to have Cuban Customs officials carrying her packages and expediting her way through the terminal.

Ramón is at his regular station outside behind the blue barriers to greet her in Havana. She is a speck in the rear window of the '56 Buick Roadmaster he drives as a taxi, the official license for his *almendrone* mere camouflage among the streetwise. Within thirty minutes of the terminal he would have Abuelita deep inside the maze of narrow streets that riddle *la Habana Vieja*.

Typically Bertrand Oliphant requires $2000 paid up front in Cuba. This takes care of his expenses and associates there. The balance will be paid per delivered passengers by their various sponsors. Other smugglers might expect payment in full: $8000 to $10,000 per passenger before their stolen fast boat is ever launched. But this is a special *librar*. This valued client has bought the full boat and has specified the night the event will take place. He must be a very talented athlete indeed, though more passengers than the ultra-valued one will be scheduled for the flight on the fast boat coming in.

These are lucrative, if chancy, sports deals being made. Family members or loved ones otherwise might be included on the secret passenger list or sent for later to protect against poor performance in the major leagues due to the player's homesickness or lovelorn blues. The traffic streaks by in the dark, and there are always those waiting, waiting to go, waiting to fetch, waiting to catch.

Oliphant operates exclusively with Ramón—his resolver, arranger, and transporter. The fewer involved the better. It is Ramón who receives his manifest and bankroll directly from Abuelita. She has separated out her own cut within minutes of meeting Elle Rousseau in a busy stall market in Little Havana up in Miami. It is Ramón then who contacts the planned passengers. It is he who instructs them about their exodus.

On this particular day his explicit instruction is for Seve Acosta to wear a red T-shirt and white trousers. Mariela, his girlfriend, is to wait at a different location with Acosta's mother, Elena. They too will be dressed in red and white. In this way the women can be observed with confidence long enough to satisfy Ramón (parked down the street) that they are not under surveillance. They will walk arm-in-arm, Ramón tells them, coming from the *Catedral de San Cristóbal* where they have been lighting candles together. When they get near Ramón's Buick, he will ask from his window, "Are you going to the party?" If the answer is yes, then the coast is clear. They will get in. If the answer to his question is no, then there's suspicion of being detected by the Cuban authorities.

Ramón is counting on someone else too. The father of a childhood friend, Capitán Alberto Osvaldo, is an officer in the *La Guardia Frontera*, the Cuban coastal guard that patrols the waters out of which Oliphant (with Bly at the high-tech helm) operates. The Osvaldo residence houses an extended family that includes Osvaldo's wife, both their mothers, and her grandmother. Osvaldo's oldest daughter, a medical student, remains in the home, as well as Enrique ("Rique"), Ramón's lifelong friend, and Rique's newlywed, pencil-thin wife with enormous brown eyes.

The stucco and tiled exterior of the house appears as dilapidated as the rest in this once prestigious neighborhood. Its faded pastel facade is streaked by rust stains lined with tannin from the drooping boughs of frowzy trees. Inside, however, there are always new furnishings: appliances, televisions, and stereo equipment, periodically upgraded over the years.

A naturally adept and quick study of technologies, Ramón has established a promising rapport with the officer. He's exploited that knowledge further to become a young man recruited into Oliphant's network. Their confidentiality has developed into a cash drop of $1000 US each night flight.

Osvaldo knows a particular sector from which he is to divert any patrol for at least a one-hour window. This feat he has accomplished easily enough by directing radio communications of suspicious activity in the opposite direction of Bly's targeted arrival. His official receipt of the bogus information would be authentic because a confidential informant (Rique usually) will make the call from a public phone somewhere in the area. Osvaldo knows the muffled counterfeit information is from his confederate, but he has

Chapter 9

his explanation—his alibi—if needed. What he doesn't have by this time (and has not bothered to tell Ramón or Rique) is that he no longer holds direct command over the Guardia patrols in the sector slated for Bly's arrival. Osvaldo has recently been reassigned and has no access at all to the schedule or direction of the patrol boats.

He doesn't reveal this news while he sits on the edge of his bed in his sleeveless undershirt. Breathing heavily, Osvaldo counts out the cash that Ramón delivers double-wrapped in thin plastic grocery bags. He takes the money with a shrug and his usual disclaimer that he will do what he can but neglects to say that what he can do now is nothing.

The fact that Oliphant's most recent missions have taken place without incident is merely favorable, random coincidence. Interceptions have been avoided, even if narrowly, by chance and good fortune, accelerated by Bly's slingshot exits away from the Cuban gunboats on patrol. Capitán Osvaldo is now taking the money and leaving the rest to *Señora Suerte*.

Chapter 10

The way to love anything is to realize that it may be lost.

—G. K. Chesterton (1874–1936)

I HEARD THE POT LID begin to rattle. Mazie Day and Linton met in the instant her mustard greens began to boil on the stove. She'd not flinched when the back door opened to the kitchen, the back serving as the front for anyone arriving from the mainland through the hammock. Mazie had been tending to me in the bedroom (where I was resting in a state of near delirium) when she recognized her son's muffled voice from his truck. Then came the rapid click of the man's shiny leather-soled wingtips on the planking of the back porch. Before he'd call out to her from the kitchen, Mazie had turned to greet him coming in.

"How's my baby boy?" she asked into their affectionate embrace.

"I'm—"

But before Linton could complete his warm reply, he was startled by the semi-conscious, grisly looking white man propped up on pillows in his mother's bed. There I lay dozing, a blood-tinged bandage bound about my shoulder.

"Mama! What ... who *is* that man?" Linton asked incredulously, stepping aside to peer cautiously into the room.

"I don't know," Mazie answered nonchalantly and went back down the breezeway with Linton at her heels, his head all but perched on her shoulder.

He whispered loudly in her ear, "You don't *know?* You don't *know?*"

Chapter 10

"No," she answered quietly. "He come up in the storm the other night." After a pause, she turned to add with a twinkle, "Might be like Jonah and the whale."

Linton adjusted his wire-rimmed glasses again and admonished, "That man's not come from a whale's belly. I can assure you of that! He looks more like he's come from a bar room brawl or maybe a knife fight somewhere."

"Gun fight, more like it," Mazie replied drily, stirring her greens.

"Gun fight!" Linton gasped, coming closer. "Mama, what have you gotten into here?"

Mazie Day shook her head solemnly and began to put away the groceries her son had left on the counter. Linton paced the yellowed linoleum floor behind her and began his interrogation.

"You mean to say you haven't let anybody know about this man, about his being in your house? He comes up in the storm in the dark of night, bloody with a gunshot wound. And you just haul him inside—Alifair here with you? Not a clue as to who or what you're dealing with?"

"You know I don't have no telephone out here. That little phone thing on your belt won't work out here neither. You know that, 'cause you'd already be pecking away at it by now," Mazie replied mirthfully. "So just what am I supposed to do, Linton? Send up smoke signals? You gonna be lookin' fo' smoke rings above the cypresses?"

"You are supposed to use that marine radio we installed for you, that's what!" Linton insisted.

"Battery's *been* dead in that thing. I don't like it no-how. All that boat talk jabbering all the time. Besides, you a preacher, son. You as good as any ought to know what the Master taught in that story 'bout the Good Samaritan."

Linton stiffened and replied, "Mama, I'm going right now to contact the sheriff's office. Straight away! Do you hear me? Straight away! My Lord, what about Alifair out here," he bleated, "with that—that *man* in there?" Thrusting a slender hand from the cuff of his starched shirt toward the bedroom, he added, "We don't know who or *what* he is!"

An Unfinished Sunset

"Him? I can handle him. Don't you worry, son. I've done dealt with worse men in my life, rest assured."

"You don't know that. You *can't* know that!"

Alifair entered through the screened door and asked, "Can't know what?"

"Can't know anything," Linton answered impatiently.

"I know somethin'," Alifair said spritely.

"Yes? What?" Linton demanded.

"I know I want one of them Red Hots you're supposed to bring."

"You go back out there and get hold of that dog, Alifair. I'm going back to town right now. And you—you're both coming with me!"

"Me and Hobo been down there to the boat," Alifair announced. "He's *all* muddy. You don't want Hobo in your truck, and I ain't a going without him."

"What boat?" Linton wanted to know.

"That boat Red Man come up here in, I reckon. Ain't that who ya'll talkin' about?"

"Red Man?" Linton wailed in a high whisper, "What kind of boat?"

"One of them real fast kind of boats with what looks like bullet holes all over it. He got his blood all on it too," Alifair added eerily for her uncle's benefit.

"My God in heaven!" Linton all but screeched. "I'm out of here. Turn that stove off, Mama. You're both coming with me. Now!"

"No, we ain't," Mazie declared obstinately, pouring dry rice from its printed bag into a tin canister she kept on the counter.

"Fine. That's just fine!" Linton sassed. "I know better by now than to stand here and argue with you two. You stay *right* here, and let's see if he cuts your throat before I can get back with the law. That *could* happen! Do you understand me, Mama?"

"What part can happen? That 'bout gettin' my throat cut or you comin' back with the law?"

"Maybe both, God help us! I just pray I'm not too late," Linton said firmly, turning to the girl. "You come with me, Alifair," he demanded, reaching for the door.

"How am I gonna do that?" Alifair asked briskly. "I got to hold Hobo so you can get to your truck without his paw prints all over your pretty white shirt. Besides, I ain't leavin' my dog out here, I

Chapter 10

told you. He don't stay in the back neither. So, is he gonna sit his muddy self on your clean seat between you and me?" the girl asked spiritedly.

As if on cue, the panting dog banged his heavy forepaws on the door.

"Forget it!" Linton screeched in disgust. "You just hold that nasty dog."

"He *ain't* nasty!"

10.1

"That there is *nasty*," a different voice says. It is an older woman's voice musing, "But it sho' is born and bred fo' the hook."

Irish is recollecting in his half-sleep a day bountiful of youth—his youth. Ray Jr., a boyhood friend, is waiting on the short bridge where Irish stops to lean his bicycle against the guardrail.

"You get 'em?" Ray Jr. asks eagerly.

Irish tells him yes and digs into an old army haversack strapped to his handlebars. He produces a mayonnaise jar stuffed with large green leaves.

"Let me see?" Ray Jr. insists, leaning in. Irish hands over the jar.

"You know the deal," Irish says, but Ray Jr. is already going down the rangy ric-rac path to the riverbank below.

Ma Doll, Ray Jr.'s great-aunt, is sitting down there on an upturned axle grease bucket scalded clean. Her complexion is the color of yellowed porcelain cracked with age. Her eyes are narrowed, a fixed expression of fierce determination on her strangely childlike face. Around dark she'll carry her fish home in that bucket she's sitting on, but for now it makes a good seat for *fishin' in the ditch* with room for a Nehi orange soda beside her. She's a small woman, the same age as Irish's grandmother, yet not as big as Ray Jr.'s twelve-year-old sister.

Folks have always called her "Doll." She's always looked like a little doll. Though Irish's grandmother tells that when she was a girl, Doll was mean.

An Unfinished Sunset

"Bad to put a frog on boys' arms. She'd make a knuckle-hard little fist and pop a fellow quick as lightning, making a knot rise up the size of a hickory nut—that kind of frog."

His grandmother says Ma Doll's always been small in everything except attitude. She's still nobody to mess with. Ray Jr. knows that as well as anyone.

Ma Doll knows Ray Jr. is behind her now, looking over her shoulder to see her nimble little fingers knot a tiny hook to her fishing line. The other end of the line has already been made fast to Ma Doll's cane pole stuck casually into the sandy bluff.

Ray Jr. asks, "You sure do like a cane pole, don't you, Ma Doll?"

She's not going to look up. Irish studies the intricate silver-haired knot at the back of her head. She is a woman who knows knots and always tests the one she's just tied.

"You askin' me about pole fishing?" she inquires in a low, firm voice. "One of the first things about pole fishing is don't do too much talkin'."

Ray Jr. is quiet then and looks kind of shamefaced.

Ma Doll is satisfied with the knot and asks, "You brung what I ask?"

"Yes 'um," Ray Jr. answers.

"That Miz Redmond's grand-youngin' there with you?" she wonders, still not looking up.

"Yes ma'am, I am," Irish answers.

"He's the one got up the tree," Ray Jr. says, extending the jar out for Ma Doll to see.

"I expect I know that," she says, taking the jar and holding it up against the low sun. You a bit too fond of them cat head biscuits, Ray Jr., to be tree climbin'."

She finds the jar teeming with fat, black-green worms from a catalpa tree. An old stand of the trees line a fencerow behind a washhouse down the road.

"Uh-huh. That's them alright," Ma Doll acknowledges, handing the jar back. "Them will do just fine."

They look nothing like the stringy black or red earthworms dug or *grunted* out for fishing. Ma Doll is famous for her worm charming. She knows all the worms good for fish bait and when to use them. Ray Jr. says she learned her sound for charming worms by watching birds flutter their wings, vibrating the ground to make the future bait appear above wet ground. Some people use a roping iron around a stob in the earth to vibrate the soil. Ma Doll's is more like a worm fiddler, dragging the dull blade of an old handsaw over the top of an ironwood stake to replicate the birds. Ray Jr. says she can fill a coffee can with earthworms in minutes, but this time of year she prizes catalpa worms above all others.

That's what the deal's about. There are five Indian-head pennies in it for Irish. Ray Jr. ends up with a good logger marble and Irish's other safety patrol badge. Ray Jr. is too old to wear it, but that's his business, Irish tells him. So now Ma Doll has only to come across with the promised pennies.

"Here you go, Ma Doll," Ray Jr. says, tilting the mouth of the opened jar.

Fast as a fisher bird's beak, her little fingers pluck a fat worm from the wad of catalpa leaf in the jar.

"That there is *nasty,* but it sho' is born and bred fo' the hook," Ma Doll announces.

The worm covers the hook, and she raises the long pole. She rocks back and comes forward, sending hook and line aloft from the sandy bluff. Folk that pole fish with the experience and skill of Ma Doll exact a precision in placement that exceeds even that of the most expert anglers. World-class fly fishermen fare no better.

"Coarse fishing," is what Irish's grandmother calls pole fishing. Victor Emmanuel has told Irish about the famous sportsmen following the trophy fish down in the Keys and across the Straits off Cuba. He has described their sleek seagoing boats, outfitted with riggings, to tease in giant sailfish or the great marlin. Yet, for Ma Doll's money, there's nothing quite so refined as the delicate placement of a weighted and baited line skillfully *plunked* in the precisely targeted spot.

Ma Doll lifts up the pole's tip again. She gently exercises exactly the right engineering of elbow and wrist to drop hook, line, and sinker squarely in the dark void between flowering water bonnets—broad lily pads downstream.

That's where the red belly will lay, Irish is thinking to himself. *And maybe the blue gill and stump knockers. Nothing says she won't take a small bass either.* He asks just above a whisper about the possibility of a bass.

"Oh yeah," Ma Doll answers quietly. "I've pulled some big ones too. But that's at night mostly, jigging. You do that when the moon is right. Full moon is best. That's when I do my jig-n'-pigs."

Irish wants to know about jig-n'-pigging. Ma Doll explains that the pig part of the procedure is derived from her use of pork rind trailers attached to a jig hook with a lead head on it. Her preference is pork rinds cut to resemble a frog.

"I can work this old pole with a short line on that jig so you nor no fish will ever believe it's anything but a sure-enough frog," Ma Doll drawls.

"She can too!" Ray Jr. avows loudly.

"Hush up, Ray Jr.! I gonna pop you," Ma Doll cautions beneath her breath.

The cork bobber has begun to move toward the bonnets upstream. The old woman whips back on the limber pole and brings up a brim big as Ray Jr.'s fat hand.

"I'm gonna slay 'em with these here catalpas," Ma Doll says. "Just you hide and watch."

That's one of Ma Doll's sayings: "Just you hide and watch." She doesn't really means to hide, but she does mean for the boys to watch. So they watch. They push and scramble for position to unhook her next catch.

Ma Doll says aloud, "Bother! I'm slaying these ole blue gills! I'm gonna be plumb gill-flirted myself by the time I'm done."

Then she has the boys baiting catalpas, taking turns with the pole and pulling fish too. At dusk Irish has the pole and pulls in a red belly big as the sole of his high-top tennis shoe. Across the river the sky is crimson through the dark filigree of the cypress trees and glistens as brightly as the underbelly of that fine fish. It is a sunset that expands lazily while they laugh. Ma Doll brags on every fish in her bucket. Irish has a treasure of five Indian-head pennies in his pocket.

Chapter 10

Ma Doll lets Ray Jr. fish. He rolls the logger marble in his hand and polishes the safety patrol badge pinned awkwardly over his T-shirt before each catch he makes, insisting the ritual is bringing him luck.

"We're all having good luck," Irish maintains.

"No, not luck," Ma Doll insists. "Blessed. All blessed."

There is no hurry about the twilight that evening. Irish Bly can still hear the spring breeze through the catalpa trees. From there he sees the sunset lingering, unfinished among these, the best of his days, in which he was so carefully instructed on the useful knowledge and value of fishing and friendship.

10.2

Consuela Doge and C. C. Moth are tending a flower garden banked against the sunny east wall of their seaside manse. Irish Bly stands nearby on the coquina shell path. He leans against a toothy rake just handed to him by Moth. Doge empties a mesh bag of dahlia tubers back into a box of peat moss. The box is one they had extracted from an ancient Frigidaire in a spacious, vault-like storage area of the manse now converted into a potting room.

"Perhaps you know," Doge huffs to Irish, "that the Caledonia Horticultural Society of Edinburgh offered a prize of two thousand pounds to the first person producing a *dahlia blu*."

"A blue dahlia? No, but I'm almost certain I've seen one. Or maybe that was the name of a book or a bar? But no, I suppose I missed that announcement. So are these," Irish asks with a wry grin, "the prize winners?"

"*That* was in 1846," Doge goes on drily. "The color blue in dahlias has *never*, at least before now, been produced."

"Dahlias do produce anthocyanin," Moth instructs helpfully, "that being an element necessary for color production. But to achieve a true blue in a plant the *anthocyanin delphinidin* needs precisely six hydroxyl groups."

"Dahlias heretofore have only developed five," Moth laments. "So the closest dahlia breeders have come to achieving a blue specimen, up until now, is some variations of mauve—some purplish and lilac-like hues we've seen."

"But not true blue?" Irish inquires in a tone mimicking genuine scientific inquiry.

"Not until now. But Eureka! Yes!" Moth exclaims, pumping her knot-like fist in the air. "We just may have it, the first True Blue!"

"Yes, well, we shall see. We shall see ..." Consuela Doge intones with caution. "Let us hope the Frigidaire has done its work. You may recall, Irish," she rambles on, "that in 1570 King Phillip II of Spain sent Francisco Hernandez to Mexico to study the natural resources of the newly colonized country."

"We're not returning to the conquests of Cortés, are we?"

"Heavens no," Consuela Doge snips. "Cortés was dead, entombed by then in the mausoleum of the Duke of Medina in Seville's Church of San Isidoro del Campo. This is the Hernandez journey, an arduous trek throughout Mexico for most of seven years. It was he, Francisco Hernandez, who first describes the wild dahlia as precisely as he would draw them. Even better in his finely written chronicles."

Doge pauses to utter a long sigh. "These are hybrids, you see," she announces, pointing with her dibble to the box at their feet. "They are the far-flung progeny of Hernandez's species, the ones he sent back later to the Royal Gardens of Madrid."

"Hybrids of hybrids," Moth laments. "But at least these are *our* hybrids. One can hardly argue against our tampering with nature when it is quite natural for us to do so, being most certainly of nature ourselves. Anyway, we're all tangled up in this thing, this quest for a deeper shade of blue. But any tampering with nature is not our purpose for summoning *you* here today, Irish."

"Well, perhaps you tamper more with human nature?" Irish jests, curious now that Doge appears to genuflect before the mossy display of bulbs.

She bends her substantial girth to take up a first tuber in cupped hands, much as one might hold a communion wafer.

"Yes, human nature. Perhaps a bit, I suspect," C. C. Moth says pensively, apparently perplexed in her careful distinguishing between the two—nature and human nature.

Chapter 10

Doge now fills her raised gardening apron with the selected dahlia bulbs. They are mounded in the pouch Moth makes beneath her sturdy grip. Moth hoists her planting dibble high in her free hand. Raising it like a regal staff, she announces to Irish, "It is time you knew exactly where and how the Mirror is to be returned to its rightful place. This is your great adventure, Irish Bly. *We* are merely the threshold keepers. *You* received your call that evening we first encountered you at the Sunset Celebration on Mallory Square. Now the great door of adventure opens to you. It opens to reveal La Malinché, our hallowed Mirror of the Jaguar Night."

"At your service," Bly answers squarely, standing erect with a straight face. "Actually, I'm eager to know just how this all comes about. I'm ready to ride, ma'am."

The slighter woman, having raised her apron broadly to receive more of the tubers, waits while Doge fills her apron with an ample number of dahlia bulbs.

"Yes, well, you will recall," Doge declares to Bly as she pours, "that we told you earlier we had entrusted La Malinché to the great artist, our dear and trusted friend Yohan Lim."

"What we haven't quite told you," Moth carries on, "is that our confidence, our trust placed in Yohan was, shall we say, an inadvertent, inescapable breach of confidence."

"It was a conscious and conscientious breach," Doge corrects.

"Very well," Moth concedes. "So it is even more important, Irish, that you know the Mirror had earlier been entrusted to *us*, placed in our safekeeping by Yohan's identical twin brother, Luis Lim."

"Identical—mirror opposites—in physicality alone," Dodge clarifies.

"Perhaps that explains Yohan's eccentric style of dress and that he would shave his head?" Moth wonders aloud.

"Yohan was the consummate artist. Luis Lim, the skilled diplomat and accomplished attaché," Doge elucidates. "Luis Lim was the delight of dinner parties, the polished conversationalist, thoroughly steeped in Cuban culture and lore and secretly the ardent, if unrequited, admirer of Marta Batista."

"Actually Luis is an utterly fanciful and failed man who has sold his soul to as many devils as will believe they have it," Doge

An Unfinished Sunset

concludes as she finishes filling the broad pouch C. C. Moth's apron makes.

"Suffice it to say," Moth observes, "that while it *was* Luis who put the Mirror in our hands, ours were the hands of faithful curators. After all, everything we did was to protect Luis from himself. We chose brother over brother, but that was as it had to be."

"Oh yes. We protected Luis from his own nature, shall we say," Doge bemoans with a sigh.

"Indeed, so we were curators, not collaborators," Moth insists. "Luis was and is all about his unrequited love, equaled in torment only by his unrealized revival of wealth. Love and lucre, if not lucre and love, are his pillars of opposites, and he is never quite balanced between the two."

"In either case," Doge stiffens to say, "Luis has been a man obsessed—be that love or money—obsessed, mind you, with what he perceives himself at the moment to have least."

"It's a double-panned scale, don't you think, Sister?" Moth asks plaintively of Doge. "One that simply will not balance for poor Luis, much as the great stone of Sisyphus will continuously roll back before he can shoulder it to the hill's summit."

"So it is with Luis's curse," Doge agrees. "For all his conceits and deceits he must continually and repetitiously weigh his thoughts. Among the most tortured of these is his failure to personally restore the Mirror to Marta Batista. For all we know she never gave either Luis or the Mirror another thought to the last."

"This is not to say that Luis is an utterly unhappy man, nor is he one who is entirely disagreeable," Doge qualifies with a raised hand.

"No, not at all," Moth agrees. "He may be what Camus concluded Sisyphus to be—happy in his own way, the endless inner struggle itself being quite enough to fill the man's heart."

"But we didn't trust him," Doge insists. "We *don't* trust him now, do we, Sister?"

"Indeed not," Moth responds. "All too often he confuses money for love or love for money. He's always in a distinguished dash for one or the other. His escapades and exploits, however discreet they may be, are all known to us. We must actually credit at least that much—all the dope on Luis—to that cad, Errol Flynn."

Chapter 10

"Takes one to know one," Doge observes absently.

"At any rate," Moth continues, "had we returned La Malinché to Luis, the Mirror might well have ended up in the hands of Idi Amin or Gaddafi or some wealthy Serbian mobster by now. Who could know?" she exclaims in genuine fear.

Doge plants a dahlia tuber, sprinkles it with water, and says, "Indeed, in his panic on the night of Batista's New Year's Eve flight, Luis brought La Malinché to us for safekeeping. He fully intended to come back for it of course. He still believed it was his courtly mission to return it to Marta. But that was a fool's errand engineered by Batista himself. There's a far more extensive anatomy of guilt in all this that exceeds Luis and outstrips Flynn. Yet another serious matter would distract us before we were compelled to say farewell to Cuba."

"So you must see that in our own urgent departure," Moth explains, "we endeavored to both vouchsafe the Mirror and protect our friend Luis from himself and this greedy, avaricious pattern he'd long established and exercised expertly in the emerging socio-political orb around Fidel."

Irish blinks slowly. "I'm not sure I'm getting all this."

"Well, most importantly here, we were fully informed of Luis's propensity for selling off the family jewels, as they say."

"Yes, whoever *they* are?" Moth seems to ask genuinely.

"So, to the point, we didn't trust Luis Lim," Doge adds bluntly. "We couldn't trust him with La Malinché, the Mirror of the Jaguar Night."

"No," agrees Moth adamantly. "We didn't and don't really trust him at all. This selling off of valuable family art and heirlooms—his or anyone else's—for filthy lucre had already made him one of those old dragons in myth and folklore," Moth squawks. "He'd hoarded up his secreted gold in the midst of utter poverty. He didn't need the money. So he became like the great beast of fairy tales in his lair, sequestering his heaps of gold coinage along with so many virgins in his cave."

"Not exactly *that*," Doge corrects. "The virgins Sister mentions as allegory."

"At least so far as we know," Moth qualifies indignantly.

"But the *point* is," Doge continues, "of what damned use has a dragon for gold or virgins either one? Now really?" Doge demands. "Yet he hoards them up, these sorry substitutes for what he cannot satisfactorily find in himself."

While Irish Bly listens, he taps at the gold treasure coin behind the faded cobalt of his Blue Rendezvous T-shirt. It hangs on the gold anchor chain around his neck, each a gift from a woman surfacing in his memory.

"Quite so," Moth says, grabbing Bly's attention. "Except that by then, by the time of our departure, Luis the courtier has begun in earnest his pilfering from the plunder of Cuba with some romantic notion that he might soon attain sufficient treasure (and thus power) to win his *Dulcinea* from that squat sergeant and pretty boy, F. Batista—a still greater dragon than he!"

"That was the better part of it, wasn't it, Sister?" Doge asks. "Indeed, the absurdity of man being *man*."

Irish Bly shrugs (as if slouching toward Bethlehem himself), realizing he has little more than a clue as to what this Luis business is all about.

"Ahh," says Moth, taking up the dibble to begin a dramatic recitation she adapts:

> Her name is *Dulcinea*, her country *El Toboso*, a
> village of *La Mancha*, her rank must be at least
> that of a princess, since she is *his* queen and
> lady, and her beauty superhuman, since all the
> impossible and fanciful attributes of beauty which
> the poets apply to their ladies are verified in her ...
> her head Elysian fields, her eyebrows rainbows,
> her eyes suns, her cheeks roses, her lips coral, her
> teeth pearls, her neck alabaster, her bosom marble,
> her hands ivory, her fairness snow, and what
> modesty conceals from sight such, *he thinks* and
> *imagines*, as rational *reflection* can only extol—
> not compare.

Chapter 10

"Ugh!" Doge says forlornly. "We had our suspicions about Luis Lim from the first. Flynn—he merely confirmed these. Luis had it going, had his little riddle wrapped in a mystery inside an enigma, as Churchill put it on another occasion. But we were on to him."

"It was all about Marta by the last of our days in Cuba. She!" Moth proclaims. "Marta Fernández de Batista, residing in the grand presidential palace of Batista. It was there that Luis Lim had come face to face with his goddess."

"That's not where I was going with this," Doge says sideways. "But yes, it was the moment in which Luis experienced a love he believed complete," Doge acknowledges gloomily. "But he is not—as perhaps he'd never prayed to be—purified by this love."

"No, Luis isn't," Moth says. "Not at all, don't you see? For, under the conditions present, she was a woman married to a man she loved, beast or not. So, rather than being edified by his love, Luis becomes even more deluded."

"Self-deluded," Doge says and takes another bulb from Moth's gathered apron. "One who will do anything for love," she notes, "must never be trusted with money any more than one who will do anything for money most certainly cannot be trusted with love."

"And," says Moth, "we knew his twin, Yohan, to be the creative, artistic one who would not sell out, shall we say. He had not and did not. We know he never would have compromised the integrity of his art. He was not some manic purveyor with a price tag for all that was within his grasp. His labors in the vineyards of creativity were priceless."

"Yes," Doge takes up the repartee. "Yohan is/was an *artiste* and inventor. In fact, he was a polymath: painter, sculptor, architect, musician, mathematician, engineer, botanist, and writer for whom this fantastic Mirror would become an inspiration rather than an instigation of the dire consequences of tainted love or found money."

"Quite so," Moth chimes back in. "As the enlightened twin we recognized him to be, he was already at a heightened stage of his own mythological journey. Yohan had long since answered *his* call to adventure—true adventure of the best kind—summoned from his own spiritual center of gravity, so to speak."

An Unfinished Sunset

"Indeed," says Doge, stamping the soil lightly with her tightly laced shoe over a planted bulb. "From beyond the veil of his struggling Cuban society, in a zone unknown, resided a fateful region of both treasure and danger deep inside society and himself. And he knew it. He had already found this distant land within himself. It was his magical forest—a kingdom underground, beneath the waves, or above the canopy of clouds. He had his secret island aloft in the brilliant sky mirrored by a jealous sea. He already knew its mountaintops, having rested there after many profound flights of fantasy."

"We knew all this immediately from his art, the works we saw," Moth says introspectively, as if this had just occurred to her. "Nothing he could have possibly said would have satisfied us in our own purposes quite as much as what we saw in the works of Yohan Lim."

"Yes," Doge adds with the elation of a passionate tour guide. "His art was a place of strangely fluid and delightful polymorphous beings where, despite unimaginable torments, superhuman deeds occur in the lush landscape of his post-apocalyptic Caribbean paintings. To gaze upon them was like being blinded to everything but *truth*."

"And so we experience an improbable delight," Moth says behind her bony hand. "Through the magical Mirror we put in his care Yohan Lim has journeyed into yet another dimension. It was as dramatic an achievement as that of the earlier masters in their secret use of a camera obscura of concave and convex mirrors to illuminate their canvases. Their techniques, though secretive, produced positively extraordinary, deeply personal images."

"We observed that Yohan was already a hero, one going forth of his own volition to accomplish the quest, as Theseus does when he arrives in his father's city, Athens, to be told the horrible history of the Minotaur."

"Quite so," Moth agrees in a hushed tone. "We saw that Yohan's artistic vision might be carried by the Mirror's reflection, much as Odysseus was cast about the Mediterranean by the winds of Poseidon."

Chapter 10

"You see," Doge instructs, "Yohan's creative adventure with the Mirror of the Jaguar Night began as his twin brother's blunder but resulted in his resourceful eye coming to see even more fantastically his frequented paths around Old Havana. The examples are multiplied, and a blossoming occurs exactly as we'd expected. By his latest portfolio he had made a mesmerizing garden in the ruins of his own country. His own *Garden of Cyrus*—heroic indeed!"

Bly shoves his hands deep into the pockets of his well-worn khaki shorts and says softly, "You are aware—I mean the both of you—that none of this makes sense. Maybe in your own orbit of course? But on what planet?"

"Harumph," Doge declares. "It *will* make sense."

"Yes," Moth instructs Irish while the two continue to plant their tubers. "If you will be so kind as to take up the rake there and cover our plantings over with more good earth?"

Bly gives the old girls a pass and rakes as they each kneel to pat the ground after him, speculating rapidly between themselves as to how blue a blue these blue tubers may sprout to be, especially as tricked by the Frigidaire into blossoming in the autumn air.

"There's a theory, a method behind our madness in planting just now, you know," Doge states. "We've carefully bred for the autumnal equinox rather than that of the spring. It could only happen here at the Southernmost."

"Yes, with our secret ingredient—crushed oyster shell laid in," Moth confesses innocently.

"Sister!" Doge admonishes.

"I didn't hear or see a thing," Bly offers courteously. "All I know is that you have your elaborate recipe for true blue."

"A gentleman and a scholar," Doge observes, returning instantly to the subject of Yohan Lim. "Consciously or unconsciously," she begins abruptly, rising and wiping her hands on her apron, "we were willing guides and mystical helpers for both Yohan and Luis. But, as mentors, we knew that the Mirror should be presented and entrusted to the hero, Yohan. Be it talisman or artifact, it would surely aid him in his loftier quest."

"Quite so, Sister. Yohan was our fine Galahad for whom the Mirror might become an amulet against the dragon forces through which he must also pass," Moth adds quickly.

"*And* to which Luis had already succumbed," Doge insists. "For Yohan the Mirror would offer a benign, protective power of his destiny. The fantasy images he produced by his talented, capable hands is a reassurance, a promise that the beauty and peace of paradise is not to be lost!"

"Oh indeed, but now you are our new Theseus, Irish, and we are playing Ariadne, giving Theseus her ball of string and a sword before he enters the labyrinth to challenge the Minotaur," Moth enjoins.

"This is all ..." Bly begins playfully, though he concludes apologetically, "Greek to me."

"No, it's not. The string is really of Yohan Lim's making," Doge insists. "The string, acting as a key, is contained within Yohan's last known work, *Caleidoscopio, Painting Number 111*."

"That's *Kaleidoscope*," Moth turns to translate. "If we decipher it correctly, as Castellan confirmed before his terrible murder, the exact location of the Mirror will be revealed to us, not ironically, via the lofty Camera Obscura above the rooftops of Old Havana. The time of this event shall be 11:11 a.m. on the eleventh day of November. We are talking mere days from now, not weeks or months. It's a very short string. And it's a key for which we are racing against others to find, we're quite sure."

Before Irish Bly can respond, Consuela Doge holds forth like a myopic college professor from a lectern. There is a Shakespearian quality to her rant.

"In the film *Star Wars* Obi-wan gives Luke his father's light saber, the object that later helps him combat Darth Vader. He teaches him to make use of *The Force*. In *The Lord of the Rings*, Frodo is given *mithril* armor, a sword, and the Phial of Galadriel."

"Without these he would have been unable to pass through Shelob's lair, would he not?" Moth coos while she wags her finger before Bly. "Here, more recently, is this boy, Harry, of *Harry Potter and the Philosopher's Stone*."

"Not that!" Doge groans.

Chapter 10

"Exactly that," Moth insists. "Dumbledore gives Harry a cloak of invisibility that aids him throughout his journey. We ought to give you something, Irish, to help you as you actually leave the known limits of this place to venture out into the unknown, perhaps dangerous realm of Yohan Lim."

"In your case, however," Doge announces, "it's not a *what*; rather it is a *whom*. A *she* to whom we now direct your attention."

"Who?"

"Whom," Doge maintains, "but whatever. Whomever. Your destiny in this rests upon Rachel Perl."

"Rachel Perl is my sword?" Irish Bly asks, looking at the Sisters blankly. "When blue dahlias bloom ..." he mutters beneath his breath.

"Your sword. Your amulet. She gave you the golden coin from the lost Cortés treasure, did she not? We gave it to her. You are wearing it now," Doge declares. "We're certain of these things we tell. Now, with your destiny clearly before you, you have the pure heart of Rachel Perl to assist you. You must go forward in this adventure, Irish. We are, you see, the *threshold guardians* at the entrance to the zone of magnified power. Beyond us, trust Rachel Perl. No one else."

"Indeed," affirms Moth. "We will presently give you your map, your string. We have told you this day wherein your power dwells, and she is like a mighty sword—however unlikely you may think it so—*she*, Irish, will ultimately be required to make your heroic return."

"Yes," Doge observes. "Despite your rather sordid past, you already see her as a fresh new face on the best hopes and aspirations of your own tainted heart. Of course, you get lost in the dark curls of her abundant hair. You find her fascinating when she swims out from shore in the turquoise sea."

"But you've never touched her, have you?" Moth asks knowingly.

"No."

"Don't. But she is far older and wiser than you know, sir," Doge tells Bly. "Still, if you touch her now, she will be lost to you. She is your secret weapon. She possesses the one thing no one else in this otherwise weird and wonderful tale possesses—absolute truth."

Moth smiles sweetly and adds, "Your hidden path home."

10.3

It is night time, and loud falls upon loud in the mix of music and mirth up on the Gulf end of Duval Street. Farther down toward the dark end of the street Rachel Perl sings in the swirl of moth shadow over a spot of light on the walk. Her big voice has attracted a bevy of tourists eddying around the muggy Coppertone-and-beer-scented foot traffic easing by.

A man adjusts his panama hat against the transfixed assemblage and leans in from among the passersby. He drops a folded twenty with a minutely written set of coded instructions into the straw hat at Rachel's scuffing feet, the soles of her Mary Janes perfecting their percussion. She sings boldly without acknowledgment of the man wearing the hat. Her eyes remain fixed upon the cloud-laden sky where the stars ought to be. Merely the whiff of incense from the head of her guitar trails after the man straightening his hat beyond the street light.

Pendarvis stops farther down and takes a cigar from an inside pocket of his rumpled linen jacket. The flame of his match exaggerates his aquiline features on the clapboard wall behind. He crosses the street to where the man-child, Estevar, reclines on the long horizontal steps fronting a row of darkened shops. Estevar's massive head, with its dark brows and curly forelock, is cocked to blissfully hear every note Rachel Perl sings. He waits and watches for a later moment when the crowd is thickest about her, and she will summon him with a lariat-like toss of her hand. He will come then from his ragged shadow to stand alongside her and sing in magnificent duet some song so sweet that it scatters away any dose of melancholy as lightly as thistledown.

Pendarvis doesn't disturb Estevar in his bliss, nor does Estevar turn his giant head to acknowledge Pendarvis while he crosses the street. Nevertheless each is acutely aware of the other. Neither knows though the careful set of encrypted instructions Oliphant has just deposited in Rachel's hat (that old western straw one with a Montana crease) so flush with cash it tilts on its rawhide-laced brim.

Chapter 10

As it happens, on this same night the flamingo-pink Citroën is parked on a side street nearby. Windows down, the Sisters listen intently and share the moment fully. The anticipated duet has begun. After a familiar, crowd-pleasing introduction by Rachel on her acoustical guitar, Estevar joins in, and they sing *Southern Cross* a cappella. They happen to be standing close by the old Southern Cross Hotel sign over the Duval Street walk.

"Absolutely extraordinary!" Doge comments inside the dark car.

"Pity Irish can't sing as well," says Moth.

"Not a lick, as my grandfather would say," Doge responds.

"Striking thought though," Moth says sadly, "a trio such as that, bringing up the curtain for our little sea urchins' opera about to unfold."

Listening pensively for a while, Doge says, "This won't end happily, you know."

"How could it?" Moth asks, as if Doge may have some other ending in mind.

Ignoring Moth's question, Doge wanders on in her thoughts as the angelic voices of Rachel Perl and Estevar soar above the elongated shadows of the banyan tree by which they'd parked.

"Irish Bly is our knight errant, is he not?"

"Yes, of course he is," Moth readily agrees.

"Don't we know enough about him to think he has practiced his whole life for the adventure he is about to encounter?"

"Practiced? Well yes. I suppose one might say that of Bly if it's a lifelong dress rehearsal that you mean. He's certainly up for the melodrama."

While Rachel and Estevar's voices blend beautifully, Moth suddenly bobs to the surface from deep within the well of her thoughts. In a voice resembling that of a startled child Moth asks suddenly, "Are we crazy, Consuela?"

"No, no," Doge answers soothingly, patting her friend's hand on the console reassuringly. "Quite simply, dear, we have outlived the value of what we know. It's about relevance. I suppose there are those who think us mad. But I'm quite sure there are just as many who see us pretending to be. Either way we are presumed

An Unfinished Sunset

to be very rich, so we are allowed our eccentricities. Let's enjoy them while we can."

"Yes," C. C. Moth responds with a sigh. "And use them to do some good, aye? After all, who else would protect and defend La Malinché? Who else would help our Mirror of the Jaguar Night find its way home and end its centuries-long exile?"

"Who indeed?" Doge stoically agrees.

Chapter 11

The best mirror is an old friend.

—George Herbert (1593–1633)

LINTON WHIRLED HIS TRUCK around in a ferocious blur, riling the patchy yard grass and ripping a red streak out the rutted trace that led back up into the hammock. He roared down the old logging road, tunneling darkly into the wet tangle of woods that were absent of any observable property line between the postage stamp of earth retained by the Day family and the vast low country of the state's conservancy. Less than a mile ahead would be the usually locked gate on the Blue Line. It was so-called because blue was the color of markings on maps delineating state land from the more easterly woodlands traded and wrought by timber companies for centuries.

The Blue Line Road snaked its way around dark-water cypress ponds, passing platoons of palmettos guarding low banks of sandy loam over drainage ditches that muck their way out to the Old Tram Road. From the main "Mainline," as many of the locals called it, the thickly wooded hammock spread for more than forty miles, unimpeded except by small hunting camps and intermittent logging operations clear-cutting blocks of timber.

Linton drove madly, far more rapidly than his cautious nature would ordinarily permit. He bounced as his truck bounced, though tightly cinched to his seat by the straps of his safety belt. Alternately praying and preaching aloud, Linton sped round through the deep stands of hardwoods and pines patched together by waste wood lattices draped with impenetrable briars. A quarter mile before the gate the road bent around the murky water of another mossy cypress pond.

    Linton gunned the truck's engine for the crossbar of the gate ahead, racing up the muddy straightaway with an anxious glance at the coveted gate key in his immaculate ashtray. But the gate had yawned open. He surged through and slowed slightly to round a gentle curve and accelerated again only to be more than surprised. Terrified, Linton abruptly crashed over a four-wheeler, a muddy all-terrain vehicle with deep-treaded, balloon-like tires abandoned beneath a gloomy crown of massive oak limbs arcing the road. The faded olive drab color and mud splatter had made the ATV almost indistinguishable from the shadows over the road. Panicked, he swerved too late and took the truck and its inanimate, mangled prey into a half spin and then mounted and mangled it before coming to an abrupt crash down the low embankment of a drainage ditch opposite the great oak.

    Coming back around the oak, a wiry straw-haired boy hurtled to the road ahead. He stood at the ditch, peering down warily from beneath the rounded brim of his camouflaged cap. The plunged spectacle of the steamy, twisted metal of the truck's red hood obscured all but a single distorted handlebar of his prized ATV. The boy waited wide-eyed and thunderstruck in oversized rubber boots, his squirrel gun crimped tightly in the bend of faded flannel shirting over his bony elbow. A dazed Linton Day wrestled himself from his previously unblemished truck to the quagmire beneath his polished shoes.

<center>~~~</center>

    By then I was sitting shirtless at the dining table by the window of Mazie Day's house. I leaned in as Alifair came to drape my chambray shirt over my shoulders. I saw my distorted face—grizzled and worn—in the bent glass of a tall china cabinet close by. I winced with a sudden stabbing pain from my bandaged shoulder, and some faint sensory recall resurrected for an instant the scent

Chapter 11

of my flesh oozing a noxious sweat. Alifair wanted to know if she had hurt me with the clean shirt.

"No," I said reassuringly and eased myself around to reposition my elbow on the tabletop. "It comes and goes, you know. But not like before."

"I think you gonna be alright now, Red Man," Alifair assured, insisting on identifying me always as she had first understood my name to be in my semiconscious murmuring.

From the table I could see through the sprawling, uneven shade beneath the rusty roof tin over the porch. Beyond the sandy yard lay the narrow shape of the boardwalk's parched timbers leading down to the small dock, more visible from this vantage point. I could see that the dock was broader than I'd first thought and the boardwalk sturdier. The planks of these were held in place by rusty nails pounded long ago into cross members mounted on the sun-scoured posts driven deep into the marsh grass and mud. The dock stood along the serpentine creek that wound its way from some glade deep within the woods behind the house to the silvery sheen of the Gulf of Mexico.

There, beyond the vista partially dappled by those small palm-shrouded isles, was the way I would go. My eyes returned to the tidal creek, and my mind formed the thought that the way out is the way in. Or so it is constant and remains for the tides. For the tides, as for the fish that feed upon them, the way in is the way out. Unlike them, however, I was marooned, fetched firmly aground in a way I was only beginning to fully comprehend.

In the small kitchen behind me Mazie Day spooned out a dripping heap of mustard greens. She'd cooked them with ham hocks that tumbled flaccidly from her ladling to partially shed the thick brown purses of skin into the simmered greens. Alifair returned to the table again with a plate of cornbread, sliced and covered with a checkered dishtowel. I massaged my shoulder around the gunshot wound and asked the girl about the creek.

"Cane Creek?" Alifair announced brightly. "We call it Cane Creek." She placed the cornbread on the table and slid in to a chair opposite me. "Some peoples say Crazy Woman Creek," the girl giggled. "Gram can tell you *all* about that 'cause this is where they growed sugar cane long, long time ago. My great-granddaddy, he worked for that man, and this was one of the houses on that place, but it has always been *our* people's house. Ain't that right, Gram?" Alifair asked over her shoulder.

The woman brought the bowl of greens to the table. "You remember how I told you," she answered the girl in a firm voice lifting with family pride.

"Yes ma'am." The girl continued, "It was *my* great-granddaddy that Mr. Detwiler turned this house and patch o' land over to, this right here," the girl insisted with a nod. "All this was his, that old Detwiler. All back in here," she gestured toward the hammock. "Him and the peoples he brung with him cleared a bunch of it in them days for sugar cane. Now the woods done come and took it all back 'cept for that old cane bunched up wild in the brakes down along the yard to the trees."

The woman came with salt and pepper and sat askew of me, nodding her approval without interrupting the girl.

"That's all there is now, this ole house and that wild sugar cane no hurricane's ever been bad enough to drag out," Alifair concluded.

A hazy, if attentive, smile formed with the downward cast of my unshaven face. I was entirely enamored of the endurance of this sturdy place. My fondness was helped in no small part by the grit and pert humor of the girl. I admired the strong dignity of the woman, her jaunty goodness, and readily perceived pride in her own place on the earth. She was large and older, yet beautiful to behold in a manner seen more clearly with age. Hers was a vast beauty—the vastness itself being beautiful, as that of a night sky—and yet she was also a solitary star upon which my tired eyes could rest.

Mazie announced that we should pray. She instructed the girl and me to clasp each other's outstretched hand. The hand of my wounded shoulder I kept against my chest. With a spirited severity Mazie asked me then if I prayed. I said I had been taught to do so but had been estranged from my catechism for quite some time. My tone was conciliatory. I said I wished that she would show me the way. The woman frowned but did so approvingly. She lifted

Chapter 11

her strong chin, closed her eyes as tight as the girl's, and began a devout blessing aloud.

The prayer was brief but heartfelt, being sparse but as nutritious for the soul as the meal before us was for the flesh. While their eyes were closed, I took a piece of ham hock from the bowl of greens and crumpled it in my paper napkin in my lap. In the deepening tone of her closing Mazie did not neglect to pray for my healing. The girl and the woman said together, "Amen." With apology in my coarse voice I said amen after them.

The talk at the table was lively, as had not been the case in our earlier, slightly solemn meals shared. Mazie and Alifair were more at ease with me now. I felt better. I asked again about the creek.

The girl sprang to revive her telling, as if it were an eager rendering of a favorite folktale. It was in fact just that: the story of a folk's life, of her own life before she was born into it. I was entirely convinced by this time in my life that we all need a story to function in the world—our own story—but that doesn't mean the story is entirely true.

Curiously enough, Alifair resumed her tale by describing the archaic sugar mill that had once stood nearby. Now, she said, it was reduced to a mound-like heap of red brick rubble, laced with an inferior mortar and serrated with outcroppings of rusted machinery and heavy timbers. It was a nesting place for the rat snake, nearly covered over by vine. The girl also told where the *big house* had stood, though Mazie qualified that it had not been a grandiose mansion nor even an elegant abode by any depiction conjured from our familiar images of a plantation house. It was simply a larger, more spacious version of the same cypress board-and-batten construction, though painted white.

Mazie added proudly, "But this one here, this is the last one standing."

"Why do you think that's so?" I asked.

"Because we live here," she answered defiantly. "We have always lived here. This is our place. We might be small potatoes," she added more lightly with a winsome smile, "but we are a family that looks after *our* potatoes. This is *our* house."

Alifair then announced with all the authority of one who had been an eyewitness that this Detwiler fellow had gone away for a while. He'd married and returned from New Orleans with a Creole woman, one much younger than he.

"Do you know where New Orleans is?" Alifair asked me innocently.

"Yes, I do," I answered.

"You been there?"

"I have."

"Are there lots of crazy women there?"

"More all the time," I answered with a mischievous grin towards Mazie.

"Well, that's where this old Detwiler got this one," Alifair rushed on. "They say she weren't so crazy when she come here, but the lonesomeness and the mosquitoes made her worser and worser. Sometimes she'd shriek out like a banshee in the night."

"You know what a banshee is?" I asked, bemused.

"Could be like a crazy woman, couldn't it?"

"Yes," I answered. "Could be."

"Well, that's what she was, and she'd rip her clothes off in the rain if that old Detwiler didn't watch her close. Only thing she liked here was the rain. Aunt Fiona, she dead now. Auntie, she was King James's sister, and she told me that woman liked the rain so much she'd dance in it. She might come out in the rain and get naked as a jay bird and—"

"You don't need to tell all that!" her grandmother cautioned.

"Well, Aunt Fiona said it weren't no sin on account of the woman was so *crazy*."

"I don't care," Mazie insisted to her granddaughter. "I don't want to hear no more about that woman right now. It's not good for my digestion."

Alifair agreed and then continued unabated, "One day that old Detwiler up and went on his mule to the courthouse at Bronson. When he come back, this land was sold mostly to a big timber company 'cept for this house and ten acres on the creek. He seen to it my great-granddaddy held the paper on that because he was the man he said he trusted most in the whole world. Old Detwiler,

Chapter 11

he put that woman in a boat that they hauled the last sugar from the mill to bigger boats out on the water. All the people that was working here stood on the dock yonder and watched while they loaded the flat boat with Detwiler's big trunks on it, and they went on out. When they was a tiny speck on the water, it was the last anybody ever seen of them Detwilers. Ain't that right, Gram?"

"Far as we know," Mazie said. "But that's enough of all that."

We were quiet for a while. I pondered on Detwiler's demise. But his deliberate departure brought another question to mind.

"I'm just curious," I wondered aloud, thinking I'd take another angle of curiosity. I mashed cornbread into some juice from the greens. "I mean, what are the chances I came off the Gulf directly to this location? Is there a light out there? Something on the water to draw the eye in the dark? In the rain?"

Mazie looked up from her plate and said, "Mister, don't nobody find the mouth of this here creek like that less they know where they's goin'."

"How could I know?"

"You tell me?" she said with a wry smile.

I didn't have an answer. At least I didn't think I did, and my appetite was improving. I ate.

After we'd finished eating, Alifair began clearing the table. I already had the crumpled napkin with the piece of ham hock in the pocket of my stained but washed and dried khakis. Mazie and I went out on the heavy gray planking of the front steps to sit. We were silent for a few minutes. The sun was not harsh, and the sea sweetened the breeze.

Then Mazie said softly, "You know that my son, Linton, is going to bring the law out here?"

"Yes," I said. "But I may not be here when they come."

Alifair came out to play with Hobo in the yard, tossing a small orange ball for the dog to chase and fetch from the centipede grass toward the boardwalk before the dock on the whiskey-colored creek.

"You still have a ways to go before you ought to be carrying yourself about," Mazie said thoughtfully. "Maybe you can just explain."

"Explain what?"

"Explain why you a guest in my house."

I smiled. "I'm a guest," I said, "because you invited me in. You could have just locked me away in that old shed out back. Slipped me some food in a pie pan once or twice a day until somebody came to relieve you of me. Worse, you could have just left me in those palmettos back there."

Mazie Day shook her head with solemn certitude, and said, "Let me ask you something. What do you call yourself?"

I looked at her, more perplexed than bemused or compliant. "Irish Bly," I said finally.

"Yes," Mazie said, looking far out over the Gulf. "Irish Bly," her assuaging tone more indicative of agreement than acknowledgment of a question asked and answered. "What do you know about the Bolita, Irish Bly?"

"The Bolita?" I asked hesitantly. "Why?"

Mazie didn't answer but continued to search the sunlit distance, waiting. In that pregnant pause I began to recollect something from my boyhood. I told her about Sporty Rey.

"Sporty wasn't his real name, I don't think. But, so far as I knew, it was the name he was known by. It suited him. It's what folks around Tampa called him anyway—Sporty Rey. He was this lean, clean-cut little fellow who drove a black '49 Buick. You see Buicks of that vintage all over Havana now, but back then it was a pretty special car, its front grill brandishing a big chrome-like smirk. The sedan was secondhand, I'm almost sure, but Sporty kept it immaculate, sleek, and waxed with a shine as fine as the day he first drove it up to his red brick bungalow off Swan Avenue."

After a moment I explained, "Appearances mattered to Sporty. He was smartly dressed, always neatly pressed, precise in knotting his tie. He worked in the insurance business for an uncle of mine. My grandmother admired his style, his fastidiousness. Sporty and his wife, at first, were among those often attending her Saturday afternoon receptions. There were always questions about Sporty though. I mean, he dressed with just enough flash to make his neighbors and some of her other guests wonder if he was really an insurance man. Or maybe he was into something else. Maybe it was the cocky way he wore his panama hat or those two-toned

Chapter 11

shoes that raised suspicions. Some said he might be a *wise guy*—one of the Tampa underworld. Could be he was connected with Charlie Wall, the dean of Tampa's crime bosses at the time. Some of Charlie's minions drove cars and dressed like that. I saw Charlie around a time or two. My grandmother pointed him out to me in front of a barbershop, and I remembered him standing on our lawn one day. But I never knew of any particular connection between him and Sporty Rey."

Mazie shifted herself comfortably against one of the front porch posts, and I went on, saying, "Wall was a Tampa native, like my grandmother. They'd known each other in childhood but had become less companionable, I'll say, by the time Charlie lorded over his central Florida crime syndicate, which he did for decades. He operated out of Ybor, a working-class Cuban neighborhood populated mostly by cigar workers back then. Wall, he bootlegged liquor, ran brothels, and virtually monopolized the Bolita games in the area. I heard or rather *overheard* all about that as a boy in knee britches, sopping up all the adult gossip. Wall's organization was expansive, extending eventually into what was called the Cracker Mafia."

"Uh huh, that Cracker Mafia," Mazie acknowledged with the enthusiasm of an amen said in church.

"They operated out of Tampa, across the state through Plant City, all the way to Daytona on the Atlantic side. That whole outfit was his operation."

I could see Mazie was growing more interested in the story.

"But later on the Italian Mafiosi started setting up shop, the Trafficante family, who began moving in on Wall's Tampa turf. There were days of reckoning and nights of retribution. Gangster stuff. Mostly before my time, this 'era of blood,' as it was known locally. So there were plenty of gangsters around Tampa in those days. But this Sporty Rey, he was an insurance man running a debt for my uncle, and that's all we knew for sure. He was just a guy with a pencil-thin mustache, a debit book, and a pretty wife. A woman who was shy to the point of being misperceived by most folks, even my grandmother, as conceited or snobbish. She wasn't though. I was only a kid, but I knew. She was just astonishingly beautiful and exceedingly shy, not stuck-up like people said. I'm pretty sure Sporty wasn't in the rackets either, at least not yet."

"What about the insurance?" Mazie asked probingly.

"Well, this was the early fifties. On weekdays Sporty would slide into his shiny Buick and disappear up Swan, turn on Nebraska, and then go who knows where. Folks out in Temple Terrace and Brandon knew where. See, Sporty worked the smaller towns in the area, mostly the poorer neighborhoods—the groves, the turpentine woods, and some of the cattle ranches or sawmills around. In the towns he'd park up a narrow street in the shade and walk door to door. He collected on the small insurance policies he'd sold. Most were just burial insurance, so maybe he collected a dollar or so a month, one door to another. It was a volume business, and Sporty stayed on the move. He was a proud man. He'd swing back that shiny car door like a matador's cape, dust his shoes with a rag from the side panel, and be off to his next debit stop."

"You know his customers?" Mazie asked.

"Not completely. Once or twice I'd ridden with my uncle on his rounds, and he'd catch up with Sporty in a little café he'd frequent or out where he was parked in some neighborhood for some reason. I did go with my uncle to a certain lady's house later. She was Sporty's customer, but he was dead by then."

"Dead?"

"Yeah, they killed him."

"Who?"

"I don't know. I just know there was an older black woman over in Brandon who was a favorite of Sporty's. She was kindly, had an easy laugh. She shared her deep, abiding faith whenever she spoke. She and Sporty, they'd sip a glass of sweet tea on her front porch, which was about as close to church as Sporty Rey ever got. They were friends, you know. They never said so, but they were."

"What was that woman's name?"

"Her name, I remember, was Emma Jakes. Emma was the first person Sporty told that his wife had left him. Even before my uncle, he told Emma. But I knew it before Sporty did."

"You?"

Chapter 11

"I had a paper route when I was a boy. Delivered the *Tampa Tribune* on my bicycle. Sporty was on my route, and one summer morning I was peddling around puddles from a recent rain, and down that street was Sporty's house. If I was lucky that day, I would soon be at their front door, gazing up at the luminous radiance of Ilene Rey."

"She was pretty?"

"You know how in paintings or glamorous photographs or sitting in a movie theater when you're young, there's this image of one before you against which you measure all others of the same gender afterward. My first glimpse of Ilene Rey seized me in such a way as to set her as the gold standard between my ears forever."

"I'll have to take your word for that," Mazie said good-naturedly.

"But on this morning as I approached by the neighbor's hedge," I continued out of an archived perplexity, "Ilene Rey stood erect out on her front porch in a black sleeveless dress and a red pillbox hat with the mesh down over her eyes. A suitcase was at her feet. I waited astride my bike as a Yellow Cab came around and pulled up to the curb of her house. She stepped down from the porch, and the cabbie took her suitcase. He opened a back door for her. Getting in, she never even glanced my way. But as the cab pulled away, she turned in the seat and looked back at me as if she knew I'd been there all along. I saw her sad, sweet smile fade away into the distance of the bricked street, the old neighborhood dissolving behind her. I knew I'd never see her again."

"And that's what happened?"

"According to Sporty there'd been no argument, no indiscretion discovered, and no note left to explain. At least that's what Sporty told Emma Jakes and Emma my uncle. I'd get most of this later, but I know from my uncle that Emma offered Sporty comfort. The kind of comfort a mama can give a son when, all the while, her own beloved husband lay gasping with each labored breath in the dark heat of the house behind them."

"Yes, yes ..." Mazie sighed softly.

"Anyhow, the next month or so after Ilene left, Sporty got around to telling Emma he now had more than insurance to sell. You asked me about Bolita. Well here's what I know, though I'm not clear whether his new enterprise developed before Ilene left or just after. In any case there were Bolita tickets stashed in Sporty's account book. I don't think Emma was any too pleased about it."

"No."

"Emma cautioned Sporty and then had a confession of her own. With her husband out of work and her own health failing, hard work was impossible. She couldn't continue to make the insurance payments on her husband's policy. As for buying a Bolita ticket, she told him, 'Nobody really wins but them Bolita bankers. And the devil, he's the biggest banker of them all.' That's how Sporty told it."

"So true."

"Months passed. Sporty never missed his regular visit with Emma, debt payment or not. They talked. Somewhere along the line it had become a game between them to forecast the next rain. It hadn't rained in a long while, I guess. They never again spoke of insurance or the numbers either one."

"That was just as well," Mazie mused and then asked, "But how exactly did that Bolita game go? I know I've heard about the game, but King James, he wouldn't do nothin' like that. Likewise I never bought no lottery ticket neither. They's about the same—your lottery and the Bolita?"

"Both a gamble, but in the basic Bolita game one hundred little numbered balls are placed into a bag, mixed, and shaken up thoroughly. Bets are taken on which number will be drawn. There are many variations on this theme and many different games. Bets are typically small and sometimes sold well in advance. Most games are rigged. That's the fact. Sometimes extra balls of a given number are included. Or certain balls are not in the bag at all. Some games cheat by including balls filled with lead that sink to the bottom of the bag, improving the odds on those numbers. Other times selected balls are iced beforehand so that they're cold and easy for the selector to find by touch. Anyway, there have always been about as many tricks as games."

"Ain't that the way."

"In Sporty's time the biggest game was out of Cuba. Somewhere in Havana was a rack of one hundred ivory balls, each with a number,

Chapter 11

laid sequentially in a mahogany rack. All the numbers were there to see. The balls were then gathered out of the rack and dropped into a black velvet bag. The bag was shaken vigorously and flung about until tossed finally to a *catcher*—one of the onlookers. The catcher would isolate a single ball and, with the aid of a knife, slit the bag to extract the ball bearing the winning number."

"So what became of this Sporty Rey?"

"Well, one night across the Florida Straits, about five hundred miles away from where he was operating in a small cabin on a lake out in the orange groves, Sporty and a bespectacled, pint-sized associate—one Ambrose Endecott—hovered around a shortwave radio. They listened to a scratchy broadcast of the Cuban National Lottery. The winning number was about to be announced, and Sporty Rey would translate for Endecott. That was his bit, but it was Endecott's task to check the *hit* or winning number against the tickets purchased for that game."

"This Endecott, he was the gangster?"

"Endecott? No, he was actually a respected local grower and businessman. He had a large grove and packing shed, a fruit stand, and a small grocery up on the highway. But after back-to-back bad harvests for his oranges, he'd fallen on hard times. Endecott wasn't just broke; he was deep in debt and in debt to the wrong people. So when he was offered $50 a week expenses and 25 percent of the profits as a Bolita checker, I suppose he wagered his reputation on a chance to get solvent again."

"There you go, that's what the devil will do," Mazie said solemnly.

"See, in a Bolita operation you've got at least four guys, each performing a particular function. You've got the *operator*. He's the head of the group, often called the *banker*. He finances the operation. The players bet against the banker. The *writer* is the guy who sells the tickets. Sporty Rey was a top writer by then. Of course, running a debt for the insurance business gave him great cover for his ticket sales. So the writer records on triplicate slips the number or numbers sold to each player. He notes on the ticket the amount of each wager and gives one copy to the player. He keeps one copy of each slip and delivers the other copy to a *pick-up* man. That's the guy who brings the tickets in from the writers. He'd put them

An Unfinished Sunset

in a paper bag and drop them off at a designated spot made known to the checker."

"What happened next?" Mazie wanted to know.

"Each Saturday afternoon Endecott would retrieve the bag of tickets from above the false ceiling in the privy behind his country store. On this particularly hot October evening Sporty and Endecott leaned toward the shortwave in the cabin in the grove, listening for the winning numbers."

"Somethin' bad is gonna happen."

"Yes, the two men didn't know it, but Charlie Wall's wife had just come home to find Charlie dead on the floor of their bedroom with his throat slashed, skull fractured, and face beat to a bloody pulp. The shortwave crackled, and the door to the cabin suddenly crashed in. Down in Havana the catcher was just making his slit in the bag when machine gun blasts riddled the interior of the cabin."

"Sporty?"

"Then it was quiet. I imagine even the screeching of frightened cranes rising from the little lake outside disappeared in the rumble of some dark sedan with its lights off, thundering back up that moonlit farm road over the hill and out of the groves."

"Lord, Lord. Sporty, he was dead right off?"

"Yes, Endecott too. Dead as Charlie Wall. Some days later a big, burly man with a crewcut ambled up the front steps of Emma Jakes's place. That was my Uncle Clyde. He was the top man in Tampa for that insurance company. Oddly enough, it was about the same time of day Sporty usually came by. But my uncle went, and I was with him because he wanted me to take a picture. Emma watched us through the screened door coming up the walk. When we stood on the porch before the door, she looked down at me on with wet eyes. Uncle Clyde was sweating profusely like he did. Mopping his head with a handkerchief, he says, 'Mrs. Jakes, I'm Sporty Rey's boss, Clyde Redmond.'"

I paused for dramatic effect, looked at Mazie, and said, "So this is how the rest of the conversation went, as far as I recall."

"You a Bolita man?" Emma, still secluded behind the screened door, asks Uncle Clyde nervously.

"No, ma'am. I'm an insurance agent," Uncle Clyde reassured her. "Sporty Rey, he worked for me."

Emma didn't speak, so my uncle went on, saying, "I'm sorry for your loss, Mrs. Jakes. Your husband, I mean. I've brung you his death benefit." He extended an envelope from his shirt pocket.

"I didn't pay all that. Had to drop it," she said.

"No, ma'am, it was paid in full, 100 percent, Mrs. Jakes. That got done for you. This death benefits check here is yours. Sporty paid it all along his self, I'm thinking," Uncle Clyde told her.

Emma Jakes looked to be weak at her knees by then.

"This one too," Uncle Clyde said, extracting a second envelope from the same pocket. "This is yours."

"What? What would *that* be?" she asked with tears streaking down her cheeks.

"That's the payout on Sporty Rey's policy on his self, Mrs. Jakes. It's a good bit more than the other. I didn't know if you knew—knew you were the named beneficiary."

I sat silent for a bit before adding, "Then it began to rain."

Mazie thought aloud, "He did that for Emma." It wasn't a question.

"Yes. I took a fine photograph out on the porch of Uncle Clyde presenting Emma Jakes with the two checks. It hung on his office wall for years until he retired."

"I never did know just how it was. But I was sure glad for Emma that things got a good bit better for her after Brother Man passed. That's what we all called Emma's husband—Brother Man. I didn't know about no Sporty Rey."

"You knew Emma Jakes?" I asked, barely concealing my astonishment.

"Emma Jakes is—was—my big sister, Irish. She's gone on ahead now. But Emma Jakes, yes sir, she was my oldest sister. There was three of us girls: Emma, me, and Elle. She was the baby, Elle."

11.1

In the modernized kitchen of the great old house on Whitehead Street Bertrand Oliphant is making two sandwiches of lobster salad on slender rolls grilled on the stovetop. A sweet amalgam of butter and olive oil sizzle over the cast-iron griddle designed into Oliphant's French-made aluminum stove. His spatula flattens the two split-top rolls, browning them then to a buttery crispness. Oliphant makes the lobster rolls exactly as he and Elle prefer them, with the bun brazed, then overstuffed with fresh salad and a cold slice of dill pickle on the side.

The smoky scent of cooking swirls from ceiling fan to ceiling fan to Elle, relaxing out on the air-conditioned sun porch. The willowy-figured woman sits in a purple dressing gown that sets off the splash of color her signature turban makes. This one is fashioned from her extensive Hermès collection of brilliant silk scarves. Sitting erect in one of the antique bamboo chairs surrounding the glass-topped table, her slender hands are folded neatly in her lap. Elle is reading from the bright screen of her laptop.

The glass walls of the porch are decorously lined with exotic plants, rendering a greenhouse-like ambiance to the room. While in Key West, Elle reads the online *New Orleans Times-Picayune* daily. Although her eyes are fixed on the computer screen, her thoughts drift erratically over the content there.

Elle absently scrolls through recent restaurant reviews. One favorable is a critique of the bistro-type eatery that she and Oliphant have recently opened on Dauphine Street. Its French Quarter location ought to be considered dangerously close to one of the city's finest restaurants—one operated, as it happens, by a renowned chef whom Oliphant himself particularly prefers. So much so in fact that when they visit the Crescent City, he and Elle maintain regular reservations to enjoy her celebrated cuisine.

There are distinct differences though between the establishments. To begin with, *Oliphant's* is more of an old-style French Quarter café—smaller and not nearly as upscale or quaint as the garden and cottage-like location of his friendly rival. And the cuisine isn't subject to contest either. *Oliphant's* offers traditional fare, hot and hardy, dished by bawdy servers on thick, white, steaming plates from the rustic Creole kitchen. This is a Vieux Carré neighborhood place. The other establishment (by the owner/chef's description) defies definition or simple classification. On her web

Chapter 11

page she says she selects the best local ingredients to craft flavorful, balanced, yet complex dishes inspired by classic cuisines from around the world. Most recently a fish recipe she'd created is said to be inspired by the cooking fires of Madagascar and is among Oliphant's personal favorites.

Elle has a more careful look at the latest menu posted. She peers through her reading glasses with a curiosity absent of competitive thought. After all, Oliphant's primary motive was to find a NOLA location to stash some cash, and a restaurant is as good a place as any for that.

Back in his own Key West kitchen Oliphant puts the sandwiches on small, festive plates and brings these with silverware tucked in linen napkins to the table. Elle's plate lands lightly on the glass between the laptop and her half flute of chardonnay.

"More?" he asks gently with a nod to her wine glass.

"You know this is all too complicated," Elle has been waiting to say. "Mixing things up as you have."

"A little heavy on the celery in the salad, you mean?" Oliphant asks bouncily, setting his plate with a click opposite hers.

"No," the woman answers tersely. "It's about your baseball player and his people and then this strange ancient pirate's treasure you now add to the bouillabaisse."

"A conquistador," Oliphant corrects, excusing himself then to return with his own full glass of wine.

"What are you talking about?" Elle wants to know as he settles in across from her.

"I'm simply saying it's not a pirate's treasure but rather an ancient *objet de vertu*, this ancient Mirror originally from among Montezuma's affects, or so its provenance goes. It was found among a conquistador's treasure trove, presumed lost in Cuban waters in the sixteenth century. I'm told it's a most exquisite object, an extraordinary find." Oliphant pauses and lifts his eyes, as if to savor the keenly detailed image held within his mind's eye, and says, "Said to be black in color."

"And gold?"

"Yes, of course, an obsidian disk artfully polished to produce a fine reflection. But yes, gold, the mirror itself mounted between Aztec jaguars cast in solid gold."

Elle's eyes narrow and return to the screen of her laptop. The newly posted menu presented by the chef on Dauphine remains there.

"Recovered from the lost ship of the conquistador," she says in a singsong tone, as if reading aloud. "The secret ship of Hernán Cortés. Every bit a pirate, to be exact."

Oliphant patiently sips his wine, certain that he has not discussed these particulars with Elle himself. He opts not to inquire about the source of her information. He merely adds blandly, as if he'd fully expected her to know and opine as she has, "But of course."

An amicable, even if arduous, competition for exact information has long been enjoyed between the two. Elle takes a small first bite from the lobster roll. She nods her approval as she chews. After tamping about her mouth with the linen napkin from her lap, she says, "But I don't care which. Conquistador or pirate, it's all the same to me."

Her dark piercing eyes level on Oliphant then. She cocks her head, as she has a habit of doing when displeased and waiting for him to speak.

"Elle, you don't trust our particular friends the Sisters?" Oliphant perceptively inquires in a fawning tone.

"Not the issue," she says tersely. "It's *you* I don't trust. You've become too greedy, Bertrand. Too self-involved. Too public. Carelessly so."

The older man lifts his head bemused, eyes wide shut. It's the visage of a Roman emperor. Elle's turbaned head in profile is no less regal.

"I'm right," Elle Rousseau says firmly. "We've always kept our business simple and our cover complex." She folds her slender arms across her trim upper torso and adds, "This has become too complicated. Even confusing. I want you to do something about it. I want it …untangled."

The authority in her voice carries a significant weight. As a matter of fact, it's business, and it's not Oliphant's money alone in

Chapter 11

play. While Oliphant does give every appearance of being, as the Sisters have put it, "the man who owns the boat," that's not entirely the case now. He is indeed the founder of the feast, the man out front, the one who makes and seals the deals. Yet, unknown to even his most trusted Key West confidantes and cronies, the fast-boat operation in particular is largely Elle's domain. It's business, but it's *personal* business with her. After all, it's about Cuba.

Elle's preoccupation with getting people out of Cuba, oddly enough, harkens back to her gratitude for her own time and fortunes on getting *in* to Cuba. In large measure this is about the Cuba she came to adore and the people who welcomed her there as a young woman, especially those who shared her passion for music and dance, for performance and dreaming, and for baseball.

Elle had first come to know something of Cuba before the revolution. As a young woman she began to perfect a dance style that won her gigs where she could find them, mostly in the hideaway clubs and bars of Ybor City, Tampa's Latin district. In all the talk and tobacco smoke around Tampa back then there was often gossip about the Havana scene, the Club San Souci, and other more intimate clubs. But always, when music and dance were the topic, the Tropicana was the ultimate conversational destination of choice. The perfumed nostalgia was expressed so palpably that she could feel the beat of congas on the tree-lined stage. She saw in her revelries the erotic whirl of feathered forms, elegant in sensual song and dance.

Such erogenous reminiscing about the music, the dancing, and the color and flash—it all made Elle want to go. She needed to see for herself the *Arcos de Cristal*, the Tropicana building composed of parabolic concrete arches and glass walls over the verdant setting of its indoor stage. She found a way down to Cuba, and that, as an entertainer and later as a businesswoman, would become her way up.

In brief, Elle had been a featured performer at the Tropicana, thanks to Arielle Vega. Vega had taken her under her protective wing some weeks after Elle arrived at the Havana docks, cardboard suitcase in hand. She'd been living as little more than a street urchin near the studio where Vega took and sometimes taught classes. Elle had already "modeled" at a seedy little burlesque theatre down in the *Barrio de Chino*. The place attracted sailors and rowdy tourists to Havana's Chinatown because, by midnight, all the provocative feathers had fallen, and the full-out shows were reduced to nothing more than those of a strip joint. Elle was mere hours from donning one of their risqué costumes when Arielle snatched her from the rouge jaws of the Shanghai.

Arielle Vega knew Martin Fox, the owner of the Tropicana, although it was his lovely wife, Ofelia, who most admired Arielle. She knew and respected her as an accomplished dancer and enjoyed her company as an eccentric young friend.

Fox tolerated Arielle. He accepted courteously her candid critiques of his shows. Martin Fox never said so, but he also respected her adamant refusal of his entreaties to perform on his stage. Many of Arielle's friends, trained and *serious* dancers, had defected to the club's far more lucrative venue. The solitary perception on which Vega and Fox entirely agreed was that Arielle Vega certainly had an eye for talent well suited to the extravagant shows on his exotic stage.

Vega admired Elle's expectant, just-off-the-boat, émigré determination to thrive in the city. Particularly so because she'd first observed Elle on the avenue outside of her dance class studio window imitating Vega's students' moves inside. Eventually Vega brought Elle in. There were *problemas*. But they were of the sort that made Vega all the more certain that Elle was destined for the Tropicana rather than the studied, artistic venues of the classically trained. Even if devoted to new or more contemporary forms and forums, Arielle Vega knew these were no platform for Elle's jazz style.

Vega was like those baseball scouts who observe youthful players on obscure playing fields where a green wall of sugarcane demarks the outfield. A scout could see instinctively that there, pitching, is one bound for New York's Yankee Stadium or Boston's Wrigley Field. The scout knows it is so because the boy pitching has already seen *himself* pitching at Yankee Stadium or Wrigley Field. So it was that knowingness that led to Arielle Vega's disinclined and reluctant nod to Martin Fox. It would be that nod of approval that first gave Elle a chance in the Tropicana's chorus line.

It occurred on a spring morning when Fox (though it was not his habit) was playing dominos. He sat for a time with his pals at a table beneath the tall palm trees rising through the roof of the club's ultramodern architecture. Elle, not yet nineteen but looking all of twenty-something, suddenly stood before his table with Arielle Vega at her side.

"You have your *las diosas de carne*, don't you?" Vega nearly snarled. "You feature this Carmen Miranda, this Josephine Baker. The world has these women—not the Tropicana alone. But this girl, Elle, she can be yours here, the Tropicana's own. Trust me. You will see. These other women, they go for the world to see them. This one, the world will come to her. They will come to the Tropicana!"

Fox was immediately enamored. The meticulous, persnickety, and already legendary performer and choreographer, Roderico Neyra, would take more time to win over. Nevertheless Neyra rapidly recovered from his indignation at Fox's intervention in the magnificent new show he was casting. By the time Elle actually took the stage, Rodney (as he was known) acknowledged that she would be a rising star in the resplendent galaxy of Tropicana talent. This was in the pre-revolutionary days, some years before the Sisters had their own illumined table, attracting in moth-like fashion the likes of Errol Flynn and 'that handsome Kennedy boy' along with the rest.

Earlier, in Elle's heyday, the Tropicana was the only club in Havana whose dance troupe was exclusively Cuban, exclusively white, or at least white enough to pass. Fox was willing to give the statuesque American beauty a shot, but there was a condition attached. She had to lighten her skin. That was the way of it then. The darker pigmentation of her skin didn't really matter to Fox but it did to most of his patrons, particularly to those arriving by Pan Am seaplane or the ferryboats out of Key West.

So a dissident babalawo (some crackpot priest and herbalist known to Neyra) applied an early version of a primal skin lightener to Elle's splendid body. It was likely a hydroquinone concoction derived from liverworts, mixed with mercury and something else to form a secret potion that eventually rendered her skin a golden honey color. Exactly the shade most preferred by the southbound patrons of that world-famous cabaret of the early 1950s.

Elle did what it took. She always had. Unlike her older sisters, who were contented with more conventional lives, Elle had ventured audaciously toward the glitz and glamour, dramatically distant from her humble coastal Florida roots. How else could Elle Day become a celebrated performer at one of the most famous nightclubs in the world? Oliphant liked the story. He liked the way she told it between cigarettes.

So that is how Oliphant found Elle Day. That's where their partnership began but only after Oliphant had befriended and prevailed upon the cabaret's bandleader to make an introduction. Oliphant, as remained his style, had gone to considerable expense to arrange it. The new watch the bandleader was wearing at the cuff of his canary yellow linen jacket cost more than the man's car.

Theirs was a brief but enchanting encounter that night, Elle would later tell. Not amorous or romantic but rather more entertaining. It was a free-wheeling conversation enabling Oliphant to demonstrate his considerable panache in that social milieu. He managed thereby to engender in Elle an implicit enthusiasm, a hopefulness of learning more before he abruptly but courteously broke from their date with a promise of continuing their playful and pleasant exchange in the near future.

Elle's newly attained celebrity (local as it was) might be more valuable than she'd thought. So the conversation did continue the next day at a bayside restaurant. It was a leisurely late lunch in the breezy shade of striped awning at a coveted table close to the old market.

"What a rare find," Oliphant greeted her in his syrupy accent. "How fascinating this occurrence, a sunlit lunch in Havana with a truly extraordinary woman of the American southland."

Elle, in a broad white sunhat, received his compliments with the wan smile of one well acquainted with flattery. But Oliphant was just getting warmed up. He had a pitcher of cold sangria brought to the table and listed three different appetizers he knew to be *exquisite* specialties of the house. Between orders from an attentive

Chapter 11

waiter in a crisp white jacket, Oliphant inquired methodically about Elle's ascension to the Tropicana's famous stage under the stars.

The tale she recounted he pronounced to be an "absolutely amazing feat," considering the start she'd described at a Tampa speakeasy deep in Ybor City. Elle said that it was there when she first began to pick up Spanish from frequently used phrases. She'd also learned the mambo, the cha-cha, the tango, and a dozen other Latin dances, as well as pure down and dirty American jive.

These were dances she would refine beneath the giant Tropicana fruit trees inside the cabaret beneath that vast air-conditioned arc of glass. On any given night more than a thousand people might meander around the gambling tables, order drinks from the bars, have dinner, and turn with the tide of celebratory guests in standing room only to see her shows. Elle recalled how she'd come down to Cuba, how she'd made her way up the precipitously inaccessible dance lines to that elite society of performers privileged enough to be featured in the Tropicana's Arcos de Cristal.

"It must be exceedingly difficult for women of Cuban origin, much less one like yourself—a woman not much more than a girl and an American girl at that—to achieve such celebrity. Unheard of!" Oliphant gushed. "A star among arguably one of the most elite troupes of entertainers on the planet."

Elle had been born a dreamer and a schemer on Florida's Gulf coast. She hadn't elaborated on the fact, however. She didn't tell Oliphant that, as a mere slip of a girl, she'd costumed herself in all manner of inventive ways, masquerading about with only the palmettos for an admiring audience. By the time she was an older teenager she'd been taught to sing in church, but she burned for a place to dance. She'd made her way from the hardscrabble life of a crabber's daughter down to the city of Tampa by bus. Her older sister, Emma and Emma's kindly husband (half her size) had welcomed Elle with open arms. They loved her and she understood this, despite their disapproval of the jazz club, dive-and-jive lifestyle in which Elle soon immersed herself.

It was true. From that small austere room in her sister's Temple Terrace home to the high life of Havana was one continuous, gigantic, jaguar-like leap. It was Elle's fearless drive and carefully calculated determination that had gotten her there.

Oliphant absorbed everything Elle revealed. He also noticed what she chose not to tell. He loved a good story. But, as she continued, he was listening and calculating as well. His thoughts retraced and then raced ahead of their encounter. This woman was not merely a *flesh goddess*, as Arielle Vega had referred to others of her ilk the day she introduced Elle to Martin Fox. Sure she had talent. Who doesn't these days, was Oliphant's guarded thought. To some other man Elle's story might have seemed much too far-fetched, one requiring a total suspension of disbelief to accept her countless twists of fate and fortune. But Bertrand Oliphant (who gave every indication of being one well born to a privileged life) knew his own story was even more incredible.

Elle had brains. He was certain of that. She also had what Oliphant was fond of calling "spine." For calculated reasons she developed as she spoke Elle offered to confide to Oliphant something concealed—a deep secret—on the waterfront that day.

"I am listening," he said. "My lips are sealed."

Elle said she had been dancing for some time with an injured back, probably the consequence of some congenital defect that was worsening by the week. No doctor or babalawo did her any good. Rum and a powdery narcotic substance a gambler acquaintance regularly slipped her now diminished daily in their affect. The adverse demands of dance and consequences of celebrity were beginning to overwhelm her.

Oliphant did not speak while a freighter (yet another irony, the *Orleans*) loudly completed its mooring close by. Then he said gently from behind his white oversized sunglasses, "Elle, I'm not propositioning, you understand? Certainly not as a lover or in any way other than business." He waited again, as if plumbing his thoughts before spilling them. "You're a big deal in Havana now, Elle, but I want to make you a better deal. The deal of a lifetime."

Elle Day nodded suspiciously from behind her tortoise shell sunglasses. She lit another cigarette and asked straight up, "What's the deal?"

Chapter 11

"The deal is that you levitate forever from the stage of the Tropicana. You, Elle, are already a fairy tale come true. Your image, as you've shaped it, remains suspended in the Tropicana's collective memory: a radiant beauty abounding in grace—not at all the pained and disturbingly distorted image you now secretly suffer to disguise."

She exhaled slowly and asked, "And?"

"And you shall become my full partner in business, in a certain venture, or perhaps several that I have in mind."

Elle looked away pensively toward the harbor. Oliphant could sense she was open to his bid.

"This is not an offer made out of any sort of pity. And so it ought not to be rejected out of pride," Oliphant hastened to add. "It's not an act of kindness of any sort. It is quite simply *business*, my dear lady. You have a charisma beyond that of your stage presence, and that charisma is valuable to me. I'm extending this offer after substantial observation, careful inquiry, and thoughtful consideration. I will make it but once," Oliphant said sternly. "But before I do," Oliphant added with a satirical smile, "as a matter of full disclosure I should tell you I'm well acquainted with your gambler friend, Mr. Rulon Rousseau. I know the score, Elle. I knew it before I invited you to our delightful lunch today."

So that was how it began those many years ago. Oliphant had only recently added the high-end Royal Street antique emporium to his assortment of New Orleans businesses. He hadn't yet thought it better to relocate the headquarters of his operations to his Key West home on Whitehead. He did want more time there and more opportunities to travel internationally for his antique and art buying. Elle could also operate another of his establishments, the popular *La Lune Bleue* in the Vieux Carré. She would become its glamorous greeter, book the talent, and generally manage the place in his stead.

By the time the Sisters were regulars there, Elle's portrait in her famous flamingo-colored plumes was adorning a wall of the Arcos de Cristal. The Sisters wouldn't have recognized her from that in Key West though. Time and the hydroquinone and the mercury had taken its toll. So had the cigarettes and after-hours cocktails and Rulon Rousseau, who found Elle again deep in the Old Quarter.

But Elle had overcome each of those challenges. After Rulon had once more beaten her mercilessly, a carriage driver plodding his horse home in the early hours found Elle in a cloying pool of lamplight on the rain-slick street. She laid there, a battered wreck of a woman, outside her pillaged townhouse in the Quarter. Oliphant had Mr. Rousseau taken care of personally. Elle thus remained in the safety of Oliphant's lavish villa in the Garden District, commencing a living arrangement that well suited each of the partners from that place and night to this.

As the two were finishing their lunch quietly on the sun porch, Elle asks again, "So tell me, Bertrand, what's to be done about this matter of your confusing my spiritual art rescue with your curious contraband, this ancient object or whatever?"

"I have a plan," Oliphant answers and stands to clear the table of dishes.

"I have a plan? Your tombstone should be engraved with 'I have a plan,'" Elle retorts drily.

"Indeed," Oliphant agrees cheerfully with his sly-dog smile—a smile long engaged to conceal his impulse to reveal along with his instinct to hide.

11.2

A line of Dutch girl scouts, bloused in red with low-knotted blue neckerchiefs, cross the pavement of the Plaza Vieja. By the time they stand in miniature before the tall door of the old Gómez Vila building, Irish Bly is out on the plaza anxiously checking his wristwatch.

Having just approached by another way, he's obliged to wait while a uniformed *Scouting Nederland* leader herds the girls into two casual columns before the doorway. Pointing upward in a statuesque pose, she summarily explains the Camera Obscura they are about to see. Describing it in elementary fashion, the scout leader says that it operates on the principles of light reflection through two lenses and a mirror located on a periscope at the top of the building. The image that's captured by the periscope (she continues while broadly cupping her hands) is projected onto a concave platform

Chapter 11

located inside the dark room at the top of the building they're about to enter. She promises that the images of the city will be sharp and crisp, especially since this is a cloudless day. The scouts will hear much of this again in more precise detail when the subsequent Cuban guide presents the Camera to them in the darkened room above.

Irish Bly is nearer now, though not so close on the old square as to intrude on the double row of girl scouts before the building's door. He is inwardly impatient, but there is time.

Having concluded her brusque introduction of the Camera Obscura, the leader barks further instructions in a more strident tone. The scouts scurry to form a single line extending beyond the oblique shadow of the Gómez Vila building next to where Irish waits uneasily in the sunny plaza.

The elevator isn't working. The visitors to the Camera and the rooftop gift shop must take the spiral stairs five stories to the top. Up and around the steps cherubic voices singing a Dutch campfire song reverberate through the building. Irish trudges up after the scouts, intermittently careening outward to peer up. Small hands appear and disappear from the arc of the banister above like small birds landing and leaving a wire.

One of the scouts' leaders is last. Not the one lecturing about the Camera Obscura. It's her assistant with a first-aid kit and water bottle holstered onto her thickly webbed belt. She's a stout woman, lamenting every step up with a distinctly sturdy huff. At each landing she sighs loudly and waits to catch her breath. Arms akimbo, she bends at her ample waist and scowls back down at Bly who has taken the gain of a step at each floor.

Now he's a mere three steps down, obliged to wait again and mask his impatience with a contrived smile. A high-pitched muttering, a sort of sputtering rattles in his head. It's the voice of the white rabbit of *Alice's Adventures in Wonderland* ringing out, *Oh dear! Oh dear! I shall be too late!* Worse yet, it occurs to Irish that the white rabbit had quickly scurried down while conversely he, by anxious fits and starts, slowly treads up.

At the top the girls are counted into the room housing the Camera Obscura. They aren't the first to be sold tickets for admission at that hour. An older British couple is already in the room. They try their Spanish with the smart, prim, multilingual guide who speaks German just as well. She'd earlier extended a greeting in that language to the tall, stark-looking man who was first to enter. It is Diebolt Krym, with his close-cropped hair, horned-rim glasses, and suspicious ice-blue eyes darting about the room as they are speaking. Wearing his dark jacket zipped to his neck, he is a dead giveaway—every feature and action conforming precisely to the description Lourdes Lim had received from her Uncle Luis. Moreover the uncle's description mirrors the one that the Sisters provided to Bly. So Krym could easily be identified by both as the jackal in the room.

But Lourdes is not in the room. She had seen Krym go up from across the plaza. She'd been closely watching him since he'd entered Hermanito's Chevy Bel Air earlier in the alleyway behind Arielle Vega's casa particular.

Lourdes and Luis Lim were in agreement: Yohan Lim's florescent solar chart foretold the significance of this day. Krym's appearance in Havana, so nearly proximate to the appointed hour, signified that he too had information about the anticipated illumination of the Mirror. They decided that it was likely that he had more intel than they did.

Krym's cautious entrance to the Gómez Vila building could only mean that he would either exit with the prize or depart the square knowing where he must go. The fact that he'd entered the Gómez Vila building provides their first clue that the Camera Obscura may well prove to be a key to the mystery of the missing Mirror.

Lourdes watches as Krym stands at the door looking around and then hurries in before the girl scouts in parade can reach the tall door. Now she is waiting observantly from a table at an outdoor café across the plaza. She orders an espresso and pays in advance.

Meanwhile Luis Lim waits pensively, not reading the newspaper he holds open before him on a bench at a bus stop behind the building. He remains consumed by the anguish he feels over the fact that others apparently have more detailed information than he. It is in fact true. Luis doesn't have the advantage of his illustrious brother's cryptic painting revealing exactly where or by what

Chapter 11

method possession of La Malinché could be reclaimed. Neither he nor Lourdes knows yet of the painting's actual existence, though a late entry in his brother's once rain-soaked journal (dried now to a crinkled bundle of fragile paper) suggested that an unexplained painting—his last, *Number 111*—was *finito*.

Consequently they have no clue as to the coded revelations Yohan's cryptic painting conceals. So of course the surviving Lims also don't know that Krym has killed Castellan for those clues. Luis Lim, however, does know and has cautioned his niece that La Malinché was a treasure for which Krym *would* kill.

And now Lourdes observes this other man, the American. He's the one over there on the plaza in faded jeans and deck shoes, wearing a thin, snug, tropical-print shirt. The sunglasses are pushed back on his head. Yes, definitely an American. The manner in which he hastily checks his watch once more confirms her suspicions. Despite his casual appearance, he's clearly anxious about his location and precisely cognizant of the exact time of day, as she'd also observed Krym to be. And now so is she.

Irish Bly deliberately watches Krym in the darkened room, having noticed him immediately there where he looms in the cool dark, his back against the wall. The girl scouts have crowded more closely around the large viewing disk, but Krym can see over them quite well as the demonstration begins. The guide describes the Camera Obscura while maneuvering the device to view the city brilliantly in a most astonishing array of vivid colors in the bright late-morning light.

All aspects of the ancient cityscape—the tiled rooftops, Romanesque domes, baroque towers, the eclectic, pastel facades of buildings and balconies (some draped with laundry)—are on display. And below in the great disk are the peopled plazas and children playing on a street where a broken water main spills. Beyond the treetops from there are the avenues, the sea, and the unblemished sky. The old city is projected with a clarity and magnificence beyond any possible unassisted view.

At precisely 11:11 a.m. nothing more extraordinary appears in anything projected by the Camera Obscura. Krym leans forward incredulously, certain that something must be amiss or terribly askew. Bly is perplexed too. But in the next instant a brightening spot of light appears in the passing of elongated seconds of the mirror's movement. The barely perceptible gleam is like that of distant torchlight in an ancient temple. It's a shimmering fleck of strange light high within the open cupola of a ruin—the storied shell of a far-flung warehouse building on the waterfront. The spot of light intensifies to a sudden burst. While the girl scouts gasp loudly, the amorphous reflection rises to a crescendo of sparkling brilliance, consuming the face of the Camera Obscura's reflective disk. It contracts to take shape then and springs with the grace of a cat-like form from the cupola out over the old bones of the city.

The spectacle could not be more telling. Its meaning to the initiated could not be more certain if Yohan Lim had himself appeared in loin cloth on the cupola's ledge, tossing a lightning bolt javelin-like to say, *It's here! La Malinché—The Mirror of the Jaguar Night—is here!*

In that instant Irish recognizes the location of the illumination. A creepy silhouette leans for the door and evaporates in the confusion of sunlight streaming through. The door has slammed back, wedged shut again. Krym is already pounding down the stairs in a spiraling descent to the plaza below. He is spry for a man of his age, but he's depending on his ploy with the rubber door wedge to buy him time. He'd never expected to be alone in his knowledge of the chamber or the exact time the location of the Mirror would be revealed. Conversely, he was quite certain his old nemeses, the Sisters, would surely know and that some agent or agents of theirs would most likely be at that location before the tick of the tock at 11:11 a.m.

Irish Bly is that man, and Krym senses the threat of his presence instantly. Bly is wading now through the frantic Dutch scouts as they swarm about their leaders. Though the Cuban guide is completely astonished by the pouncing light and the slamming of the door against it, he reassures the frantic girls that they are safe. But their horror grows with the sudden jarring sound of Irish Bly banging his shoulder in the dark against the jammed door. Panic sets in full bore behind his pushing against the wedge, edging fractionally back.

Chapter 11

On the street below a young man in a black tank top, sporting a bleached Mohawk and a large sun tattoo on his mahogany shoulder, has casually propped himself against a lamppost. Luis Lim eyes him suspiciously from above his newspaper. Parked down the street, Hermanito has kept a sleepy eye on the blue Zongshien motorcycle chained to that lamppost. Now he watches warily as the man with the sun tattoo seems stealthily to examine the bike while he smokes. Then he walks on, sort of rolling like a billfish that has inspected a teaser and swims away.

Irish barrels from the Gómez Vila building, the assistant scout leader having successfully assisted him in dislodging the door wedge with a serrated ruler/fish scaler unfolded from her large Swiss Army knife. In the early confusion Bly had lost sight of Krym in the darkened room. He'd not actually seen him go out, nor did he hear his footfall on the stairs either below or behind him. Bly conjectures as he skips every other step that Krym slipped out of the room perhaps earlier than he'd initially thought. In any case it was Krym or an accomplice perhaps who had planted the doorstopper. Who else?

In a single motion Irish Bly unlocks and tosses the cable securing his motorcycle. He's fully aware that the old Lim warehouse (with its distinctive cupola) is down on the port behind him. He knows the city well enough. Also the Sisters have instructed him well in the Lim legacy and the whereabouts of their prerevolutionary properties. He's equally certain that the German won't be ahead of him by much if at all. Krym may even be waiting and watching to stalk him now to the Mirror of the Jaguar Night.

Actually Krym has only just landed on the back seat of Hermanito's Bel Air. Though exhausted, he slaps the yellowed cream vinyl of the driver's seat. It sags back with Hermanito's massive shoulders, and Krym pounds alongside demanding, *"Mach dich bereit! Mach dich bereit!"* Hermanito *is* ready as Krym shouts his non-interpreted orders; he just doesn't know yet *what* to be ready for.

Krym jabs a bony finger toward Bly who's turning his motorcycle west on Muralla, now wrenching the handlebars for speed toward the capitol building with its towering dome so similar to the

An Unfinished Sunset

one in Washington, DC. Krym immediately suspects this route to be a diversion tactic. But he doesn't know the city as Bly does, so he opts to make a chase. Hermanito hammers the accelerator with the sole of his giant athletic shoe. The Bel Air lunges forward like a big blue bull struck with an electrified cattle prod.

Irish knows within the instant that he's being pursued. Or, at least as he roars past lamppost after lamppost, he thinks it sensible to act as if he is. Rather than take the direct route to the port he now races for the Paseo di Marti and the Prado, which will be busy in the approach of the noon hour. He can more easily recognize and lose anyone in pursuit more easily.

"Na los!" Krym shouts from behind into Hermanito's conch shell of an ear. *"Beeil dich! Beeil dich!"* Krym rages. *"Beeilung!"* And now in Spanish: *"Rápido! Rápido!"*

Irish swerves around two women in florescent yellow spandex, standing as mirror opposites in the middle of the street. They're trying to thumb a ride rather than take the approaching, crowded, pink passenger bus, one of the many eighteen-wheeled beasts that roam the city. Made of two Soviet-era buses welded together on a flat bed with humped front and rear sections, the clumsy steel fabrication is maneuvered in the narrow streets by a driver in the separate cab of a heavy-duty truck. The *camello* pulls out ahead of Bly now and lurches almost immediately to a stop. A woman pushing a baby stroller hurries across in the musty shadows of tropical trees. Irish darts opposite the baby carriage, leaps past the bus, and cuts back to find a narrow lane through the congested traffic ahead.

It is a byzantine dodge six blocks up to the Prado. The race is on through Old Havana. Despite his size, Hermanito is an agile and perceptive driver. Irish escapes from view, nearly laying his motorcycle down on the oily pavement while leaning to slide up a narrow one-way street. Knowing the city better, Hermanito corners precisely his next right turn with Krym pounding the back of his seat demanding to know why this particular turn.

Irish squeezes past a man pushing a dolly loaded with greasy truck tires. He lands on the crowded street merely two cars ahead of the Bel Air. To Krym's sudden delight Hermanito has actually gained on Bly.

Chapter 11

Irish pulls out, taking the lane ahead close aside an old Mercedes truck with a cluster of habaneros standing in the battered dump body. He accelerates beyond its dented bumper in a blurry zoom, streaking for the Prado ahead. At the bronze lions Irish leans in on the avenue onto the Paseo del Prado. He pulls upright to weave through the congestion of horn-honking traffic.

The congested street is colorfully and frightfully akin to those in Cadiz or Bombay. All along the leafy avenue there's the scaling of ancient pilasters. Towering exterior walls now expose old brick in the deterioration of their colonial facades. Here and there small plants grow high in the fissures. Broad expanses of exposed brick across the walls are covered in layers of biotic growth. Plant roots lift stone slabs along the balustrade of once-opulent edifices even as the sidewalk below (once smooth and accustomed to finely cobbled shoes) is splintered with bone-jarring fractures Irish must traverse.

The lush shade trees of the linear Prado dapple Bly's shoulders like spots changing on a leopard's skin. He rises on the seat to see into the muted versicolor of the street traffic ahead. He glances back. Hermanito has lost ground.

Bly rips through four, now five cars nearly a block ahead in the torrid air of the street. Down by the bay in front of him the pavement shimmers with the heat-bent sun rays in a silvery blue, mirage-like affect. It's the color of water, brighter and bluer than the quaking waves behind the seawall on the Malecón dead ahead.

Hermanito has squeezed past another slow bus. He wobbles side to side, scoping out the way over his padded steering wheel. Krym alternately hides his eyes and slaps the back of Hermanito's seat, cursing and yelling in German for him to stay on the motorcycle. Hermanito (in appearance) is impervious to the German's profane instructions, yet he steadily presses, weaves, and bobs like a boxer in pursuit of Bly on the Zongshien. Then suddenly he locks down on his brakes. A gaggle of school children in mustard-colored trousers or skirts streams across the busy street against the light. They are in no hurry.

Krym is cursing again before a high-pitched whine drowns him out of Hermanito's ear. Another Chinese motorcycle zooms by—a flash of red and chrome on the sidewalk beside them. The rider expertly jumps from curb to curb, leaping a drain for rain to be channeled through the walk. Krym watches wide-eyed behind his spectacles, silenced as he observes incredulously the second motorcycle jumping then from the sidewalk back to the Paseo de Marti.

Irish, still wrangling through the laurel shadows of the Malecón ahead, sees the rapidly approaching rider in his rearview mirror. The other motorcycle is also red, and the driver works the same weave through the traffic. A slender form in black is hunkered down like a jockey reaching for speed. Long black hair streams from a shiny red helmet, a dark visor obscuring the face.

Irish rips back on the throttle and jumps back onto the sidewalk, racing his own elongated shadow on the surprisingly vacant pavement down to the Malecón. Where the walk abruptly ends he jumps the curb back to the avenue with the Castillo de San Salvador and the Maximo Gomez monument standing watch on the waterfront ahead. Bly swerves round onto the Malecón and races south with the sea splashing up and sliding back in silver rivulets over the immense mossy rocks beneath the famous seawall.

The Bel Air is behind another bus, stopped again nowhere close to any designated bus stop. Apparently there are simply those who wish to get off there. The sooty bus disgorges passengers into the traffic while other cars whiz by. The steady stream of cars stalls Hermanito's leap for the lane in motion. He considers the sidewalk, but that is crowded too.

He's a better, more aggressive driver than this, but things have gone wrong. The irate German in his back seat has no visual of Irish now. He's unmistakably angry but speechless for the moment. Hermanito's eyes meet his passenger's in the rearview mirror. Krym's eyes bulge as the pressure cooker that is his brain builds with rage. Hermanito is competitive enough to want the chase, but his apparently unruffled countenance would seem to indicate otherwise. This nonchalance is likely something of an emotional defense mechanism, but his fierce passenger is disinclined to make such a kind analysis. To Krym, the young colossus at the wheel strikes him as one less than spirited in the chase and more like one who prefers a nap. There is gloom in Krym's momentarily silent rage of

Chapter 11

conflicting attitudes, and the Bel Air is now a distant third in what has otherwise become a race of the Zongshiens.

Hermanito is still stalled behind the bus. He ignores Krym's sudden burst of belligerent demands to push through the throng that's in no hurry to depart the bus. He shrugs his massive shoulders indifferently, as if to say simply, *This is Cuba*. He tunes Krym out and turns up the volume on the *timba*—this salsa on steroids—that blasts Krym back in his seat.

Krym will have to wait. Cuban law prescribes jail time for motorists who injure pedestrians even if they aren't crossing in designated areas. Hermanito taps his fat fingers on the steering wheel and imagines himself in sunglasses live on stage up in Miami. The blinding strobe lights of the South Beach Club Cameo reveal in erratic flashes the most beautiful people in the world gyrating to his rap.

Out on the Malecón Irish Bly barrels ahead, tracing the coastline past the port and down the broad avenue to the warehouse district. The motorcycle rider behind him has expertly kept both a disarming distance and a direct visual on him. Bly is cognizant of the absence of the blue Bel Air, but he's increasingly certain now that there's somebody else in the game. He stretches his motorcycle out with speed on the bayside avenue. The rider behind him does the same, so the distance between them remains the same.

Far back, Hermanito swerves onto the Malecón in his *Yank tank*. But no sooner does he gain speed than two rock-ribbed boys dash across the thoroughfare in front of him. He hits his breaks as they scurry across carefree, oblivious to the traffic coursing in either direction. Krym watches out the back window in utter despair while the lithe brown *muchachos* launch themselves from the grand seawall to the balmy surf rising up to embrace them.

Irish makes a sudden dart from the Malecón, gearing down to divert up toward the Plaza de Armas. The historic square, once an ancient element of the city's defenses, is now a popular daily fair for booksellers. Their crowded stalls chocked full of all manner of books and magazines turn the shady quadrant into a literary haven. Only pedestrian traffic is permitted around the plaza, which is bordered by high baroque buildings. Yet it occurs to Irish that he may well lose his mysterious motorcycle pursuer in that maze of book racks. Then, building speed once more, he calculates his undetected escape from the plaza's arabesque shadows, darting out and away again between marble benches beneath the sprawling trees on the square. Irish turns inward and revs up on the cluster of horse-drawn carriages waiting with a line of vintage cars. The taxis idle ahead for tourists in the parking area guarded by the *Castillo de Réal Fuerza*.

Ignoring the startled and cursing gestures of angry drivers interrupted in their conversations, Bly roars on. His is a direct shot for the square. The other motorcycle driver soon makes the turn, unwittingly closing in. The trap has been sprung. The outrage of taxi drivers is even more aggressive in the second blast by. They step out and shake their fists so that the second Zongshien must slow and swerve out to avoid them.

Bly also veers away into the plaza, provoking the other motorcycle into a hot pursuit. He whizzes between two bookstalls and then back around between two others, unintentionally snagging a strand of unplugged Christmas tree lights. These—long hung there for some supposedly attractive effect—now fling their colored glass blubs whip-like after Bly, lashing from stall to stall until they catch and upend one onto the cobbled plaza. The second Zongshien swerves shakily to avoid the scattered books. Its front wheel clips the coral stone base of an old hitching post. The unbridled motorcycle spins out then in a long vertical pitch and crashes the driver headlong into a toppled, peeling, leather-bound collection of Cervantes. Lourdes Lim lies prostrate in the square. Loosening her chin strap, she rolls exhausted on her back. She stares groggily up at the glistening noonday sun, bright and confusing through the filigree of ancient oak branches over the Plaza de Armas.

A boxy white Russian-made Ladia cop car, with its blue light flashing, scurries out from a side street. It narrowly avoids Lourdes to give chase to Irish Bly who's already back on the Malecón. Bly leans in on his handlebars and kicks the Zongshien into high gear. There is of course the downward pull of gravity, the friction between the tires and the asphalt ribbon round the bay, and Bly

Chapter 11

plays against the slant of the bike. He holds the outside lane around the turn, allowing the centrifugal force to stand the bike back up.

Amazingly enough Bly is riding the best he has ridden in his life. Perhaps it's because he's riding (or so he now perceives) for his life. The blue and cream Bel Air is back in view. The white *Policia* Ladia suddenly sinks deep into the swells of heavy traffic on the Malecón. It's sputtering to the curb as the Bel Air comes by.

Bly screams ahead past the old ferry terminals that once connected Havana with Key West. Other wharves and tall port structures border the water—dirty white with wainscotings of lime green or turquoise or red. They are marred and gashed at their corners by heavy carts or streaked along the walls by the throngs of stevedores, port workers, passengers, and passersby. Decades of salt spray, weather, paltry maintenance, and sheer abandonment take their toll. Just past these a tall buxom woman stands out with her bare bronzed midriff at eye level from the Zongshien. She wears vertically-striped spandex leggings and flashes an inquisitive smile as Bly blazes by in the high noon.

After the Malecón, Southern Habana Vieja is enclosed by Avenida del Puerto. But before it becomes the Avenida Desamparado, there's another stretch of the waterfront avenue. Here stand the scruffy haunts of old Havana docks and warehouses, like the P&O docks where the ships out of Miami used to port. Just ahead Irish rushes by the old Pan American World Airways terminal where white clipper ships (those classic flying boats) once motored in.

Before the Desamparado stands the forsaken Lim wharf with its immense, ghostly storehouse in ruins amidst other commercial warehouses. The roofless edifice is long shorn of its tall louvered shutters. Its massive oak doors—once adorned with iron hinges, rings, and latches—have been removed. The brick hulk now makes a windy canyon in the rubble, crowned by the still distinctive cupola. That remains intact with its pagoda-like roof of stylized terracotta palm fronds turning up at each corner. Even those who know nothing of the place find this peculiar feature part of a curious landmark: an oriental-inspired tower on the Cuban coastline.

Irish roars in through its gaping side street door. He skids to a screeching stop on its vast cement floor. He looks around. There's a room (once an office) remaining beneath the cupola above the broad street door. Irish hurries up the metal stairs expecting to find a way from there to the vault of the cupola above. That must be the way to the Mirror. It all seems so obvious now.

The office door hangs open, the darkened room emitting an ammoniac stench of wet, moldy paper and pigeon droppings. Irish peers in and sees that a door opposite is opened to a metal balcony. He passes through and wonders dreadfully what sudden, startling warmth has just brushed his face. It was, he thinks, putting a hand to his cheek, as if some *live* thing—dark and unseen—had come extremely close in the rancid dark. Looking back, however, there was no sound or movement he could discern.

Fortunately for Bly, in the absence of any other ceiling, he sees ahead of him the back landing of the box-like office. There he finds a loft ladder attached to a brick wall. It slides up or down, rattling and screeching on its corroded runners as Bly pushes up. He climbs as rapidly as he is able, keeping a tight grip on the dank steel until he reaches a grated shaft. The heavy grate lifts under the palm of his raised hand. He presses it upward until it slides aside awkwardly. Now there's room enough for him to shift his weight and edge up into the vault of the cupola. His head clears the floor, and his ears fill instantly with a whirling sound in the downward thrust of air. The tower walls seem to quake. An electrified bolt of fear escapes down Bly's spine as a startling burst of pigeons on the wing explodes out of the cupola's open arches.

It *is* there! In the flurrying dispersal of wings, Irish Bly gazes up at La Malinché—the Mirror of the Jaguar Night—where Yohan Lim had so exactly mounted and positioned it to be obscured until the precise moment he intended.

11.3

Across the Florida Straits the Sisters have set up a listening post in the second-story library of their Key West manse. They stand at the tall windows with an unobstructed view of the Atlantic on a perfectly clear day. Consuela Doge rests her hand regally on a boxy satellite phone situated on a marble pedestal for the occasion. She

Chapter 11

wears a white pith helmet. At her large brass telescope mounted on a tripod of polished teak C. C. sports her grand Kentucky Derby hat boasting giant roses swathed in tulle. They say these — the hats — are worn for good luck.

"One ought to see straight down to Havana on a day as clear as this," C. C. Moth sighs, turning from her telescope.

"But we don't see that far, do we?" Consuela responds drily.

"No, indeed not. You'd think though that the rascal might call," Moth adds. "Our Irish Bly ... his spymasters pacing about by the sat phone here at our very own Vauxhall Cross."

"Well, it's entirely possible he's quite busy just now," Consuelo Doge says drily.

"So, you do still think we can trust him?"

"That quite depends."

"Depends? Oh, most certainly. Everything *depends*, doesn't it?" Moth says pensively. "We once thought there were two sides to every story. Now we know there are as many sides as there are people involved. Everything's a thousand things. It's just that simple. Each time we remember a thing, turns out that we're actually remembering the last time we remembered it. You recall the anecdote of the ancient Asian sage, don't you? The one who dreamed he was a butterfly?"

"How could I forget?" Doge replies with a wince and barely a nod, remembering distinctly the narrative when last told. She then takes a turn at the fully extended spyglass, knowing Moth will continue on with or without her affirmation.

"He awoke from dreaming that he was a butterfly, didn't he? And wondered then if he was *truly* a man awakened or *was* he actually a butterfly dreaming he was a man?"

Looking from the glass abruptly, Doge queries blandly, "Your point?"

"My point? Our dear Mr. Bly hasn't known if he is man or butterfly. Doing that which is good comes quite as easily to him as doing damage," Moth says vaguely.

"And vice-versa if I take your meaning," the larger woman expounds. "That is, he doesn't know if he's a good person with a propensity for doing bad things. Or is it that he's bad by predisposition, while often enough he does *do* good?"

"Hmm. I expect we're about to find out," Moth answers.

"Well, I must say," Doge says firmly, as if issuing a judicial decree from the bench, "and I've thought this all along, that Irish Bly will come through for us in the clutch." With that she snaps up the spyglass to have another look.

"Yes, I agree," Moth continues, while perceptibly surprised by Consuela's bold optimism about Bly. "Though let's not make things more complicated than they already are, Sister. The truth is that we hardly know the man even with everything we've been told. That sets up a problem for us, one of possible contagion, don't you agree? Some sort of guilt by association is inevitable, I mean."

"It's his maestro, Bertrand Oliphant, whom we know is unworthy of our trust," Doge says bluntly with a sharp glance back. "Let Oliphant shoulder guilt at the wheel if there's any shouldering to be done."

"But trust Bly we must," says a strong if raspy female voice from behind the map table. "That is, we trust him to be *who he is*," Elle Rousseau interjects, joining the catty exchange.

Sitting erect in a high-backed red velvet chair, her hands resting on the carved lion's paw at the bend of each oak arm, she adds, "I mean, who better to know and operate the logistics necessary for your rescue of the Mirror than he who knows both sides now?"

"Oh, we quite agree," the Sisters say together.

Elle extends a hand to sweep over the nautical map flattened on the table and asks, "Hasn't he the proven network of collaborators in place to keep him straight?"

"Indeed, my dear," Doge assures. "Your turning of *Monsieur* Oliphant's suspicious crossings to our good purposes has bought and therefore brought art and artifice every bit as imaginative as it is practical. You have been entirely in tune with our universal longings from the first note."

"So right, Sister," Moth agrees, pointing a bony finger in Elle's direction. Then to Doge she says with a slight slump, "But there's this too. We simply don't know people ourselves as we once did. That is, we don't have our own people, do we? Sea captains, private

Chapter 11

investigators, the whole gambit—gone now. The best we ever knew ... they've just timed out on us, perished, or were put away."

"Sad but true," Doge adds sorrowfully. "Those *characters*, respectively, were really our fathers' people, weren't they? A different time, a different code by which to live and get things done. All *disparu*. We really *have* no organization of our own now. None at all. There's Henry, Henry of the Hive of course, but ye gods and little fishes!"

"Yes. Yes, a slow coach on the old line, but financially not so much as a charity, dear," Moth laments. "Nor any sort of nonprofit, even if merely for cover."

"We should've been better about that," Doge muses. "I fear our stodgy old trust accounts have made us complacent about the future."

"Indeed," Moth deflates further with a sigh. "Though not quite so flush, we're still well-fixed but just a couple of old steam punks these days, I'm afraid."

Elle Rousseau stands slowly. It's perceptible now that her turban, formed in an intricate Moorish style, is the same red color as the velvet upholstery of the high-backed chair.

"You've both done well enough," Elle says, crossing the room. At the window on the Atlantic she adds solemnly, "And now you must leave *well enough alone*."

Just then a screaming sound comes over the manse. It rips the drift of sunlit perihelia beyond the great window, tearing like a great marlin spearing sea foam in the crystalline sky. The Super Hornet, a jet coming off Boca Chica, is already out over the Florida Straits.

CHAPTER 12

All of this, I repeat, seems to me curious, obscene, terrifying and unfathomably mysterious.

—from *Let Us Now Praise Famous Men*, James Agee (1909–1955)

WE HAD LINGERED AT the dining table in casual conversation, nothing more than a scrap or rind remaining on any plate. Mazie's curious revelations of sisterhood might have alarmed me, yet she'd disclosed effortlessly and with such nonchalance the names of her siblings. These disclosures fairly rippled over the pond of my settling mind. Something sedating had occurred while eating together from those warm bowls. I kept my poker face easily enough, offering merely a nod at each disclosure, as if to say, *but of course*. By a strange twist of fate, the gentle Emma Jakes of my early youth was, as it happened, Mazie Day's older sister. And, by a bizarre conspiracy (however benign), Mazie's Elle became *the* Elle out of my feverish dreaming—Bertrand Oliphant's associate and confidante, Elle Rousseau. *But of course*.

So you'd think I might have asked. I mean to say, I could have confirmed outright as true these identifications. After all, Mazie hadn't exactly said that her sister, Elle, was the Key West Elle. A twinkle from her unfathomable eyes had certainly indicated it to be so. Moreover it occurred to me in the undulating swell of these curiosities that a subtle messaging was occurring. Familiar tradecraft for old smugglers, but Mazie managed just as well. Her facts were lean, though breaded with story. Why spoil her intrigue with unnecessary interrogation? Her tone alone was enough to alert me

Chapter 12

that she'd telegraphed a crafted message. I respected that, particularly as the woman had offered care and comfort without hesitancy or problematic questions of her own.

It hadn't escaped my notice either that Mazie had addressed me just then as *Irish*. That appellation brought with it a sense of familiarity not evident in any earlier conversations between us. The lift of her shoulders, her confidential tone leaning in, the narrowing cut of her eyes—these revealed more than she'd actually said. I'd also observed at the moment of her concluding that she looked sharply away. Mazie was silent then, as if to say, *I grant you this, nothing more*. But when she looked slowly back to me, that welling twinkle of her eyes baited to say at least, *not yet*.

And so, while she diverted to the topic of the weather and storms, I kept watch on her bright eyes to contemplate coordinates she'd seemingly signaled for the map in my mind. I now had a pretty good idea where I was and the direction I must go. This was most certainly discreet and useful information; it was passed artfully and not clumsily spilled by accident. It came as no coincidence and was my good fortune to receive it.

Good cops and smugglers alike will tell you there are no coincidences. You make your own way just as you make your own luck. To that end—be it for good, bad, or indifference—if you manage to live long on the jagged edge of life, you soon learn that the questions you ask may cause more trouble than those you don't. That's where I thought myself to be with Mazie Day. We were lingering, as I've said, but I knew too that her panicked son, Linton, was not. Still, I was operating on *her* time. I wanted to wait.

I thought, after all, that it was Mazie who'd prompted (provoked really) my Bolita story. Hadn't she cleverly dredged up my recollection of Sporty Rey? How could I tell Sporty's story and not come to Emma's front porch? Then Mazie dropped Elle into the calculus. It got easier to connect the dots as Elle's story unfurled, as if in a Caribbean breeze. These stories had the feel of old stories retold surprisingly new.

We all have old stories we make new again, the things we tell and twine from time to time. Everything we constantly connect to everything else in some sort of cosmic passive-aggressive buzz passing over the planet. Entirely original thoughts are as rare as the diamonds born of asteroids. There are none here but talk about talk. For each of us has his or her own amalgam of tales rife with memories, the anecdotes and yarns we spin like rag strips shorn and woven on the tapestry loom of our own histories.

Maybe we begin with something as unintended and inadvertent as an encounter of the eyes on a busy city sidewalk. The gaping lion's mouth of a brown river somewhere in Southeast Asia makes a start. An ancient coin is twiddled between wizened fingers, and suddenly a particular *something* (as one bookman tells) becomes *something happened*. As with the pilgrims who trod the chary path to Canterbury with their tales of yore, our stories collect to shape and populate the pantheon of our personal mythologies. I don't mean these are altogether untruths or outright lies. But rather, poignant word portraits, vignettes with which we may mask entire epochs of personal experience.

Even so (and this is not solely for the chronically melancholy), we may as easily dismiss a time in our lives with some spark of the eyes or mischievous gesture, a nod being as good as a wink. We also know we are sometimes caught in our own web of stories. We wrestle with the knots of these and sometimes flap wildly around the deck. Held to the mast, we take the poet's defense: "Just because it never happened doesn't mean it's not true."

I've hung out in marinas long enough—no better laboratories for an analysis of human longings exist—to observe fabrication become fact. Most exaggerations you know. It may be said they reveal more about the teller than they do the tale. It is especially so for those told repeatedly from a ready repertoire of particular yarn. James Joyce called this phenomenon the personal myth or *monomyth*.

I'm no scholar, but I am experienced in the marinas, as I've said. I've known fellas to tell a few whoppers in their time and keep telling them until finally, by damn, they made them true. There's yet another marvel by which truth becomes stranger than fiction. I'm reminded of the title sequence of the old TV show *Alfred Hitchcock Presents*. Remember the legendary movie director in silhouette, inching forward while Gounod's "Funeral March of the Marionette"

Chapter 12

plays? There he is, merging into that iconic image. Hitchcock completes it, eclipsing his own caricature fully drawn and awaiting him at center screen. Now there is no difference between the two.

None of this did I complete as fully fleshed thought at Mazie's table, though a rain of lost love reminiscences did wash over me. Nothing provokes such presumptions in relationships as a love that will not quite extinguish, drawn out like the endless smoldering of a scented candle's wick.

For example, there was this pretty Georgia girl on a long Daytona boardwalk back in the sixties, leaning to the railing with wet eyes watching the surf. She was awkwardly, rebelliously smoking a cigarette in the night breeze. I didn't have or want a cigarette, but I asked her for a light. Something happened.

At first light another young woman — raven-haired and statuesque — waited dreamily for me between the great columns of the Lyceum Building up at Ole Miss. The mist brightened into a Maxwell Parish painting. We drove in an old car down an old road to an old house behind a stone gate. We went down to Mendenhall. Something happened.

By now I couldn't pick either one of those women out of a crowd, yet I reminisce and make new again (for better or worse) what happened or might have happened or happened next that makes any sense at all of the human heart.

Through the kaleidoscopic lens of time we scatter one moment to the next. I look upon one when the autumn light cascades over warm bed sheets beneath a frosted cottage window in New England. Something has happened, she tells me on her side toward the cold pewter hue of the window. It halts your heart to hear something so intensely told. I don't forget the scent at the nape of her slender neck, nor that my lips dared not move then against her pale skin.

There is also the insidious damage of things unsaid, the unintended consequences that attend wrong time, wrong place. I have my story too, but she knows it already. She is both attracted and repelled by it. She admits that the more restless the heart the greater its attraction. She says she wants me to stay as a way of assuring I go. This is a tactic of the mistaken or reckless to purge an encounter such as we had made. There is some prospect for redemption, some hope that the misbegotten may lure now the star-crossed dreamer, storm chaser of the human heart, to search the purple horizon from that doorstep. Or maybe it's simply some fleeting notion that by romancing the wayfarer we assuage a pained heart, offering something like the dulcet delight of a winsome troubadour's song before venturing on.

Perhaps there's a more coarse explanation for one's courting compulsively those who compose their love letters in disappearing ink. I think of a feeble neighbor from my childhood. He lived in a great house with his older sister until she died at ninety-four. I'd come around to collect for my newspaper delivery to find him in his rumpled old herringbone jacket, this broken man, bent and trundling through empty bottles in wood slat crates in his shed out back. He was mumbling something about "hair of the dog that bit me."

Self-conscious and self-indulgent as it seems now, I was most certainly weighing my losses against the liberties I took. In the transience of poignancy, solemnity and penance waited. It was an intense, if brief, immersion in the river of time passed and passing. It was an immersion, I confess, having almost nothing to do with nostalgia and almost everything to do with self-pity.

There was a woman with her sunglasses pushed back over her sun-streaked chestnut hair. She smiles back at me inquisitively while smacking the sand from her sandals in an arched doorway in the South of France. We'd parked her vintage convertible in a locus grove and found a field of lavender to lie in beneath a cloudless sky. Another day and yet another version of *les journées*. As a glint of sun through a magnifying glass may spark a flame, this encounter ignites another romance.

But before queuing-up the romantic ballad or lifting arms to swell a stirring symphony, let me tell you what's troubling and what I reckon with under mortality's spell: this damned, if discernable, scar, this stain that is a pox upon the page of another's life. There, in the port in France, I saw it by candlelight while we dined in a restaurant called *The Cave*. I wore a plain white shirt, the only collared shirt I owned at the time, I'd said. I was honest with her at least about that. In truth, however, I've always lied about the future but never the past. So this hadn't happened yet. Her laugh

Chapter 12

was warmed by wine, full-hearted and free, until it tugged at her scar, and her beautiful eyes winced against the candlelight.

And so I sat now in this sturdy, quiet, enduring house of Mazie Day's. Here this proud woman—beautiful in her way—was content and confident with the time and place of her life. Except for the weather nothing changed here except by birth or death. Another place setting to make at the dining table, another day there's one to take away. I imagined Mazie at the table with her King James. They must have been good for each other. Mazie bore no discernable scar, as I've mentioned. I've heard it said that no sane creature fouls his own nest, but some people make such a mess growing crazy together.

This observation led me to my acquired notion that two good people can be bad for each other, bringing a voluptuous Puerto Rican woman to mind. She was the one dancing and laughing louder than anyone else in an eccentric old bar with parrots painted on the walls. Her fastidious pet monkey fidgeted on her bronze shoulder. It was delightfully startling to find (despite our different cultural orientations) how many of the same songs we each knew by heart. You sing. You dance with a woman like that, one who dances because she loves to dance. That scar I tell of is there. It's as telling as the rose tattoo pierced by a dagger atop her ample breast. But this is a woman who has inflicted as many scars as she carries, let me tell you.

Walking arm in arm, we went through the dark to her upper apartment, lit by a multitude of candles dripping over cracked and peeling colonial furniture. She quotes from poets I've read or should have read or want to read because she shares them with such passion. She has matched me whiskey for whiskey. She is as drunk as I am, though she remains alert to the sacred—crossing herself reflexively in passing the old cathedral across the plaza. She knows all the prayers by heart. A large crucifix hangs above her bed.

I already want to think that because we've sung the same songs and read the same books that now we can read each other's minds. That is the first turn (however gently made) toward less than eight weeks later getting my clothes tossed down one night to the wet cobbled street below. My old sea bag, still bearing my name as stenciled in boot camp, is emptied and set afire with a burning candle from the headboard of her bed. I salvage my papers and everything else I can wad under my arm. It's a vile and serious threat made when her favorite uncle's name is fiercely invoked, this bludgeon-eyed boss of a (not so) secret police cadre operating in San Juan at the time.

"The crazy bitch, why did you have to deceive her?" I scolded myself. I'd gambled her monkey away! It wasn't fair. But then she never was who I told her she was anyway. She couldn't be. And all the truth I'd told about myself came to no better by then than a pack of lies. So there was nothing better to do than shrug toward the harbor and find a freighter going out on the next tide. The way out being the way in—the wayfaring stranger moving on. I played it straight.

This scrolling through my head at Mazie's table turned even more tragic. A man comes to know loss best through his failed relationships. Yet for once—only once—there was a time when the months did give way to years, good years. But through the decades these became increasingly anesthetized by loss and routine.

I had a loving wife and a respectable life selling and writing ads. But I became a self-possessed remote control, clicking away at a small TV in a house with terrazzo floors. They were the exact same floors and TV everyone else had around that cull de sac in Miami. The days began to churn, click after click, the staccato trap and release of snippets and frames from incessant reruns, all depicting the humdrum of mundane daily living. We'd lost a child fourteen years earlier. After that we lost everything else, a wet eyelash at a time.

You know these things about yourself, and you have to truly admire a woman like Mazie Day. You hanker to linger. Your stories are easily enticed. She's a woman as pure and unsoiled of heart as any, and yet she doesn't wince at your dirty laundry. Her innate wisdom tells her that your stories are romanticized and sentimentalized versions, no matter how truly told. She is a storyteller too. By their continual telling they become more tragic or comic than the actual events. Sometimes we shape these further to our own purposes.

In down time, particularly in the rainy season on the MeKong under some tarpaulin heavy with rain, I must've heard a dozen

Chapter 12

different versions of a dozen different stories. Most were shaped around the bones of a familiar plot like, say, the cop who finds a teenage couple naked in the darkened back seat of a car parked down some obscure road (usually a cemetery road). The cop makes an indecent proposal only to find that the girl in the back seat is his own daughter. It's a tale personalized to either attract or repel listeners in some way or other. Sometimes we tell stories to put in a fix. This turns on something some US politician—Bill Clinton, I'm pretty sure—ginned up much later to cheer the nation. This notion that there's nothing *wrong* with us that what's *right* with us can't fix. Well, I got to tossing that around down on the Key West docks one night. Like I told Rachel Perl, sometimes it seems we tell the worst on ourselves, wagering we'll somehow redeem the best of ourselves.

So I don't remember all the times over the years I've told my Sporty Rey story in one version or another with one intention or another. Mazie beckoned it by raising the Bolita connection. She must've already known the story (some version) well enough at least to skillfully summon that nexus between her sister, Emma, and me. From Emma we got to Elle.

Elle Rousseau must've told Mazie about Emma and me, though I'd not said anything to Elle directly. I think I told Ducky Durban about Emma and Sporty Rey one rainy afternoon at the bar in the Blue Rendezvous. Reciprocal reminiscences of youthful bliss fronted that particular version. It was just casual bar talk, some balmy recollections on the energetic stirrings of sensuality and eroticism in early youth. More explicitly in my case, those as first aroused in a boyhood unintentionally by a woman ripe with years.

So often there *is* that one woman—the magnificent female who's ever the paragon of beauty in one's deeply personal collection of magnificents. She is forever gorgeous and her splendor indelible, as memory magnifies her beauty and time unremitting preserves her beyond compare. Ducky Durban had his story on that theme. I had mine. I stood that day in high-top sneakers astride my bike, a blissful tremor brought on by the awe-inspiring image of Ilene Rey turning slightly from the taxi with an inquisitive smile to look my way.

An Unfinished Sunset

I first saw Ilene Rey on Sporty's arm at one of my grandmother's lawn parties. I last saw her on the steps of their pink house—the one with perfectly squared hedges off Swan Avenue—the day a yellow cab drove her away forever. Over the years though, I have to say, I thought a thousand times that I'd caught another glimpse of her: in bus stations and air terminals, in Times Square, down a beach near San Diego, or somewhere in the crowd on a dirty street near the American embassy in Saigon. I was almost certain I saw her years later while feeling out of place in a posh shopping district in Rome. Ilene Rey was getting into a limo that suddenly pulled away. I've looked for her in every woman I've ever loved.

It had happened again in a different way. On yet another occasion I'd come to tell of Ilene Rey. In the fullness of that telling, Sporty Rey, Bolita, and, before the rain had stopped, Emma Jakes.

The way I figure it now Ducky Durban was sizing me up pretty good by the time I got down to my Ilene Rey story. There was the nexus with her husband, Sporty, his connection with Emma Jakes (Emma Day Jakes, as it turns out), and so the nexus I now knew as a far-flung consequence of having tagged along with my Uncle Clyde that fateful day.

I figure too that Ducky was checking me out early on for the fast boat gig down to Cuba. Surely he gave my story to Bertrand Oliphant who, as is his nature, would've delved for every detail. Later on I'm thinking Oliphant gave it all to Elle Rousseau if she wasn't in the room with Durban and Oliphant at the time. That's also likely. After all, the trafficking out of Cuba was really Elle's show. Oliphant, as Oliphant was always wont to do, played impresario: directing, casting, choreographing, lighting the set. Elle knew everything he knew, but perhaps Oliphant didn't know everything Elle knew. That's my guess now.

Long before I put Key West and Tampa together in what precipitously appeared to be the scheme, there did seem to be an unwarranted, immediate affection Elle Rousseau held for me. Terms of endearment gushed, though she'd never said nor so much as signaled a single impetus toward her kindness. Yet from the first and at each encounter afterward Elle's bright eyes emitted warmth in greeting that nuanced a depth, an endearing, shared history about which I had no clue. I was attentive to the fact that something beyond the ordinary (however brief) was evidenced in our casual exchange of pleasantries. We were, in the first instant, old friends. Her eyes said so and I believed her.

In retrospect Elle's eyes were as unfathomable as her sister Emma's. Like those of her eldest sister, Mazie, Elle's eyes could plumb the subtle knot of body and soul. And there was also a quality the three had in common: each spoke lucidly and precisely, as if meticulously unraveling long threads of truth, all the while saying little to nothing of any truth they knew outright.

I was familiar with the style. So I accepted Mazie's obscure revelations as nonchalantly as she'd offered them. Everything she said I took in quietly, with little more than a nod of acknowledgment at my good fortune of these gifts. Of course, Elle was the first dealer, but the deck was now in Mazie's careful hands. As it happened, I now held better cards, and the game was falling my way. I'd been tossed a pair of aces from the bottom of Mazie's deck. While she made a time and a way for me to leave, her absence of actual knowledge of my parting or possible whereabouts would stand as devout and plausible denial.

When we'd go to our respective rooms for a nap, I knew there was a boat not far, though I'd have to row a good ways to make Cedar Key. The rustic sun-bleached fishing village, with its high and low rooftops variegated with sable palm shadow and red rust, rose in my mind's eye there beyond a jagged crescent of oyster bars. Someone would be waiting for me. I'd know in time, as in the offing I now knew: it was no happenstance that had brought me to Mazie Day's door.

Moreover I could be sure by then that this was *not* something Oliphant knew. Elle had to know it had been Emma Jakes who cared lovingly for 'Miz Lydia' until my grandmother's dying day. Oliphant wouldn't have overlooked that as a possible leverage point with me. The spry cuss couldn't have helped deceitfully suggesting, "Not to speak of it, but ..." He'd actually subsidized Emma's meager domestic's pay. In logic as mercurial as fuel oil over water I reasoned that Oliphant certainly didn't know of the

An Unfinished Sunset

connection his housemate, his business associate and confidante—Elle—shared with me.

No, as tactically gallant and cleverly courteous as Bertrand Oliphant could be, he knew nothing of Mazie Day or the simplicity, gentleness of heart, and quiet dignity she so effortlessly demonstrated in the domestic details of her daily life. Elle would have purposefully protected Emma, as she would young Alifair. Albeit inadvertently, by my presence she had now permitted the stain of her own refined iniquities to bleed to Mazie's door.

Alifair stood and dutifully cleared the table. The dark billowing sails of a small storm mounted the horizon of the languid Gulf. The conversation between Mazie and me predictably dissolved to the subject of weather. While we watched the distant purple roll of the expanding clouds, I contemplated the gravity of the message she had earlier relayed.

If (as I now had reason to suspect) my safeguarding by Mazie was sustained within an elaborate design for my protection, then this time with her and Alifair would be but the calculated turn of one escape wheel upon another. It was clockwork not of my own devices, and I reckoned with that. This reckoning comprised incredible and elaborate configurations of occurrences, like the ones divulged in the Arthurian grail legends written by Sir Thomas Malory, each of which my grandmother read aloud to me as a boy. Accordingly I reckoned myself now to be somewhere in the tropic of Sir Galahad. I should take the cues coming on as subtly as they were being offered. In a short time I would spring for the next wheel already turning up toward me, its cogs budding with increasing clarity.

Yes, there was catharsis in my recognition that I was not at her table by random happenstance. Mazie spoke of past storms and hurricanes in a nearly amorous manner. I think that was because she—her family and that sturdy shanty—had endured them all. Meanwhile my innermost thoughts increasingly settled and cleared when suddenly, with a start, *it* was there before me—the boat! *The* boat I saw in reflection, in relief, as if by the aid of lightning over turbulent nocturnal surf. I recollected this boat clearing gloomy swells, as Mazie described, their dark crests pitched forth with sea

Chapter 12

foam illuminated to a glaring white in the storm noir. This was not the custom-designed, go fast transport I raced out of Cuba and drove in madness out of that earlier buzzing in my head. This was another boat, a blue-hulled Challenger, waiting in my flight from Cuba somewhere off Marathon.

In that instant I recalled the Challenger's instrument panel nodding and blinking before the helm. Its acne of florescent orange and green reflected over the chrome wheel I'd held fast with my good hand. The GPS coordinates by which I'd been steering out of Cuba had already been programmed in. It was the boat in which I must have made the Vica Cut, taking a round in my shoulder from the man on the bridge as I blasted through into the green waters of the Gulf of Mexico.

So it only made sense now that I'd run up the coast into the night with the storm coming on. I hadn't consciously recalled the canvas bag containing La Malinché nor anything in the Gulf until that moment when I'd fetched the creek's bluff by the house before dawn. How did I know the GPS was already programmed for that location? I tried to think on that and must have flinched or winced.

"You alright?" Mazie queried kindly.

Alifair was returning to the table. "What's the matter?" she asked her grandmother.

"I don't know," the older woman said with a perceptive smile. "I thought maybe your Mr. Red Man there saw a ghost or somethin'."

"Ha! You can sure make somebody see ghosts, Gram. You know that." Then looking toward me, the girl said, "Gram can tell the best ghost stories you ever heard, Red Man."

"I like ghost stories," I told the girl with a slow smile. Then to Mazie, "Especially true ones."

"We *all* have our ghost stories," Mazie said drily.

"Yeah, but Gram, she know lots of good ones!" the girl added, wiping the table top with a damp cloth. "Don't you, Gram?"

"Sometimes I think I know more stories than a body should," the older woman sighed. Then with a playful snap to Alifair, "Girl, you get this table finished off. Don't you be messin' with my afternoon nap."

An Unfinished Sunset

"I want you to tell that Molly Garth story again, Gram," the girl insisted.

"No," Mazie said stridently, pushing from the table. "Not that."

"That's a scary story, and it's true too, the way Gram tells it," Alifair said to me. "I really like that story, Red Man!" Then to her grandmother, "I just don't like you to tell it at night no more."

"I already told you that story ten times," Mazie contended in a higher pitch.

"Tell it one more time," Alifair beseeched. "Tell it eleven times, except this time in the day time."

Mazie held to the back of her chair and mulled the girl's fervent request. "Maybe I will," she said finally. "You get that kitchen finished, and come out on the front steps with me and your Mr. Red Man. But baby, you know I always take my nap after dinner," Mazie cautioned. "I might tell it. I might not. Might be a reason to tell it. Might not."

12.1

Possessing a general license for visiting a *close* relative in Cuba, Ambuelita is booked on tomorrow's 8:00 a.m. charter flight from Miami to Havana. In recent years the grandmotherly Cuban émigré has proved to be exceedingly effective as a courier for rescue operations planned by Rousseau and Oliphant.

Ambuelita's apparently commonplace, inadvertent encounter with Elle Rousseau occurs again in an open-air market up in Miami. There they transact the initial pass of the *sobre*, the envelope in which an encrypted manifest and abundant cash are enclosed.

After an early morning rain, the colorful stalls stand close together in the eclectic marketplace busy with Saturday shoppers. Before a booth of fresh-cut flowers the two women browse in plain sight. Elle, tall and slender, is dressed in casual Hermès, a colorful silk scarf turban, and $800 sandals. Ambuelita, by complete contrast, is nearly dwarf-like, squat in her washed-out cotton clothes and dependable orthopedic shoes. Of dissimilarity too is Elle's rather staid countenance, a sort of detached elegance by which she moves from stall to stall, making studied selections that appear to

Chapter 12

bore her. This is opposed to Ambuelita's eagerly engaging, constant pecking about through the produce and other offerings, an enamoring, saintly smile fixed on her adorable face.

The two search for items according to their own styles in the midst of buckets and great bundles of long-stemmed flowers covering tables on the wet pavement. When Ambuelita is close enough, Elle maneuvers the thin plastic bags containing just a few chosen vegetables and fruits. She selects a bundle of flowers—this one or that one—on the table before her. She pays the dowdy vendor in cash from her large gold leather purse and moves on.

At the next booth closer to the chain-link fence gate is a small table constructed of silvered cypress planking across sawhorses. On it sits a wide assortment of honey and beeswax products, each bearing the distinctive label: *Henry of the Hive*. Elle selects a ribbed glass bottle of orange blossom honey and places the flowers she's already purchased beside the cash box where a gregarious little fellow in a white linen jacket yellowed with age waits. His sweat-stained panama hat is pushed back toward the crown of his round face. He greets Elle engagingly in a heavy accent, thick as his honey and discernibly of the Deep South.

They exchange pleasantries anonymously. Elle's earnest, practiced absence of accent is in contrast to everything else about her to the stout older fellow with a schoolboy grin gesturing before her. With a tap to the wilted brim of his old hat, he brags as profusely on the ornate silk turban she wears as he does his amber honey. This gesture is a signal that he has detected no one else paying particular attention to either Elle or Ambuelita, who now turns from the buckets of long-stemmed flowers to make her way to his rustic table.

Elle's envelope is obscured beneath the green waxed tissue paper around the stems of the flowers she lets drop to the table so as to better handle her purchase from Henry of the Hive. Ambuelita is standing steps away with her oversized shopping bag draped in the crook of her elbow. Her hand begins to examine a waxy balm said to be good for healing cold sores or fever blisters.

The sobre is quickly exchanged in the separate purchases made in plain sight. Henry makes the pass with the deft skill of a carnie

An Unfinished Sunset

working a shell game. The pass is made, and the sobre is safely inside the fold of one of an array of Henry's slapdash promotional brochures. He slides these with each purchase into one of a selection of salvaged paper bags chosen by size from an odd stack in the shadow of his ancient pickup's bold sideboards.

Elle is already well away by the time the sobre is carefully tucked deep inside Ambuelita's shopping bag. Ambuelita parts with Henry's abundant expressions of appreciation, spoken unabashedly in a honeyed Spanglish, viscous with the intonations of the old man's early Mississippi delta youth.

Parked nearby, Ambuelita's niece has waited behind the wheel of her small ordinary car with a flamboyant assortment of beaded trinkets and charms hanging from the rearview mirror. While the motor purrs drowsily with an occasional hiss from the air conditioning compressor, the niece reads an erotic romance paperback of which her elderly aunt has already expressed stern disapproval. The cover photo alone is sufficient to draw the older woman's quiet denunciation.

Ambuelita taps at the curbside window of the locked car. The younger woman lowers her book with an expression of annoyance. She apathetically trips open the door lock, and Ambuelita trundles in her shopping bag more nimbly than one might expect. She slides her purchased wares quickly to the floorboard where there remains ample room for her small feet. She enters the passenger seat and buckles up as the sultry niece tosses her book to the rear seat.

The younger woman looks back over the street side shoulder of her lavender tank top and exposed luminous green bra strap. With a spontaneous indifference she enters the flow of traffic disappearing ahead down Meridian. Meanwhile her wizened passenger—dear Ambuelita—has made sticky her fingertips with the waxy balm. She is already counting her cut from the sobre into the lap of her long plain skirt.

12.2

At Elle Rousseau's expressed direction Oliphant operates in Cuba exclusively with and through Ramón. Ramón's grandfather,

Chapter 12

a popular regular at the fabled Tropicana, had been a gregarious gambler *with connections*. His wife, a former dancer, had been a close friend of Elle.

After the Revolution, things went badly for Ramón's grandfather, as well as for his grandmother and mother. A Cuban firing squad ultimately executed his grandfather and two Americans against a wall on Pinar del Rio. The trials for all three had occurred in a single day, and each had been immediately convicted, sentenced, and summarily executed for alleged counterrevolutionary activity. Whether his grandfather had actually participated in such activity remains unknown to any of his family, yet the bitter resentment against the regime smolders on silently from generation to generation.

Only Ramón's grandmother, though now deceased, knew her picaresque grandson to be the sole operative for Elle Rousseau and Oliphant's rescue operations. He alone is their covert arranger and transporter in Cuba. The fewer involved the better. His older sister's droning voice is the one broadcast from the makeshift numbers station Ramón operates, but the original recording was made some years ago and for a purpose she didn't know.

Now Ramón carefully edits each recording for his deceptively random broadcasts. Some are meaningless sequences, merely diversions or distractions. Oliphant's decoding device detects those immediately. Otherwise Ramón selects and edits for play a precise sequence of numbers indicating the exact time and location for each rendezvous with the mysterious fast boat his grandmother's friend dispatches out of the Florida Keys.

Until recently it had been only Bly who'd entered Ramón's coded rescue coordinates into the highly sophisticated GPS systems aboard his rapid craft. Now Rachel Perl usually makes the entries on *flights* down in the dark. Sometimes too she drives in the wide-open stretch across the Straits. Twice she has actually maneuvered for the pickup, remaining at the helm within three miles of the watery landing zone where their still more exact DHOBI radar guided system automatically locks on to Ramón's flotation device. The transmissions from that device hone the speeding boat in with

An Unfinished Sunset

a frightening pinpoint accuracy—so precise that there is virtually no margin for error.

Bly (whom Ramón knows only as *el barquero*—the boatman) has managed repeatedly to hit his mark along the Cuban shoreline with swift exactitude. The acute accuracy of their high-tech turnabouts allows an astonishingly rapid snatch-and-go blast back across the Florida Straits. Elle Rousseau has flawlessly choreographed the coordination and execution of each mission. Only unpredictably foul weather conditions have ever interrupted any flight plan. When a detection of their activities on either side of the straights has occurred, it has done so too late for any real response. Theirs is an extraordinarily high success rate, especially and appreciably so considering the hundreds savaged by the unscrupulous smugglers or the thousands lost to less well-equipped and often pitiful attempts at flight on homemade flotation devices.

But the odds here are much in the favor of el barquero largely because he operates an adroitly designed and technologically enhanced super craft that Elle Rousseau herself has carefully researched and insisted on. Oliphant ordered the exact V-hull specs from a meticulous Marathon private boat builder to give it good handling qualities even in turbulent water. The boat has both speed and a shallow draft, a mere three feet required for its churching, high-speed turnabout. Its meticulously muffled diesel engines are both powerful and reliable. Couple these with specially engineered water jets and the craft can deliver fast, near rocket-like acceleration from the coast while diminishing the so-called rooster tail effect that makes typical fast boats easier to locate and track.

The craft's low silhouette also reduces its radar signature. Rendering it even more difficult to detect is an amazingly effective light diffusion system that camouflages the boat in any degree of light or darkness. It operates like a squid, using a bioluminescence to counter-illuminate its presence so as to match the brighter sea surface above. In this manner Bly's rocket-like boat can virtually mirror the usually moonlit sea over which it is racing, but the system is just as effective in daylight.

Ramón knows only the technology he operates, some of which has been tossed to him in earlier operations by el barquero

Chapter 12

who, until this night, has remained a mere silhouette to Ramón. Unbeknownst to Ramón, Bly isn't doing the flying this night. He is already there in Havana. Unidentified by name to Bly, it is Ramón he is about meet for the first time.

The cunning, streetwise Ramón knows everything else that can be known about the operation on that side of the Malecón. He has deciphered his manifest contained within the sobre, the envelope also holding ready cash for his operative purposes, payouts, and payoffs.

He has received this directly from Ambuelita's hand inside an imposing, pallid-pink, deteriorating apartment building. There the labyrinth of hallways peels back, descending floor by floor to a once-stunning, multi-level galleria. The open lobby spills over unpolished terrazzo inlaid with tarnished brass. At its center is a rosette depiction of an ornate compass at whose four cardinal points stand four doors, each framed by a crumbling frieze portraying great sails furling with ropes to a windlass and spire. Beyond this the exterior coral, turquoise, and white cityscape of the ancient Vedado is awash with sunlight, rolling back like architecturally designed breakers in a tropical sea of versicolor.

So it is Ramón who de-codes what appears to be a loving letter within the sealed sobre. The letter explains profusely the benevolent purposes intended for the envelope's ample cash. It isn't what it seems of course. The letter is composed by an unnamed loved one to an intended recipient. The addressee is never identified by name but rather by one term of endearment or another. Even more gratuitously, the writer makes plain that the disarming grandmother knows nothing of the thick envelope's content that she is so obliging to deliver.

The calculated, intended vindication hasn't mattered. The Cuban Customs' officials and police patrolling the Havana terminal wave Ambuelita through as usual. The most gallant have scurried to assist. They carry forward, as far as they can, the packages of scarcities she brings—such simple things as soaps, shampoos, or other ordinary provisions she lugs in her wrapped bundles.

Subsequently Ramón makes covert contact with each planned passenger. He is careful, however, to make these contacts fit

An Unfinished Sunset

inconspicuously within their daily routines as well as his own. His cover is typically one that deceives the intellect (rather than the eyes) of anyone watching. Ramón rather notoriously and flagrantly deals in the black market sale of music CDs. His best, most frequent customers ask for hip-hop, but the trunk of his Buick is chockfull of CD cases boasting artists from Sinatra to Santana, Shakira to Queen Latifah. The underground business he operates out of the back of his car has something for everyone in an economy where virtually nothing better than his bootlegged CDs is available, much less affordable. So, oddly enough, Ramón obscures illegal acts that could get him shot or jailed by another one—the sale of black market CDs.

On the day of departure, when Bly discovers and recovers La Malinché, Ramón's explicit instructions are to be carried out. Each passenger is to wear blue with white. A blue shirt or jersey is easy enough for Seve Acosta, as royal blue is the color worn by his illustrious baseball team, the *Industriales*. So the blue shirt with white trousers is entirely familiar to Seve, as they are to his fans, although Ramón is no baseball aficionado. Blue is blue and contrasts well with white—blue being on the darker end of the color spectrum and white the opposite. More than half of people asked list blue as a favorite color. White is neutral and noncompetitive. The contrast between the two is distinctive. Ramón's chosen color combination is as simply summoned as that. His is a scientific mind, eschewing the muddle of amorous thought, unlike his (as yet unmet) cohort, Irish Bly. For Bly might, with momentum and no particular impetus, drift half a day on the symbolic connotations of the color blue alone.

El mapa is made in Ramón's orderly mind. Mariel, Seve Acosta's girlfriend, is asked to wait with her mother at a specified location different than the one assigned to Seve. She is to wear a blue blouse and white jeans and her mother some variation of the same. Dressed like this, the passengers may be observed with certainty long enough to satisfy Ramón that they're not being shadowed or watched. The mother and daughter will walk arm in arm, as if coming from the Catedral de San Cristóbal, where they might have been lighting candles together. As they near Ramón's Buick on the street he will ask, "Going to the party?"

If the answer is yes, then both mother and daughter believe the coast to be clear. If Ramón's question is not asked and should he remain silent behind the wheel of his Buick with his elbow removed from the opened window before they pass, the two will know that he has detected danger, and they should continue casually on. Or when Ramón asks as planned, "El ir a la fiesta?" and the answer comes as a cautious no, he is thereby signaled that surveillance by the Cuban authorities has been detected. The two women will continue their promenade toward the Prado. The flight will be aborted, satellite phone connections established, and arrangements made for another date, time, and sequence for similar actions to carefully play out.

On this night of passage, however, everything has gone smoothly. Earlier there was a rallying of police over at the Plaza de Armas. But that, though it occurred nearby, had not provided a complication, so far as Ramón knew. The convergence of police dispersed rather quickly. Perhaps fortune has smiled upon him. Or so Ramón still believes. He sees in his side view mirror the women in blue and white approaching. The talk on the Prado and along the Malecón earlier has been that the authorities are determined to apprehend the motociclistas—a diversion of their usual attention that Ramón hopes will work in his favor.

He puts his elbow out for Mariel and her mother to easily see. He has no idea that one of the motorcyclists pursued is to be waiting at his final stop before the coast road that night. Ramón knows only that an anonymous male "fugitive" (clad in blue) is also to be invited to the party. This surprising and entirely unusual instruction was also contained in the letter of the sobre. It crosses Ramón's mind again like a cloud shadow of unease while he watches in his mirror Mariel and her mother coming toward him.

"*Vas párr la fiesta? Si.*" The backdoor at the curb pops open, and the women pile in hurriedly.

"*Ves con cuidado!*" Take it easy, Ramón cautions in a stage whisper. "*Tranquilo!*"

An Unfinished Sunset

Ramón has been watching his mirrors as he drives. His eyes dart from rear view to side view for any suspicious vehicle following. A soft misting rain has begun to fall from the darkness descending over the city. Where the mist is not swept away by the brittle blades of his loud windshield wipers it bejewels his glass with reflections of iridescent street signs along the cobbled maze he travels through Old Havana.

In his rearview mirror Ramón sees Mariel and her mother huddled closely together, ridged with fright, frozen arm in arm against the backseat. They have not spoken since he'd barked beneath his breath as they were getting in. Their eyes are pleading. With no other choice they must trust Ramón.

Now the women in the back look around expectantly, abruptly alert to the narrow street. Ramón has entered the Cerro district of the city. He turns cautiously down a side street near the *Estadio Lationoamericano*. This is the great Havana stadium known in Cuba as the Colossus of Cerro. It's the home of Cuba's most successful and famous baseball team, the Industriales. They are the New York Yankees of Cuban baseball, loved and hated across the island. But in Havana they are as gods.

It was in this stadium that Seve Acosta first saw a no-hit game pitched. And it was here, in the midst of all the fervor of a rock concert, that he pitched his first no-hitter for the Industriales. It's a pitchers' park, the prevailing winds off the sea at night favoring their throws. But arguably (and it's argued passionately) Seve Acosta is the best to pitch in *El Coloso del Cerro* in a very long time. Maybe ever. Maybe better even than his personal hero, Orlando Hernández—*El Duque*—whose unique pitching with a distinctive high-leg kick Seve had mimicked as a youth. Hernández too had played for the Industriales. His career-winning percentage was the league record before Acosta's best eleven years later. But by then El Duque had long since defected to the US, gaining asylum first in Costa Rica, where his agent negotiated a whopping four-year, $6.6 million contract with the New York Yankees.

Nowadays Cuba's top-rated defecting players are getting upward of $60 million. It's well known in Cuba that prices in the US for top players skyrocketed when the league capped spending on the draft and other international amateurs. Cuban aces, aged twenty-three and older, then ranked even more highly. As top-flight Cuban players entering the US from an intercessional country they aren't subject to the rigors and restrictions of the draft. They are immediately true free agents. All they have to do is get out of Cuba.

There have always been nefarious characters vying for that lucrative business. But the players have to get out safely. Now the gangs in Mexico have a tatted and bloody hand in. So not all do. But when they do, all across the Straits can be heard the sound of some stadium's cash register ring: *chaaa-ching!*

Ramón turns off *Cuatro Caminos*. A few strategic turns later he comes to a slow stop before a darkened doorway on the *Calle Concordia* and pulls over past the restaurant on the quiet end of the street. As he has quickly instructed her, Mariel rolls down the back window on the curb and calls out, *"Oye! Vas párr la fiesta?"*

There's no movement on the sidewalk. Then, two darkened doors down, Seve Acosta steps from the shadows—a tall, handsome god of El Coloso del Cerro.

12.3

Bly's climb down from the cupola above the old Lim warehouse with La Malinché is more perilous than the climb up. Absent another startling flurry of doves, the weight of the object alone heightens the level of difficulty in descending.

The solid weight of the object bears down like an anvil where it rests in the crook of his arm. His other arm strains as it braces into the metal ladder. He tightens and then loosens his grip on the rust-corroded ladder's stark decline to a metal balcony extending like an observation deck from the rear of a railroad car into the caboose-like office below.

Bly reckons the relic now in his embrace to be somewhere in the neighborhood of forty pounds or more. That thing seen in movies—someone effortlessly tossing a pack of gold bars about and racing off—it just doesn't wash when confronted with gold's true weight.

There's no time for an accurate calculation of the material value, particularly as Bly doesn't have a clue as to the current spot price for gold. Though somewhere in his frenzied thoughts it occurs to him that by factoring in the magnificent emerald eyes La Malinché may be worth a million dollars or more in material value alone. He doesn't know really. And it doesn't matter because his job is to get it back across the Straits, and he hasn't yet gotten it to the floor of the warehouse ruins.

Bly hears the metal clang (not unlike the closing of a prison cell door) as he drops to the steel grate of the balcony's floor. Then he hears an automobile on the street outside coming up fast on the Calle Desamparados just in front of the warehouse's gaping door. Others before have whizzed by. But this car is now slowing, and the high-pitch squeal application of its bad brakes is audible over the wheeze of an exhausted engine as the driver gears down.

Bly reasons that his motorcycle is out of street view. He's left it lodged at the foot of the metal stairs to the suspended office. Now he navigates in darkness to make his way back through. Something holds the stench and insipid warmth, felt as a rancid breath upon his neck. Bly thinks the weight of La Malinché seems lightened now by his forward momentum, and he won't slow his stride on the heavy metal mesh of the steps. He slings a leg over to mount the thick bar railing and rides it down. It's a maneuver he first perfected on the grand banisters in his grandmother's house when he'd first invented *Irish Bly*.

In the instant he stands erect at the foot of the stairs the street outside is suddenly and eerily silent. He steps out solidly on the fractured oily pavement, waiting and not wanting to breathe so as to better hear. Then the big engine of a car rumbles to life. It has to be the antique Bel Air coming after him around the Malecón. Revving up, astonishingly, it speeds away.

He places La Malinché on the grated landing, darts around the Zongshien to lift its seat, and removes a tobacco-tan canvas bag with heavy leather grips from the compartment beneath. Now he has the objet d'art zipped in the bag. But it's clear that it won't fit back into the storage compartment, and riding with it exposed before him presents too much danger. So he decides quickly that

Chapter 12

the motorcycle is now useless to him. Bly calculates that traversing the back streets or hailing a cab is better for him and the priceless treasure in the canvas grip. He knows his rendezvous point is distant through the maze of the old city behind him. Astride the metallic blue Zongshien on the Malecón, the police—maybe soldiers too—will certainly be on the lookout. Not to mention the German and God knows who else.

So Bly rolls the bike back rapidly, running it to the rear of the massive brick ruin that caves to the bay. Across the way container ships come into full view, hunkered down along the quay of the shipyards. Bly makes a clutching motion with his right hand, rears back on the machine with all his might, and the motorcycle roars to life. Its rear tire scalds the pavement in a cloud of silver smoke. The motor wails like a banshee and the bike surges outward, rising higher on its rear wheel before lunging off the potholed cement pier into the murky channel below.

Bly no sooner has his hand back on the bag than he hears the ogre-like engine of the Bel Air returning full bore. He doesn't wait for the behemoth to come bursting through the gaping entrance before him but runs obliquely for the line of tall arched windows divested of anything but the vista of distant roof tiles over Habana Viejas.

Bly decides that the canvas bag containing La Malinché already feels like an albatross around his neck. He hauls it up the refuse-strewn embankment to Calle Desamparados. The sound of the Bel Air skidding to a stop inside the warehouse ruin is behind him. Over his shoulder now stands the pagoda-like cupola—this portside landmark with its stylized terracotta palm fronds turned up at each corner.

Bly slips inside the dense shadow below the terminal eves of an adjacent warehouse. His back is up against the wall of shattered stucco and exposed brick. His shoulder blades scrape along the fractured facade. He's expecting at any moment to see someone peering from the Lim cupola. From that vantage point anyone would see where La Malinché had been, and he or she would surely spot him.

Just across Desamparados is an unpaved turnout where a cream-colored Moskvich is parked. Inside the small Russian-made

An Unfinished Sunset

car sits a woman eating a dainty sandwich. She looks familiar. Yes, Bly believes he recognizes her. It's all well and good to ignore coincidences, but one can't ignore their consequences. Why would the interpreter and guide at the Camera Obscura be here having her lunch? With his back against the wall, Bly clutches the canvas bag with both hands and catches his breath.

The woman is indifferently observing him now. She looks quickly back to the Lim warehouse and appears to peek up from beneath her sun visor to see to the pagoda-like cupola. She glances back at Bly, frozen against the old brick in the shade of the warehouse eves. He's not certain at first, but she certainly appears now to be gesturing to him to come toward her. The slight movement of just two fingers on her hand in the lowered window is slow and mechanical. Yes, she's waving Bly toward her. Suddenly her hand is flat and stilled, the palm extended with fingers flexed, the universal signal to hold.

His crouch is instinctive but slight. Bly turns his head slowly to look back down the Desamparados. He sees no movement other than that of ordinary traffic on the road, accompanied by a swish or swoosh, depending on the size and speed of the passing vehicle. Then the woman is gesturing again for him to come, two fingers wagging more rapidly to beckon Bly to her car.

It's a chance he takes. In a few rapid strides he's behind the Moskvich, its paint chalky after so many years of harsh sun. Bly peers through the glass at the woman eating solemnly again and beyond her to the channeled view of the yawning Lim warehouse door. There's a streak of motion behind the third of four arched windows he can see through the car at that angle.

The woman gestures impatiently for him to enter, keeping her hand low over the well-worn car seat. Crouching down to wrestle the door open, Bly hears a muffled shout from within the ruin of the warehouse. The Bel Air rumbles awake again as he lugs La Malinché in after him. The woman is still eating slowly. Not yet uttering a word, she signals with a wag of her head for him to roll the grip over into the back seat. Her eyes remain fixed on the warehouse door. While her left hand holds the sandwich crust, her right directs Bly to the floorboard at his feet. He is immediately crumpled and bent with his nose near the shapely calf of the woman's leg. He waits. The Bel Air thunders by, its cranky rumble diminishing back toward the Malecón.

"Gracias," Bly says out of his contortion. Unfolding himself to sit upright in the car seat, he adds haltingly, *"Estoy muy agradecido. Soy bueno."*

The woman takes a small paper napkin from her purse, tamps her lips, and says drily, "I think it is better we speak English."

Irish agrees readily. He recognizes with certainty now the same well-fitting suit worn by the guide in the chamber of the Camera Obscura. Though absent any insignia, he thinks it rather martial in style and color, a gun-metal blue.

"You are the guide from the Camera Obscura?"

"Yes. *You* are the man who butted the door like a crazy bull, but the smart Dutch woman with the scouts got you out."

Bly settles back in the seat. "Okay," he says slowly, as discontented with her characterizations as he was willing to let them pass. It was the least he could do in appreciation for the surprising shelter she'd given. "So, how do you happen to be ... here?" he asks with true astonishment.

"I don't just *happen* to be here. I am here the same as you. I saw the flash. It is my lunch, so I came to see what all the confusion was about. I know this place. You found something?"

"Yes, obviously," Bly says blandly, with a glance for reassurance over the seat back to his canvas bag.

"Yes, I think you did. Something to do with Yohan Lim?"

"Lim? Why would you say Lim?"

"Why? Why not? I knew Yohan Lim. He came up to the Camera often," gesturing in a circle. "I know the history of my city." She points down across the Desampardos and adds, "That is the warehouse built by Yohan Lim's father. See the oriental cupola? It is not so complicated that I would associate Yohan Lim with this place. So I saw, as you did, this was the place of the light I have seen many times."

"Many times?" Bly is both confused and astounded by the casual statement.

"Yes, of course, many times. But not like today. Today was glorious, no? So I came."

"Yes, I suppose, why not? You know the history. You saw the flash. You knew Lim. You know this location."

"Exactly. He was brilliant, and I had a feeling he was up to something at the end." After a long pause, she says pensively, "And he was very kind. One of the great talents of Cuba and a very kind man."

"And you are kind," Bly says turning to her, not meaning at all to pander.

"No, not really," she says, meeting his earnest gaze icily. "I simply want to know what you are up to."

"Forgive me," Bly says in a quandary before finally extending his hand. "I'm Irish Bly."

The woman smiles softly. She is pretty when relaxed. She does not take his hand but replies, "I am Rafaela."

"Pleased to meet you, Rafaela. Thank you."

"That is not a real name — Irish bly," she says, returning the used napkin to her purse.

"It is a name by which I am known."

"You are known by many names, no doubt. Not all nice names, I think."

"But none more true than Irish Bly. I decided that long ago. That's my story. Irish Bly is my story, and I'm sticking to it."

"Sticking? Whatever. So, Irish Bly, will you tell me what is in the bag?"

"It's just as well you don't know. But as my new best friend, I will tell you this—"

"No, don't tell me. You would not tell me the truth anyway." Rafaela reaches for the ignition of her car, and its engine is aroused abruptly.

"Where are we going?" Bly asks, as if it really mattered.

"I am going back to my work. Where are you going?"

"Back into Havana somewhere, I guess ... with you. I'm waiting for a ride."

"To where?"

"To where? I don't know where."

Chapter 12

"I think you do," she responds, making a rapid U-turn and driving back up the Desampardos toward the Malecón.

"You think I'm a bad guy."

"I think you are a bad guy? I bring you to my car? I don't think so. Why do I bring a bad guy to my car unless simply I am a bad woman?"

"You are not a bad woman. So why did you?"

"I am curious," she says thoughtfully as she drives. "That should be my story name; I am *curiosa*."

Bly thought he heard, "I. M. Curiosa," or so she made it sound.

Rafaela continued to speak, finding it impossible (as with most Havanans) not to integrate bits of the city's history into conversations. She names the spires and rotundas coming into view in the old city, as if identifying family members on the street ahead.

In just this manner she also says, "What I saw at the Camera Obscura and then in the Lim tower. I knew you were the same man wanting out the door so fast after the big flash. Whatever made that flash is why you are here. It is why the tall German man is here, but there is something evil about this man. I could almost smell it when he came in. Not you."

"Yes, he is the man, the passenger in the Chevy."

"I know. The blue and ... how do you say, tan? I saw him going by."

"Cream. Blue and cream."

"Yes, cream, that is better."

"So if you could tell immediately that the German—his name is Diebolt Krym, by the way—is evil, then you must have known as quickly that I am not," Bly says in an inquiring tone strange to him. It sounded almost juvenile, a beseeching for reassurance.

"You are not evil, I don't think." She looks at Bly earnestly and says, "But you are not good. You are ... how do you say ... in between."

"Yes, that's probably a safe bet, I'd agree. You can let me out up ahead at the—"

"What will you do now?" Rafaela interrupts.

"Wait."

253

An Unfinished Sunset

"You stand out like some sore finger, a Yuma with that big heavy bag. What time does your friend come?"

"After dark."

Driving pensively, Rafaela says, "I have an intern this afternoon. He is intelligent. Maybe a young man more confident than he should be just now, but he is good to take the afternoon duties. I had thought this before now. Anyway, there is something important I must do. You will come with me. I will make coffee. We will see what is best to do after that."

Bly puts Rafaela somewhere in her late forties. She is attractive, intelligent. She has a discerning, dry wit about her that with her ready admission curiously deflects a sense of threat from her. As a man who has long depended on the kindness of strangers and as one who has long believed in earthbound angels, he watches the towering Lopez building come into view. Bly decides Rafaela just may be one—still another unexpected angel put upon his path.

Then they are back on the Malecón, and before reaching what remains of that monument dedicated to those lost in the sinking of the USS Maine, two giant Corinthian columns appear supporting a short lintel with the word *Libertad* inscribed. Rafaela suddenly jerks the wheel of her small Russian-made car to dart up a narrow street into the Vedado.

"There was once a big American eagle with wings spread wide on top of that monument back there," Rafaela says matter-of-factly. "Fidel had it removed. I am not political in that way."

"In what way then?"

"I am political as Yohan Lim was political. I am passionate about this city. Conquistadors come and go, but this city remains. It prevails."

With the bay behind them Bly is looking back instinctively to see if any other vehicle has made the same turn. Seeing none, he says to Rafaela with relief, "I don't think they're on to us."

"Who knows?" she says with a shrug. "In Cuba we never take these things as sure."

"It is interesting you use the term *conquistador* just now," Bly says after a silence and another turn.

"Is it?" Rafaela says more than asks.

Chapter 12

After four or five blocks and a few more turns, the pale yellow facade of the Gómez Vila Building comes back into view.

"You stay in the car. No getting out. Now I will park," Rafaela announces officiously, nodding toward a small parking lot just off the Plaza Vieja. "This is for me to do. I will be back soon. You must stay in the car, you understand?"

"Yes," Bly agrees, looking back and then all around as the woman came to an abrupt stop in a parking space to which she seemed to have some claim.

"Maybe it would be good if you have a nap on the seat, you know, down like that. Rest and wait. You look like you need sleep anyway," she adds observantly. "Lock the doors."

She is out immediately, walking with an erect, almost military gait toward the eclectic building whose top floor houses the Camera Obscura—the very point at which his madcap escapade over the recent hours had begun. Bly experiences a sense of having returned to the scene of his own crime. He takes one last look around before his nap and thinks to himself, *What crime?*

The size of the car itself makes a near fetal position necessary in order to rest out of sight. Bly is no sooner as comfortable as he can make himself than a white van drives slowly past on the street beside him. The driver is a mahogany-faced older man with silver hair combed neatly back upon his handsome visage. Slumped in the seat beside him is a woman with raven black hair, dressed in the distinctively padded leather of a fitted black motorcycle jacket.

Chapter 13

If art reflects life, it does so with special mirrors.

—from *A Short Organum for the Theatre*, Bertolt Brecht (1898–1956)

Mazie and I sat together in the oblique wedge of shade the rusted roof offered over the front porch steps. Alifair came around from the back with Hobo plodding sloppily ahead of her. She'd hung wet dishtowels on a wire inside the smaller back porch where little socks already dried alongside the girl's canvas shoes rinsed of mud.

"Dead men don't sniff no money," Alifair recited sassily, throwing herself to the planking over the steps below us. "Tell about that, Gram." The girl gathered in the hound between her pink flip-flops. "Start with that old Clegg. He always say (her voice ringing out then in her theatrical, low-pitched rendering of a baritone): "Dead men don't sniff no money!"

Mazie smiled, looked dreamily out across the bay, and began, "That's right. That Jack Clegg, he said that. At least that's how I heard it. See, this all happened a long, long time ago when the Prohibition was on."

"They couldn't sell whiskey," the girl footnoted without looking back.

"That's right, child," Mazie said. "So these men, that Clegg and the Porter fella, they were rum runners. They say Clegg had his raggedy cruiser boat down from Cedar Keys tied up on Henry Creek up yonder, next one up of any size. Pretty deep too, that ole Henry Creek is," Mazie said, nodding to a point northwesterly

Chapter 13

in the general direction I now knew the fishing hamlet of Cedar Key to be.

"That's what this Clegg said his pap used to say: 'Dead men don't sniff no money.' At least that's how this other man, Porter, told it on Clegg. It was on account of Clegg having this dead woman in his fish camp on the creek yonder. Porter, see, he's the one spilled all this out to some men that was delivering stuff out back of the Island Hotel. It was whiskey talk, don't you know, so you can't tell it's true or not. Some part might be. Anyhow, like Porter tells it, he's on Henry Creek and calls up from his skiff to Clegg, him sitting cross-legged up on his boat, 'You sure she's dead?' Clegg says, 'She couldn't be no deader ifin' she *was* a doornail in the camp yonder. Cold as a wedge.' He says, 'I held my watch right under her nose for the longest time. Nary bit did the crystal fog.' Then Porter says, 'You saying she fell, hittin' her head with a gash like that? You don't think we outta take her on back up to Cedar Key?'"

Mazie was telling the tale masterfully, setting the scene, and skillfully altering her voice for each character.

"They's talking about Molly Garth," Alifair informed me over her shoulder. "She's the one that Clegg man kilt!"

"*I'm* telling this," Mazie advised the girl.

"I know. And it be good too," Alifair said in a stage whisper.

Mazie continued, "Clegg tells Porter, 'Look here, I took her in my arms my own self, right up this shell bank here to the cabin. I laid her out pretty as you please on the table. I cleaned her up good too and made her look presentable-like. Her people is gonna wanna see she was done proper, not lugged around like a side ah beef!' Porter tells him that her people ain't gonna believe none of it. Clegg replies, 'Oh, they's gonna believe 'cause you, my good buddy, is going to get up yonder and tell you seen the whole thing. It was on accident. Say I done all I could, but there weren't no bringing her round. And 'bout me, you tell 'em I'm grievin' to pure death. Say I'm near mad with the grief, and you don't know as I might not do harm to myself so to be with her eternal, like that. Say you couldn't pry me from her body with a crowbar. You tell 'em, just like that, like I say! Say you never seen such misery. You fetch the law too. Bring 'em all along so!' 'Bring the law here … to the camp?' Porter,

An Unfinished Sunset

he wasn't sure about that. 'Sure. I won't be idle my own self,' Clegg say, holding up a bag of money. 'I'm gonna stash this money up in that hollow cypress back in the slough, there behind the cabin. It'll all be clean as a whistle back yonder.'"

Mazie explained to me that there were rum bottles in crates behind that cabin, adding, "Still is some, empties and the crates most rotted away back in the woods. See, that's what them coasters did—run that dark rum out of Cuba. When they wasn't fishing, they did. They didn't fish much no how 'cause they weren't going to work that hard. They sure wasn't going to mess with no oysters or crabs, not men like Clegg or Porter. Anyhow, Clegg, he tells Porter to sure fetch the law, saying, 'Everything will be plumb fine. You bring them Garth boys and the law with 'em. Plum fine, I say. I'll be pitiful as any man you ever seed.'

"Porter says he don't like it none at all. Says, 'Them Garth brothers of hers ain't never liked you, Clegg. They's decent folk. Honest grocers, butchers both. True Irish, clannish as when they kin come off the boat. They won't take kindly to this here—no how, no way!'

"Clegg, he jumps down to that little boardwalk they put in and says real mean like, 'You get goin', Porter. You have 'em back here soon as you can. I'll take care of the rest.' Porter says, 'Alright then,' and pushes from the cruiser and snatches the pull on his outboard. It was one of them four cylinder kind, big and blocky as one of them rum crates."

Mazie stopped for a moment to observe Alifair's rapt expression and then took up the tale again.

"When Clegg's cruiser came in from its night engagements, way out with some boat out of Cuba, then they'd offload some on Porter's smaller outboard kicker boat," she explained. "That was better for running them smaller loads under catfish traps. Not so much suspicion up the east pass onto the Suwannee by the moon. Clegg run the boat for that. They say Jack Clegg knew the Suwannee—every bend of it—like the palm of his own hand. He knew every sand bar and where he could cut through. He'd run to ground most anybody coming after him. There's one bar up there, a good piece upriver, where the sandy shallows run in a big crescent

Chapter 13

for near a quarter mile down river. Jack Clegg knew exactly where that narrow pass lay along the near bank, not where you'd think, so close in. He was some kind of famous for losing anybody who'd come after him by that bar there. Some say it got named for him later on — Jack's Sandbar.

"But on the afternoon I'm telling about, it was his sidekick, that Porter fellow, running the boat out Henry creek. Out past them islands you can see way up yonder. Yes sir, Porter set his cap for Cedar Key, which he intended to make before dark."

Mazie sat quietly for a while. Alifair looked back curiously in the long silence. The dog squirmed with a whimper, and the girl hushed him. I kept my eyes fixed on that distant point where a tangled copse of palms now stood in deep indigo against the pale sky. Mazie resumed her story.

"Clegg, I reckon he went back up into the trees to the cabin where Molly Garth was laid out on the table. He saw her like she was in a deep sleep. Her hair was redder than rust. Dark like brick — that kind of red, they say. She lay with her arms crossed over her womanly breasts. Her blouse was bloody, her skirt was long, and a solitary shoe was on the one foot. That's how Porter said it was later. But everybody knew Molly Garth was a sassy gal, smart-mouthed, as they say. But just as likely to laugh big as sass. Yes sir, always said to be full of life, laughing one minute but quick to anger like she had a talent for it. As quick to anger as every other appetite she had, I'm saying. Molly Garth, she was the only daughter in a passel of brothers. By the time she took up with Clegg, them brothers had fought most of this county to defend her honor whether she deserved it or not. The way it's told they were a lot more likely to defend her honor than she was. That Molly, she was a wild one!"

"Yeah, I knew a woman like that one time," I said vacantly, without quite meaning to. "She had a little monkey for a pet. Or used to."

"A monkey?" Alifair asked excitedly.

"There ain't no monkey in this story I'm telling," Mazie snapped.

"Forgive me."

An Unfinished Sunset

She continued, "Anyhow, Jack Clegg was exactly the man Molly Garth's brothers hoped she'd never meet."

Mazie closed her eyes slowly. I thought she was disposed to her nap, but her eyes opened again quickly, and she leaped back into her tale to linger over every word. Her telling was now in a different, dreamier, near trance-like tone.

"Clegg loved that Molly Garth, whatever kind of love it was. I see him standing in that fishing shack door and admiring his Molly Garth—her all laid out there before him—admiring her for what seems like the first time. He's done told Porter he might've had remorse if Molly hadn't always been so quick with her switchblade tongue. So now Clegg, he sits in that hide-bottomed chair by the window, getting to whatever he's gonna feel at the bottom of that bottle in his hand. Porter says nobody ever fought like them two nor ever made up any better or more fierce than them two did. I expect he knew what Clegg was thinking about, sitting with that bottle in that chair by the open window. It's still up there, that chair and that bottle, turned over in the cobwebs below Clegg's window."

Alifair girl perked up then and interjected excitedly, "Gram saw that chair and ole empty bottle! She and King James went up there in his boat."

"No, honey-girl," Mazie corrected. Then she looked squarely at me. "I said that I *said* King James would *keep* a boat up there. It was some rowboat and some crab traps he stashed up under that old cabin. It sits up, near about head high on what they called stilts, them pilings, and you can see that little stilt house up through the trees when you get close coming in from the hammock. There's room underneath for that ole boat and them traps King James put out up yonder. Henry Creek is the best creek in this country for them good blue crabs. They eats anything and anybody. Anyhow," she says with an emphatic nod, "that same *boat* is right yonder."

"Oars too?" I asked matter-of-factly.

"Sure enough," Mazie answered with a slight wink disguised by her teasing frown. "The boat's turned bottom up and the oar's handles I seen was peeking out from underneath."

I realized then the greater purpose of her story, a sort of second telegraphing that she did. Mazie, the raconteur, picked up speed

Chapter 13

from there. The girl noticed her excisions and insertions but only wrinkled her nose or furrowed her brow, keeping with the improvisations and bluesy rhythm of the story as Mazie was telling it now.

The window for Linton's returning was closing rapidly, as each of us knew. Mazie's little trail of storytelling bread crumbs had taken us past the old sugar mill of Alifair's innocent folk history of that place. Past that brick relic to the distant creek where the Clegg camp lay. As sure as I was that Mazie's Elle was Elle Rousseau, I was sure now that near that far point there was a boat at my disposal, somewhere upstream of the purple patch of palms on which my attention was now focused.

Mazie concluded her tale with Porter returning. He brought with him a sheriff's deputy named Simes, she'd tell, and the Garth brothers. All three of them.

But before that, there was the strange, haunting scream in the night. Mazie blinked her eyes slowly again. They opened wider than before as her tone changed, lowering nearly to a hoarse whisper. She described the hammocks' dark shadows swallowing the cabin slowly, and then the shadows swallowed themselves to bloat with the dark. After a while she said a wisp of moonlight tailed down from an opened spot up in the trees. I could feel my skin crawl. Alifair rubbed her bare arms nervously while Mazie described that wisp of moonlight as "slithering down the dark crowns of them trees to take the shape of the silvery creek going out in the night."

Alifair rolled her eyes back to me with an impish grin that said, *Told you so!* In the chilling manner of true raconteurs of the macabre Mazie seemed now to conjure her tale more than recite it.

"Back in the cabin on the creek Clegg must've waked to a terrifying sound. From out in the slough came a far-off cry, something like that of a terrified young'un or woman might make who was lost out in them dark woods."

Clegg, she told, sat upright with the bottle in his lap and leaned to look out into the dark. He heard the cry again closer, reverberating all around him. He looked to see the body of Molly Garth as it lay fixed and still on the table. Then it was quiet. Too quiet. Clegg, mighty scared now, set the bottle down beside his chair to

An Unfinished Sunset

get to the bottom of it, Mazie said. He waited. Nothing ... then he nodded back off to sleep.

"Porter and them other fellas come out of Cedar Key at dawn, but it was too late for Clegg."

Mazie suddenly demonstrated the wild cry that had jolted Clegg awake before daylight. It was a screaming not like a human but a panther or some other big cat. A jaguar maybe. Clegg was shaken to his scuffed shoes. He sat up straight with his eyes wide, not sure what wild, uncivilized thing he'd heard. Molly Garth lay motionless in the moonlight.

"The moon had gotten down and crept back from the creek to the cabin now," Mazie told in a low voice. "Clegg, he stood and worked his way round the table near Molly Garth. He found his old navy pistol in the flap of a battered travel bag by the bed. That's where Clegg sat then on the cot-like bed to keep watch on the unhinged window across the room.

"Then it come again! This time the scream was deafening, the most tortured sound a body could make, and it was everywhere at once, even if it seemed to have sprung full force from Molly Garth's own dark lips!"

Mazie unexpectedly demonstrated the sound again in an even more ear-piercing shriek. It was so horrific that Alifair and I pitched back with a start. The hound jerked about too and barked back at Mazie furiously. We were all laughing then while the girl soothed the dog. When we settled down again, Mazie finished the story.

"That's when something large and dark, quicker than the black shadow of a night bird, rose up between Clegg and the window. He fired blindly with his trembling hand. The whiskey already had him, and the cruel darkness covered him up. Clegg got off another shot. In the pistol's flash he saw those wild cat eyes! The great cat was the darkness as much as the darkness was the cat. Clegg felt his throat catch fire as he rocked back, the screaming and scratching and clawing so fierce that the heavy table overturned like in the blow of a hurricane. Clegg fired once more. The painful burden of the darkness over him was like a ton, and it held him to the floor while the night reeled and roared like a whirlwind of pitch black fire, disappearing down his gaping mouth, ripping

Chapter 13

out his torn throat. Then there was nothing," Mazie rasped slowly. "Nothing at all."

Mazie paused a moment for effect. Noticing the spellbinding effect of her narrative, she went on.

"In the full light of day Porter's boat came creeping up the mouth of the creek. The men were standing in the boat, skulking to the bend where the stilt camp house sat. The cabin cruiser was tied and leaned near 'bout down to the mud on such a low tide. Porter got alongside. One of the Garth brothers leaped to the boardwalk and tied them off. Up the bank the men followed Porter on the shell path up to cabin's door. Porter called out as he came, 'Jack! Jack Clegg, we're ah comin' in now. Me and Deputy Simes, Molly's brothers, too. They come for her, Jack. It's time!'

"No sound came from the cabin, no mournful moaning or sobbing as Porter was thinking Clegg would put on. So Porter braced his shoulder against the clapboard door, and it lay back on them rusty hinges with a low screech. Quick, he let out a gasp and flattened his back against the side of the door. Deputy Simes peeked in after him with his hand on his sidearm. The Garth brothers leaned in from behind."

Mazie stretched out her legs on the porch step, readying herself for the dramatic ending.

"Clegg's scratched-up hand lay in the shaft of light from the opened door, his spent revolver close by. Over him lay Molly Garth, bloodied where a bullet had exited her back. Clegg had taken one in his throat. More awful than that, Clegg's face was scratched and gouged and swelled up to such a gruesome sight that even the Garth brothers shivered. Worst of all was his mauled and mangled left ear, which they saw clenched between Molly Garth's bloody teeth."

We sat silent at Mazie's gory conclusion to the tale. I couldn't know of course the veracity of such an account, though it sounded to be a tale of many different authors. Be it art or artifice I felt sure her location of the camp and description of the boat were accurate and meant for me.

Alifair shook her head solemnly. She turned slowly and looked back, wide-eyed still. "Gram," she says, "that is just a strange, scary kinda story, now ain't it?"

"Might be. But it's our naptime story for today, honey girl. It's way past time we laid down. Red Man too. He's got to get his strength back, pull his self back together." And then, as if she'd deciphered my every intention, said to me, "This little breeze we got before that cloud yonder will sho' be nice through that front window by the bed, won't it?"

"Yes," I replied, standing with a shy smile, my hand on Alifair's knot of a shoulder for balance. "I know you'll wake me," I said with a wink, "if I'm still napping by the time your son gets back."

"Yes," she said softly without looking my way. "I expect I will."

13.1

Rafaela backs away rapidly from the looming shadow of the Gómez Vila building. Bly adjusts himself upright out of a half-sleep in the squat Lada. There is a fortunate gap in the erratic bursts of traffic. Rafaela's double-fisted snatch against the stiff wheel wrestles the steering to right the car in the outer lane. She accelerates quickly, the shift of gears clanking with each ascending jolt. The woman hasn't said a word.

Bly careens around to look for any suspicious vehicle following. Rafaela remains expressionless except for a curious glint in her intelligent eyes—eyes Bly had earlier thought dark amber. He now notices them to be gold-flecked and in that light lending toward deep green.

Rafaela is not oblivious to Bly's inquisitiveness but opts to meet his ocular curiosity with silence. They have made a dodge down three city blocks, and silence reigns. She isn't inquiring about Bly's apparent confusion over the color of her eyes. Such curiosity has occurred many times in her experience and ordinarily come to conversation she did not want.

In the afternoon sun the Lada dissolves into a traffic swell of pre-Revolution US auto leftovers. Bulky Soviet work trucks squeeze upon Russian compacts, numerous ones repainted brightly in unconventional designs. The interiors of these have also been modified with glitz and dashboard displays of assorted curios: miniature figurines of Santeria and Christian saints, erotic nudes, or creepy plastic skulls. But Bly observes that the durable cult of the customized Lada is now giving way to the increasingly prevalent Chinese compacts. Most of those are of Daewoo design, like the one buzzing by.

Rafaela jerks the wheel, changing to a temporary lane. Another series of turns takes them deeper into the old city. Three cars ahead a motorcycle cop blocks the intersection of a major thoroughfare. Bly slumps slightly in the seat and adjusts the bill of his ball cap just above his inquiring eyes. He watches to observe an expressionless Rafaela. The rapid series of turns remain unexplained. A white-helmeted motorcycle policeman stands astride his bike blocking the intersection ahead. Rafaela merely sighs as she brakes for the stubby line of stalled traffic. Bly is about to ask about the road block when a dark string of black Mercedes limos rip through the intersection, and the cop leans after them to bring his motorbike upright in the aft of the political cortege.

The waxed canvas bag containing La Malinché rests on the floorboard, wedged securely between Bly's well-worn deck shoes. Whether the recent radical turns are because they're being pursued or this is simply Rafaela's customarily erratic (if not insolent) charge upon the city's traffic isn't clear to Bly. They are moving again in the traffic, sorting itself out after the roadblock. Without averting her eyes from the street ahead Rafaela responds to Bly's unspoken perplexity.

"Everything is good, not a problem," she says flatly in her mild accent and attractively husky voice. "Work is fine too. Jorge is fine, as I went to see. He is learning but will be alright. The interpretations will be fine until I return. They will occur this afternoon as usual. Anyway there is something I must do. It is my obligation, but you will be safe while I do this. Then I will telephone someone to trust."

Bly nods with a shrug, intending his apparent indifference to her plan as an indication of acquiescence. Now the traffic narrows. Rafaela splinters off to the left, down an angular avenue lined by drab buildings splashed with color here and there where political signage has been pasted. Some newly fastened political billboards boast the visages of revolutionaries who have not resembled those

An Unfinished Sunset

pictures for fifty years. The street is made even more surreal by the irregular buildings looming ahead. They protrude on either side and resemble rotting molars in the elongated jawbone of a giant sea fossil.

The street is tree-lined on the driver's side, the gnarled trunks thick, their ruddy bark smooth except where pocked or pitted up to a canopy of broad leathery leaves. The trees do little, however, to mute the exchange of staccato beeps and steady blasts of car or truck horns. These communicate driver attitudes more often than the driver's intentions.

There is also the music, always the music—the rush of cacophonous blasts, as ocean waves roll in a steady, jarring sequence. Oncoming auto stereos, music from boom boxes alongside on the street, music from shops ahead or opened apartment windows above breaking loose before morphing into the mix of sound down the avenue. It is as if the street itself amps up a constantly streaming scan of music along the arc of a radio dial.

At Bly's shoulder the street is now virtually walled by the bleak and forlorn fade of old tenements. They are ochre and gray except for patches of colorful clothing drying from balcony railings or on lines toggled between tall windows. Peering up, some windows Bly sees are boarded over. Among the highest are those that gape to the open sky, not unlike the monumental ruins in more ancient cities where they crumble under their own weight in the carbon exhaust.

"Jorge has a new tie," Rafaela says, as if thinking aloud. Her eyes remain fixed on the traffic ahead. Then to Bly more deliberately, "He is very proud of it. It is black silk but nicely textured, I think. Geometric patterns—I like those in the fabric. You see this if the light is right. It is Armani, the designer. Jorge showed me the label. So it is a very fine tie, this one?"

"Yes, I suppose," Bly answers over the traffic noise threaded by music. "And a very expensive brand, last time I looked. But I'm a jeans and T-shirt kind of guy, you know? Not exactly a clothes horse."

"Horse? A clothes horse?"

"It doesn't matter." Bly glances back over his shoulder again.

Chapter 13

"No, I want to understand," Rafaela insists emphatically. "I don't want to feel stupid when you say something." Her countenance is rather serious.

"You are far from stupid. I'm quite sure of that," Bly says, perplexed that an idiom might mean so much. "A clothes horse," he begins slowly, "is a way of saying one is passionate about clothes, finds pleasure in shopping and buying clothing—usually fashionable things. A clothes horse is someone who has lots of clothes, closets of clothes, boxes of shoes, if you see what I'm saying."

"Yes. So many clothes—enough to *choke a horse?*" Rafaela says with a spirited smile. "I have heard this one, 'enough to choke a horse.' I understand it."

"That works for me."

"Anyway, the tie, it looks very nice with Jorge's white shirt. He says this tie was a gift to him only yesterday from a tourist woman, *mujer China*. I don't know," she says with a shrug.

Rafaela turns sharply left on a blue-and-white tiled corner to a side street, stopping abruptly on the narrow pavement. A shirtless black man wearing a horizontal striped T-shirt in the arrangement of an Egyptian headdress steps from the curb. His statuesque torso approaches her window with an ample block of white cheese extended on a strip of cardboard. Rafaela is already flagging a few pesos for his other outstretched hand. The rapid exchange is mute and apparently familiar to them both.

"Please?" Rafaela inquires, offering the cheese to Bly to hold. "This, I think you would say, is *farm cheese*."

Bly balances the weighty cheese on the cardboard in his lap while Rafaela returns to her usual route. The street view ahead is opening over lower buildings with a huge cluster of taller ones against the skyline ahead. It is an image Bly abstractly summons as a monumental carton of fast food french-fries standing on end. In their shadow Rafaela turns sharply up into a double row of massive cubical apartment buildings. She veers for a vacant parking spot and, coming to an abrupt stop, says, "You don't talk very much."

"No, not very much," Bly says, "except when I talk too much."

"You are a very strange man," the woman says parked. "I wonder if you are capable of a straight answer?"

An Unfinished Sunset

"Is that a question?" Bly asks, admiring an old red-and-white Meteor-Cadillac ambulance that apparently hadn't moved in years from the parking space beside him.

"No," she replies. "I don't think so."

All around them the massive apartment buildings stand now like gigantic encyclopedias, dingy-white, frayed volumes squared in light. They are virtually mirror opposites, the structure on each side of the street devoid of any architectural features other than the same dreary color and rectangular shape of their concrete facades. The arrangement of the apartments is at once logical and clear, though as devoid of creativity as an arithmetic problem. Bly suspects and Rafaela soon confirms that these are communist-inspired, Russian-supervised constructions. Detecting Bly's bleak assessment, Rafaela chattily addresses the sameness.

"The Soviets," she says with another pronounced shrug, "this is their sentiment. Everything and everyone equal completely. They are buildings for classless communities. You see that. There are many more everywhere in Cuba. Even the unfinished ones, many of our people live in these. They are as they were abandoned to us, and we make them livable by salvage and rummage. The Russians, most of them, are gone now, but many people still live in their boxes.

"Who knows what our economy is now? The Spanish, French, Canadians, Israelis—many more—they come to invest in hotels we never see, citrus groves that produce fruit not for us to eat. They fish, eat lobsters from waters where it is unlawful for us to fish. The *turistas* eat beefsteak; this business too is entirely controlled by the government. It is too expensive for us anyway. So you go to prison for butchering a cow on land your people farm with their sweat. Everyone is here but the US," Rafaela says. "Your magistrates think it is your money, the strength of your embargo, your ego. You think this is so important to our economy. Maybe it is not that."

Rafaela massages her chin as if shaping an imaginary beard, the commonly used gesture to identify the famously bearded Fidel without saying his name. Then she turns in her seat to continue.

"You have your embargo, and so *you know who* has his excuse to say we are a poor and oppressed nation because of your harsh policies. We must tighten our belts," Rafaela announces in a deepened

Chapter 13

newscasters voice. "We must resist the oppression of the *Yanquis*. No! The US government is much more valuable to the leaders of the regime as an arrogant enemy than it could ever be as an economic ally. All of this is my pleasure to show the amused guests of our country each day in a mirror upside down. I say nothing but in that way. Anyway the problem is not between our people. It is between our governments. You see this?"

"I'm not into politics either way," Bly says blandly in response to Rafaela's diatribe. "At least I'm not political like that." Bly seeks to change the subject. "Where are we, by the way?"

"Not *in that way* political?" Rafaela persists. "In what way then are you political?"

"I don't know. Most of you Cubans talk politics like you talk baseball. I don't try to keep score. I see everybody's running a game. If it's local, maybe I'm interested. But saving the world, saving one country or another—been there, done that, got the T-shirt. Got my ass singed," Bly responds with an equal measure of emphasis. "Pardon me."

Rafaela's brow furrows as she makes an intolerant frown and says, "You are being evasive again."

"Okay," Bly elaborates. "Say a certain ordinance to limit the hours of operation for local taverns is on the city ballot. That was a local political issue some years ago. I paid attention to it. But even that doesn't matter to me now. All politics is local for me, but I'll acknowledge it's increasingly global for the world. Politics is just one big briar patch into which I may burrow incognito from time to time, but I try to steer clear of the thorns."

Rafaela observes Bly languidly with mild bemusement. Her eyes appear now to have darkened to the color of freshly washed grapes. An indistinct smile emerges from the shadows at the corners of her pretty lips.

"This is where I live," she says, opening the car door to exit the Lada, "in the thorns. I live in the thorns."

She makes a friendly gesture for Bly to follow. Up a dank stairwell Bly holds firmly onto the thick leather grips of his heavy canvas bag. He's following Rafaela to an austere door on the fourth floor. The poised, dignified woman turns to him then.

An Unfinished Sunset

"This man inside—he is like my own father—is not well. I must make sure he eats. He is not my father, but I must see how he is now. I have my reasons. You will see. We will make a coffee and not stay long."

Bly nods without the slightest reason to trust Rafaela beyond some instinctive sense of survival he possesses, sparked by the beatific light of the woman's eyes. Bly doesn't consciously consider this rationale for trust. It is not deliberate, though it is sensible within the similar pathos of that memorable closing line from the Tennessee Williams play, *A Street Car Named Desire:* "Whoever you are, I have always depended on the kindness of strangers."

Bly enters the apartment after Rafaela, and he is in another world. The interior is neat and orderly yet entirely divergent from the building's insipid, staid exterior. The walls are bursting with color, covered virtually from floor to ceiling with oil paintings bright with tropical hues. Given the similarity of their style and distinctive, vibrant shades of the Caribbean, each is evidently by the same artist. There is no illusion of depth; elements of Spanish and Cuban folklore are assimilated with elements of pop culture. The paintings are sensual and surreal yet oddly integrated with an array of ordinary acts and objects presented in unordinary ways. Some larger pieces are bound up, curiously enough, in grandly carved antique frames. It occurs to Bly that they were not meant for the art upon such walls. These are massive, rusticated frames displaying abundant, leafy, gold profusions of overlapping and intertwining scrolls and volutes. Generous frames of this type Bly associates with the grand traditions of depth and light as celebrated in the art of Renaissance painters featured in premier museums. He completes his thought with the names of only two: Michelangelo and Caravaggio.

The abstract paintings before Bly, he decides, are evidently more concerned with the construction and arrangement of their colors than any sort of realistic representations. By whatever design or definition they overspread the white walls of the entire living space. Dozens more painted canvases (most unframed) lean together, standing in stacks against a wall. Of the extensive

Chapter 13

collection Bly blithely considers non-authoritatively that such modern art isn't really modern any longer.

Putting away the cheese, Rafaela observes Bly from the kitchen to be perplexed by the altered human forms and disproportionate objects in the art. He has not yet perused the artist's small sculptures and painted ceramics arranged or stacked on tabletops throughout the apartment.

Mildly amused, the woman says, "Do you know this? 'We all know that art is not truth. Art is a lie that makes us realize truth.' Do you know who said this? He was the biggest liar."

"No. I don't know anything about art," Bly says. "Or women," he adds, magnetized now by a larger painting on the opposite wall made entirely in shades of blue. A beautiful nude woman with large breasts is misshapen there, waist deep in azure concentric circles of water. "Nor can I accurately quote anyone who does," he adds slowly.

"Anyway, as you say of things, 'it doesn't matter.' But to me it does," Rafaela laments returning to Bly's side. "These," she says with a circular gesture, "are this man's paintings that I was telling you about. He and Yohan Lim were, I don't know what you say, *rivales* maybe?"

"Competitors?"

"Yes, that is better. They were in competition, but they were almost friendly. They never said they were in competition, but they were. That is how I know Yohan Lim. These," Rafaela sweeps her hand about the room, "these are the paintings of this man who has always signed his work simply with an *S*. Simply that," she says softly. "Now he does not want his name said at all. Only *S. Ese*," she interprets.

"Okay?"

"This is the kitchen," she says with a gesture to follow. "I must make something. You also have not eaten, I know."

Rafaela rapidly sets about heating a pot of black bean soup on a hotplate while continuing in a hushed tone to speak of the man who is apparently in a room with the door shut at the opposite side of the apartment.

"He went to Spain when he was young. This was before the Revolution. Then to France for many years, but his heart was always here in Cuba. I do believe that. He came home to us when I was already seventeen. I never knew him except as I remembered a completely bald man with a regal bearing and workman's body who rolled a large bright ball around on the beach—on the *cayo*—for us to chase with a child's laughter. When he went away, he imagined that my mother wept for him always, but she was only insane without him. She never would see him when he returned to Cuba. Never. He would come to the door, but she would not see him again. So maybe she wasn't so crazy, eh?"

Bly looks back from where he leans at the kitchen's doorway to the blue woman in the blue water. It occurs to him that, despite her misshaped body above the water, her painted reflection over the rippling azure surface of the canvas is perfectly proportioned, not distorted, because the water is correcting and clarifying rather than the more realistic reverse.

Rafaela continues without looking up from the slices and crumbles of cheese she is putting on a split loaf of bread. As if reciting from a reverie, she recounts, "He taught me French and how to make and fly a paper kite. And how to walk like a ballet dancer. He could be very silly. In English, it is *ballerina?*"

"Yes, ballerina. And this is a little awkward," Bly says, looking back to her, "but the woman in this blue painting, she looks a lot like you."

Rafaela laughs reticently. This is the first time Bly had heard her laugh, and it is as enamoring as her speaking voice.

"No. No," she says hurriedly, putting the bread in a baking pan to heat and soften the cheese. "That is another woman in another country long ago. *S* loved her, I think, but it was an unrequited love, as the poets say. She was much older than he. Older than you see her there," Rafaela asserts with a nod toward the blue painting. "Older when first he found her and went to her enormous stone house with a rotting roof in a village in France above the Côte d'Azur. She was an artist, almost famous, but a recluse. Each day he would come to ask her to be his teacher. She was once very beautiful, but later she was not, and she drank and smoked cigarettes very much. Some

Chapter 13

days she would say, 'Yes, come in, come in ….' Other days she shooed him away, as if he were simply a troublesome schoolboy grubbing at her door."

As he listens to Rafaela, Irish Bly wonders to himself how her story must surely reveal some obscure piece of the La Malinché puzzle. And so it does, though what she tells is also a puzzle unto itself.

"Yes, she was older than he," Rafaela continues slowly. "But he must have loved her, been in love with her. My mother thought this too. She knew from his letters. In these *S* told everything because he wanted her to know everything. Even if it hurt her. There were also the dozens of portraits of this woman he loved. This is one. Some my mother saw in the catalogs from the gallery he sent from France. She never spoke of it because …" Rafaela halts, as if to reconsider what she might say next. With a shrug she concludes, "My mother kept his letters and paintings because she did love him in that way one cannot love anyone else. But he was a poison she drank each day.

"When *S* did come home, that painting had already been here in Cuba for many years in our house on the cayo. She knew it was this other woman who was also an artist, but she kept it in our house because his love was in it, she said. Even if it was not love for her and it was cruel of him to send it to her, she hung it in our home so that the sea air might destroy it as she could not."

"It didn't."

"No. The sea … no. It did not destroy the painting. If anything at all, the sea sent its breeze to enter the painting and made more exquisite the shades of blue. Anyway all the stronger was my mother's resolve. She would refuse to ever see him again, though really this was because she was dying. I think he knew, even if he says he did not. All the paintings he sent back to her, like flowers for forgiveness—sometimes by the crate full—they hung in our home while she lived. You see many of them here now."

"Sounds complicated," Bly says.

"It is complicated," she agrees as she prepares the lunch.

Rafaela hastily sets a bowl of the soup by Bly at the small table in a dining nook within the kitchen. "You must eat," she says, putting down a saucer laden with the grilled cheese toast she has pressed flat under a heavy cast-iron pan.

"What about you?"

"I ate in my car," she says. "Earlier, that is what I was doing. Waiting."

"Waiting?" Bly asks, taking up a spoon.

"Waiting for you. But you must excuse me now. I have this for *S* to eat."

It is quiet behind the closed door. Minutes pass, and a muffled conversation intones intermittently from the bedroom. It has been quiet again when Rafaela returns to the table to sit askew in a chair across from Bly. She begins to speak, then stops to rest her head in her hands with her elbows braced against the table.

"You okay?"

"No." Rafaela looks up to ask rapidly, "Where is your bag?"

"Here." Bly gestures to the canvas sack between his feet under the table.

She looks uncomfortable with what she is about to convey and says finally, "He wants to see you."

"Who?"

"*S*. He wants to see you."

"Why?" Bly is authentic in his surprise.

"It is what he said. He wants to see you. This is what I know. Trust me."

Bly looks quickly down to the bag at his feet.

"Bring it with you. You are safe here. I have told you that. Go in, please, and I will make a coffee now."

Bly takes up the heavy bag and lugs it with him toward the bedroom door. He enters. A strange older man sits by the window in a heavy antique armchair. His skin is the burnished tan color of an old baseball. Stocky and bald, he sits bare-chested in nothing but a diaper-like wrap of sheet cloth. *S* awaits Bly with a toothy grin of yellowed teeth and large, piercing, black eyes, shiny as the obsidian of the Aztec Mirror in his grip.

"Come in! Come in!" the ancient one croaks in a rasping voice.

The bedroom is also covered with paintings from floor to ceiling, with more unframed pieces six or seven deep leaning against furniture. There is a distinctly ominous quality about these. They are more recent, and the room is redolent with the scent of fresh oil paints in rot. Bly experiences the paintings viscerally all at once in the same recoil he experiences from the decaying fecal stench of the room. He stands erect with an inquisitive cast of his eyes toward *S*, the canvas bag held fast before him in a double-fisted grip.

"You are Irish Bly?" *S* states more than asks in an accent more French than Spanish.

"I am."

"Liar." The old man says in a raspy tone and laughs aloud, as though the joke is on him.

Bly shrugs. "You asked."

"Yes. I asked," *S* admits with suddenly suspicious eyes. "No one lies now better than I do. I don't allow it." He laughs heartily and then gasps for air to demand, "It is in the bag now, is it not? In the bag?"

"It?"

"It!" *S* virtually shouts with a gesture inviting Bly to sit at the foot of his unmade bed. Yes, *it!*" He reiterates harshly as Bly sits with the hidden Mirror positioned before him. "I am speaking of Yohan Lim's device of course. Rafaela pretends not to know, but I know anyway. Did you make Rafaela promise not to tell me?" the old man asks in a sing-song tone with a wagging of his thick finger.

Bly catches himself before answering impulsively, as he is about to do. He says instead, "I have nothing to show you."

"Of course you do. All of you were coming, and I knew it all the time. Who do you think told me? Luis Lim, eh? *Nooo*. Maybe those two, 'the Sisters.' Everyone in the galleries knows them. Consuelo Doge, C. C. Moth? *Yesss,* I know all about them and their fascination for Yohan's device. This fascination was fatal for Sergio Castellan, no?" *S* all but snickers.

"And now I come to Herr Krym. Ah yes. You've seen him around today, haven't you? Diebolt Krym? Hmm, I think you do have something to show me. It is not as if I don't already know … something." *S* announces with steely eyes. "That will be the device Yohan used for making his art lately. I *know* he had a way of seeing by using some mirror. My lover told me. She knew instinctively. She *knew* a convex mirror was involved in Yohan's technique. She saw his paintings in the gallery in Paris, just the same as your friends the Sisters. She knew instantly this *autre Cubaine* was using a mirror device, so she told me. I remember the exact moment. It was when I held a lit candle to her cigarette in that long, thin trumpet of a cigarette holder of hers. Her hands cupped mine. They were beautiful hands even then. Her fingers were slender and elegant with perfectly manicured nails of scarlet. You see her hands everywhere in my work for a long time. Look there!" *S* barks, pointing up to a cat-like portrait of a woman, her dark hair pulled tightly about her elegant head. They were precisely the fingers described—their pointed red nails splayed before her face.

"Do you know who offered me safe passage anywhere in the world for this piece? Simply that. I will tell you." *S* crosses his arms across his bare chest and frowns smugly for dramatic effect. And in a burst he exclaims, "Bertrand Oliphant, hah!"

"Oliphant?"

"Of course. Do you really think your Key West is not such a small place? But don't worry. My lover, my friend, my mentor, she knew Oliphant all too well. She is dead now, you understand? She would have told me that night—the last night we were together—if she had known exactly about this Mirror. She loved me that night. This was after she had hated me for weeks, and then she loved me again before she would hate me the next day. It went like that. She returned to her apartment in Paris. I came back to Cuba. I don't know how it ended for us on the last day. Love me, love me not; I don't know. I wanted the Sisters to tell me when they'd come and go, but they were cruel about this and gave me no news from Paris. Everything was about Yohan."

S is suddenly pensive, adding, "She died alone in Paris, and I had become a stranger in my own land. Now, I want only to see the Mirror. I want to see what Yohan Lim saw. I want to see what she knew."

Rafaela comes into the bedroom with a tray raised before her. Arranged on the tray are three small cups of stout Cuban coffee, made syrupy thick with sugar.

Chapter 13

"Ah, daughter, you are only too kind," *S* gushes in a voice laced with mendacity.

"I am *not* your daughter. You know that irritates me for you to say it," Rafaela states blandly, as if for the thousandth time.

She extends the tray to Bly first and then to *S* before placing it on a bedside table and removing the remaining cup. The high dose of caffeine and sugar sends a jolt through Bly.

"So," *S* says after a loud slurp of coffee, "now we are having coffee together, and we are all friends. Let us see what is in the bag, and we will love you. Then you will go, and we will hate you, but it is possible that we may love you again. So what do you say, Irish Bly? One look, eh? A mystery for me solved, a dying old man decomposing before your very eyes. May he rest in peace?"

Bly looks to Rafaela seated primly on the unmade bed.

"Why not?" she says with her now familiar shrug. "If any harm would come to you or your mysterious object in this place, it would've come before now." She nods gradually toward *S*. "He is wicked but helpless," she says with a sigh. Maybe it will do his soul good to see as he has not seen, only imagined as you see in such bitter envy."

Bly, having earlier considered that but for Rafaela he may well have fallen victim to Krym's zip gun, moves his hands over the heavy zipper of the bag. Except for her he might well not be in possession of La Malinché at all.

Bly sets his cup aside and opens the bag. He extracts the weighty Mirror amidst the old man's gasp and braces it atop his knee. So there it stands at last for *S* to see. The polished obsidian Mirror mounted between golden jaguars with emerald eyes. The male and female, nuzzling at the top of the piece, their bodies angled out so to shape the triangular mount with the cats' hindmost, long, entwined tails forming the Mirror's thick base across Bly's leg.

S appears astonished at first, his countenance almost fearful. And then he begins to laugh aloud, his dark, bulging eyes wide shut as a raucous sense of mirth seems to overwhelm him. This wheezing laughter follows Bly from the bedroom and continues while he returns the Mirror to the grip.

An Unfinished Sunset

"It will only be worse if we stay," she says. "He is trapped here by his own vices. And after his laughter, he will become a raging bull. Believe me, I know. It is better we go."

They stop at a blue door one floor down and east of the stairwell. Rafaela tells Bly, "You wait here. One minute, please. Just that."

At the door she raps twice before a woman with a child on her hip opens the door widely while welcoming Rafaela in. The banter between the two women is instant, profuse, and congenial. Apparently oblivious of Bly they disappear into the cilantro and cumin-infused shades of the faintly lit apartment. That the door is left open offers the only indication that Bly is invited in. Instead he waits with his back against the balustrade on the open corridor with the Havana skyline behind him.

Deep within the shadows of the room a wan, wispy woman, dressed in a white gown and housecoat, sits motionless in a chair against a far wall. She appears to be a living statue, like the painted buskers that strike their poses on city streets for tips. But then the ancient woman swats a fly from her nose. Her arm drops to the exact position it was before lifting it. She is a seer or living statue again. Rafaela is in some other room, apparently speaking into a telephone. The child cries out and is hushed. The abrupt rotary whirl of a floor fan rushes over the cool tiles. Rafaela's voice reverberates more loudly above the sound of the fan.

Bly understands enough Spanish to interpret roughly her account for being delayed in returning to her work. She is evidently familiar with the official she's called—affable but formally courteous. She must have been asked about the incident involving the jammed door and the frightened Dutch Girl Scouts earlier in the viewing chamber of the Camera Obscura. But when she resumes her duties, she promises to make a full report.

"*Ay. Si, pronto! Pronto! Caio,*" she says, hanging up the phone and turning to go.

Back in the Lada they drive to a distant suburb of Havana. Rafaela tells Bly, "This place, *Cubanacán*, used to be Habana's, so to say in the US, 'Beverly Hills.' The Communist party officials preferred it here. These are very nice homes. You see them here, there, and there, yes?"

Chapter 13

"Yes, so the Communist party bosses, they didn't go for their own boxes to live in?"

"No. Those are for *the people*. The bosses, as you say, they are not the people. They are the bureaucracy. So different. But this over there, see that? Before now it was the *Escuelas Nacionales de Arte*. Today it's called *Instituto Superior de Arte*. Anyway these are some of Cuba's national art schools."

Off the driveway lay a strange configuration of brick and terracotta structures rivaling the most startling illustrations of science fiction architecture around.

"All this," Rafaela says, extending her hand to to the sloping terrain, "it was one time an important club for golf. Very nice. Restricted. Fidel and Ché—Ché Guevara—they famously played a game of golf here and decided it would be a better place for the art schools. So they did that.

"Historians of the architecture say these are the most outstanding architectural achievements of the Revolution. As you see, even now they are very ... innovative, no?" Rafaela parks on the street above the schools built along a tropical forested gorge. "Those domes, the bricks and tiles, they are placed lengthways in this type of construction. It is an ancient way and common in the Mediterranean."

Bly sees that the domed structures, nearly a dozen or so, are organized along two distinct arcs with curving, colonnaded walkways connecting them. Other structures are accommodated in a contrasting block-like design that wrap in with the colonnaded paths so that from an aerial view the successive and overlapping domes must resemble an organic paisley pattern descending the still recognizable golf links.

"These, they were the pride of the Revolution, but like so much they were never finished, and soon the architects too were ridiculed for something so strange and not the same Soviet forms, the boxes, as you say. There were accusations."

"What sort of accusations?"

"The School of Fine Arts was said to be the incarnate *Ochún*, the Afro-Cuban fertility goddess. This series of domes, they were said to be modeled on women's breasts, which may be true, but what does it matter? I am not comfortable telling you this, but I will.

An Unfinished Sunset

The famous 'papaya' fountain sculpture in the courtyard over there. That was supposed to be another outrage. Papaya, as I'm sure you know, is a crude Cuban slang for vagina. Then some other peoples, they say they think the design is maybe homosexual. I can't even explain that. You will have to think of it. Anyway all this became very problematic. I think the design was incompatible with the Revolution. Simply that. So anyway this is a good place for me to say good-bye."

"Good-bye?"

"Yes. You see just down there, by this path?" Rafaela points down the nape of the gorge. "This is the school for ballet. You will know it. It was built down there into the hill's side. It is, I think, the most beautiful unfinished school of all. Now it is a good place for you to be obscure, and before some time I will come back. But I must return to the Camera Obscura just now. There might be questions. It is better this way; I promise you that. I will come back for you."

Bly, as apprehensive about the circumstance as he feels strange in the sprawling architectural before him, is profuse in his appreciation. After an awkward embrace in the car, he springs for the path with his valise. But before he can turn back to signal again his gratitude, the Lada is gone from view.

Bly makes his way down the narrow path through the jungle-like terrain of the earlier golf course's ravine. The path below is cleaved with a notch to drain off rain water. At some distance in the decline the bricks and mortar of the ballet school complex are revealed through the over story, like an ancient ruin bunkered within the lower space of the ravine. At a narrow plateau made by overflow Bly can see now to a cluster of domed structures seeming to levitate in the lush landscape. Outwardly from aloft it is apparent that among these are a series of large domed structures connected in a layering of successive vaults. They resemble giant scallop shells lain upon each other along a steamy serpentine path.

Bly stops in awe before the deep shade of the entrance, there where the winding passage ascends to link the various pavilions of the unfinished school. Not far within is the gaping entrance to the pantheon-like space of what would have been the ballet

Chapter 13

performance theater, the great unblinking eye of a round skylight at the apex of its tiled dome.

Where the inner corridors connect with their sanctums of this forsaken place they do interesting things with the air, elongating it and twisting it into shapes. All sound borne upon the acrid air is strangely wrought in this way, making it more difficult to find the limit of a particular sound or the possibilities that sound may present.

Deep within the pavilion Bly turns to the recurring and descending metallic scrapes that form and decay over the water-stained concrete of the corridor's floor. The sound tightens and becomes more reverberant as it nears. The heavy scuff signals someone large approaching. Bly lurches away from the cusp of light spilling softly from the pupil-like skylight in the rotunda overhead. He stumbles backward over his canvas duffle and reaches to bring it around to rest in the dusky shadows against his heels.

13.2

A dark, sleek performance boat is coming in fast off the choppy bay, its onrushing roar of four 350 HP outboards blare in its rapid approach. A towering rooster tail of sunlit spray arcs high above the channel marker as the boat comes round to enter the mouth of the Waccasassa. Slowing only slightly into the gaping mouth, the coffee-colored water of the river churns to wake aft in a frothy inverted V that snakes after the fast boat.

Inward bound, small waterfowl flutter and scurry from the salt grasses. Larger birds flap from tall cypresses along the near bank while the boat zooms on up river. A big alligator slides from a drift log that has fetched the muddy shore.

As the river narrows languorously into the palm-fortified banks of the headland the deep-throated roar of the powerboat throttles down again to a lower octave. The sound of the engine reverberates more throatily upriver while its sleek bow knifes through the mercurial camouflage of light and shadow. Watery-brown hues change and shift in shape upon shades of myrtle and hyacinth green. The

An Unfinished Sunset

rough wake of the advancing boat washes over wispy eddies of sand and tidal flats flecked with shell in the midday sun.

Deeper in, above the county boat ramp, pole fishermen sit on their tackle boxes or on the flat of upturned plastic buckets. An older man and woman wearing matching straw hats are settled comfortably in their collapsible lawn chairs. They each hold a long cane pole, their fishing lines descending slackly over the lazy water. Three others stand fishing from the jagged contour of the riverbank along the grassy parking plateau. Older pickup trucks and a late-model economy car are parked in a disheveled smudge of mottled colors close behind. Trailing those are newer blocky trucks with unburdened boat trailers perched above the public boat ramp.

A younger man with sleeves rolled above his knotty biceps is fishing down on a narrow spit of sand. He casts his bait with a rod and reel. A conical bobber, red over white, wags outward to plop on the dark water. He raises the tip of his rod. The float is held taut against the current, allowing the lead weights plied to the line to sweep back. He waits anxiously with the sound of the approaching boat, his baited hook falling back beside the submerged contours of mossy locomotive wheels holding fish.

Now the menacing sound of the oncoming boat turns all heads down river. Some fishermen rapidly pull in their lines. Others brace themselves, gesturing with frustration as the aggressive yellow boat blasts by, leaving the air heavy with its oily high-octane fuel exhaust.

The older woman hoots loudly when the wake crashes back upon her bobber's placid float. The surge slaps the shins of the younger rod man down on the bank. He raises his clasped fist and curses out after the boat, his angry eyes following the continuous splash ripping up along the root-riddled river bank.

Behind the boat's center console sit two suspicious-looking characters. Expressionless, they streak by with total disregard for those fishing from the bank. Not so much as a glance from behind their dark wraparound sunglasses toward the leisurely but serious enterprise they've disturbed. Suddenly the driver tucks his shaved head. All bone and sinew, shrouded with gruesome tattoos, he turns the craft down rapidly and brings its shark-nosed bow

Chapter 13

around to creep into the private canal of the Waccasassa Fishing Club's marina.

Those gathered around that marina get a better look at the men in the overpowered boat. They will later describe the two at the helm as rough looking. The driver is lean and taut as a fighting dog. His eyes are eerily bright, his tats utterly horrific. The other, standing at the console beside him, is taller. Square-jawed and beefier, he is equally tanned to an unctuous red-russet—the color of dried blood. In stark contrast to the shaved head of the driver this one sports a thick, old-school flattop that's bleached a peroxide-tinged yellow/white and waxed flat as an upturned scrub brush.

Two club members in fishing shorts and ball caps stand out on the boardwalk in front of the marina's store and clubhouse. They watch warily as the powerboat creeps in. Then they see a third man, this one sitting as if poised to strike from a bench seat behind.

The onion-headed driver leans forward to the chrome wheel, slowly surveying the circumference around him as the boat rumbles by in a creep. The other one remains upright, posing a flexed, soldierly bearing as he moves his head around to scan the marina compound in a jerky robotic motion. Together they expertly scope out the entire marina, examining thoroughly each boat along the docks, trailered or in bays. There is no humor about these men. They are obviously looking for something or someone, and they are not friendly about it.

Gradually the boat is brought menacingly about before the marina's broad ramp. Its mighty outboards gurgle back at the silent onlookers lounging by a fire ring on the bluff. Apparently they haven't found what or who they're looking for. The third man stands abruptly. He is much older, tall and lean and apparently fit for a man of advanced years. He wears a fishing hat with a back flap to shield the sun from his long ashen neck and seems to be searching with a wild, turkey-like jerking of his head. He appears incredulous, his piercing eyes wide behind wire-rimmed glasses. His facial expression is one of irritable imploring, as if he fiercely intends to verify the vacant report the driver has given in a rap-like cadence.

The tall man lifts his bony chin and shouts something unintelligible above the rumbling of the big performance boat going out. A craggy-faced World War II vet by the fire ring will tell Levy County deputies that the man's distinctive accent sounded German to him.

13.3

Linton is soon to be within the spotty reach of a cellular tower. A flannel-clad hunter with a thick shock of salt-and-pepper hair and lettuce-green eyes drives him out of the Gulf Hammock hunting woods. He is the esteemed patriarch of the Maddox family, great-uncle to the boy whose four-wheeler Linton had crushed earlier. His status among the Maddox clan renders him the highest ranking among all of that family's members, which includes by marriage the business and political alliances of Fallons, Warrens, and Earls.

Earlier, after nearly an hour of walking out the through the slough along a narrow maze of deeply-rutted berm roads, the boy had shown Linton a shortcut via a game path. It skirted a stand of sturdy cabins clustered around a long cookhouse with a bathhouse nearby. It is on this rocky patch of higher ground that the Boatwright Well camp stands beneath spreading oaks growing since the time of Hernando De Soto.

There, by the smoldering burn of a fire built before first light, the entire camp has returned from the morning hunt and has gathered in a huddle around Linton and the boy. Looking around anxiously, Linton holds forth in his best prayer voice with a remorseful account of how the accident back on the Blue Line happened. He deliberately omits the reason for his frantic haste. He prefers that his mother not be implicated in some future matter should the disreputable stranger harbored in her bed prove to be an outlaw, as his practiced paranoia predicted. The boy, Tobin Maddox, nods in reassuring agreement with Linton's humble statements of fact.

The pastor is winsome with his apology, but it is Patton Maddox's thoughtful attentiveness and kindly demeanor that set the attitude for the rest. It's after Maddox removes the old fedora he wears for hunting and wipes his brow that the camp, in a cascade of murmurs, echoes their prelate's cordial sentiment, "At least no one got hurt."

Chapter 13

    This so assuages Linton's pounding heart that his voice settles to a business tone. He then produces from his wallet an insurance card and summons quelling assurances that all damages will be remedied. But the crowd has largely dispersed back to their duties in the camp, while several other boys speed off on four-wheelers of their own to find the scene of the calamity.

    Afterward Patton Maddox is driving Linton in his pearly white pickup—still redolent with the scent of new leather—out to the highway. In the back seat Tobin leans forward to rest his elbows on the console between Linton and his uncle. By the time they are on the Buck Island grade Linton maintains that this ride need take him no farther than the highway. He'd have a cell phone signal from there.

    On the massive swamp tires of the vehicle Linton bounces as easily as the straw-haired boy beside him on the bench seat. Linton and Tobin appear equally forlorn, now some hours after the mishap on the Blue Line. Patton Maddox, genteel and gregarious, tries to keep up a conversation with Linton. He is accustomed to good-natured banter and entertaining persiflage to sort out personal connections and relationships.

    Maddox also knows Mazie and recalls that for many years she had been the much-beloved cook for the county jail. So popular was her cooking and consoling nature that inveterate prisoners—black and white alike—took to calling her "Mom," Maddox recalls. He knew of Mazie's praises because he'd been a county commissioner for all the years she had stirred and ladled her tasty fare at the jailhouse stove.

    "That Mazie changed more lives than those steel bars ever did," Maddox says with a reassuring nod.

    Despite the amicable observations, for Linton it is a protracted forty minutes from the camp out to US 19. He converses on auto pilot, remaining preoccupied with how dangerous is the unnamed man back at his mother's house.

    US 19 runs north and south for long stretches mere miles inland of Florida's Gulf coast. Despite the vast asphalt ribbons of interstate and turnpikes crisscrossing the state, Hwy 19 remains a familiar corridor for those traveling from Tampa/St Petersburg up

An Unfinished Sunset

to Tallahassee or down the other way around. Where 19 and the Buck Island grade intersect there is a derelict store with abandoned living quarters above the bridge over the Waccasassa.

The hunters drop Linton off at the storefront. There he profusely expresses his genuine gratitude for the ride and offers again to pay his fare out. The older Maddox touches the tip of his dusty fedora, and with the engaging smile of a consummate politician, he refuses.

"My best regards to your mama, son," Patton Maddox says soothingly. "You're quite sure we can't take you on in to town?"

"No sir," Linton assures eagerly. "I'll be just fine right here."

The expensive truck cruises back up to the sandy Buck Island grade. The boy, remaining in the back seat of the cab, feebly waves back at Linton Day, who is already frantically dialing the sheriff on his cell phone.

CHAPTER 14

Life is a pure flame and we live by an invisible sun within us.

—Sir Thomas Browne (1605–1682)

BEFORE I KNEW IT Krym's hard charging go-fast was already roaring out the Waccasassa, that dark serpentine river with its gaping mouth on the silver sheen of the Gulf of Mexico. They were looking for me—Krym and his goons. I had just settled in for an afternoon nap, realizing they'd be after the grip. I did know that much.

So I wouldn't sleep. Mazie and Alifair were already slumbering in the girl's bedroom behind me. That was the way they'd slept while I lay healing in Mazie's bed. The woman's soft snore was familiar to me now, as was the subtle manner in which she revealed information. Most recent were her boosts for my impending departure. There was this too. Mazie repeatedly raised her full anticipation that Linton would be returning in short order with the law. After all, her anxious and alarmed son had declared his intention loudly and plainly enough within my earshot. I rolled to the window with full expectation that Linton Day would be back at the door at any moment with a sheriff's deputy or two.

My first impulse had been to play my game out with the law. I could come up with a story good enough to keep me from being cuffed and hauled away so long as Mazie played along. I'd stay cool and talk my way out of being taken in. There was nothing unlawful they could pin on me at the moment, I thought, but then what did I actually know about what they actually knew? These things became increasingly clear to me as I lay pondering the situation. I couldn't know what Mazie knew either or if she actually knew anything at all about my escapade. Still, I had it in my head that I might well offer myself as a man who'd washed up in the storm, injured by a loose gaff or busted rod that ripped across my shoulder. I had no identification but could say that my wallet had been lost in the storm when I was tossed from my boat and had to swim for my life.

But, as was immediately apparent to me, my beached boat was a problem. All identification numbers had already been irretrievably scraped or sanded away. I still wasn't thinking as clearly (dehydration having some part, I suspect), though it had occurred to me as tradecraft that the Challenger would be stolen and its ownership obscured. That would raise questions in and of itself. In any case, what I really wanted was to lie low and undisturbed at Mazie's for a while longer. It was just too bad that Alifair had spilled to her uncle about the location of my wrecked and bloody boat on the creek. That put in check any innocent or cavalier invention I might conjure.

So there was the Challenger, a problem to be sure, even if the girl hadn't spoken of it. It wouldn't take long for law enforcement or Krym to spot my boat. It could likely be seen from the dock. Most any police officer would have his obligatory look around, checking things out. Yes, the boat was a problem. Even in an approach by water the beached boat would be visible soon enough.

And then, among the litany of things I didn't know at the time, an alarming media broadcast had everyone on high alert, reporting that men in fast boats had carried out a gambling boat heist on the night of the recent, unpredicted storm. An exchange of gunfire had "… pierced the sheets of windswept rain in the stormy night at sea." The initial facts of that heist (given my unidentifiable boat wrecked ashore on that same night) would certainly ensnare me. Why wouldn't it? Here I lay, a wounded man with a powerboat smashed on the storm tide against a creek bank, its windshield riddled with bullet holes and bloodstains settled in crimson ripples where the oily rainwater collected in the aft. I'd have never

Chapter 14

satisfactorily explained away any of that, not to mention how high the bar for doing so would be in light of the gambling boat hit.

Lying on the patchwork quilt over Mazie's bed, I was examining my deck shoes on an old wicker chair in the faintly purple shadow across the uncluttered room. I could slide barefoot into those easily enough on the hardwood floor. I wouldn't have to disturb my wounded shoulder at all, though that consideration brought me to an uncertainty about how fast I might move with my left arm and shoulder bound up as they were.

Mazie had that arm folded against my chest. It was wrapped tightly with strips of bed sheeting to immobilize the deeply grazed shoulder packed with gauze. When she'd changed my shoulder bandage that morning, there wasn't a trace of fresh blood. The gauze pad she showed me was stained with the fading remnant of some lime-green salve she prescribed for healing anything that "itched or blooded-up." There was that on the gauze and a narrow viscous streak of some opaque healing serum my body now produced in recovery. I was uncertain about how the bandage might do absent the binding around my shoulder and arm, but I had to be rid of it.

In this quandary I set about to let myself loose. But apparently I had decided without determining all the consequences. There was the boat and my bandages and a good many other things I was uncertain about just then. These included other matters I might not examine or linger over at all if I were a wiser man.

In this odd musing mode, for example, I had never been quite certain about the color mauve. Lilac and lavender and violet—these I identified readily. Violets, I remembered, grew wild on a fencerow along a country road in my youth. Purple lilacs were my great-grandfather's favorite flower, or so my grandmother insisted within the legend she managed. There was an accommodating florist over on Swan who could sometimes procure the purple variety he preferred. Grandmother put them in a special crystal vase, broad at its base and fluting upward. Slim and tall, it stood to trumpet at its crown with a wide scalloped mouth. This shape allowed the lilacs to tumble in luscious clumps down over the glass.

That crystal piece (which my grandmother predictably identified as *the lilac vase*) had its special place on a round mahogany library table. There it long stood above a gilded picture frame holding a yellowed photographic portrait of the great man himself. Behind the frame glass a certain cast of the old man's eyes betrayed an otherwise stoic countenance. His eyes, I'd finally decided before joining the Navy, revealed some tacit capitulation to the tedium of his monetary endeavors. Worse, they carried a frightful glimpse of the dissatisfaction each celebrated success must have brought without the next. And, as far as I know, he never went where lilacs grew.

Of the color lavender, I later saw immense leas of lavender growing in exact rows over the undulating countryside in the south of France. I was a young seaman by then, anxiously hitchhiking from Paris (where I'd reveled too long) to catch up with my ship in Marseilles. I was sleepless but aboard before she left for Rota in the dawn. I was at the rail as she traveled out with some faint remnant of that color in the sky. The memory brought me back to amazement at such vibrant hues I saw over those fields the day before. That amazement did not diminish before Spain, nor has it to this day.

And so I lay blue in Mazie's bed in an idle contemplation of purple, unwrapping the broad cotton strips from my chest. I folded one of these and then two more back over my shoulder until the strips of adhesive bandage were exposed. The purple hues of my recollections washed and merged, melding and separating out as watercolors on heavy paper do. I wandered through the vagaries these purple patches made. The bindings were painstakingly removed. This brought me to a pause. I questioned my purpose in purple, looked around, and saw it for what it was: inexplicable, even if the whole of it had transpired within a millisecond.

Then I heard the dog. Hobo moaned in his dreaming and stirred in the cool sand where he'd hollowed a spot under the front porch just outside my window. I was wasting time, or so anyone more lucid or practical than I would certainly insist. But, as I've said, all this washed over me in an instant. Though there was an instant more, I wondered why I should think such things at all. Perhaps it

Chapter 14

was because I'd made quite some rapid recovery shrouded by this same shadow (mauve, let me now say) in those hours of midday. And I wanted to take the color with me, I suspect, as I had earlier recollected the fields of lavender near Marseilles. So I did, deciding at that moment to cure my uncertainty finally by describing the shadow cast about the room as most certainly *mauve*.

To the more sensible such an aesthetic exercise would seem entirely useless and without any action. But I wanted to put my errant thoughts then (as now) within a different context. After all, this reverie had taken up time in a house where time in the conventional sense seemed not to matter much. At least not time as a clock says nor as the turned page of a calendar might. Here, in Mazie Day's house on the Gulf, time was more told (as it always had been) by the sun and moon, by the changing of the tides, by the turning of a child's head toward her mother's milk, by the waning pulse of a man deeply loved. Or by the coming of storms or the going of thistledown aloft on a late summer's breeze. Colors, by their hues, told the time of day in Mazie's world by shade and cloud shadow. At least these told all she needed to know.

I sat upright on the edge of the bed. Something I'd read about an old Indian rattled about in my head. A certain US Army general had presented him with a fine pocket watch, insisting to the native he'd henceforth tell *real* time with this precise device. But the chief admonished the general sagely, saying that this *real* time he spoke of made no more sense to him than did the general's implication that his US minted coins—also offered—represented *real* money.

I shuddered and blinked to clear such cobwebs from my head. I had to think forward and try not to reminisce or engage in such thoughts, as I was often admonished as a boy for doing. The present being entirely ephemeral, it was said that I better think ahead. But I had no aptitude for thinking ahead. Frankly I found my talents (such as they were) better fitted to revising the past so that it suit me later rather than portending or somehow scheduling my future. The present, I decided early on, could rarely be depended upon. The future had historically and most certainly been the least reliable of all.

That's just the way I ruminate. I suppose it's why I prefer my life as Irish Bly. Regardless, one may well agree with more than several who have thought my reinventions dubious. They've said as much, and such idle thoughts have cost me long-term friends a plenty, certainly a good wife, any number of steady jobs, and more money than I've ever claimed to make, even in the most nefarious of my pursuits.

Old news is good news. You're not as likely to get tangled up in it. If you think about it, the starlight a sailor steers by is some thousands of years old by the time he or she sees it to calculate that star's significance to the intended course. No matter how proficient with a sextant, the seagoing navigators who found the New World steered by old news. If you don't think that's relevant to your life, it's not. Of course, you wouldn't chance to lose your girlfriend's monkey in a poker game down in Puerto Rico either. So you'd likely not see or even know by now about La Malinché. You'd not know how to find the Mirror of the Jaguar Night except by someone as wayward as I. I've seen the Mirror. As I sat on the edge of that bed it was illumined by torchlight in my mind's eye.

Outside, beyond the silvered timbers and rusted roof of the old house, the daylight had descended to reveal a cavernous opening in the undulant scrub before the tall hardwoods of the hammock. A lenient breeze lifted, revealing an indistinct path through the scrub. The hour for my departure from this heretofore safe haven had arrived. The night was coming after me. If it were only the night, I would have been more fortunate. I had been helped and cared for—healed up mostly—and was about to make off again with my hidden treasure. But as an old Carolina mountain fellow, sharpening his butcher knife, once wisely observed to me, "The fat hog is not always in luck."

Down by the creek my canvas grip lay concealed. I'd tossed it that tempestuous night into the taller grass where the bag remained partially submerged in muck. I'd thought more than once that Alifair's dog, Hobo, might go bounding out that way. But each time he'd darted off the girl had called him back. The dog would stop and turn with eyes that seemed to say, *But don't you want to know what's out there? There's something there that wasn't there before!*

Chapter 14

Alifair would stamp her foot and call Hobo back another time in a yet more demanding tone, and the dog would dutifully plod back up the muddy path to her with a slump that seemed to respond, *Okay, fine. It's not as if it's something to eat out there. Not as big a deal as that.* Then the dog would slow and look questioningly over his haunches again. *But there is something* ... his eyes told in looking back again. But the girl would rather that the two of them played with the large rubber ball she was booting between her feet soccer style.

And so she'd make her kick, and Hobo chased after the ball again. Alifair rewarded him with sugary praises, but his heart wasn't always in the game. The ball was nothing to eat either. Sometimes he'd freeze the ball with an outstretched paw. He'd look over at me, sitting on the steps in the soothing sun. His eyes would narrow in some accusatory manner with a glare sufficient to say, *I know you know what's out there. I'm watching you. It better not be something to eat!* And then the girl would demand his attention again, and the ball would be put back into play.

Indeed, I did know what was out there. And it was time to dislodge my treasure from the quick of that mud, make it out of the grass to the hammock, and be gone.

The Reverend Linton Day had gotten the sheriff on his cell phone by then. Such was the privileged capability of Caldwell's former classmate (Linton), now shepherding a large church congregation with a demonstrated voting record. Virtually simultaneous was the roar (though not yet in my hearing) of Krym's sleek racing craft completing its outward arc from the river's mouth. It would now be at a good running depth, bearing down on its deliberate northerly course.

Those two goons Krym had hired would be standing erect at the helm, muscles flexed with opposite hands gripping the stainless steel side rails mounted on the boat's console. I would soon see them coming up the creek, as if the boat itself was in a crouch. Linton would be bouncing in beside the sheriff, his Crown Vic racing down the ruts of the Buck Island grade with the deputy's car behind, fishtailing in the sand.

14.1

At the passenger side window Lourdes Lim's raven hair tosses and flags, releasing the faint scent of Oud Wood to the sultry air streaming through her uncle's van. Lithe and athletic, Lourdes has suffered surprisingly few injuries from her motorcycle crash—merely minor sprains, scuffed knees and scraped elbows. Entirely competitive by temperament and incessantly self-analytical by nature, more serious is the blow to her ego.

Lourdes sits stoically upright in the seat in her black leather jacket unzipped to the waist. Her arms lock around a single knee raised before her, a raspberry abrasion exposed through a tear in her black leggings. Lourdes rests her chin where the tear isn't, staring straight ahead at nothing on the narrow backstreet of a bleak inner-city neighborhood. The sky is the somber ash gray an indolent sun makes on sultry, overcast days. Virtually everything else is the color of rust. Old men in sundry shades of brown play dominos at tables on the sheltered street corner ahead.

Lourdes is as inwardly agitated now as she was when her Uncle Luis first rushed to her side at the crash scene. The traffic by the Prado and around the Malecón to the busy plaza having been kinder to him, Luis had reached his dazed niece by the upended bookstalls almost immediately. He'd helped her then to raise and roll away the damaged bike.

As they drive, Lourdes is replaying in her pretty head the crash and its aftermath. So vivid are the images she recollects that they project like cinema frames behind the dark glassiness of her almond-shaped eyes. By her abysmal reflection Lourdes is immersed again within the gawking swarm of onlookers prattling and flailing about as Luis helped her to set the motorcycle upright. The two at the handlebars, each opposite of the other, lean into their push. The bike's wheels wobble to the van parked up a congested side street nearby. With the help of a shirtless stranger the battered machine is hoisted into the rear of the van. The small throngs of spectators clamber after like crabs in a bucket scrambling to be on top and see out to the yawning back of Luis's van.

Chapter 14

It is the shirtless workman who directs the mulish onlookers back so that Luis can shut the van's double doors. Two miniature patrol cars with flashing lights flicker now down by the old fortress on the waterfront. Unfortunately for Lourdes, despite her insufferable impulse to take back up the pursuit, the police approach from the same direction she last saw Bly go.

Luis insists to her that their pursuit is at an end. In fact, some contingency is clearly necessary now if they are to evade the police themselves. So the white van lurches off in the direction opposite the police now, overtaking the tatterdemalion bookstalls of the Plaza de Armas. Luis loudly and insistently waves oblivious pedestrians out of their way down the cobbled street. Albeit his appearance is somewhat frantic, the uncle gathers his thoughts methodically to examine his alternatives. Luis Lim is a survivor, a diplomatic manager of crises. He is also skilled most adeptly at saving his own skin.

By contrast Lourdes is silently, sullenly introspective. Her fixed facial expression is a precise characterization of that dazed, unaccepting gaze omnipresent among the fiercely competitive when suddenly and surprisingly confronted with defeat. The uncle looks to his niece inquiringly, though he knows full well her condition. The accounts that trumpet her prowess among the best swordsmen in the world are not exaggerations. Lourdes Lim has the heart of a champion. She will snap back in her vowed change of engagement.

She is surmising about Bly's trajectory around the Desampardo, being uncertain of his exact destination. Meanwhile Hermanito's frantic backseat driver has remained in a distant, dogged pursuit. Krym thought twice he'd lost Bly, but there he was again where his temporarily airborne bike landed back on the tree-lined avenue by the waterfront. Hermanito seems oblivious to Bly on his bike, but Krym desperately directs his attention to the Zongshien that's already dissolving into the colorful traffic ahead.

Hermanito and the hysterical Krym are catching up before losing ground again. The beastly Bel Air heaves and swerves to jerk back into its lane, regaining some distance before Bly escapes once more from Krym's line of sight.

Though the Bel Air is momentarily too far back to see Bly, Hermanito continues around the avenue tracing the waterfront to the Desampardo and the portside warehouse district. But that can't matter to Lourdes now. Evading the Havana police and their certain inquiry into her activities in Cuba does matter. She must figure out not where Bly is but rather where he will be. Not here in Cuba, not for long, but there, over there across the Florida Straits.

Numerous individuals in the crowd behind them will volunteer eyewitness accounts of the plaza incident, offering effusive descriptions of the white van and the *porcelana de la gente*—the China people—fleeing in it. A radio alert will go out instantly for the conspicuous van because it isn't a make and model frequently found in Cuba. It's another mistake that Lourdes regrets aloud while her aged uncle sweats behind the wheel in his once finely tailored but now tight-fitting suit jacket.

Luis loosens his necktie while driving at erratic speeds. He shoots across chaotic intersections, accelerating where least likely to be observed by police in the heavy shadows of these byzantine backstreets. His thick hands tight on the wheel, Luis zigs then zags a route back around toward the Prado. It is a seemingly uncertain and circuitous way he takes, albeit one calculated to confound and evade. Luis himself is continually confronted with frustrating turns onto increasingly narrow streets that flush the van into one-way streets or send him city blocks awry of a more immediate route plotted aloud and argued by an increasingly alarmed Lourdes.

In more than twice the time it would have taken to drive directly, the van skulks into the shadowy back alley behind Arielle Vega's apartment building. It's the 1940's-era office high-rise facing the leafy Prado on the Paseo de Marti, known notoriously before the Revolution as the Doge Building. Here, in the obscured alleyway behind, the van can be concealed. Luis has already insisted to Lourdes— *"Sin duda, indudablemente!"* —that Arielle Vega can be counted on to aid them further. After all, it is she who had informed Luis of Krym's recent contact. It was she who provided precise details of Krym's ultimate arrival and possible purpose in Cuba. It was she, Arielle, who had cleverly volunteered her nephew to be Krym's driver so as to keep close tabs on the guileful German.

Chapter 14

~~~

Always *una historia*. Arielle and Luis, as it happened, had remained close associates from the time of Marta Batista. It had in fact fallen to Luis (at Marta's persistent request) to arrange an introduction between *el presidente's* wife and the exciting new dance phenomenon that was Arielle Vega.

In the camera flash of time in those heady days before the precipitous fall of Batista, Luis (entirely in Marta's service) continued to escort the first family to cultural events and performances at the ballet. *El presidente* himself was not much interested. Luis was his diplomat, and there were bodyguards with eyes on him and another within and anywhere around the First Lady's entourage. It was she who had a keen fondness for the ballet, and this attention became especially pronounced after its principal dancer, Alicia Alonso, was away.

Alonso, world famous among the cultural elite by then, had found a budding international audience that was more endowing and less suspicious of her than were Batista's secret police. Arielle Vega pirouetted to prominence in Alicia's Alonso's stead. As the First Lady had entreated, Luis dutifully arranged for Marta and Arielle to meet. They were friendly from the start and spoke frequently and at length, often in Luis's presence, including backstage after performances of *Ballet de Cuba* and occasionally at formal receptions presided over by Marta in the grand chambers of the presidential palace.

Alicia Alonso had plenty of ardent and faithful admirers. Letter-writing gossips were quick with their pens. Courtyard chatter traveled by airplane and dirigible. Word of the burgeoning friendship between Arielle and Cuba's First Lady got around in toe shoes too. In the fantastic salons of Paris, as from behind bouquets in many of Europe's theatre dressing rooms, denizens of the dance world were only too eager to whisper in Alicia's ear.

Unknown to Arielle Vega and Marta Batista, however, was a tantalizing entreaty Alicia Alonso had recently been sent. It seems the prima ballerina in self-exile had received a secret communiqué from a revolutionary leader holed up in Cuba's Sierra Madres.

El Comandante, as she would discreetly confide, had assured her that a victorious Revolution would name her director of the National Ballet.

The guerilla leader was at the time little more to Batista than a mild pestilence off in the hills. That would change. And so it was with mild chagrin that Alicia Alonso would hear of the deepening liaison developing between Arielle Vega and Marta Batista. After all, Alicia was quite sure the days of Batista in Cuba were numbered. So too would be the diminishing spotlight on the good wife of *El Mulato Lindo*, as the strongman was known in the streets. But *El Hombre* would soon resemble Humpty Dumpty in his famous fall. Contrariwise, Alicia Alonso's revolutionary admirer would gather his throng by the thousands, and from their shoulders he would mount the wall at Batista's palace gate. Alicia, along with his minions and foes alike, would thereafter know the victor simply as *Fidel*.

Nonetheless Arielle's life had begun as a child dancing for her life in the streets of Havana. Over the ballast stones of Spanish galleons laid for pavements she twirled spritely for coin with a long wisp of bright silk streaming from her raised hand. Survival was her only politics then, and Alonso knows she is as innocent of politics now as then. Anyhow Arielle had only the muffled rumblings in the cafés to inform her of what loomed for Cuba beyond the bellicose shadows spreading from the verdant Sierra Madres. At the time an unpretentious and apolitical Arielle Vega was as nearly enchanted with Marta Batista as was the First Lady's attaché, Luis Lim.

Out of this rather elegant simpatico Luis and Arielle also became friends. And, as the Cuba of the Batista's crumbled, they became confidantes and later co-conspirators in Luis's trafficking in plundered Cuban art and antiquities. It was and is Luis's nature to pursue relationships of every description for self-aggrandizement and profit. Be that as it may, with surprising sincerity and apparent warmth he had come to refer to Arielle as *manita*, his little sister.

As things go, and much to Luis's displeasure, another of Arielle's passionate, if not obsessive, admirers came to inhabit her private life. This one would impose himself on her not as a

Chapter 14

Machiavellian brother like Luis but rather as a boorish brute of Shultzstaffel proportions. The interloper was a considerably older and obstinate ex-Nazi, one Helmut Krym.

This was after Marta fled with her deposed husband on the fateful New Year's Eve of '59 that ushered in the Revolution. Soon after, Helmut Krym was among the several former Nazi SS officers recruited to confidentially advise the new government. Totalitarian regime building aside, Krym the elder was only too eager to haunt Cuba for a far more compelling reason. A shoddy military historian, Helmut Krym was infatuated with his own discredited history, *Cortés, Eroberer des Jaguar-Gottes*.

It was in the pages of *Cortés, Conqueror of the Jaguar God* that Helmut Krym divulged his extraordinary find of the Lopez Codex in Mexico, its treasure inventory listing and detailing the drawing of the Aztec Mirror that would come to consume his thoughts for decades. Krym was only too eager to haunt the Cuban museums and galleries in his quest to find mention of (much less recover) this crown jewel of the lost Cortés treasure. Little did he know, but he played persistently and purposefully to the youthful Arielle's sensitivities and vulnerabilities.

While the city feigned normality in its Havana nights, the brutal Prussian (more lately of Argentina) often slumped oddly teary-eyed out in the red seats of the historic *Teatro de la Habana*. Under the stage lights Arielle still whirled gazelle-like—a fluid blur within the distorted prism of Helmut's lurid gaze. She was not the effortlessly ethereal being that Alicia Alonso was and so was largely ignored by Alonso when she'd returned to the theater.

While Arielle remained rather mesmerizing in her visceral style, the spotlight abandoned her for Alicia Alonso on her return. Arielle's now timid admirers would later insist behind their hands that she was the more athletic and perhaps Alonso's equal aesthetically. Nonetheless she was fortunate to have merely been returned unceremoniously to the chorus line. There, having wisely made anonymity her new best friend, Arielle escaped the dire consequences of being on the wrong side of the Revolution. Unfortunately she would not escape the wicked obsessions of Helmut Krym.

"Arielle, she was sensual," Luis describes her in a feeble attempt to distract Lourdes from her preoccupation. "So vibrant and vivacious in her dance. You would have seen this at once. She was, I think, more the enchanted forest creature than the romantic angel, as was Alicia."

～～

None of these reminiscences mattered to Lourdes now except as they returned her thoughts to Diebolt Krym. Her uncle dawdled on, telling again that it was no coincidence those decades later that the sociopathic son of Helmut Krym had advanced his coming to Cuba through his father's suspected Cuban paramour. Luis would insist that this much could be known: an inheritance of absence occurred. Ultimately each Krym held no interest in Arielle Vega exceeding a lust for the Mirror, La Malinché. For reasons marginally different both Kryms came to covet above all things this objet d'art. The elder believed himself to be entitled to it, as it was he who first discovered its existence deep within the Lopez manifest in that peeling leather box archived in Mexico. And it was his sullen son, Diebolt, determined to best his disapproving father, who verified the actual existence of the Mirror as described in the ancient codex. In the Florence penthouse above the Arno it was Diebolt Krym who had killed for it.

Among the papers and notebooks Diebolt's father left in his estate was in-depth and intimate information about Arielle, her friendly association with Marta Batista, and the rumored location of La Malinché. It was all there in Helmut's minuscule, meticulous hand. Diebolt, the dissolute and avenging son, had poured over these materials with an amalgam of intrigue and revolutionary fervor of his own. The notations regarding Arielle were blatantly written with boorish bravado and filed without restriction, redaction, or remorse. There was malevolence in what his father had written. For, despite overwhelming the youthful Arielle as he did, it had brought him no closer to the Mirror.

Removing his wire-rimmed glasses from his angular face, Diebolt must have looked up with pleasure registering in his eyes

Chapter 14

despite his cruel sneer. His father had been too late for Arielle to have had any actual access to the Mirror's whereabouts by then. Helmut's only consolation had been a fragile news clipping she produced as confirmation that the Mirror did in fact exist. It had been found and was whispered to have been enshrined in Batista's palatial bedroom. But it had gone missing again in the diaspora. And Arielle didn't know what Luis Lim knew about that.

Luis knew enough of the Krym invasions to explain Arielle's hushed disdain for Helmut Krym as the embodiment of bad seed. Now, nearly a half-century later, Arielle would play out her contempt by personally hindering Diebolt Krym's hunt for La Malinché. He would appear in Havana all these years later, a taller and leaner version of his father. At first sight of the son Arielle would cringe with revulsion in her recollection of his father. Her long-suppressed memories of Helmut covered her instantly like a mask of wasps before she'd twirled into her theatrical greeting of Diebolt at the airport. Nothing disgusted her more than the recollection of Helmut's naked, boar-like shoulder against her eyes wide shut—an inexplicable butcher block's scent of raw meat muting the flare of her youthful nostrils.

~~~

Luis knows how to let Lourdes into the building through the heavy door on the shaded alleyway. Deeper in, cardboard boxes and a drab tarp obscure the van behind them like a large garbage bin. Luis lets the door clank shut behind them.

In the cool of a dimly lit back stairwell Lourdes follows her uncle up the terracotta steps. Muffled music with a heavy reverberating beat grows increasingly loud as they climb within the yellowed and fractured plaster of the stairwell's high walls. Most of the former offices high in the storied building have been renovated as apartments appointed with an eclectic mix of 1950's-era hotel and office furniture. Other pieces are as much as a century old, though most are contemporaneous with the Revolution itself. Many of Arielle's tenants and lodgers are in Cuba on business. Others have scholarly associations with one of the nearby universities.

An Unfinished Sunset

None is a Cuban national. Just ahead there's a small arched door to the mezzanine level that overlooks the expansive lobby below.

At street level on the lackluster marble floor of that vast antechamber Arielle is conducting a neighborhood Zumba class. The heavy thud of a recognizable samba rhythm resounds within lofty white granite walls hung with colossal and forgotten tapestries and Eden-like images woven in wool and silk on a heavy cotton warp. These were commissioned of the Merton Abby mills by Laurence Hobbs Doge himself. On opposite walls they depict exotic images both exquisite and bold. In one, two nude figures (male and female) raise hands filled with fruit to the stylized radiance of a corpulent sun. On the opposite wall the same two wade with garlands of fruit around their necks toward that same sun, now set upon an undulant sea.

Between these towering walls a colorfully attired throng of gym shoe-clad women in irregular lines gyrate anxiously to the former ballerina's brassy instructions. Energetic, if aged, Arielle leads the group loudly before the milky plate glass windows on the famous paseo, her brightly colored hair bouncing to the beat in ponytails protruding on either side of her head.

With Lourdes at the landing behind, a breathless Luis appears on the swirling marble mezzanine above the choreographed gyrations of the class. Braced before the substantial balustrade, he observes with an amused bewilderment the dervish-style syncopation occurring below. The class mounts the vigorous crescendo of their finale set for that day with Arielle shouting out and dancercising onward as energetically as she had begun.

Class dismissed, Arielle scurries the exhausted women (all younger, though heavier and more ripe with perspiration than she) from the chattering echo of the cavernous chamber to the sidewalk outside. While the doors remain open, Lourdes and Luis have a partial view of the Prado below, gamboling through the laurels that shade the median of the paseo. Luis's thick hands flinch upon the stone of the balustrade as a police patrol car eases watchfully by.

Arielle, her dance tights boasting no less than three florescent and distinctively contrasting colors, comes up the sweeping marble steps to the mezzanine, a frayed towel swathing her swan-like neck.

Chapter 14

Her expression does not register surprise when she asks her unexpected visitors, "What are you doing here?"

Luis telegraphs by the incredulous cast of his eyes that there are complications to explain. The lines in Arielle's waxy face betray her age as she approaches. Lourdes and Arielle lean into an air kiss on either side of their cheeks.

"What has happened?" the older woman demands of Luis more sternly than she intends. Though before either can answer, Arielle releases a machine-gun fire of exclamations and demands: "Tell me. You are not supposed to be here now, you know that! Hermanito—oh my God—he's had an accident!" Her eyes narrow, and she asks, "No? He did get the German confused?" She probes more suspiciously in another blast of anxieties spiked by her severe declarations, asking, "Where is Hermanito this minute? If you do not have the Mirror, who then? I will slap him! If he has not done exactly as I say, I will slap him!"

Suddenly perplexed, she adds, "I found a painting, I must tell you. It is by this Yohan Lim, cut from a picture frame somewhere. Do you know this? I'm sure of it. It is in the apartment I put the German in, on the bed there right now. There were notes and drawings like a picture map on strips of butcher paper. I know something: It is *S*—that miserable *viejo libertino!* I saw these on the bed after the German Krym went out! *S* does this!"

"Show us," Lourdes demands firmly.

"Come with me!" Arielle says, already in a lean toward the back stairs.

The oil painting is on Diebolt Krym's tightly made bed exactly as Arielle described it. Both Lourdes and a wheezing Luis bend at the waist to examine the distinctively unmistakable last work of Yohan Lim. Luis also knows the fanciful sketches and small, boxy script that deciphers the purloined work of art.

"It is *S*. Papa, ay ay!" Luis slaps his forehead in self-derision as he stands erect. "The warehouse on the waterfront! Of course, the port. The Mirror must be there!" Luis yelps. "Why would I not think of this?"

Looking at her uncle blankly, Lourdes says softly with hard eyes, "*Was* there."

She recognizes an elongated, distorted depiction of the building where the Camera Obscura is housed, but the Lim warehouse she is thinking of is in the Barrio China at the other end of the Prado. Not on the port.

"No!" her frustrated uncle explains with a wide-eyed Arielle looking on. "There was also the port warehouse. It is still there, the ruin of it." Then, as if reasoning with himself, Luis continues, "Though really it has been gutted and is without a roof, a ruin long before Yohan's death, I'm sure. Ay, you idiot!" Luis claps his forehead, chiding himself over again. "Of course! But the cupola above the raised office, the roof tiles are intact there. The vaulted windows of the pagoda open to the sky! The Mirror, it *was* there! Ay ... ay ... ay!"

Lourdes gazes at her uncle quizzically. What has he not told her? There's another warehouse, a Lim warehouse on the waterfront (exactly the direction Bly went). So now Hermanito has Krym out there somewhere on the avenues along the port. Bly must have recognized and targeted the exact location from the towering heights of the Camera Obscura just as her benefactor had told her he would. And so she had been waiting, ready to leap like a tigress after him. Yes, he would himself be the unwitting rabbit to take Lourdes to that warren where the ascending ladder to the Mirror would be found.

Mere minutes later, still wearing her florescent lime, orange, and turquoise workout togs, Arielle is barreling out of the back alley on her flamingo-pink Italian motor scooter. Clutching at the slight paunch of her waist from the passenger seat behind is Lourdes Lim still dressed black. They are soon buzzing up the Malecón, diametrically opposite the location of Irish Bly. He has continued to evade Krym by skirting the massive walls of old brick and peeling plaster of the waterfront warehouses. Rafaela waits, perhaps for nothing, in her car. But Lourdes knows no more of Rafaela's involvement than Rafaela know of Lourdes or Luis in the chase. Arielle, however, now sees just how the cogs of both wheels turn. And, as soon as she sees that, they turn upon each other.

Chapter 14

Bly has waited in the slender shade by the weathered planking of an enormous door, hinged and locked shut with an antique padlock the size of his fist. La Malinché weighs heavily in his grip.

Krym has lost Bly's trail over the pocked and rust-stained concrete. His outrages echo in the Lim ruin behind Bly. After all, Hermanito has adeptly and deceptively delayed Krym's pursuit just as his imperious aunt has stealthily instructed. Never mind that Hermanito is roundly accused by Krym of being inept. He enjoys an identity too harmonized with his erratic music to be injured by Krym's appraisal of his driving and surveillance skills. Besides, he's already been well paid, and Bly has gotten away.

Hermanito, with both car doors flung wide to the vacant roofless exterior of the Lim warehouse, lumbers far back to stand at the loading dock on the water. He peers up at a giant derrick in the shipyard across the way. Down from the upper office stairs beneath the pagoda Krym is approaching noisily. He rants and rails again against his colossal driver—a colossal mistake. Hermanito adjusts his cheap sunglasses and points out to a derelict wharf.

Exactly opposite of the direction Hermanito indicates Bly is waiting and watching the compact car parked across the Desampardo. Rafaela Vélaz sits in that car, calmly eating her dainty sandwich.

~~~

Lourdes Lim holds tightly to Arielle as she scoots along in a madcap race for the Marina Hemingway. "Twenty minutes now, no more," Arielle tells Lourdes in the wind over her shoulder.

That's if she keeps pace. The swell of traffic has thinned as they buzz past the seawall with the sunlight withdrawing from the water's stony edge to the pastel plateaus of rooftops under the darkening sky. Lourdes knows what she must do. Bly is Oliphant's man in Cuba, but the powerful motorcycle he has waiting for Irish at the marina is exactly like the one Elle also has waiting for Lourdes in the Barrio Chino. It is in fact the same (though a different color) as the motorcycle Lourdes has in secure private parking at the Toronto Pearson International Airport, out of which she makes her frequent flights to Havana. That's because it is she, Lourdes Lim, who recommended the Zongshiens to Elle Rousseau.

There is this too. Besides the location of each delivery, there's one other distinction between the two bikes. Expertly concealed beneath the false bottom of the storage compartment under the seat of the one delivered to Lourdes is a subcompact Walther 9 mm. That handgun, recovered from the crashed bike while in her uncle's van, now rests against her spine beneath the sheer leather jacket she wears.

Lourdes knows the Sisters have paid well for La Malinché's ticket to ride. The flight down and back is Oliphant's plan. They don't trust Oliphant. They never did. They don't totally trust Bly either, though admittedly they've wanted to.

"We do trust Elle," C. C. Moth says, her long finger tapping a crystal ball she rolls between hands that appear mummified from her years of gardening in the sun.

"Indeed," agrees Consuela Doge, "We trust Elle because Elle trusts no one."

That's true, as Lourdes also knows, at least to a varying degree. Elle acts as she must to make things go her way but stops short of making her way entirely her own. That's the difference between Elle and Oliphant. Unlike her constant companion these many years, Elle tells the truth, though never the whole truth. Take for example the fact that Elle alone knows Ramón's full identity and scope of operations on the island. Oliphant can rig the game, but Elle owns it. Bly knows only the protocol by which he must connect with the shadowy Ramón to make the rendezvous. It's the same with Acosta and company. At the appointed time and place, which neither Oliphant nor his boatman knows with exactitude until mere minutes out, Ramón's charges will be found.

Pendarvis knows what Oliphant knows: the obscure location and hour a flotation device will be activated, transmitting then its engaging signal from Cuba. The fast boat out the Florida Keys will be closing on the island rapidly enough to immediately switch its navigation from the GPS approach, bearing to the precise honing signal that pinpoints the true extraction zone on the north coast of Cuba.

Chapter 14

Elle knows, despite Oliphant's deceptively casual and demure interest in La Malinché, he will want it for himself. She has overheard telephone calls to his exquisite antique emporium on Royal Street back in New Orleans. He's had inquiries made as to how valuable on the black market the Mirror might be. In any case Oliphant cannot resist possessing the treasure himself. It's his nature. The Sisters should have known he was a snake when they picked him up to pet. That's Oliphant's take. Estevar, the Pavarotti of the *Mercy*, will bring La Malinché to him. Pendarvis has put in the fix.

Bly won't know the worst of it any more than Pendarvis knows the reverence by which Estevar holds his song bird answering in the night, Rachel Perl. So there's Bly, off in fabled Havana with the Mirror. He's thinking his way out is the water-bound rocket Rachel Perl drives (just as he taught her) with dutiful Estevar at her side. Pendarvis's take on the subterfuge Oliphant intends is as cynical as it is clean-cut. His senses that Bly won't care which way La Malinché falls so long as he gets paid and comes out alive. Oliphant qualifies that prognostication to say in his inimitable syrupy style, "Bly? He'll care. He just may not care enough."

The fact is that Bly fully intends to convey La Malinché to the fast boat via Elle's covert operatives on the island. Failing that, he has been instructed about the backup plan. Pendarvis and Captain Cobb will wait in the Marina Hemingway until Pendarvis ascertains that La Malinché is northbound in the night. Barring that, Bly has twenty-four hours to make it to the *Mercy*.

Elle also knows the backup plan, and so Lourdes Lim knows where the *Mercy* (as backup) will be. She is banking now that Bly will make the connection with Ramón. Elle knows Oliphant's backup plan too. Over at Pepe's at breakfast she'd hatched it out with him beneath the bougainvillea. Neither one prefers to have all eggs in one basket. In this case what Elle knows, Lourdes Lim knows, and so Lourdes knows the *Mercy* waits at the Marina Hemingway. She's hoping that Bly, having evaded her in the havoc he'd wreaked at the Plaza, has kept on course for his rendezvous with Ramón and ultimately the fast boat coming in the night over the Straits. Wagering on Irish's legendary luck, his backup plan becomes hers, known by the code words Elle has covertly disclosed: *big tuna*.

Down in the *Mercy's* salon Cobb and Pendarvis are already well into a bottle of Havana Club rum. Seated next to Pendarvis on the creamy leather couch is a beautiful young woman, introduced to him earlier in the day as Mariposa. She is, as the taxi driver waiting just outside the marina gates had proclaimed: a woman *normal*.

"Buy her two packs of cigarettes of her choice and she will be your girlfriend and translator, not a prostitute. Just a friend for the day. Or buy as many days as you like. Anywhere you want to go, my friend. But these things cost money. You know this already," the driver tells Pendarvis over his shoulder.

They are on their way to a small *tienda* in nearby Santa Fe where cigarettes are available. Pendarvis knows the place. A small selection of cheese and long loaves of fresh bread also will be for sale. Conveniently there will be three bottles of Havana Club rum on the counter. Only three. Always three. Mariposa will want one of those too. For starters she performs for Pendarvis an excellent (if demure) imitation of youthful shyness. Coy as Mariposa may seem coming back to the taxi, she holds a second bottle of the rum by its slender neck.

When back at the boat in the marina, Mariposa makes herself immediately at home. She assists Cobb in slicing the cheese atop thick slices of bread to make sandwiches.

"I like this one," Cobb croaks over at Pendarvis mixing drinks. "This one's a good girl in the galley."

Pendarvis is slicing a lime, one the agricultural inspector had winked at in exchange for a Diet Coke.

"Let me show you. Better we do it like this," Mariposa demands, taking the kitchen knife from Cobb.

Suddenly the unzipped flap containing the air-conditioning to the enclosed bridge above slaps back. Lourdes Lim stares down at the two men with a scowl that becomes a sneer. Her regal composure regained, the men and Mariposa see that Lourdes holds the Walther flat against her well-defined thigh.

"Get her out of here," Lourdes demands with a nod toward Mariposa. "We are going out. It's *big tuna* time—now!"

Chapter 14

 Cobb and Pendarvis know the protocol. They know the code. "Big tuna" means big trouble. Pendarvis is genuine in his pleading to Mariposa's understanding and forgiveness. The sixty US dollars—more than a Cuban doctor makes in a month—soothes her obvious, overly dramatic disappointment at being escorted dockside. Mariposa slaps at Pendarvis's outstretched hand and then insists he offer it back with his ballpoint pen. She writes her cell phone number in serial killer script across his palm and keeps the pen. With a sporting sashay of her ample hips, Mariposa makes toward the marina gate, her heavy purse chockfull with cigarettes and rum and American greenbacks, far better than the usual take of a woman *normal*.

14.2

 A frantic Linton Day bends at his narrow waist toward the derelict storefront on the upper bank of the Waccasassa. On speed dial, his cell phone is pressed tightly to his ear. Linton waits anxiously at the fragile outermost proximity of a cellular tower. The slight signal of his call begins to ring through as he plugs his other ear with a finger to block the road noise behind him. A heavy duty sunburnt-orange Ford pickup with pale blue doors rumbles by in the northbound lane. Prominent in passing are the truck's high sideboards. The playful lettering arced upon these depict the iconic image of bees buzzing around the thick straw coils of a conical hive. There goes Henry of the Hive.
 Sheriff Lad Caldwell congenially answers Linton's call in his diffident smoker's baritone. In a frantically high pitch Day gasps and strains mightily to inform him of the mysterious stranger back at his mother's place on the Gulf. A square-jawed Caldwell, sporting a deep fisherman's tan, listens intently from behind a pair of stylish tortoiseshell sunglasses. Even so, every fourth or fifth word of Linton's complaint is lost to the scratchy swarm of interference in his ear. Caldwell lights a filtered Camel with his Zippo lighter that bears the well-worn insignia of his former NATO Allied Forces command unit.

Uncharacteristically in this time of clunky polyester uniforms, the sheriff is as always smartly dressed in a tailored suit and silk tie. His suits are made-to-order by a fine clothier up in Charleston—the same preferred by the former sheriff, Caldwell's father. They're closeted in an array of colors in his spacious country home: suits in fine fabrics ranging from dark navy and rich olive to summer seersucker or the winter white flannel he wears on this autumn day.

Linton Day's caller ID is entirely familiar to the elected sheriff who has always counted on Pastor Day's considerable congregation and influence at the polling place. So he listens carefully from his unmarked unit, a Crown Victoria parked out behind the red brick sheriff's office and county jail complex.

Caldwell's been watching orange-clad inmates in a fierce game of basketball. The *Shirts* are playing the *Skins* in a loud disarray of fast play within the fenced compound. A burst of laughter, laced with expletives and exclamations, emanates from the game of hoops. A tall shirtless inmate has just slam-dunked the ball with the force of a giant catapult. Caldwell looks up again from his leather notebook wherein he makes notes in a flowing hand while the urgent caller scrapes on.

Linton Day, having let loose his plugged ear to gesture broadly with his every word in the mode of an orchestra conductor, pauses breathlessly now in his urgent message. Taking advantage of the gap, the sheriff announces that this character out at Mazie's place just might be one of the *bad actors* who pirated a gambling boat out of Crystal River a few nights back.

"It was one of those Aztec Del Rey evening cruises the night we had that unpredicted storm. We know at least one was shot up real bad," Caldwell tells Day. "They say his was the boat that got away with the money bag too. How about that?" Caldwell drawls in conclusion with his rhetorical trademark close.

"O my God!" Linton Day responds.

Caldwell has more. He says his office had earlier received a call from the Waccasassa Marina saying that some very suspicious characters in a high-powered boat—similar to those manned by the Crystal River bunch—had been observed scouring the premises.

Chapter 14

"I've got Deputy Jakes in route now," Caldwell assures Day. "I'll radio him to meet you back at the Buck Island grade there on 19. Let's get an investigator on the way too—Leland Roy. How about that? You know Leland. You can point our men in from there, Pastor, straightaway to your mama's place. How about that?"

Linton Day is okay with that but not comfortably or completely so. The wily sheriff immediately picks up on the fact that in a matter as urgent as a perceived threat to his mother and young niece his influential constituent would be expecting the "high sheriff" in person.

"Tell you what," Caldwell declares firmly, "I'll be there *myself*. You just hold up right there at the old store. I'm on my way now, Pastor. Jakes may get there before me, but we'll all go in hard together. How about that?"

"Yes! Yes. I appreciate that, sir. I certainly do," Linton Day announces above the radio chatter.

Through the static bursts, much to his relief, he already hears (as the sheriff intends) Caldwell issuing instructions to his deputies with dramatic command. Their scantily audible responses are immediate enough to be impressive.

"Hold on to your hat, Pastor. We're 10–76 in route!" Caldwell blurts back into his cell phone. "How about that?"

14.3

On this night of passage everything has gone smoothly, with Ramón making good time out the coast road from Havana in the steamy dark. Seve Acosta sits up front with Ramón who attempts to engage the baseball hero in innocuous small talk. He knows fully of course that it is the heralded young lion of Cuban baseball who watches pensively out the front window. Yet Ramón avoids any discussion of his baseball fame or future fortune in the game. Acosta must be handled as anonymously to Ramón as any unknown, as anonymous to him as Acosta's girlfriend and her mother. All who are game for his passenger list dissolve into nameless taxi fares.

Acosta makes his feigned anonymity easy for Ramón. He is not as sullen as he appears but is Spartan in manner. *His is the profile*

311

An Unfinished Sunset

of a warrior, Ramón thinks to himself. Meanwhile the women are huddled anxiously in the darkened back of the Buick's spongy back seat. The intermittent street lighting streams in versicolor over the windshield of the lumbering car but fades before the clasp of the women's hands interlaced on Marina's taut thigh.

Through these miles Havana lights disappear behind them, and the two women speak quietly to each other in gloomy whispers. Now their hands crinkle over flimsy plastic shopping bags in their laps. Inside them are a change of clothing and a few basic toiletries. All items new, their receipts are stuffed in for corroboration of a ready claim to have merely been out shopping earlier that day. *Sólo eso.*

Yes, only that. Ramón's charges know exactly what to say if inspected, though Ramón has little confidence that the mother will maintain her composure under pressure. She has been shaky from the start, tremulous even now as they travel the coast road without incident. Keeping a careful watch behind, Ramón has seen the older woman in the rearview mirror on the verge of tears. But she is the one among them who has witnessed the violent consequences of resistance against the Revolution.

As a child she'd seen the spontaneous execution of dissenters on her neighborhood streets in Matanzas. They were the fathers of two of her playmates, she's told her daughter. The two men standing together were convicted, sentenced, and executed on the spot. They were felled where they stood, against crimson-red mandevilla vined on a courtyard wall. She'd recounted in strained whispers how the slain men were then hung from ornate lampposts to bloat in the sun. Though earlier known to be ardent revolutionary guerilla fighters in Castro's cause, these men were subsequently accused of being anti-communist insurgents. The crude signs around their necks proclaimed them dissenters and insurrectionaries in the post-revolutionary *Lucha contra Bandidos*. In the so-called War against the Bandits, Elena witnessed their horrible deaths as a child with a little toy boat in her small hands. How ironic was that—*el pequeño bote*—the small boat, she wonders now.

There is this too. After the executions, she'd lived in constant fear that her own father would be lost to the madness. She'd tended

Chapter 14

that fear with a child's heart until the very day his death was confirmed to her as an adult — an adult and a married woman by then. So there was finally the realization that her father's death had come, not at the gunpoint of executioners but in a misguided, impulsive attempt to go out with the night surf. By then too old and feeble to survive the Florida Straits, he had floated out with the rafters in a last gasp for freedom and had been lost to the sea. The same sea that now awaited his daughter these troubled years later.

Approaching the Rotonda de Cojimar on the Via Blanca, Ramón decelerates to a crawl. He blinks his lights in the manner of unlicensed taxies signaling each other. Inside his Buick he announces rapidly what his passengers should expect next.

The car rolls slowly through the roundabout. Bly bolts from the back of a pink scooter parked in the dense shadows. He snatches open Ramón's passenger side back door, and, in a continuous motion, he lopes in with his bundle held to his chest. Albeit this rendezvous had been forewarned an instant earlier, Elena (nearest Bly) is horrified as he shoves in beneath the spiny shadows of palms. Bly pulls the car door shut more firmly now with a solid snap. He exhales loudly and smooths back his silver hair. With a sigh of relief he lets the canvas grip slide from his knees with a subtle thud on the threadbare floorboard.

Ramón rises in his seat, keeps a steady hand on the wheel, and extends back at arm's length his bare knuckles. *"El barquero!"* Ramón exclaims in the rear view mirror as Bly brings his fist up for a bump.

In the faltering staccato of streetlight the women are already cutting glances at the bulging canvas resting at Bly's feet. There would be no explaining the bag. They all know that immediately. Bly most assuredly has no rational explanation for La Malinché. He doesn't even have one for himself. The story to be given earlier is that Ramón is merely a hire, taking the other Cubans out to Matanzas to visit an aged and ailing aunt. That will hardly wash with La Malinché aboard. *This Yuma, a yanqui friend of the family with an Aztec treasure first looted over three centuries ago? I don't think so,* Bly thinks to himself with a shrug.

Ramón's on the same wavelength. He drives a little faster while the women silently inspect the new passenger, as if something foul and fetid now rides with them.

"Hola," Irish Bly says to them both, brandishing a disarming smile.

Elena remains aghast. Marina smiles wanly, keeping her cool, though her bright eyes and raised eyebrow signal confusion. Conversely Seve seems to pay no attention at all. He has his game face on, intently focused on the road before them, occasionally casting a wary glance at the side view mirror for any suspicious vehicle that may be tailing. Ramón has been doing the same. He steadily quickens the V8 again, accelerating smoothly in a deceptively rapid glide through the drowsy dark.

The night nods with cloud-scattered moonlight over the barren landscape. Ramón cautiously puts distance between his Buick and the roundabout on the Via Blanca. The coast road is a long, waxy ribbon ahead. Out either side window is a patchy profusion of thicket and dark willowy shrubs. With a bouncy lift the heavy car courses the rippling lay of the costal terrain.

Far from the Rotonda de Cojimar or any street light before Matanzas, Ramón comes to a rough turnout on the surf side of the road. A narrow beach path disappears from there through a stand of gnarled windswept coastal trees. Ramón parks so as to completely obscure the sandy path from the roadway. He gets out in the absence of any interior light, leaving the door agape. In plain sight, except for the darkness of the night, Ramón comes around quickly and lifts the Buick's heavy hood. He disengages a sparkplug wire so that it's not left as obvious to someone on patrol or to some curious passerby. He leaves the hood up.

Ramón crouches behind the car to extract a small backpack from a hidden compartment high in the wheel well. The road is quiet, disappearing in profound darkness in either direction. From this position he slides free the license plate and fits it in a sheath at the rear of his pack. If interrogated later, he will swear that it was stolen when he went for assistance for his immobile car. Ramón slings the black pack over his shoulder and hurries his passengers from the car's dark interior. As he instructs, each one exits low from

Chapter 14

the surf side opposite the road. They let Ramón pass between them and eagerly follow him down the meandering path, through the undulating dunes of a coastal nature preserve, to the beach. From that dark cove beyond the dunes ahead—northward beyond the horizon—appear the scattered lights of the Florida Keys.

It is from there, near Boca Chica to be more exact, that the sleek profile of an exceedingly fast boat has come quietly out with the tide on Geiger Creek. Rachel Perl has entered the GPS coordinates she'd decoded from Bertrand's Oliphant's twenty-dollar bill. She accelerates steadily out toward the Straits with the formidable Estevar at her side. No running lights are lit.

Just behind their mitigated wake Ducky Durban sits in his sun-bleached, electronically equipped van by the lofty boathouse on Geiger Creek. Through a headset over his tattered ball cap Ducky monitors the radio frequencies on which the US Coast Guard and air control and pilots out of Boca Chica broadcast. He and Rachel communicate now solely by coded clicks of the mike when keyed. So far the coast is clear.

The moon is rising behind the mercifully ashen guise of a still-overcast Florida sky. Steering seaward, Rachel smiles reassuringly at the long-haired titan at her shoulder and activates the defused lighting system. Instantly the racing boat is camouflaged perfectly within the prevailing conditions. For all its power the stealth of the boat's design minimizes its wake. It will morph in countless colors and camouflage many times over with each emergence of increasing import by its rapid return.

The US Coast Guard planes are on patrol at an altitude of about 1500 feet, equipped with sensors that pick out shapes on the water's surface miles away. A giant cruise ship may look like a smudge on the horizon. Sailboats appear as white dots with long wakes. Rafters are harder to spot but possible. Pilots look for anything suspicious: waves that don't seem to break quite right, some dark fleck in the cloud shadow, the wink or glimmer of an item tossed overboard, or the shimmering ripple of a wet tarp.

Thirty-eight minutes out, Rachel takes up a satellite phone and watches its face light up with florescent green insignia and numerals. A little over fifty miles away the satellite phone Ramón

An Unfinished Sunset

has extracted from his backpack lights up concurrently. He stands up in the sea oats above the beach and begins to dial. A sea bird lifts on the breeze, squawking loudly into the powdery blue night along the coast.

Bly, Seve, and the women crouch deeper in the copse of misshapen trees with waxy leaves in the lea of the dunes. The bird disappears with the soft sound of the surf lapping at that sandy strand along the obscure cove.

"No estamos aquí," Ramón says urgently into the sat phone. "We are not here! *Abortar! Abortar!*"

This of course is the opposite of the material fact and is a tactical method of response to be carried out in the operation. Interception of the satellite phone communications by security operations on either side of the Straits would be difficult though possible. The sat phones Oliphant had deployed earlier are programmed with extra layers of cipher software, making any eventual decoding (however rapid) not to be in real time. Minutes in intermission—even seconds in these operations—determine the success or failure of the *rescue*.

Down through the sea oats, behind the dune from which he has made his call, Ramón retrieves an inflatable life raft buried in the sand. He brings it back up and drops to his knees to lay the raft out flat and release the inflating mechanism. This raft has never failed Ramón. He drags it fully inflated toward the sea as far as he can and remains concealed in a spot before the sea oats begin to thin. He rolls inside the raft to lay low and wait, resting his head on the tightly rounded gunnel to watch the moon appear momentarily from behind a cobalt cloud gilded with purple. There is for that instant a lighted path over the dark water, or so Ramón thinks. He rests upon his elbow, watching and waiting as he has told the others to do in the windswept grove behind him.

They wait—the others, the passengers. They wait, weary with waiting. Seve Acosta hunkers down with his famous arm around his girlfriend, Marina, who has proved to be as strong and resilient as he. Her frightened mother is heavier and more uncomfortable crouching. She now sits flat upon the sand that's rippled with dry seaweed washed up in storm tides. She clutches with one hand

Chapter 14

the crucifix she wears around her neck. The other holds fast to her daughter's free hand extended in the leafy shadows.

Ramón pats the inflated gunnel of his life raft with confidence and watches more closely the thin leaden line of the empty horizon. He is oblivious to the absence of any protections Capitán Osvaldo once offered such missions by misdirecting La Guardia Frontera patrols in those waters. Osvaldo remains on the take, folding the cash from Ramón's envelope into his hiding place beneath a tile in his bedroom floor and nothing more. Ramón contents himself with the quiet and darkness all about his chosen *zona de aterrizaje*—the landing zone—deceptively clear at that hour. But he is merely hiding behind the skirts of Señora Suerte, and Lady Luck is about to step away.

Although the sky has begun to clear and the sea is settling, one of the speeding boat's powerful engines runs roughly, coughing in extended fits. Rachel remains at the wheel while Estevar lifts a floor panel to examine the erratic engine. An adjustment to a fuel filter seems to have fixed the problem. Estevar returns to Rachel's side.

"Gracias, gracias, amigo," she calls out above the engine's muffled roar. Estevar shrugs modestly.

Behind schedule, according to Rachel's GPS calculations the fast boat remains about thirty minutes out from the pickup point. It is time to have Ramón position the passengers for extraction and set the honing beacon in his backpack. Rachel takes up the satellite phone again.

Ramón's sat phone begins to flash in dim lime-colored flickers that silently announce an incoming call. He doesn't have to answer it. He knows what a call within that time frame signals. If there's an immediate redial, then everything is on go. No need for more risky voice communication with the sleek cigarette boat coming on.

Ramón races barefoot down the sand dune toward the water with the raft sliding woozily behind him. At the water's edge he extracts the beacon from his backpack on the floor of the raft. In an instant he mounts the beacon on an inflatable flotation device.

Everything's ready on the beach. Ramón runs in a hunched position between the forward dunes to the low copse of trees where his passengers wait. His voice is reduced to a forceful whisper: *"Rápido sígueme! Sígueme!"*

The Cubanos follow, Seve Acosta in the lead. Marina hurries her mother before her. Only Bly remains to cast a careful glance back up the gritty moonlit path by which they've come from the car. Seeing nothing to indicate an alert, he sets out after the rest with La Malinché under his arm. His deck shoes sink more deeply into the sand from the Mirror's weight.

Bly is not far behind when the rest reach the beached raft. In stage whispers Ramón instructs the passengers to take up the raft and hurry into the low, barely distinguishable breakers of surf washing up and sliding back at the water's edge. They are wet to their waists. The sand floor of the small bay is firm beneath their feet, though the pull of the water surges sand over their bare ankles. Bly balances La Malinché on the tightly inflated gunnel of the raft. Ramón, standing before the bow of the raft, activates the beacon. He knots a cord attached to the float into a belt loop of his knee-length britches. Without looking back, he tells Seve matter-of-factly to help the women into the raft.

Seve does as instructed but first lifts himself on the gunnel like a gymnast mounting a pummel horse. He rolls easily into the raft. With extraordinary athleticism he then pulls the women in after him, her mother first, as Marina insists.

"Ahora," Ramón says with a nod askew toward Bly. But Bly politely waves off Ramón's direction, indicating he can control the weight and balance of La Malinché better from outside the already crowded raft. Ramón concedes with a serious glance seaward. Controlling the raft with its gaggle of passengers, he wades farther out to a distance in the water that puts him in up to his neck.

Bly, taller than Ramón, stands with the water high upon his chest. A banana wind has begun to rise out of the southwest over the water still warm with tropical sun. La Malinché has become more difficult for Bly to balance. Seve has his cool eyes fixed on the gaping mouth of the bay. Both women notice Bly's difficulty. Elena shirks back with her hand clasped before her chest to avoid any contact with the suspicious bundle. Marina conversely repositions herself on her knees in the raft to assist Bly in keeping the

Chapter 14

Mirror stabilized on the gunnel. Ramón tells Seve where to toss out a sea anchor to help stabilize the raft. A flash of light no larger than a bright star in the sky blinks "-.—-.—."

"Ahora!" Ramón says excitedly with quelled breath. Long seconds pass with the salty biota scent of the quaking brine filling their flared nostrils. The first faint drone of the speeding boat's powerful engines reaches their ears. But it seems to be coming on earlier than Ramón expects.

The *barco de la raza del cigarillo* will be coming in fast and furious, Ramón cautions again. *"Tu lo sabes,"* he says firmly to Bly with a tilt of his head, as if to say, *You know this, but it is different now, eh?*

There will be no light, he tells them all. Only the moon and her angels—the clouds. The driver of the boat will target the honing device and attempt to slide broadside by the raft in the boat's quick turnaround. That is when each in turn must spring from their step to the raft's broad gunnel to be pulled over into the speedboat's cockpit. Seve will go first. This is the protocol Ramón is instructed to follow. The girlfriend next and then her mother. Bly, the tagalong, is to be last. By the time his last shoe drops over the fiberglass gunnel of the speedboat, the driver will be throttling up again. If all goes well, each and all—including La Malinché—will be safely aboard in that swift, unbroken turn toward immediate acceleration *al norte*.

The night is warm with the banana wind, but everyone in the raft is shivering as the roar of distant diesels rises. Bly, while having coolly stood at the helm on the other side of this maneuver dozens of times, finds his own heart now dancing in his throat. He knows for sure that marine engines are approaching, but a low oncoming droning sound seems to be beneath the first one of a higher pitch. This one seems to be rising from behind the eastern point below the cove. Ramón acknowledges the same sound. Some other combustion-mechanized rumble confuses that of the night flight craft approaching out of the Florida Keys.

Then suddenly the undertone whirrs more deeply, churning to an apparent stop. The abrupt absence of the undertone doesn't elude Ramón. He immediately demands that everyone in the raft lay low. This precaution at least will make detection more difficult by anyone on watch with night goggles.

Without a word between them Bly and Ramón search with eyes wide all along the iridescent wake line before the jetties out at the point. Each instantly thinks he's detected movement beyond there, and in that instant some tall, black, jagged form lifts higher in the bob of the surf.

"There!" Bly whispers in alignment with the jut of Ramón's chin.

The dark boat extends only slightly beyond the line of upright leaning palms draping the sandbank. It is a Guardia patrol craft, both are certain. The con tower and the array of antennae make it likely one of the Russian class commissioned in '85 with a .50 caliber machine gun mounted on the bow. It doesn't matter. It's plenty big enough and fast enough to block the channel, a maneuver that would contain the fast boat while a smaller rapid assault craft could charge on to intercept.

Ramón and Bly each know the drill. It's not too late to signal the speedboat to abort, Ramón thinks to himself. But, before he can get to his backpack for the sat phone, the sound of the oncoming liberator heightens and intensifies—a clear indication to the raft that she is not about to back down.

The emerging unlit speck is racing even faster now, bearing down on the bay with a throaty, if muffled, scream like a battle cry. Ramón alone knows the sound from the blue-black water's surface.

Beyond Estevar's lofty pointing finger Rachel Perl has seen the Guardia patrol craft hovering around before the jetties. With merely a determined glance at her colossal defender she's rammed the throttle forward again. The liberator is now rocketing into the gloomy bay with the Guardia patrol boat lighting up and powering forward to close off Rachel's escape.

Undaunted, she uses precisely the reading produced by Ramón's honing device in florescent display on the console of the zooming craft. A spotlight from the darkened point flashes in a long searching beam broken instantly by the speeding boat. The light jerks around to track the silvery gash of Rachel's vanishing slipstream fading to the bobbing raft. She turns the fast boat suddenly, throwing a broad obscuring spray as she slides upon a homing buoy.

Chapter 14

Seve Acosta springs from the raft with the grace of a great cat to leap aboard and be steadied by Estevar, who's already extending his thick hands to Marina. He catches and lifts her as if she was a tiny ballerina to be steadied on the deck. Estevar turns and bends then to take the older woman up from where she teeters on the raft's nodding gunnel. He has the woman by her girth and hauls her aboard inelegantly but safely. By the time Bly gets his soggy canvas valise with La Malinché into Estevar's eager grip, a predictable smaller searchlight tightens the white-hot focus in the bright iris eye of the patrol boats coming on.

Now the stifled voice of someone shouting instructions over a megaphone grates the low rumble, gurgle, and spittle of the idling liberator rocking in the shiny light on the night surf. Poised and ready at the helm, Rachel looks back over her shoulder, perspiration beading in the light on her brow. She knows that interception by the whaler-type craft buzzing in is imminent. The larger patrol boat navigates at its depths to block escape. Apprehension or the injury of all on board will be unavoidable unless she launches now with all the power her long boat can summon. Rachel rams the throttle forward at once. Irish Bly and Ramón are snatched aboard in a huge two-fisted grab, tumbling on the deck together in a bruising heap. La Malinché, cloaked in canvas, lies between them at Estevar's massive mahogany feet.

Bly is instantly at Rachel's ear. He calls a run taking them in a sharp westerly maneuver intended to outflank the Guardia through treacherous protracted reefs he's plotted out before. They can outrun the smaller craft, and the rat-tat-tat-tat spray of its machine gun fire is faintly audible above the liberator's boxed roar. But now the .50 caliber opens up from the heavier Guardia craft closing on the precarious waters the fast boat foxhounds. The rapid-fire thuds volley over the water astern, and then they are aft over the quicksilver of the roiling fade of the Guardia's searching lights.

The quicker and more lithe boat evades the gunfire in a rickrack dart among coral reefs blacker than night where their scarcely submerged chasms open to the sea. Ramón watches the lights of the Guardia boats peel back with blinks and nods, back into the dense night off the wild coast. Ramón has no intention of fleeing with the rest to the US. Not now. It has been his dream to do so but not yet. To get away from the Guardia's light boat, that is what necessitated his leap aboard this night.

So now the speeding boat is running westerly with only an irregular jig or jog in her course. While she runs virtually parallel with the island's shore and the distance from the Guardia boats opens, Ramón signals his intention to Estevar. The colossus acknowledges with an ambiguous shrug. In two bounding steps Ramón leaps high from the racing boat to tumble back into the froth of an uncaring sea.

It is a long swim back to his island, a long walk to recover his equipment on the beach if he can. And then there's surely a circuitous creep through the dunes and scrub to see that his Buick waits alone and without other eyes upon it. The situation, as he finds it ashore, will certainly forecast what his own future may be. Flashlights on the beach and dunes back at the cove that night—or not—either way, there is cleaning to be done and distance to cover.

In fathoming Ramón's leap, Rachel Perl readily relinquishes the wheel back to the usual barquero, Bly, who knows these waters better for their full-throttled escape. He is already turning to sweep northerly so as to shoot a narrow gap through the last barrier reef.

Twenty-five miles out from Marathon, the still-racing boat remains on autopilot, with Bly pressing where he can for more speed. He has the vessel now at maximum surge, given the light chop of the surface conditions over the Straits. The long broad nose of the fast boat skips the occasional patch of white tops and rises again on the sea rushing under it. A low-flying jet roars overhead in the broken overcast, backlit by a heel print of moon. It is seen in a far-off minuscule flash for an instant above the purple plain of the sea. The anonymous plane has come near, as a low-altitude jet may, but Bly expresses doubts to Rachel that their detection has been made. Or, at least as he reminds her, that had been their good fortune with similar flyovers on earlier trips.

Rachel catches a final glimpse of the diminishing flicker of the jet's positional lights in a blue patch of sky on the easterly horizon ahead. A shadow of uncertainty can be detected deep within the well of her bold brown eyes.

Chapter 14

The chop is heavier now in the blustery torrents of the Gulf Stream. The door to the small passenger cabin pops opens to bang back against the bulkhead. Rachel holds on to a safety bar by the hatch with a tight grasp. She angles to position herself downward to fasten the latch. Bly leans past her sun-burnished shoulder to see their passengers crowded below. Each peers back hazily from where he or she sprawls on beanbag chairs under the cabin's muted light. The bulky seats are huddled closely together. With the boat's special construction they absorb the roughest pounding and pummeling of the surf.

"*Es bueno!*" Rachel shouts down comfortingly out of the wind, even as her expressive eyes ask of her uncertain passengers the same. The three merely pull around themselves more tightly their soft blankets and nod variously according to the intensity of their separate need for reassurance. Twelve miles out from Marathon, Rachel tells Bly it is almost time for her to take back control of the boat.

"No, I'm good. Keep watch on the sky," Bly yells back over the wind from the cockpit, a sudden bust of ocean spray showering up beside the lunging boat.

"Yes, Irish! It's time. It's like this, Irish. I have to put La Malinché back into your arms. There's another plan for you, for the Mirror, for another boat. Do you get me?"

"What *other* boat?" Bly asks incredulously. He looks back instinctively at Estevar, who maintains a firm grip on La Malinché inside the sturdy canvas bag.

"Listen," Rachel says, sliding up from the driver's seat. "There's a Contender coming off the Sombrero Light. You're jumping ship there with La Malinché. It's the way. Trust me."

Bly locks down on the wheel to hold firmly through another rough patch of surf as Rachel lowers her head closer to his beneath the salt spray. In a whisper only he can hear she tells Bly she must retrieve for him the Mirror from Estevar.

"He doesn't understand. He's been given other orders, but that can be undone. Though not by you, Irish. You don't have a weapon for that, I promise you."

Bly glances anxiously over his shoulder to the giant on the seat behind them. Estevar glares back at him suspiciously while he hugs the Mirror of the Jaguar Night more tightly in massive arms brought close to his barrel chest. "Yeah," Bly agrees with a wry grin. "Maybe you're right."

Six miles off Marathon, the only lights on the water are those of shrimpers working a vast swell on the ocean's floor. Now, silent as a shooting star, a second jet flyover occurs, arcing back inwardly upon a distant trajectory from far out at sea. While the jet flies clear and away and there is only the sound of their own boat knifing through the night sea, Rachel approaches Estevar—beauty before the beast.

"You must give me the bag, Estevar," she says firmly. "It isn't ours to keep."

"Señor Oliphant?" Estevar asks plaintively with a child-like wince.

"No," she replies more loudly against the thrust and monotonous moan of the boat in the wind. "It is *not* his. Do you understand? It is not ours. It belongs to a volcano in Mexico."

Estevar looks down at the bag he'd dutifully guarded from the instant he'd taken it up from the wet deck between Ramón and Bly. Now it is locked beneath the defined musculature of his sleeveless arms.

Confused, he asks more slowly, "What I have? What I hold? Why? For Señor Oliphant, no? For the volcano? The *valcano*, yes?"

"Yes," Rachel answers, resting a small hand lightly on his thick forearm. "The volcano. In that bag is magic, Estevar. It is amazing to see but awful to keep. We must return it to the volcano. It will only cause more harm. Even Irish doesn't know this yet. We must tell him, Estevar."

Estevar's dark eyes dart to Bly who has turned to wrestle the wheel in an oncoming swell. Bly looks back again briefly, thinking he'd heard his name invoked in whatever was being said. Rachel is bent at the waist, slightly askew of Estevar, with the slice of moon over his thick shoulder. There stands the silhouette of a fairytale princess before a giant befitting the beanstalk fable. The gentle curve of her palm extends to the slender fingers of her hand. That,

Chapter 14

held flat, waits with sweetness to receive the gold the giant holds. To Bly's consummate surprise and relief, Rachel draggles the canvas-shrouded La Malinché in the rush of salt air to the vacant seat beside him.

"Rachel, my *sword*," he murmurs in amused puzzlement, a recollection of the Sisters' mysterious forecast, the image of that moment fixed like a frozen sepia image in his head.

Rachel slides in with a satisfied smile—La Malinché between them—and shouts above the sound of the boat in the night, "Really, Irish, it's time I take the helm."

Off the speeding boat's port bow Rachel first detects a light already too large on the vague horizon to be a star. The light is emerging steadily out of the humid night. Coming closer, the distinct ambit of a searchlight more powerful than anything seen coming out of Cuba ignites. Instantly it races out over the ticked surface of the sea, streaming ahead like a hunting hound before a stalking horse. Behind that light vaguely protrudes the great underbelly of a giant Chinook helicopter.

Helmeted crewmen, four in rapid succession, now descend a rope ladder within the shimmering glare. The *whap–whap–whap* sounds of thick rotary blades signal an agile descent, though the sound is absorbed by the overriding diesel whine of the fast boat. The spectacle of the lighted Chinook coming in low directly from behind is startlingly reminiscent for Bly. Shades of the Mekong Delta dart across his eyes. The taste of danger is on his tongue while he directs Rachel to "Let her rip!"

Rachel has counted four, each down a rope ladder to the high-powered pursuit craft, rigged on hoist cables beneath the powerful chopper. The ocean spray beneath the helicopters blades intensifies and catches light. The special boat team is positioned in the ridged-hull inflatable boat powered by turbocharged diesels entirely competitive with any fast boat out of Cuba. But this is exactly the fast boat they've been waiting for.

Bly takes up the canvas grip from the wet deck beside his passenger seat in the cockpit and stabilizes himself behind Rachel rocking at the helm. A reluctant Estevar, while confused in his heart, reclines languidly on the deep pleats of the bench seat deep

An Unfinished Sunset

within the inverted U of the fast boat's cockpit. He's not sure anything matters now, nothing but getting Rachel safely back to Key West. He appears almost insolent as Rachel looks back out of concern for him. He merely lifts an immense arm to point out another light coming into view.

Ahead now is the distinctly visible Sombrero Light. An aid to navigation—red, nearly black in the first light—the pyramidal structure is a cast-iron skeletal frame rising some 140 feet above the treacherous, stunningly beautiful Sombrero Reef.

Holding La Malinché like a big baby on his hip, Bly looks back impatiently to the giant helicopter hovering low and close enough to discern the boat beneath. Suddenly the Chinook is lifting and rolling back in the dawning. But the ridged black hull of the pursuit craft, with black-helmeted men leaning in, is dimly defined against the gunmetal-gray sky. It darts now over the quaking surface of the sea to get between the fast boat and its passengers and dry land.

Rachel sees ahead the shadowy nod of the well-powered Contender in the chop out from the light. "There he is!" she shouts to Bly, without taking her eyes from the oncoming Contender, already revved and cutting back on a trajectory to scoot within Rachel's own arc.

"You can make it!" Bly shouts beside her in the cockpit. "Cut 'er hard! She can take it!"

Rachel does just that, snatching the wheel away from the Sombrero Light, rolling roughly with the weighty Estevar sliding to the boat's rubberized gray decking, the passengers below juddering about in the midst of tossed blankets and muffled screams.

The stabilizing performance handling system spontaneously rights Rachel's boat. It minimizes the jolt as they lunge and plane out again over the mercurial seascape. Now Rachel has the fast boat racing alongside the Contender, and Randy (yes, Randy of Randy and the Reefers notoriety) is close enough to flash his not yet famous Cheshire cat smile.

"Go! Go!" Rachel shouts back to Bly, already squat and positioning himself on the gunnel for the leap. "Go! I've got this!"

Bly looks back with a curious grin of his own. Then the Mirror of the Jaguar Night is in the air and he with it. They land

Chapter 14

more solidly in a slide than he'd intended, sprawling now with La Malinché safely in his arms on the cushy pair of those useful beanbag chairs Randy has waiting.

At Rachel's signal she lets back on her throttle. The fast boat's speed decreases just slightly enough to allow Randy in the Contender to shoot ahead and safely crosses in a streak before her.

Randy, tucking back like a running back reversing field on a defender, is behind the pursuit boat in an escalating chase to overtake Rachel. He is putting increasing distance between his Contender and the other boats racing opposite. While Randy has the boat in an even glide in the ashen cast of early sun seaward, Bly watches solemnly over the gunnel while the Contender's reflection jitters over the smoky glass effect of the water. Emerging ahead is a barnacle-like continuum—a rangy shoreline of iridescent desert mirage colors spreading over the vista. There, somewhere in a widening void of that smudge coming into view, is the Vica Cut.

"She's all yours, Bly," Randy shouts over to Irish, coming now to his side.

"What?"

"Hey, your destination is locked in. Extra fuel in auxiliary tanks port and starboard. You're good to go, brother. Here's my ride now, man," Randy nods ahead. *"Adios!"*

There's a small fishing skiff not far off the Contender's bow. Two long-haired, rail-thin guitar guys in T-shirts and a muscular dwarf drummer in a tropical print shirt keep up their morning ritual chant calling out with extended cans of beer.

"Ham and eggs! Ham and eggs!" they chant above the oncoming buzz that consumes their voices as a roar, though not their antics in the Contender's rapid approach.

He doesn't have to hear to know. "Ham and eggs!" Randy rejoins with a troubadour's last strum and lift of his hand high in abandoning the helm. Bly lunges for the wheel to keep control of the speeding boat.

Looking back in the instant, Randy is already scrambling into the jostled skiff bobbing in the sheen. Obliging hands reach through suds and surf in virtual suspension to latch onto Randy's board shorts. The mantra, "Ham and eggs! Ham and eggs!" froths like spilt beer from their lips.

The shadowy pursuit craft, apparently disinterested in the Contender, is now close enough for Rachel to distinguish the body forms of the coxswain and the three other crew members. Estevar is abruptly at her side with Bly's combat shotgun, grasped from the dry locker under his back seat in the cockpit. Rachel searches his stern eyes, dark as those of an octopus shrouded in the tangle of his black curls. Estevar's massive jaw is set with serious intent.

As the pursuers intercept, a mere nod from Rachel means Estevar will open fire, fiercely pumping the ribbed slide handle with all the automatic efficiency and deadly force the close quarter weapon can deliver. But Rachel has him lower the weapon with a subtle cast of her gleaming eyes and slight turn of her head.

"Put it away," she tells her great admirer. "Put it back now, Estevar."

She borrows from Bly something he'd said to her on an earlier flight, perhaps also to appeal to her assumed Quaker sensibilities. "When vastly outgunned," he'd advised, "it's better to be fast than fierce."

Estevar acknowledges her caution with a bestial grunt, lumbers aft, and puts the shotgun back beneath the seat. It is almost certain now, as they are running, that the specially designed US Navy vessel will outflank and then engage Rachel as she runs at high (if erratic) speeds in the increasingly choppy surf. Their distance apart steadily narrows with the possible point of intercept ever closer. The special operations team will fire on her—warning shots first— if she is relentless as she goes. Searching ahead, Rachel leans in on the wheel. Running more northerly now, she is virtually parallel with the low cloud line, a darker shade of pale over the wispy sliver of mangrove and upper keys off to the west.

As the Navy pursuit craft bears down and the crew is positioning for action, Rachel suddenly snatches down on the wheel. She affects a maneuver not unlike one that Bly had executed in shooting the reef out of Cuba. In that instant she ducks in behind the black pursuit craft and targets Marathon Key. Out of that churning flash she makes a roaring streak over the tide inward

Chapter 14

with no regard for anything more than making land — fast as she can — at Sombrero Beach.

Despite the shadow and light disguise of her boat, the heat-detecting technology aboard the pursuit craft has sensed Rachel's trajectory and all the while marked her frothy path in the chalky green sea. Close in and at the lift of first light her every maneuver registers on the Navy boat's console screen. The rapid blips in the orange-on-black display only confirm with pinpoint accuracy what the skilled coxswain's eye immediately suspects.

Now he turns too, though necessarily in a more sweeping arc than he would've wanted to effect. All helmeted heads and goggled eyes aboard turn with the boat giving chase. Although they are battle-tried warriors familiar with fanaticism in combat, an emblazoned incredulity forms in their eyes. It is astonishing to see this woman at closer range now. Her jet-black hair is loose and streaming as she throws 2700 horsepower into the leap and flight of a rocket ride to ply the Kevlar of her Deep-V hull upon the gritty terra firma of Marathon Key's Sombrero Beach.

Eerily simultaneous with her impact, across the sound a rifle shot rings, and gulls scatter from the highway bridge spanning the swift aqua glare over the tidal rush through the Vica Cut.

Chapter 15

I understand what lies hidden beneath beguiling words. I understand the trap beneath extravagant words. I understand the deceit beneath depraved words. And I understand the weariness beneath evasive words.

— Mencius (372–289 BCE)

I WAITED FROM MY BED, propping the pillows to look outside the bedroom window. Beyond lay luxuriant leas of tall grasses, swaths and patches interspersed in puzzle-like pieces of green and russet. Spreading fanlike was a vast shade of indigo to the horizon.

I felt empty, vacant from myself at that time of day when the fiery chariot of the sun mounts the great emerald crest of forest filling the wilderness coast. Here, before the swaying grasses in that moment magnificent, the light was just catching the mop-headed thatch of sable palms on the spiny little islands sprinkled about. Wide creeks mirrored the sun in shimmering rivulets rippling with the tide. In the languid afternoon the light ebbed from the stark horizon and washed back, altering shadows in shades of blue over the seascape and marsh.

Sunlight aslant genuflected under the rusted tin covering the rough-cut eaves of this house, scoured an off-white by the seasons. It slowly lengthened to lay lithe as a luminous jaguar resting outstretched beside my bed. I blinked slowly. My eyes flinched before opening again.

"Why do you talk like you do?" Alifair asked me warily from the chair by the window.

Chapter 15

I had been thinking without thinking I was asleep and must have said something aloud. She most certainly had, though now I saw the girl's lips pursed, her eyebrows hitched up in expectation of an answer.

"I didn't say anything," I answered.

"No? Well, it sounded like something," the girl insisted, leaning in, her chin cradled in small hands braced between knotty elbows on knobby knees.

Not moving, I eyed her blankly and said drowsily, "I don't know why I talk like I do," I conceded.

She didn't stir. She sat motionless, piercing eyes aglow with guarded curiosity.

"So how do I talk?" I asked.

"Like you'd been reading out of some old book or somethin'," she replied matter-of-factly.

"What book?"

"I don't know what book," Alifair answered impatiently. "Your book maybe. Must be. I don't know. There's lots of it is all I know."

"My book?" I inquired, my throat dry.

"Maybe that's what it is. Do you even know who you talkin' about?"

"Who?"

"Who?" she echoed with annoyance, sitting up straight. "You don't know who? Maybe you jus' be crazy, I don't know. Maybe you jus' love words."

Love words? *Love words?* I nearly smiled through the moan I made repositioning myself. The turn of that phrase took me back to a bleak winter's day and an old English literature professor of mine. I hadn't reminisced about this for years. I was on the last leg of my unsuccessful tour of southern universities before lighting out for the Navy. It was the first day of the winter term up at Ole Miss. I'd walked up through the corridors of worn brick to the upper-story classroom where other students entered before and after me to take vacant desks. Against the high wooden frame of an arching window behind his lectern an elderly wiry-haired professor in a bedraggled tweed jacket leaned dreamily. Outside that window lay a panoramic

An Unfinished Sunset

view of the town and fields and after that a forested mauve in the distance beyond the campus gates.

It was minutes past the time for class to begin. The room was stone silent, but the old professor kept his wistful pose. Along with the rest of the assemblage I sat transfixed in this Dickensian tableau: the rumpled lecturer posed theatrically at the high window. He gazed pensively beyond the frosted glass to the far-flung smudge of winter against the cold sky. With the timing of a skilled dramatist the professor turned slowly. Then in the most devoutly sublime manner he extended his arms to say slowly to us all, "I love woulds."

I love words. That was what he said in his syrupy-smooth accent, thick as resin with romance. *Woulds* was words. It had never occurred to me that such a connoisseur could exist or that his penchant for language would in any way be annuitized to me. I learned that I also loved words that winter, though by spring I'd learned little else.

Coming back to the moment with Alifair, I knew it overwrought to tell of things as I do. I admitted as much then to the girl.

"I am flat on my back, searching these bare rafters just now for something better to say," I said next. "Something wise and meaningful to leave with you."

"I don't need that," Alifair answered pensively. "You might just make me worry or be unhappy with that kind of talk. It's alright for you to go and not say nothin'. It might even be best that way."

I closed my eyes and a while later opened them again. The chair by the window was now empty. In the next room (Alifair's bedroom that Mazie had shared during my stay) I could hear the older woman's hushed, familiar, pant-like breathing when asleep. I heard the girl next to her make the tender sighs she often made during sleep.

I sat up with a start in fear of the time. Avoiding my still-bandaged shoulder, I levered myself with my opposite elbow and sat fully upright, feeling a sudden sharp pain behind my swollen brow. Through the dissolves of decades the sweeping of such fine sand from the pine laths over the floor had made a satin finish. Rising to my feet, I put the heel of my hand to my eye and let the pain dissipate while sliding into my scuffed deck shoes. From the

Chapter 15

spindle-backed chest I took a clean, if threadbare, chambray shirt that had belonged to King James. Mazie or the girl had left it for me, I supposed. My shoulder had healed well enough but remained stiff and unhelpful. I slid the shirt on with considerable effort, careful to ginger my thinly bandaged wound.

From the cool sand of his wallow under the front porch the dog, Hobo, stirred with a melancholy groan. I waited a moment to survey the yard fully from the opened window. I admit I was hesitant, though that couldn't matter much longer.

When I made footfall on the dry patch of grass in front of the house, the dog poked his long snout out with a low, teeth-baring snarl. I was as ready for him as he was for me. He crouched and watched with great suspicion or possibly anticipation while I fished out the crumpled paper napkin waded around the pork rind in my khakis' pocket. Hobo was getting impatient. That little grub wouldn't occupy him long anyway but long enough for me to make my way, once I had my canvas grip in hand, over to the marsh grass by the creek bank. Hobo crept from under the house with a growl that swelled to a sudden bark, but I tossed the fatty rind to him, napkin and all. The dog caught a whiff of his vittles and then pawed the napkin to get to the tough fatback. Meanwhile I was making a hobbling run for the tall grass by the boardwalk.

That's when I first heard the approaching drone of a powerboat coming up the creek on the incoming tide. By the time I got down the low bluff beyond the catwalk out to the dock, the approaching boat had throttled back its engines. Argumentative conversation scattered above the idling outboard. The scuttle of voices carried over the tall grasses obscuring the nearby bend from my view. The water was shallow in that spot over outcroppings of limestone that held a sandbar.

I was pulling a red safety kit from the console of my beached Contender. Somebody down creek was shouting that the bottom there was scored by the prop of another craft surging through. Excitement could be heard in the responses to this discovery. I didn't recognize the voices, which sounded strange and muddled by the breeze. I hurriedly uncapped all fuel tanks and loosely wicked an oily rag into the throat of one. It was awkward going in the rainwater and scum where the foul water had settled inside the stranded boat.

I could no longer hear the voices. Hobo was barking over-fiercely, racing down the yard to launch out over the catwalk to the creek. I was wet high on my shins, sloshing in my deck shoes as I lugged the grip against my hip back up the low-slung bluff.

The boat down creek powered up again. There was the crack of a pistol shot behind the tall grass. The dog whirled around, barking in a lower pitch now toward a glint of light streaking out from the wood behind the house. Two vehicles were coming, bouncing in tandem out of the hammock. I saw law enforcement green and whites—SUVs with dash mounts flashing an aggressive whirl of striking blue.

I stood amazed and amused. This was not the kind of thing you can schedule or structure into any plan. But it's just the sort of Hollywood coincidence that seems to happen when I'm into my full Irish Bly. I had to wait another instant, entirely entertained by the improbable, if convenient, collision occurring before me. I could make matters worse and I would. I took up the flare gun fitted with one of the 12-guage flare cartridges.

The approaching boat was churning mud from the bottom up, its yellow bow only now coming into view. Testosterone-fueled shouts railed out at their sighting of the Contender's jutting outboards resting unevenly at my wrecked boat's stern. The cop cars were just then sliding to a stop behind the house, and I squeezed off the first flare.

I scurried across the bluff to the copse of scrub oaks and palmettos that had been my initial hiding place before the hound had found me. The first tank exploded with a fiery blast. It was beautiful. Everything slowed down, and a Tom Waits piano riff went through my head. I steadied my aim on the low branch of a scrubby oak and let go another flare into the immediate vicinity of the far fuel tank. Gas fumes ignited in a fantastic flash, collapsing instantly over the tank to explode down through to the fueling bowel and blast out, taking apart that side of the fiery boat.

Somebody on the boat coming through the pitch-black smoke let loose with an automatic weapon. I don't know what or who

Chapter 15

the gunman thought he was shooting at, but the cops were coming below on the bluff with weapons drawn and readied in that two-handed grip they're trained to affect. The officers returned fire rapidly through the now billowing black smoke flecked with orange flame. There was an exchange of more gunfire, but I was turning away by then.

Over by the house Alifair was snatching back Hobo by his collar. Mazie had the girl by her arm, and Linton had them both at the waist, ushering his loved ones frantically back toward one of the cop cars. I was ducking up under the low canopy of sparkleberry at the forest's edge. My intention was to scatter blithely as thistledown up the narrow trail through the briar and thicket back into the dark hammock. I heaved mightily on the canvas grip and caught a last glimpse over my shoulder of the girl through the sparkleberry. I felt frightened for her, for Mazie too. Then the girl looked out from her uncle's grasp to catch my specter on the path, her smiling eyes saying, "Go ahead on, Red Man! Go ahead on!"

From the path, which wasn't more than a game trail back into the swampy woods, I heard the powerboat's engines slash about and the boat thud and scream until her outboards choked on mud and wet grass. Muffled shouts drifted from the creek. It sounded to me like the boat was being overtaken where it was wedged in the mud bank. I didn't know who was coming for whom, but I was moving on.

After making a dash as far as I could before running out of breath, the devastation that was Detwiler's sugar mill loomed ahead on the path. Its crumbling limestone masonry—wrecked by time and hurricane winds—gaped open where it wasn't overtaken by vines. The high brick chimney was streaked with rot-inducing rain. I came to rest at its cairn-like gate and slumped to lean against my treasure on the leafy ground. I listened beyond my own heavy breathing and looked around. From the gateway lay an open view of the massive iron gears and fractured cane press deep in the half-light permitted by sunny breaches in the morning glory vines over the ravaged, roofless ruin.

Sound carried spirit-like through these wet woods. I thought I heard a command given, something stern but incomprehensible, muted by a distance thick with the mottled bark of tall trees. I heard Hobo's yelp corrected by a small voice I supposed to be the girl's. There was a thump that might have been a car door slammed shut. I kept moving. If I understood Mazie's version of the Molly Garth tale, there would be a way by boat out old Henry Creek to Cedar Key.

My progress on the trail was steady, if not sure. The murky way forward was barely perceptible in places, a mere break in the briar around fallen brushwood that a deer might leap or a wild hog burrow beneath. Then there were open spaces sweeping to coastal vistas. A small savannah lay broadly over a sandy flat spotted with squat palms in groups and patches of dry, harsh, waist-high grass.

I had come through one of these, a wisp of savannah on the marshy coastline with the trail winding through massive clumps of wiregrass. The damp sand was marred by the downy tracks of raccoons and the sharp lacerations of wild pigs. The tracks led away back into the wet thickets of the hammock. I sidled up a sand bank bedded upon ancient oyster shell, the thick stratum now weathered like ashen relics tinged with a pale rose hue in the low sun behind me. Before me lay the woodland, darker than before, though a recently gouged logging road tunneled a bluish light through the wild stand. I stood apelike on top of the berm, clutching the canvas grip with both hands. My eyes adjusted to the primordial gloom through which the trail opened to reveal a cypress dome.

In the distance the bare trunks of pond cypress rose to great heights at the center of a dark pool. Nearly perfectly round, the tops of the taller trees extended to those of lesser heights circling the edges. I trudged on.

Among the broad bases and woody stalagmite-like roots of the pond cypresses I wedged in with my grip against a tree trunk that, cut into slabs, would have shaped a clover leaf. But not a four-leaf clover. I lay back, the thick loam receiving my tired body. An acrid scent—redolent of muck and drying canvas—arose that I associated with a waft of the military surplus haversack I'd used when camping as a boy.

I felt numb except for a strange, prickly sensation I thought might be a heat rash. It was nothing observable though. There were a few scrapes and scratches on my arms and chest from plowing

Chapter 15

through underbrush where the trail narrowed or had to be found again. But I certainly felt this rash over my upper body, branching down under my elbows and forearms. And a sullen ache throbbed beneath the laceration over my eye. My shoulder wound merely itched, though differently from the more intense rash sensation.

    I forgot about these when I thought I heard a dog bark. I heard it only once, far away, and not in the direction from which I'd come. I waited a while and didn't hear another bark, which I thought was strange. In my quandary I considered that the dog had been silenced. Looking around me, the color red caught my eye, and I saw the brass of two spent shotgun shells on the ground nearby. They hadn't been there long. Despite the dog bark and the sensations crawling over my skin, I was so exhausted I half-dreamed of sleep.

    Something large stirred near the far root-ridden bank of the pool. It made a splash. In a slow glide out of the concentric circles that the splash made two knob-like eyes surfaced and rippled in my direction. I know alligators well enough to know they're not likely to come at you unless you're kicking around in their space. If you rustled a nest or got between a cow and her hatchlings, you were in trouble. I'd done neither of these. But now, as this bull continued easing my way, I had no interest in any dispute over what or where his domain boundaries might be. He could have the place.

    I caught my breath. Lethargically calculating the seemingly increasing weight my valise had taken on, I walked out of the yeasty shade of the cypress dome. Looking back just once, I kept a steady pace on the meandering trail, skirting the cut-down pocked with twisted piles of waste wood until I was back up into the woods. The itching sensation had sequestered itself by then on top of my scalp and was manageable there. I looked over my shoulder and ran a dirty hand back through my hair. Nothing but a breeze moved over the ground I'd crossed. A hawk circled in the sky but was lost to me when it disappeared into the cypress dome behind me.

    After a long stretch of mercifully easy walking on the leafy trail, I caught a whiff of wood smoke—oak perhaps. Up ahead I saw a broad wave of roofing tin and a column of wood smoke rising thinly in the aperture formed by dusky tree boughs. More than one mirage has appeared to me over time, but this was something rising and sure.

I watched an unattended cooking fire for a while from thick cypresses in a muck bottom off from the shack. The slough was muddy but nearly dry of standing water except for a narrow drain where it lay putrid in a drain disappearing hazily behind the shack. The low fire had begun to smolder. Around it several larger drift logs had been pulled up for benches by the fire ring.

I bent down a branch to better see the fishing shack. Just as Mazie had described, it stood five or six feet high on stilt piers. But the original plank steps had rotted down or been washed away in a storm tide. The tread half of a rickety painter's ladder now leaned up to the latched door. Beneath the shack King James's small skiff (as Mazie had also described) was turned over on its gunnels and rested on its oars set crosswise. Behind the shack I could see his rust-brown wire crab traps, stacked and disheveled like so many frail loaves on a ransacked grocery shelf.

Something moved, and my eyes darted instantly back to the cooking fire where the smoke shifted its shape again on the breeze rising from the Gulf. It occurred to me to leave the canvas grip at my feet by the tree trunk while I had a look around. But then I thought better of that and reached back.

At the fire ring I could see down to Henry Creek where a sun-scoured turquoise-and-white fishing skiff was tied. It was easily recognized as a "birddog," as boats of that design are called by Gulf coast fisherman. The boat is steered from the bow, the bow usually banned (as was this one) with a spray shield. A well is built up for the outboard motor to be mounted near the bow. The prop is in the water, so she runs well in the shallows with the propeller riding up in the water column. The stern has a cutaway transom, so a gill net can be run out the back. An angler can circle a good school of fish in a hurry like that, particularly as the driver is in prime position up front to "birddog" for his netter.

This boat had seen plenty of use but not lately — not as a net boat anyway. Two long poles lay alongside the nearest gunnel. The well-worn, scraped-up net deck was absent the usual heap of net with its float line and lead lines hauled in. By the appearance of things the

Chapter 15

boat had been tied up recently, I surmised. It was tied fore and aft to old wooden pilings that might have formed the mooring place where Jack and Molly once tied. I looked around deliberately, but nothing more than the fire ring said anybody was about.

A still-warm fry pan holding bacon renderings and crusty adheres of fish skin lay askew on a flat rock by the fire. Someone (as I'd suspected from the path) had made supper by the shack. He announced himself about then from behind me.

I heard a tobacco and whiskey-whetted voice croak, "Whatcha got in that bag?"

I turned around slowly and clutched the rolled leather handles of the grip more firmly. Standing behind a sawed-off shotgun pointed at my chest was a smaller man with a scruffy face and a bad haircut. The oily flaxen curls that crowned his head were buzzed close if unevenly around the sides.

"See here, friend," I offered, "I'm just passing through. I don't mean any trouble at all," I said, slowly letting the grip ease to the ground and extending my open palms from my sides.

"Yeah, well, this ain't exactly the turnpike out here, you know." He raised himself, leaned back a whit in his white rubber boots, and added, "You kinda off the beaten path now ain'tcha, Holmes?"

"I'm easing my way up to Cedar Key." I pondered a second and explained, "I bear the compliments of your good neighbor, Mazie Day." I didn't think invoking Mazie's name to a local could hurt.

The man squinted and spat aside without moving his shotgun a fraction. "You say you know Mazie Day?" he asked suspiciously. Before I could answer, he insisted abruptly, "How do I know you didn't kill that poor woman and burn her house down, Holmes? Come to think of it, I seen smoke down that way this afternoon."

"No, nothing like that. See here now, Mazie told me all about this place, all about that fella Jack and ... uh ... Molly Garth. That's right, isn't it—Molly Garth?" Seeing his blank look and the shotgun fixed on me with both hands, I dared to prod him gently, "This *is* the place, right?"

The man nodded gradually. "I could ask you about that nasty gash there above your eye," he said, squinting, as if to see far off. "But I reckon you'd jus' tell me a lie."

He pressed his tongue to the inside of his cheek, standing there cocksure in his grimy "wife beater" undershirt and threadbare suit pants stuffed into the tops of his rubber boots. He looked me up and down like he was inspecting something that didn't smell right.

"Whatcher name?" he asked crankily.

"Irish Bly," I replied with a nod.

"What kind of name is *that*?" he demanded.

"I call myself Irish Bly," I said with a disarming smile. "What do you call yourself, sir?"

He didn't answer immediately but brought the gun up to the burnished lump of muscle that was his shoulder. It was an encouraging gesture from my point of view.

"I think I'll just call myself Holmes," he replied with a sardonic sneer. "I call everbody Holmes."

"That'll be fine, Mr. Holmes," I said, squatting cautiously so as not to cause alarm. I put more kindling wood on the coals of the fire as a companionable gesture. "I do appreciate your hospitality, Mr. Holmes. Nothing like a warm fire to do a tired body good."

"Yeah?" he asked unhurriedly with wariness remaining in his voice. "Well, alright then."

The sun had set behind a purple line of clouds on the horizon. I built up the fire while Holmes went down to his boat to plunder an ice chest. He lit a cigarette and looked back twice to see what I was doing. By the time I had the fire going, he'd brought up a rasher of bacon in a wad of butcher's paper, a yellow onion, and a plastic baggie with two small filets of fish that looked like flounder. He stood there, watching me organize these items with the sawed-off shotgun still tucked under his arm. When I had the foodstuffs laid out on a flat piece of drift by the pan, Holmes adjusted the shotgun and took a pickle jar out of his pants pocket. One slice of dill pickle floated in the greenish brine.

"You kin have all 'at. I done eat," he said and went to sit on the opposing log with a half pint of cheap whiskey in his hand.

"I sure thank you, Mr. Holmes. And I apologize for this, as we've just met. But I don't have a knife or utensil of any kind to do this cooking."

Chapter 15

He took a slow sip from the half-pint, let it trickle down the back of his throat, and said with disbelief, "Whew! You ain't even got a knife?"

"No."

Holmes held out the whiskey bottle and rested his other elbow on his knee, absolute incredulousness registering over his rough face as he leaned forward.

"You ain't got a knife? You come traipsin' round here a totin' your big bag o' secrets, and you ain't got *no* damned knife?"

"No."

"What kind of man *are* you, ain't got no knife?"

"I don't know," I answered earnestly. "I guess just a man *who ain't got no knife*."

With his free hand Holmes dug down in his white low-cut rubber boot, fished out a Barlow knife, and tossed it to me. When I responded on impulse by reaching out with both hands to make the catch, my shoulder wound felt like I'd caught a sharp snag there. An awful pain shot down under my shoulder blade. I made the catch, but Holmes saw my grimace and cocked his head curiously. He took another sip from his half pint and scratched his ear, more like he was dusting it off.

He said, "Somethin's up with that shoulder too now, ain't it?"

"I suppose I banged it up, same as my head," I said preoccupied with opening the pocketknife, which I managed without a wince.

It was an old knife, and at least a quarter of the larger blade had been whetted and honed away. I sliced off two thick cuts of bacon and halved the onion. Then I diced up the peeled onion coarsely and dropped it in the pan with the sizzling bacon. Stirring the mixture with the blade of the knife, it made a savory bed for the flounder.

"You right smart with that cookin', handy as a shirt pocket, now ain'tcha," Holmes pestered.

"Guess I can do alright. I get by."

Holmes took a good swig of whiskey and wiped his mouth on the back of his hand with the bottle in it.

"You must batch it like me," he said without apparent regret. "See here, I do my own cookin'. Laundry too. Of course, I got a

An Unfinished Sunset

woman what comes round," he hastened to add, "when she ain't waitin' tables at the restaurant, that is. She has a boatload, but been 'round cookin' and mess. That, with two young'uns—both roughhouse, hard-tail boys with bottomless pits fer bellies. So she don't hold no truck with laundry washin' and foldin' neither, but that's alright by me, Holmes. She has other talents I prefer to cookin' and cleanin' if you get my drift."

"I do," I acknowledged wistfully. "I surely do."

"I'd offer you a drink of this here whiskey, but I ain't got nary a glass," Holmes said all at once. "And I don't drink after nobody I won't kiss on the mouth."

"That's as good a rule as any," I said.

The flounder broke up in the onion. Holmes was increasingly lubricated and never stopped talking. I did a sort of sauté, using the bacon at the tip of the Barlow blade to mop the rest around. It wouldn't have passed at the dankest dive on the worst wharf on the Gulf, but it looked pretty good to me right then.

"Damn," Holmes said, squinting over the top of his whiskey bottle. "That ain't hittin' on much now, is it?

I just smiled and flagged a piece of bacon at him from the point of his blade.

"Say, Holmes," he continued, "did I tell you about that ole pit barbeque I did right about Khe Sanh? One of them wild pigs over in Nam. We got 'em. They's rank round cher, but them was some tasty little bastard bobs over yonder, you hear me?"

I was stirring my pan and heard, as if in a delayed broadcast, what the man had said.

"You were in Nam?" I asked with the fervor of one war veteran reaching out for another.

"Hell yes! And don't you damn dare say you's in Nam too ifin' you weren't!" His eyes bulged as he leaned forward on the log and jabbed his whiskey bottle at me like a K-bar knife. "You hear me, Holmes? Don't you never say that!"

I waved at my mouth to cool the scald of a seared shred of bacon. When I could finally talk, I didn't say anything about Viet Nam per se. I just said I respected what he was saying, that I knew exactly where he was coming from.

Chapter 15

"Good," he said, settling back on the log. "That was a world of shit, Holmes. Too many good men died in it. I might not be much now, but I stood Khe Sanh. I damned sure did that. I'd cut somebody over that kinda lie," he said sadly to his boots. Then, looking up with a drunken smile, he added, "But hell, you got my damned ole knife! I can't cut nobody. You got my knife, bud!" and he began to laugh. He laughed so hard it took two tries in earnest to get the near-empty bottle to his lips again. "Hell, I'm going to bed," he said after that.

I was still scraping from the pan, but I hurriedly wiped the blade of the man's knife clean on my britches leg, folded it shut, and handed it up to him as he tottered past on his way to the shack.

"Thank you, Mr. Holmes."

"Don't mention, don't mention it," he muttered at the foot of the ladder in the dark. He just stood there hanging his head.

"I'll help you up," I called to him from the low fire.

"If I needed any help, I wouldn't have done this before," Holmes scolded.

And he went up the ladder and was knocking on the shut door, as if there was someone inside to let him. I thought there might have been. The door opened with a screech, and Holmes crawled in from the ladder on his hands and knees. In a short while the cabin door screeched open again, and out of the deeper darkness inside someone tossed a folded tarpaulin that hit with a heavy splat on the ground between the fishing shack and me.

I didn't know what time it was. I didn't know what time Holmes climbed up to bed or the time when I rolled myself up in the thick canvas sheeting given me for bedding. I just know I slept that cool night by the smoldering fire ring, bundled up in that old canvas as well as any tired man could.

When I awoke, the gray morning was breaking with a brisk breeze flapping the corners of my makeshift bedroll. I rose to my feet beside the fire ring bed with cold cinders. The ashes had been pocked by sparsely fallen drops of rain. The fry pan was not there. I looked quickly around to the creek still running out with the tide. The boat was gone too.

15.1

In a satellite close-up the gleaming white fishing skiff would appear to be floating on Van Gogh swirls of aquamarine and cyan green with a swath of cobalt where the channel lies. In a bird's eye the Sisters sit astride their cushioned seats facing their nearby limestone manse—the grand house bedazzled with sunlight—while the usual profusion of gulls swarm around its tiled roof. The women fish to the sounds of big band music piped down from WLCK Miami. There has not been a word between them for quite some time.

"You seem ... well ... ponderous," C. C. Moth says, preferring dialogue to the vintage tunes.

"I'm thinking about today," Consuela Doge responds wearily.

Moth lifts her head and observes, "Today, yes. Sluggish here in the sun today. We should have boated a snapper or two by now, I should think."

"I think more," Doge yawns, "which is unusual, since I usually think more than do you."

"Do you?" Moth probes.

"Of course," Doge assures her. "To wit, has it not occurred to you that today we are the oldest we have ever been?"

"Yes," Moth answers cheerfully. "And so we are also as young today as we will ever be again. So there's that, isn't there?"

"I suppose that's the other way to look it," Doge acknowledges with a shrug. "I must confess, however, that I have begun to wonder if we are, shall I say, holding out at our finest."

"Ah ha! I see. It's about the Mirror, isn't it?" Moth observes. "Haven't we concluded that it was best to remain unaware of the location of Irish Bly and our misbegotten Mirror of the Jaguar Night?"

"My, my. How declarative," Doge stiffens defensively. "You were almost beside yourself with angst last night, were you not?"

"Yes. But that was last night," Moth replies spritely. "Night is night and day is day. The night is more hospitable to angst, trepidation, and all manner of unease. But this is a fine day. A very fine day—excellent and clear."

Chapter 15

"Frankly," Doge snaps, "I'm surprised at you, Sister. You seem rather inexplicably to have recovered rapidly from anxieties you made a pox on me. So, *ce qui sera sera* ... is it?"

"No. *Sang-froid sous pression*," responds Moth in a nasal tone. "That and a stiff upper lip. The sort of thing you yourself always lecture about."

"Exactly so!" Doge agrees assertively.

Moth's monofilament fishing line begins to move outwardly in slight darts and squiggly fidgets. Both women steady themselves to watch eagerly for the next quiver or a sudden squeal from the open-face reel spooling out against the drag set. Moth purposefully raises her fragile wrist from which dangles a modest waterproof watch. She is ready to set the hook, though now the line slackens limply. Moth's bony shoulders slump beneath her sun shirt.

"Must have been the live shrimp," she says with a tinge of mock loathing.

Out of a broad westerly arc behind them a sleek powerboat is now coming into view. As it nears it is clearly the vintage mahogany launch owned by Bertrand Oliphant, the same one often admired by the Sisters on their sunset walks down by the hotel docks below Mallory Square. The Sisters turn around and set aside their fishing rods, shading their eyes. A woman is at the wheel. She's wearing sleek sunglasses and a military fatigue cap pulled tightly on her pretty head.

"Hmm!" snorts Consuela Doge. "Guess who?"

"Wicked witch of the West?"

"East. You know how it goes."

"Indeed. Go westerly long enough and you end up in the East."

The polished launch slows to a slurping, descending drone as it comes round to bob in the effervescent vanquishing the boat's wake makes of the placid surface of the sea. Lourdes Lim positions herself slowly on the luxuriantly pleated upholstery to face them full-front.

"Hello, ladies," she says with a saccharin smile.

"Well, well," says Moth. "Aren't you the glamorous one!"

"I'm the curious one," responds Lim pleasantly.

"Ha! Curious yourself, or is it about something or someone else you're curious?" C. C. Moth wants to know.

An Unfinished Sunset

"Both actually. Curious about someone and some *thing*."

"Hmm. So, now *we* are curious, aren't we, Sister?" Moth pipes up.

"Ah, curiouser and curiouser," retorts Lourdes Lim.

"Yes. Yes. We get the allusion," Doge comments drily. "And we know quite well who owns that boat. So out with it, tootsie. What's your business with us?"

"Let's make a deal," Lourdes rings out delightfully.

"We don't play that game," Moth insists instantly.

"We don't have to," Doge avers.

Lourdes Lim is undeterred and says patiently, "Tell me where to find your fine Mr. Bly and this ... damned Mirror, La Malinché, and—"

"And don't waste your breath, little missy," Doge interrupts. "There's not enough tea in China!"

"Besides," adds Moth, "we already have plausible deniability. What else do we need?"

"Indeed," says Doge. "Honestly we don't have a clue where Irish Bly or the Mirror is just now. We have never actually known. Apparently neither do you."

"Exactly," Moth snuffs down her nose. "We haven't known where this business was really going from the very beginning. You could put bamboo shoots under our fingernails. We'd be lying if we told you a single thing!"

"Oh my!" gasps Lim theatrically, eyes wide, slender fingers to her cheeks. "Aren't we melodramatic today!"

"Over the top! That's what we are," Doge jousts. "Over the top!"

"Up tight, out of sight, and in the groove!" announces Moth with a raised fist.

"And don't think for a nanosecond that we've achieved such satisfaction as we now enjoy by knowing very much," Doge asserts.

"No, indeed," rejoins Moth. "Why, if we really knew anything, we'd be in a heap of trouble, wouldn't we?"

"Oh," says Lourdes Lim firmly, reaching for the ignition switch. The launch rumbles to life, and the bow of her boat gently nods away. Back over her shoulder Lim scolds, "Same old paradise, don't you know? Well, I know. I know now exactly where to go. *Laissez les bon temps roulez!* Girls! *Bon temps roulet!*"

Chapter 15

And with that, Lim is rocketing back across the water, the sky reflecting in the mirror of the sea a day excellent and clear.

15.2

Beyond the floor to ceiling panes of glass, banana leaves riffle as a backdrop to gently nodding lilies in bloom. Lush zebra-stripe shadows cascade down the bent bamboo furniture and spread over the blond parquetry of the floor. Here, in the sunroom of his Key West house on Whitehead, Bertrand Oliphant sits reading *The Herald* from his laptop on the glass-topped breakfast table. He shifts his white-and-tan loafers and takes up his turquoise cup beside an antique crystal bowl of beach glass pebbles.

Elle Rousseau enters with a coffee cup of her own, stately and statuesque in her plush robe, a loosely bound paisley turban wrapped around her head. She waits at the windows with a view across the white picket fence to the tree-lined street outside. The coral cup she holds is cradled in her hands just below her lower lip. The silence in the room is redolent of coffee, toast, overripe pears, and the citrus scent of bergamot.

Oliphant, out of his preoccupation with the latest news feed, says vaguely, "Lots more here about the mysterious fast boat that crashed on the beach at Marathon. Oh, and witnesses coming forth now. They all say the boat's passengers and crew, though indistinguishable as to which was which, *scurried*—that's my portrayal— from the beached boat to a white van apparently waiting there in the parking lot."

"Interesting," Rousseau responds vacantly.

"I don't suppose you know anything about that white van?" Oliphant queries wryly without looking up from the laptop's screen.

Elle Rousseau takes a slow sip of coffee and observes in the window glass Oliphant's owl-eyed reflection. He sits erect. He waits expectantly, raising his horn-rimmed reading glasses above his deeply tanned forehead to rest evenly over his thinning hair.

She responds slowly, "I know a plumber who drives a white van, but he's up in Miami now."

An Unfinished Sunset

"I see," Oliphant says, resting back in his chair. "And this ... plumber? I don't suppose you've had communication with him here lately?"

"Well, certainly not since I spoke with him last."

Oliphant, possessing a patrician's bearing (even if in a workman's physique) crosses his arms over his barrel chest and asks, "Just where and when might that communication have occurred?"

Elle is not hurried. Two finches flit and bathe together in a mossy birdbath atop a ceramic pedestal among the lilies.

"Somewhere on the turnpike between Stockbridge and Boston," she says finally with a faint smile, taking another sip from her cup. "Although I'm not entirely certain. It's been a while."

"Sweet," Oliphant utters drily.

"Yes."

Oliphant lowers his glasses, returns his eyes to the news on the screen, and comments without sentiment, "That was a damned expensive boat. But you do know that."

"Yes."

"Well, it was always a gamble, that boat. But I never wager more than I can afford to lose," Oliphant says resolutely. "Do you, Elle?"

"No."

"No?"

The quiet in the room is palpable.

"Well now," Oliphant observes, breaking the silence. "Here, in an apparently related story, we find that another boat—yet *another* boat—was fired upon the very same day. The shots, it says, were fired by an assailant on the highway bridge over the Vica Cut at Marathon. Apparently he fired repeatedly on a speeding craft racing beneath the bridge and out into the Gulf of Mexico. Imagine that."

Elle nods, saying, "Yes, well, you can tell me about that one. I'm sure you doubled down in the game. A shooter sounds more like your play than mine."

"Really! So did you *really* think I'd trust Bly to turn over an ancient artifact likely worth millions to those giddy old gals in the pink Citroen?" Oliphant asks tellingly.

"Yes," Elle Rousseau assures him, turning to her rankled inquirer. "You trusted him to do exactly that. That's why you had your little

Chapter 15

baseball business going right along so. You thought you'd pick him off stealing in on a slide for home. And you almost did."

Laughing, Oliphant counters, "You, Elle? A baseball analogy? I'm amused."

"Hmm. I know the game quite well," she says with a cautionary glance.

Oliphant stiffens and rejoins, "Actually, I'm only surprised that you've trusted me at all."

"I didn't have any doubt as to how you'd play out this Mirror business, Bertrand," Elle says mildly. "I've only had to trust you to trust me. There was difficulty in that, but you did. You did, and now you've done the right thing in spite of yourself. So now we both would do better to let it go."

Oliphant carefully massages the temples of his burnished forehead, adding with languid reluctance, "Yes, I'll let it go. But you understand that a certain type of clockwork is set in motion by events such as these. I can't turn that back. I can't stop wheels already turning beyond my own."

Elle comes to Oliphant's side. She rests a slender mahogany hand laden with diamonds and emeralds on the shoulder of his long-sleeved French naval Tee with the Breton stripes. The scent of bergamot is more pronounced.

"Let it go, Bertrand," she implores softly before returning to the kitchen.

On the street, beyond the slant of picket fence visible from where Oliphant sits, a white jeep with the top down is parked. Lourdes Lim stands outside. She is waiting with her back to the freshly painted jeep. The morning breeze lifts her raven-colored hair. A telltale coin hangs over the dark silk of her chemise.

"I'd better take the girls for their walk," Oliphant calls toward the kitchen.

There is only the sound of coffee percolating in reply. On the ivory Italian stove with polished brass fittings an egg begins to bob in the boil against a saucepan on the blue flame.

Chapter 16

There is [in every man] one direction in which all space is open to him. He has faculties silently invited him thither to endless exertion. He is like a ship in a river; he runs against obstructions on every side but one; on that side all obstruction is taken away, and he sweeps serenely over a deepening channel into an infinite sea.

—Ralph Waldo Emerson (1803–1882)

A LOOSE CORNER OF MY makeshift bedroll flapped and snapped back over the sandy spate before the piers of the old fishing shanty. I awoke to that. A dappled gray morning unfurled on the brisk dawn breeze. I stood gracelessly erect above the laps of sailcloth to stretch and scratch, to look around, kneading my now-festering shoulder wound beneath the heel of my hand.

Behind the camp the densely wooded bayou was still confused by darkness, though the welter of its cypresses flecked here and there with an amber morning light. Out over the marsh the misty rush of a zephyr suddenly frisked the salt grasses. I heard the hollow barking of a dog break on the breeze before dissipating easterly up a slough, out there some place before the swamp scrabbled to the pine plantations. At my bare feet the fire ring of tepid cinders smoldered, pocked by sparsely fallen drops of rain. The fry pan I'd eaten from the night before wasn't there. I reeled around to see down to the creek and instantly dropped to my knees. Burrowing back under the musty canvas, I confirmed the whereabouts of my valise.

It was there—deep in the distended folds of mottled cloth, heavy with my treasure. I looked in, gathered the bag to me, cast

Chapter 16

off the weighty cloth, and rolled upright with profound gratitude. When I'd managed to get back on my feet, I studied the shell and muck path down to the boat landing on the creek. I had my morning relief there while I stood and suspiciously surveyed the landscape.

The entire creek was vacant. As far as I could see nothing more than a soft mercurial sheen lay over the tidewater meandering out. The boat was gone. That certainty brought on a cold apprehension there at the water's edge. I hadn't yet asked after it, but some possibility of being ferried into Cedar Key by this fellow, Holmes, had crossed my thoughts while sharing his fire. Now there was only a lone set of shoe prints scattered in the silt patterns over the wet sand. A hoary rope dangled to the drift from a weathered cypress post where Holmes's birddog had been tied last night. A broad gash over the bottom, which the boat's bow made putting out, was still healing beneath the whiskey-colored ebb of the current. So much for plan B. Then a startling bang sounded. I winced and crouched while the loud, shotgun-like report reverberated out over the creek.

The door above the ladder to the fishing shanty had come loose in the erratic gusts. I saw it bash loudly again against the roof tin nailed up for siding. So that's what the banging was: the cabin door loose in the wind gusts and flailing away.

Back up the path I considered stashing my valise under King James's old boat beneath the shanty. A man of six feet or so could stand erect under there. I rummaged around and spied a long locker behind the boat. It was made of rough-cut boards and constructed coffin-like. The proverbial pine box was painted a battleship gray. An open padlock hung awkwardly in the hasp, a brass key still in the lock. I could hide my cargo there. Pocket the key.

Thinking better of the idea, I went back out front instead and climbed the ladder with deliberate care, lugging the heavy bag up with me rung by rung. At the topmost point I latched on with my wounded arm and set the valise down inside just in time to fend off the heavy door swinging back again.

I leaned forward with the door pressing against me. Pungent warmth permeated the cavernous dark. In boot camp in the Navy we'd softened shoeblack for spit shines by holding a lit Zippo to the bottom of the parade polish can. There was something of the same burnt and waxy scent about the place. And something more that put in mind the peculiarly industrial odor of electrical sparks raining in a dank, oily atmosphere. That and a warm, dense, rising scent that resembled moist earth sweetened by fallen fruit.

A box of kitchen matches beside a small kerosene lantern lay at my hand on the floor planking. I lit the lantern. It made a pitiful dint in the darkness, and I climbed in after it. There was a large, rusty screwdriver protruding from the pocket of a well-worn tin cloth jacket hanging like a bat's wing on the wall. I pushed out on the door and jammed the tool just below the upper hinge to hold the door open for better light.

When I turned around with the lantern raised, surprisingly enough, there stood a strange Victorian bed. Its ornately carved headboard rose high against the back wall. The bed was much too large for that constricted space and was peculiarly lavish considering the otherwise rustic interior. An eccentric contrivance, to be sure. Nappy old blankets and ragged quilts were mounded on the bed in a billowing heap, wadded together with what appeared to be a large flaccid pillow on the stained mattress ticking.

Bringing the lantern to my right, its light fell against the shuttered, latched window. There was one kitchen chair, its red plastic seat cover slashed with a tuft of exposed stuffing. I slowly brought the lantern back around to see a wooden fruit crate standing upright against the window's opposing wall. The partitioned crate had been set on end to make a crude cabinet. A five-gallon can, smudged with roofing tar, served as a bottom weight to stabilize it. The floor made a leathery creak beneath my feet like a saddle being mounted. On closer inspection I found the improvised cupboard chockfull of rusty hardware, a tin cup, corroded cans of reel oil, waxed twine, spooled fishing line, greasy small engine parts, and all sorts of tarnished whatnots. I raised the smudge pot of my lantern to turn and look around again. The crate, the messy bed, and the slashed chair were the cabin's only furnishings.

In a shaft of light by the gaping door I'd begun to examine the tattered cuffs of the stiff jacket hanging there when a strong, feminine, softly spoken voice said from behind me, "You might need that jacket."

Chapter 16

I wheeled around and asked, "What's that?"

In the unsteady light of the lantern quickly thrust high, a woman—honey blond, voluptuous, and buxom—sat up out of the mare's nest of tatty bedding. Her thick hair cascaded generously over bare shoulders, rounding away to the bed's shadows.

She said again, "You just really might need that jacket." Adding in a sly tone, "I don't know if you're *ever* going to close that annoying door or not."

The woman gazed at me with a strange serenity while I stammered to apologize for my unannounced entry. She was evidently entirely unaffected by her state of complete undress. She smiled then, as if mildly amused by my stammer. I assured her once more that I'd certainly thought no one else was around. And except for the pesky door I'd never have intruded.

"Yes, I know," the woman sighed, gathering the blankets and quilts up above her waist and no further. She lay back against the absurdly high headboard and added with a teasing smile, "It's alright though. *I'm* not going to hurt you."

"Well, that's kind of you," I said, courteously lowering the lantern and noticing the stack of old books high by the bedside. Their deeply embossed leather spines were cracked and peeling with age.

She said, "I heard you and Quinn out there last night carrying on in your back-and-forth conversation. I didn't come down to fix you supper. You'll just have to forgive me for that. I'm still, shall we say, rehabbing out here. I haven't been anywhere in a hundred years, or so it seems."

I was about to speak, but she burst on, "I don't feel right, you know? I mean ... what am I saying? I'm not right. That's just it, you see. I'm not *right*."

The woman laughed delightfully, though in the next instant she became entirely contemplative and demure, adding, "Besides, Quinn is reluctant to introduce me to anyone. It seems he has great difficulty in categorizing our relationship."

"Quinn?"

So he's Quinn, is he? I told her I understood completely about the relationship dilemma. I understood that it was what it was, not why. I explained that I hadn't a clue about this Quinn fellow, as she'd now identified him. While I expressed my appreciation for his hospitality (such as it was), I had received no indication from him that neither she nor anyone else was in the camp.

"It was the door banging that brought me up," I said reassuringly.

"Hmm ... an intruder in the dust. That's just what you are," she cooed, half her pretty face lit and one ample bosom exposed in the sepia light above the gentle folds of blanket around her belly. "Yes, so here you are!"

"Exactly so. Here I am," I answered anxiously with a shrug. "It happens like this to me all the time."

"Like what?"

"Like this. Happens all the time. It just seems that wherever I go, I look around and well ... there I am."

"That's funny," she said drily, suspecting it, I'm sure, to be a threadbare line of mine.

"Yeah, well, that's just how it is, you know?" I said, mimicking her dry tone.

"Yes. So, whatever will you do ... now?" she teased softly back.

It began to rain. The drumfire of a sudden downpour raked over the tin roof, and a steady downpour ensued, turning me around.

"I was thinking," I said above the sound of the rain, "if you don't mind, I might just try on this jacket here after all."

"Suit yourself," she replied, nonplussed.

The jacket fit well enough. The pallid green buttons of corroded copper popped through the twice-sown buttonholes. It cradled my neck. The heavy cloth was overworked and needed wax, but I felt better when it was on. That I'd had considerable difficulty getting the jacket over my wounded shoulder didn't escape the woman's notice.

"Are you a cripple?" she asked languidly.

"No." I told her. "It's just a thing."

"Huh. I just bet you've been shot," she said with that eerily serene smile returning.

"And why would you think that?"

"I don't know. You just seem like a man who ought to be shot, that's all," she said plainly with a shrug.

Chapter 16

"Yeah? Imagine that," I said, looking squarely upon her visage, which I thought then remarkably similar to that of winged Liberty on the Mercury dime.

I'd turned away and was watching out the open door toward the Gulf. The rain still tormented the surface of the low, molasses-like creek. I watched it come and go in torrents from the dark fingers of storm cloud rolling down against the quicksilver dome of the cold sky.

In a lull there was another water sound behind me—the unmistakable tinkling noise of a woman letting water into a metal pan. I didn't turn back to verify. I didn't have to. I heard the vessel being slid back under the bed, and then the mattress creaked and sagged as the curvaceous woman climbed back in.

After a while I said over my shoulder, "Seems, intimate as we are, I ought at least to know your first name." I didn't wait for her to respond but came about to add, "I should've been polite enough to offer mine. It's Irish," I said squarely. "Irish Bly."

"No, it's not," she said out of a theatrical pout. You say it like 'James. James Bond' or something."

She was lying on her stomach now, rolled slightly forward to reveal a shapely, swimmer's shoulder deep in her blankets and quilts. Her truly magnificent mane rested in soft rivulets over her bent arm as she said drowsily, "Irish Bly's *not* your name."

"No?"

"No. I heard you telling all that twaddle to Quinn last night. Irish Bly isn't truly your name or any true name at all, I don't think. And, believe me," she added with a pained sigh, "I've heard them all."

"You want to give *me* a name?" I asked warily.

"Oh, I don't know," she said hazily. "I can just call you Buster, I suppose."

"No. I mean, do you want to give me *your* name?" I hastened to clarify.

"Okay. So ... it's Millicent. Millicent. It really is ... Millicent. I would never say anything different. I'm simply Millicent, and that's how it is. I don't like my name, but it is what it is," she said firmly.

"I see," I said. "Well, it's a pleasure to meet you, I'm sure, Millicent. And when the rain stops, I'll leave you to your private abode here and be merrily on my way."

After a long silence Millicent said slowly, as if divining letters on a lighted wall chart in an optometrist's office, "I've read the essays of Sir Francis Bacon and have in mind more particularly, yes, his work on love. Bacon's love letters. He makes clear that there is *nuptial love*, which 'maketh mankind.' That's at the height of all." She raised her pointing finger upward here. "But there is also *friendly love*, which 'perfecteth' love. Per-fect-eth ..." she said with added emphasis. "He was brilliant, Bacon was. You know, some say he was the true author of the classic plays now attributed with such great acclaim to William Shakespeare, the Bard of Avon. But you know all that, don't you, the thing about Shakespeare? That it wasn't really him?"

"No," I answered abruptly, mildly astonished at having been regaled with such literary gossip, particularly from the likes of one who might well have been sent up from central casting for a Viking woman warrior au naturel. I mean to say that it seemed astonishingly absurd—all this about Bacon and Shakespeare—there and then.

"Sorry, I took you for an accomplished conversationalist," she said almost bitterly. "Seems you could have come up with ... something."

"Well, I am interested to know when you think your Mr. Quinn might be coming back. Your thoughts on that?"

"I can't say anything certain. He left before daylight in a foul and fetid mood. It's that temperament he takes on when I give him too much to think about, when all he really wants is the solace of his drink and sometimes the carnal yelp that comes with visceral release. But I've wondered lately if that too is more an aphrodisiac for sleep than anything else."

I didn't know what sense to make of what Millicent had just said but replied, "So, about Quinn, are we talking hours or days here, you think?"

Chapter 16

"About Quinn? Could be weeks. Of course, he's just the sort to cut somebody, get shot himself, or simply lounge around as the mood takes him."

"Yeah. I get that about Quinn."

Millicent sat back up against the high headboard and looked piercingly at the mud-spattered valise at my feet. She asked, "You have anything to eat in that?"

"No," I said. "Not a crumb. Old rags is all."

"Umm. I'd like a dark coffee and beignets."

"Yeah, well, another time. Another place."

"Yes. Pretty to think so."

When the rain stopped again, it had ended entirely that day, as evinced by a final roiling wake of deep purple coursing the sky southward that left behind nothing but infinite blue. I lowered myself down the ladder with my valise dangling from a loosening grip. The wind had begun to build behind the rain. While I examined King James's skiff more closely, the distant drone of an outboard came within my hearing. As suddenly as it had come, the sound of the boat's motor diminished to the ambient sounds of the coastal surround. Now a swamp jay barked from a skeletal branch up a twisted bay tree close by the shank. The whole of it was splotched with fine mosses. A versicolor of green and brown, it felt like infinitesimal velvet smoothed beneath my hand from stem to stern. Low in the aft was an irregular pattern of four small holes—bullet holes below the waterline, to be sure. They'd have to be repaired if the boat was to be of any use.

I looked up in dismay to notice shapely feet and legs descending the shanty's ladder in front of me. Millicent came down in a loosely joined housedress and stood at the foot of the ladder, turning thick golden tresses from her pretty face. Standing in the full light of day, she looked taller—more of a voluptuous blond tabloid celebrity than a Norse goddess. I gestured my exasperation with the boat and returned my attention to its damaged hull.

"You going somewhere in that thing?" Millicent asked demurely.

"That's my plan."

"It's got holes in it," she said with a shrug.

"Yes. Yes, it does."

"Quinn sits by the fire at night and drinks, just like last night. And when he drinks, he gets mean. Just like last night. My daddy was like that. Daddy'd say he'd get that way over too deep a cup while contemplating the futility of all human endeavor. I think that's what Quinn does. He gets like that, but he doesn't say what it is he's thinking or can't think. He just shoots his pistol off in every which direction in total disgust. Seems like everything around here's got holes in it."

"Yeah, that's the hell of it, isn't it?"

"Well, your story's got lots of holes in it too," Millicent said distantly, as if distracted by her own commentary.

"My story?"

"Yeah, like who you are and where you really came from and where you're going. See, you've got no beginning, at least as far as I can make out. You're just kind of, well ... stuck in the middle out here ... in the middle of nowhere," she said, her hands gesturing absence or emptiness. Then, in an almost childlike expression of dismay, she added, "And I surely have no idea how this is going to end with me and you. Do you?"

"Yes. I'm going to fix this boat."

"With what?" she wanted to know.

I asked about that large can of roofing tar up in the shack. She said it had been there for as long as she could remember and had no idea about its content or condition. I told her that I could make do in any case and would bring the bucket down myself. Millicent offered to help, but I suggested that she build the fire up in the fire ring if it was something she could do. She said she could but that there was a gas cooker in the locker behind me. We could use it to heat the roofing tar.

I got the tar bucket down, and she already had the propane burner set under a welded metal frame to support a cooking pot. Millicent didn't want to use her good cast-iron Dutch oven for melting down the tar, and I said we'd just heat it in the bucket, as it appeared someone had done before. This brightened her attitude about the project, and she offered to scare up a pot of coffee. Then she said she had eggs on a block of ice in a well-stocked cooler kept in the locker along with a loaf of light bread. There was

Chapter 16

more. Bacon was added, and she volunteered to make us some fried egg sandwiches, which sounded pretty good to me any time. We had quite the regular little housekeeping chatter going on while I searched for some small driftwood. I'd whittle some down to pegs for plugging the bullet holes and tar over them in the boat that I christened *The King James*.

So we had our breakfast together, sitting in *The King James* on the sand out from the shack. We looked out to the Gulf, felt the pleasant breeze, and spoke of the day itself and nothing more. Having finished my meal, I crumpled into a ball the waxed paper on which she'd served the sandwich. Millicent said she knew I was ready to go. She asked about my shoulder and didn't wait for an answer, getting out of the boat and positioning herself to tug opposite me on the oarlock. The profusion of hair that spilled from her head was so thick and golden in the light that it cascaded audibly against the boat's hull as she bent. When she lifted, her upper torso heaved with abject femininity. My God, she really was a beautiful woman. The fabric of her dress fairly washed up and down again over the hull.

We slid the skiff out of the shanty's shade into better light and more space in which to work. I'd come around and gotten beside her to heave the boat up and over on its keel. We cleaned it from the inside. Close by, her fragrance was of someone unwashed but damned near intoxicating—something distantly citrus, the memorized but long-forgotten scent of a warm night breeze through waxen leaves of blood orange trees in an Italian grove. I don't know where that thought came from. I didn't know where it was going. It was just stunning, the scent of her. She smiled back at me inquisitively and walked back to the shack.

While I pared down and sighted and finished the wood plugs for Quinn's bullet holes, Millicent watched from the ladder. She said directly after a while, "I hope you're right in the head."

I nodded perceptively without looking up from my pocketknife scaling the piece of drift in my hand and replied, "I hope you are too."

"I already told you I'm *not*," she said resolutely.

I used a block of sawn wood as a mallet and plugged each hole firmly. Without my asking, Millicent hoisted the tar bucket from the grate over the low blue flame of the burner. She'd fashioned a swab from a narrow strip of marine ply board, wrapped and bound with a bit of dingy terrycloth. When the plugged holes were mopped with molten tar, we sat in the boat together again. Our dispositions seemed to resemble each other while we solemnly and wordlessly gazed out over the swollen tidal creek below. Our shoulders touched dreamily, and we lingered like that for a few moments. It was a cozy silence.

"This almost feels like we're going somewhere, you know?" she said.

"Yes," I replied. "Almost."

The tar cooled and adhered in an unsightly blotch on *The King James*, though the boat now seemed sturdy and as seaworthy as I could make it. Millicent helped me dray the boat down to the landing. The oars were dry and rough with the weather, but they fit the oarlocks and would make a good pull, I reckoned. I knelt and washed them well in the rising tide, and when I looked around, Millicent was nowhere in sight.

I climbed back up, and she was lying again in the big bed on her stomach beneath the blankets with my valise close by. I sat near the edge of the mattress by her magnificent head.

"I'll be going now," I said.

"Nice knowing you," she said into her pillow.

I tried to think of the right thing to say next but only said awkwardly, "I have no talent for this—the good-byes."

"It's easy," she said, muffled by the pillow. "If you try."

I rolled into the bed and lay beside Millicent without thinking why, just shaping myself to her inviting body. She turned toward me, coming to me softly, strongly, as my hand knotted into her luxurious hair. Then she leaned into me peacefully. I felt her waiting breath against my wind-burned cheek. I've made worse mistakes, I can tell you that.

An hour later there was no wind as I went down to the water. The boat listed slightly, its bow up firmly on the sand. I hauled my valise over the low side. Millicent remained in bed and didn't answer when I whispered my reticent farewell behind her ear. A soft, sweet moan from her pillows—something I fancied as a subtle suggestion of lingering regret at my leaving—was all she answered. By the time I got the skiff astern and set my pilfered water jar down, Millicent was standing up in the shanty doorway in her housedress, a bare shoulder against the doorframe, her wild honey hair in fantastic disarray.

I lifted an oar to pole *The King James* back into the swiftly running current. Looking out to me, the woman raised a reticent hand to fan flatly, slowly, side to side in that motion commonly made on such partings. I nodded back, set my oars in the oarlocks, and brought the bow around. My back was to the camp, and I was with the tide when I raised my hand to mirror her farewell.

16.1

Clearing the grass points out Henry Creek, the islands that make up the Cedar Keys lay low ahead against the pastel sky in linear shapes and shades of brown-smudged avocado. The open Gulf laps at the boat's hull while I sit to recon my course. I can just make out the hazy structure of the distant lighthouse on Seahorse. So I am westerly of my intended landing at that languid little town of Cedar Key itself. There's a blue bandana in a pocket of the old work jacket. I knot it around my head, stiffening my back for the long pull it will be for that landing. Despite the nagging pain in my shoulder, with each tug on the oar I begin to make headway.

Favoring an inward passage, I sweep through expanse after expanse of dark water reflecting the clouds above. Between these are the scattered lea isles and keys that dangle along the grass lines off my bow. I continually adjust my course according to the coastline and the depths beneath my oars. Uncertain about the weather as I am of the currents below, I reassure myself that this is the better way to go. Crossing directly (as a bird may fly) could bring on unintended consequences. Any kind of trouble on the open water in a small, unseaworthy rowboat would likely bring unsolicited attention and perhaps radio chatter the authorities might pick up on. There might also be Fish & Wildlife officers around.

An Unfinished Sunset

As for going as the bird flies, there's a profusion of water birds all along the shoreline route I've chosen. The branches of coastal trees on many of these islets seem laden with white waterfowl. Frigate birds cross high above and before me. A brown pelican sits atop a sun-scoured post set as a channel marker. His countenance is that of a jurist presiding as I float by. A white ibis wades out from the egrets closer in. A little blue heron congregates next to a great blue heron that's frozen against the grass except for the constant dart of his eye. Out from a spiny little island ahead willets scatter in noisy whirls from exposed oyster bars.

Over on a small island off my port side stands the stubby ramparts of a long since decayed corral of sorts. It was likely constructed on that sliver of beach to serve as a pen by turtlers of old and was the remains of a turtle *kraal*. Made to keep their live catch while they'd camped on the island. Up on a low-slung bluff behind the kraal an osprey has left its roost amid the skeletal branches of a lightning-struck pine. Far ahead on the grass line cormorants cavort like geese, changing directions over the mirror of the now placid bay.

The birds are a blessing. I let my mind take up with the wings of these, hoisting my thoughts from my shoulder's pain, my chafing hands, and the parching heat of the sun. A certain delirium—some strange feverishness—seems to be creeping over me, not unlike what I'd felt in the palmettos before Hobo had found me.

Then I spy something rise just off my port side. Given the large boil and relatively small turtle's head that peered out from the water's surface, I'm almost certain that a green turtle (though it is actually brown) has shown itself. A rare sighting these days and an ironic one, as I hadn't gone far past the turtle kraal relic.

It takes a flight of imagination now to conceive how plentiful these turtles once were. The old ships' logs report that their migrations sometimes prevented sailing vessels from passing for hours at a time. Historical accounts tell of vast shoals of the green turtle in particular, so thick "a man could walk from the back of one to another for quite a distance." Huge numbers at a time might be spotted in a single shoal (as these groupings were called) hundreds of yards long, adrift in the warm green waters of the Gulf.

Chapter 16

With my now measured pull of the oars I recall how they had come nearly to their demise. The green turtles were most prized because their meat was truly delectable when cooked as steaks or stew meat. Around the turn of the twentieth century one culinary delight—green turtle soup—became popular as far away as the cafés of London and Paris. Combs, hair barrettes, and implements such as letter openers and guitar picks made from turtle shell were also fashionable. Craftsman in "scale work," as the making of such items from the scale of tortoise shell was called, were factors too. Though scale workers favored the Hawksbill turtles for these purposes.

The harvesting of sea turtles was done by both land and sea. Boats of conchs out of Key West and coasters down from the Cedar Keys plied the Gulf waters for turtles taken in great nets or harpooned—*pegged* as the act was known. My grandmother often engaged the same verb with a vigor that suggested an actual harpooning of another sort to have occurred, saying, "She sure had him pegged!"

The typical turtling net, I've been told, was a hundred feet long and eight feet deep with meshes a foot square. In my near-deluded state I begin to visualize these among the mirage of boats not far away. They're coming about slowly, flickering in the web-like dance of light extending before the drowning sun. I imagine I see working skiffs letting out the great nets buoyed by cork floats along their top lines. I think I hear the sound of men's voices shouting from skiff to skiff. Vast numbers of a heavy shoal are being corralled and captured at a distance. I can scarcely see, or so it appears, that a great turtle's outsized flippers are tangled in the heavy net.

I blink, and the salt of sweat from my brow burns my eyes. A ways out two men in yet another skiff, one sculling from the aft and another at the bow—the *striker*—are stalking turtles floating idly by beyond the netting. When the striker is close enough, he plants his harpoon in the massive shell bobbing by on the swells. The thrashing and plunging of the sea beast sends up an enormous gush of spray that is soon crimson red and falls like rain over the skiff's bow. In a bright flare of that illusory blood rain I see a rifle pointed down at me. The flash comes as a gull screams, and I slump over instantly, losing an oar.

I lay on my side against a gunnel with my better hand trailing in the water. The lost oar is afloat not more ten or twelve yards astern. I splash my face with water from over the side and then let the last of the warm water from my jar slide down the back of my parched throat. It feels strangely just then to have the consistency of condensed milk. I am revived enough to fit my remaining oar into a sculling notch (fortunately found on the stern of *The King James*) and go after the other one.

The sculling skill was one I'd picked up from an old Brit in the Bahamas years ago. There are different strokes, but with a single rowing oar this one works well enough, operating the blade like that of a single-edged knife cutting downward in a slalom pattern in the surface of the water. This becomes my power stroke, the oar rotating slightly so that the lower-leading edge slashes across the stern in one direction, rotates back with a twist, and slashes the other way. My technique brings the blade as much sideways as downward on the grip. Held vertically after each propulsion, the blade then becomes my steering oar until I can come around and reclaim the other on the silvery surface.

By late afternoon I have the framework of the town in my hazy view. Farther out fishing boats are coming in. A crabber in a ball cap approaches fast in a birddog. For a moment I take him to be Holmes or Quinn or whoever he claimed to be. And, for the obvious reason, I'm not altogether pleased that it can well be the man himself. The boat comes on fast only to weight back abruptly before a line of crab trap buoys that I hadn't brought into focus before then.

The crabber stands, watching me warily for the longest time, never making a reply to the friendly lift of my sore hand. I imagine he is wondering what kind of idiot is in a rowboat out there. I'd indicated no signal of distress. But if I had, I suspect the old crabber wouldn't be much concerned.

So I dip the bandana from my head and let the cool water sooth my ruddy face again. My eyes burn, but they clear to a depth of field better than before. I return to my oars and am well away when

Chapter 16

I hear the crabber rev his outboard. Over my shoulder I watch him make a wide arc back out and around toward the town.

I get close enough in to make out the boat docks, the broad parking lot above the boat ramp, and the lofty ramshackle line of restaurants and shops lining Dock Street that hooks around to enclose a snug little boat basin behind. By this time the sun is setting in a fiery blaze behind the westerly keys. At the quay before my bow a tour guide (calling himself *captain* something or other) is wiping down his pontoon boat broadside the seawall. At the little beach by a city park a family is eating dinner at a picnic table by the bandstand. Children chase seagulls or come in tandem down a bright yellow playground slide.

I land on the sand of the park beach, scattering the gulls there gliding around the eaves of the motel behind the park. Two of the children hurry over curiously, wanting to know if I have fish in my boat. I politely dismiss their busy questions and stand stiffly to lug my valise out after me. That's when I can see, unobstructed by the seawall or tour boat shacks, to the boat trailer parking lot. There's the sunburnt-orange, heavy duty pickup with pale blue doors, the tailgate down with an array of amber jars I know to be honey on display. Standing by in his battered panama hat is none other than the ubiquitous old goat himself. Yes, as advertised on the truck's high, canvas-topped sideboards, it is Henry of the Hive.

16.2

"The hell you say?" Henry hoots, slapping his headlight on while driving out from the island town. The high beams jostle the dusk, channeling more darkly between the scrubby silhouettes of cedars and cabbage palms lining either side of the road. There's a distant sprinkling of blue lights out beyond the bridges on Highway 24. Reflectors on the Number Four Bridge before the mainland pop into view. The blue lights we'd seen coming out flash atop the county sheriff's car parked on a sandy turnout on the other side.

There is another vehicle a good ways ahead. We see its orange tail lights blink twice in the dark as the driver comes to a stop before the blue lights. The oblique blur of a flashlight is moving

An Unfinished Sunset

side to side, the shadowy form of a uniformed deputy in a western hat leaning in. His orange safety vest becomes increasingly illuminated by the low beams of Henry's oncoming truck.

"Roadblock," Henry announces matter-of-factly.

It takes the deputy manning the roadblock considerable time to clear the vehicle ahead of us. It's an old Ford Bronco, jacked up with off-road tires and packed with smartass teenagers wearing ball caps. We have our windows down and can hear well enough all the joshing going on.

Though the deputy apparently knows the youthful driver and his younger brother riding shotgun, the boys cheerfully make identification of the passengers in back difficult. The deputy holds firm. The boys, especially the younger one, persist in addressing the deputy by his first name and jest to the point that provocation of a search and seizure action seems imminent. My guess is that such an action might bring about confiscation of the beer and weed they likely had stuffed up under the seats.

The deputy is rapidly approaching his limit with their aggravations and obfuscations. I think an older girl in the back seat picks up on that, and in short order she directs a cooperation that gets them begrudgingly waved through.

It's the advancing Bronco lights that reveal a second car deeper in the turnout—an unmarked silver Crown Vic. In a flash of the passing light, I can see a man through the window glass in a white shirt, wearing a necktie and talking on a cell phone.

Henry pulls up to the line the deputy's flashlight lays before us.

"Evening, officer," he says gregariously, leaning through the rolled down window with his hat back on his head. "Whatcha got he'ah, a DL check?" Henry's driver's license is already in his thick hand.

"That's correct, sir," the deputy says, taking up the license officiously to examine before the glow of his flashlight. "Seen your truck plentiful here and about through the years," he muses. "Everything alright with you tonight?"

"Oh yes. Fine as frogs' hair," Henry chortles.

Chapter 16

The officer courteously returns the license to Henry. "How about you, sir?" the deputy says suddenly with the handheld light in my face.

"Oh him, he's my nephew, deputy," Henry hastens to declare. "He ain't got good sense. He don't drive," Henry rambles on through a possum's grin, "but he sure is good with the bees. Helps me move the hives with a better back than mine nowadays, fo' sure."

I smile awkwardly, still squinting into the light. By my matted hair and disheveled appearance it is evidently a smile that does not discredit Henry's disparaging description of my intellect. Nonetheless the conscientious deputy goes on to inquire if I have any identification.

"Well yes, some papers he'ah," Henry injects immediately, reaching up in his shirtsleeves to fumble through the thick stack of yellowed and wrinkled folds of paper clipped behind the sun visor. But by then the slender, well-groomed man in a shirt and tie, a badge clipped to his belt, has come from the Crown Vic to stride up to Henry's window.

"Hello, Henry," he says warmly.

Henry's head bobs back to the window like that of an old turtle peering out over a log. "Why, hey, hey, sheriff! By golly, sure is good to see you."

"You too, Henry," the young sheriff says slowly in a voiced that registers high with sincerity.

"I was just thinkin' the other day 'bout your ole daddy—the legend," Henry declares. "Of course, he was sheriff round he'ah when sheriffin' was fun. Them were good days, boy. Your bootleggers and grifters, they was more mischievous than mean. They weren't out to kill nobody!"

The young sheriff smiles pensively and comments, "How about that? Daddy bought many a jar off this ole truck."

"He sure did now!" Henry exclaims with delight. "That Sheriff Caldwell the first, he never did let me get by without gettin' hisself a good dose of that orange blossom. I had some healthy hives up a beautiful grove there about Ocoee in them days. That man loved my orange blossom honey on them buckwheat griddlecakes he always bragged your mama made."

An Unfinished Sunset

The sheriff nods slowly and says, "Just about every empty jar my mama put up her jellies and jams in had a *Henry of the Hive* label on it at one time or another. Those bottles she got from Daddy, she put up her pepper sauce in too."

"Yeah, yeah," Henry says solemnly with a bowed head, "your mama was real sick there at the end. That evil old crab cancer was eatin' her alive," he said with true sorrow.

"Yes. I know you helped there too, Henry. I know how you did for her," Caldwell says delicately at Henry's ear. "But better we remember her happy doing for others in her kitchen. She dearly loved those cold winter mornings we'd all be pulled up at the kitchen table, enjoying her griddle cakes so light they'd have floated off if it weren't for that orange blossom honey worth its weight in gold, Daddy'd say."

Henry smiles gratefully, and then, as if to get me to the table of the sheriff's homey breakfast scene, he lights up to Caldwell with, "Hey! See he'ah, sheriff, this man," Henry jabs a thick thumb across his chest at me, "he's my nephew! You know my sister, Mavis. It's her boy, Jack. We call him Jack. Jack, he's simple, but he's good help and good company on the road. You know a travelin' man like me do get weary," Henry concludes mournfully.

The handsome sheriff bends to look in and observe my easily acquired impression of a village idiot's self-conscious smile. "My pleasure, Jack," the sheriff says to me, touching his brow with a leisurely two-fingered salute. Then, resting an elbow at Henry's window, he leans closer to the old codger's unflinching eye.

"Henry," he says, "Several days ago we rousted a fella out of hiding down where he'd held up with a good family off Dry Creek. We got the dogs in, but they lost him somewhere in the Gulf Hammock swamp. We have reason to believe that the man was part of a pirate bunch that hit a gambling boat on the Gulf here a while back. You get around, Henry. Have you seen anybody recently, some suspicious looking character? How about that?"

Henry scratches broadly at his left temple, appearing to be tossing through a disorderly Rolodex behind his eyes.

"No. No, not suspicious," he says finally with an easy smile, which he instantly clouds over with a slow blink of his pale blue

Chapter 16

eyes. "Well now, maybe, I mean now that I think about it. I did see this fella looked like he was floundering about alongside the highway. That was a few days back. No vehicle around there on 19, down to the old store on the Waccasassa Bridge."

"Can you give me a description, Henry?" Caldwell prods politely.

"Sure. I'd say he was a dark-skinned fella, a growed man but small and not too tall, kinda tight-waisted like a dirt-dobber, you know, like his belt had him synched-up and pulled in ... nice threads though. Real nice from what I could see. I'll say that's it— what I saw—*if* he'd be what 'cha call *suspicious*."

"I see."

"That sound like the fella you're a lookin' for?" Henry asks meekly.

"No. No, I'd say this fella was closer to Jack's description over there," Caldwell answers squarely, nodding in my direction with a knowing smile.

"Lord, not exactly, I hope!" Henry screeches under his breath.

"No. Maybe not exactly," Caldwell says pensively then. Slapping the window frame firmly, he adds, "You drive safe tonight, Henry. How about that?"

"Yes sir! Let's get rollin' here," Henry rasps with relief, and I fix a simpleton's grateful smile to the sheriff's narrowing gaze as it lifts from the window.

Henry sets his jaw on the luminous white line over the road ahead. I lean to the dash to watch while Caldwell and the deputy go darkly into the flashing blue lights of the cruiser. We are by then rumbling on into the wet night.

The road runs east, straight, and level through lowland that smells like marsh weed and fennel. We proceed without a word until Henry takes an abrupt northerly turn onto a narrow tar and crushed rock road that he announces to be Shell Mound Road. He said that way will provide greater obscurity while we skirt around through the coastal scrub.

We come out on another country road. This one takes us over Florida farmland, vast fields out there in the dark where sometimes a lone sable palm stands, as if it was the solitary pillar remaining of some ruin. Hazy house and barn lights flicker occasionally like

An Unfinished Sunset

fireflies frozen against dark-blue gauze. Presently we come to the little town of Chiefland. This is up on US 19, back on the four-lane that will remain our route all the way into the Tallahassee hills.

The conversation between Henry and me afterward is light and bare of any accounting for the days I'd disappeared until our Cedar Key rendezvous. As well-laid contingency plans go, ours had necessarily offered a rather inexact backup strategy. We'd relied more on our familiarity with each other's habits, the confidences and close association we'd shared over some forty years rather than any particular precision in making a solid plan. In any event it had worked. I was being spirited away through the night by the ageless old goat who had been as much a mentor to me as an associate and co-conspirator for decades.

The Gathering Table restaurant sign is still lit on the dark end of Chiefland's Main Street Shopping Plaza. I stay in the truck with my valise while Henry ducks inside with a jar of his honey in each hand. It's a regular delivery, but he is up for some eats too. I can see through the plate-glass the woman who owns the place greeting Henry like a favorite uncle, as most everyone that knows him is wont to do. As for me, I am past being hungry but not so far gone that I don't know I need to eat. Moreover I need to sleep.

While Henry drives on with his coffee, I balance a tall Styrofoam cup of milk, and we each eat a hamburger sandwich from a paper wrapper. Between bites I remind Henry that I am ever in his debt. This, as I've said, goes back a ways. You see, Henry has been artfully freighting sundry contraband beneath his honey crates stuffed with straw since the early fifties. The ubiquitous Henry of the Hive goes all around Florida from the Keys back up around the Big Bend and on out to New Orleans. That is kind of his beat—Key West to NOLA. He gives every appearance of being more or less egalitarian in his trade. But before I was in big-boy britches, Henry was taking care of the "special" needs of a rather prominent, predominantly small-town clientele that preferred his discreet deliveries to being observed at the local tobacco and local liquor dives where "decent people don't go" if you know what I mean.

There's this too. Henry is businessman enough to know that the markup on the obscure and primo, the connoisseur and aficionado brands (especially those with the sensual allure of having been smuggled in from Cuba) puts extra ready cash in the big pockets of his rumpled, ill-fitting white linen jacket. My own intrigues are wired into the masterful import machinations of Henry of the Hive early on in my nascent buccaneer career.

Not coincidentally (at least insofar as a *traveling man* goes) Henry is a true highway historian. As one who's ridden many a mile with him over the years I can tell you that Henry eloquently unravels as he goes a prolific highway history of Florida and all the Gulf Coast states through Louisiana. In his most authoritative announcer's voice he delivers (while driving past) a flowing recitation of construction particulars for each stretch of highway — be it any highway bridge or roadside historical marker. Henry's recitations, always spiced with colorful socio-political commentary, inevitably include the governor at the time, his "silk-stocking cronies," and all scandalous gossip contemporaneous with a particular project's administration. He has the inside scoop from trusted clientele and confidantes in the highway construction business too. Old Henry knows the nitty-gritty, for example, on shiny new pickup trucks delivered in the night (with keys left in the ignitions) for a friendly DOT highway inspector to find upon retrieving his newspaper the next morning.

It is always amusing and entertaining, even if I'm at the point of complete exhaustion (as I was this long night), to hear Henry of the Hive breathe such ribald life into the old girders and political bones of the states before the coming of turnpikes and enormous shopping malls. Be that as it may, by the time we clear the highway bridge over the Suwannee not twenty miles on, I am fast asleep.

16.3

Cloud shadow in roughly the shape of a colossal manta ray drifts over the general aviation end of the Key West International Airport. Behind the parting sweep of its densely blue tail a burst of sunlight reflects from the mirror-like livery of a large seaplane with its wheels down on the tarmac. It's a Grumman Albatross, long retired from one of the Bahamian runs of Chalk's Ocean Airways.

An Unfinished Sunset

Now the classy amphibian is listed among the private stock of a renegade charter outfit operated by a couple of excommunicated CIA agents in Homestead, outside Miami. Behind its elevated windshield an older pilot with a crisp flattop haircut makes notations on his clipboard. His copilot, a man of about the same vintage wearing a bad toupee, polishes oversized aviation sunglasses on the tail of his loud tropical-print shirt.

A burnt-orange windsock flaps above the squat flight service office nearby. Behind the front counter a young woman brandishing a boyish haircut and a too-tight Island City T-shirt jacks the automatic gate opener permitting vehicle access to the airfield. A vintage turquoise-blue Jeep Grand Wagoneer comes around and parks close to the charter. Mercer Pendarvis hurries out from behind the wheel to open doors for his passengers and attend to their cargo of boxy white-and-black leather luggage strapped to the roof rack. Pendarvis's white shirt tugs in the sun from his khakis as he tips up in scuffed alligator loafers to take down another of the heavy luggage pieces. Their thick skins, except for the blemishes and travel scars, are monotonous with posh repetitions of a dead designer's waning global trademark.

Consuelo Doge and C. C. Moth are attired in traditional safari dress, though Moth eschews the white pith helmet that Doge wears for an embroidered black mariachi sombrero. While the women assemble watchfully behind Pendarvis, who's hauling down their luggage from the roof rack, a line guy out from the flight service office loads luggage already on the tarmac to a wobbly luggage cart he'll shove to the Albatross.

"Oh dear!" Moth exclaims to no one in particular. "I wonder, do we always over pack?"

"Ye gods," Doge sniffs, "How any years have passed since the decades after our Eurail passes expired, and you ask this? I mean, we never did hoist Army and Navy surplus backpacks to travel by train or plane either one now, did we?"

"I suppose you're right, Sister," Moth whines.

"Not necessarily," says Doge, disallowing simple agreement. "Haven't we always gotten as much in as there's room to pack? So,

Chapter 16

seems we pack unnecessarily simply because we have more luggage than we ever need."

"No matter," acknowledges Moth. "But doesn't it come to the same thing?"

The luggage is loaded into the cargo hold. The copilot secures the hatch and escorts his peculiar passengers up into the white flying ship. Pendarvis stands back in his Ray-bans to observe preparations for takeoff. Out in front of the plane's now whirling propellers the line guy is signaling with his wands extended. The Albatross begins to turn slowly, sputtering in jerky half measures before taxiing almost gracefully to the runway.

A shiny aluminum airliner bound for Boston lifts from the far end of the Key West International runway. Up in the terminal's tower the air traffic controller tells the pilot that he's cleared for takeoff. Like a true Albatross with his tail feathers on fire, the clipper races down the rubber-streaked runway and takes heavily to the air. Beneath the hand that shades Pendarvis's eyes the plane is up and comes back around above the salt ponds and coconut palms to disappear into the sunlight of a mottled sky.

Chapter 17

> I can no longer tell dream from reality.
> Into what world shall I awake
> from this bewildering dream?
>
> —Akazome Emon (956–1041)

Henry of the Hive drove with the windows down and chomped a cigar he'd never actually smoke. A highway bridge drenched with rain surfaced ahead like the dorsal of a great fish rising in the amber night. Beneath its crest the jittery lights of New Orleans spread like sea sparkles roiling out in a blue-black ocean below. Henry latched the cigar stub between his forefinger and the thick steering wheel. Rolling on down, he broke from an abrupt nod of his rumpled panama to roust a gravelly version of the blues tune, "Three O'Clock."

That's the time of morning it was. Three o'clock. I was awake and had been for miles, resting my head on the folded jacket against the side window. The glass hung perpetually at a quarter down, dappling differently as we went. Now streetlights popped up ahead like incandescent pompoms misting a tawny light over the exit signs and guardrail down the ramp to a wet street that flushes out on Canal.

"What do you think, Henry? We good to go?" I asked, sitting upright.

Henry glanced at his rearview window again and assured me, "Oh yeah. Not a jaybird in sight."

Chapter 17

The elongated shades of date palms planted along Canal Street burst over the burnt-orange hood of the truck. Hazy neon diversions of light peeled from electronic billboards high in the cityscape. The ricochet of urban lights washed back over Henry's windshield to the truck's colorful sideboards, swaying with all the glee of a carnival come to town.

I checked the side view mirror too for any indication of a tail. A handsome Cadillac, a red '58 or '59 Bonneville, turned off slowly onto a side street. No other vehicle approached from behind. Canal was clear back to Basin Street. On the other side of the median a stream of vehicles lolled out of the French Quarter slow as beads of molasses cooling. There were two late-model cars on the street ahead. Both plowed through some runoff from the rain. Henry took the puddle next. The water scudded beneath the pale blue truck doors with a diminishing roar. A squeaky swab of the windshield wipers ended in a solitary thud.

It was quiet in the cab for another block. I looked back again. A lonely trumpet was reminiscing softly somewhere down a dark alley. Closer to Bourbon a few fatigued revelers—stragglers late in the saturnalia—ambled along. Others clustered in smudges of silhouette before the drowsily lit windows of street-level shops and restaurants closed for the night.

Out beyond the contours of Henry's terrapin-like profile the wild heart of the Quarter was faintly pulsing at that early hour. The Ritz Carlton, its distinctive flags streaming high across the white stone exterior, was ahead across the median. Farther down the median two of the city's iconic red streetcars sat idle on the sidetrack. They'd be offline for several more hours.

"This is far enough, Henry," I said. "I'm going to walk on from here."

"Sure, you do that, son," Henry replied, pulling to a stop at the curb past the Walgreens. "Might do you good. But keep your eyes peeled, your ears pricked, and walk a jagged line, you hear?"

I opened the door with a little help from my sore shoulder. Henry was leaning toward me with a faithful grin. He didn't look tired or exhausted in any way. In fact, Henry seemed as impervious to time as he was to any kind of weather. He'd endured curiously unchanged from earlier times, the man entire who'd long coursed these highways of simple ribbons unfurled on uncluttered times. I adjusted myself to hoist the heavy canvas grip up from the floorboard before me to the seat I'd left warm.

"There she is, Henry," I said with a pat to the thick leather handles.

"Pretty little thing," Henry responded, broadening his grin.

"You can take it from here."

"Oh yes, I got it. I always look out for you, son. You know that."

"Yes, yes, you always have, Henry. And I thank you."

I began to shut the truck door. Henry raised an alerting finger.

"See here, boy. Listen to me, now," he cautioned with piercing sincerity. "Don't let your Irish Bly overpower your Jack Redmond. You hear me? I got this," he said firmly with the flat of his thick hand now atop the bag. "I've got this if you've got that. Understood?"

"Quid pro quo?"

"Quid pro quo," Henry affirmed with a nod and straightened himself up in the truck seat.

I shut the truck door with a solid click and walked into the white glare of a sanitation workman's flood light over a safeguarded manhole in the sidewalk. A block back, high in the structured shade of night, hung the unaffected Roosevelt Hotel sign. Minutes later I was drifting over the cool tiles of the gilded lobby beneath crystal chandeliers and by the polished brass of the Sazerac bar room. At that particular hour there was no one to notice a haggard vagabond silently wandering the shiny corridors, silent as he went with his dubious tales of a drifter's gold.

I popped out on the opposing street and came back around, zigzagging my way to St. Charles Avenue above Lafayette Square. There was still a considerable distance to go. Although I felt a little lightheaded, I was confident I could make the pull out along the St. Charles line into the Garden District—a good hour's stroll.

The leafy walk was erratically lit but vacant, so far as I could tell, as was the scarcely discernible streetcar track streaming out the median. Several cars nosed together along behind their low beams in the early morning murk back toward the business district. The last was (I was almost certain) that red Bonneville I'd seen turn off back at Canal, though this one was clearly a convertible,

Chapter 17

and I hadn't observed that fact earlier from the side view mirror of Henry's truck.

Only once was I disturbed as I plodded on. A sound came from behind on the irregular pavement of the sidewalk. The incessant ringing of a small bell gained steadily until suddenly, over my shoulder and passing by on a bicycle, a diminutive black man dressed in white appeared. He was wearing a paper cap like soda jerks used to wear. His hollow eyes never looked my way as he breezed closely by. Nor did he let up on the bell, though its cautioning diminished in the darkened distance ahead.

When the bicycle's bell's ringing had vanished from the night completely, I came to my destination, a lane in the denser shadow of a spreading live oak. Down that lane stood a high wall of old brick. Bamboo spilled over it before a tall cast-iron gate. There was a trick to the latch that locked that gate, and I knew the trick because it was my gate. I let myself in. Beyond the wall and thatch of bamboo, where a topknot of Chinese tulip trees would bloom early that spring, lay Jack Redmond's secret garden.

I awoke to the soft, slow clack of a ceiling fan above my own spacious bed. The pillows there were undisturbed and remained neatly arranged under the quilted silk spread. I was slumped comfortably with my sore shoulder resting against the rolled arm of the leather chair. My grimy chambray shirt and roughed-out jacket were draped over the other.

I'd slept only a few hours there, though they had been deep and restful. My eye caught a ruddy spot on the chambray of my shirt. I sat up all at once to examine the blood spot. I wanted to see that it was really there. I touched my wounded shoulder. It was there. Deep inside the mists of my own imaginings back across the Gulf I felt Mazie Day and Alifair rejoicing with me that I was safely home.

I managed to shave in the shower of my steamy bathroom. This task was not done without difficulty, however. I rested my head against the white stone wall, letting the warm water wash my wound and stream down over my sore thighs to my raw toes on the pebble stone floor. *Henry's likely out I–10 in Texas by now*, I thought to myself. My mind's eye honed in, focusing in aerial mode on Henry's old truck rolling out over the flat earth. I recollected

An Unfinished Sunset

then the stark image of a Mexican border town across the river with an ancient bank building—a solitary and bleak little fortress by a leafless cottonwood.

When I'd gotten on my robe and brushed my hair back below the nape of my now leathery neck, the rap at my bedroom door was an announcement that required no response. Grace came in, holding before her a breakfast tray with a carafe of coffee, cups, rolls, and condiments for us both. Medical supplies were also on the tray: gauze, adhesive tape, and scissors—the usual items for bandage making that she left on a small table before the window curtains. In a great *swish* from the extended arms of her slight silhouette Grace threw back the heavy curtains to let in the late morning light.

The garden outside was not at its most colorful this time of year, but it was for me that day, as the saying goes, "a feast for sore eyes." We were each content and comfortable with the quiet in the room. It had always been that way between us, though it was particularly so from the time I drove her in her new Land Rover back from California. Left behind was a wrecked marriage she really didn't want to talk about, but I knew it had been a bruising relationship that began as a fairy tale and ended as a nightmare. Her telephone call to me had come late in the night, the first I'd heard from her in more years than I like to remember. The long drive back was my idea—time to decompress, time to talk if she wanted to.

This reunion of ours was about the time the movie *Forrest Gump* had come out. Grace hadn't seen the movie, she said. So I offered my version of the plot as humorously as I could make it, going lightly over the fascination Forrest had for his "one and only best friend," Jenny. Somewhere before New Mexico I said I supposed she was *my* Jenny. I confessed that having the privilege of galloping to her aid was a pretty big deal for me—a knight in shining armor and all that. Grace placed her hand on mine where it rested on the console between us and gave a reassuring squeeze.

"Lots of men know what to say," she said to me. "But you always know what not to say, and that's a real special difference, you know?" She looked at me warmly and turned in her seat to add, "That's why you will always be my Irish Bly."

Chapter 17

Grace and I had that particular history, an intimacy involving both reliance and absolution that required no rekindling regardless of the time or space between us. There'd been some recent discussion of that *history of us*, prompted by a pet project Grace had newly undertaken. It entailed her careful selection and cataloging of photographs I'd taken in my youth. She sorted through hundreds of my flash photography pictures from battered file boxes she'd found. These would be for a select private printing, one long overdue, she insisted. Consequently, previous to my latest departure, our morning coffee at the kitchen table together had elicited my ramblings upon fond recollections, remembrances lost, and brusque disregard for occurrences I didn't care to recall.

At any rate, coffee and breakfast were usually my job. But of course I was late in rising, and Grace was not needed that day, she said, at a certain charity to which she regularly contributed both her time and money.

"I won't ask about your day or time away," she offered as she tended my shoulder while having our coffee at the foot of the garden window.

"I'm afraid I'm a rather unreliable narrator, Grace," I said.

"Yes, you are that," she agreed vaguely while applying to my wound an ointment that smelled faintly of a moldy cantaloupe. "You are a complicated and contradictory man, to be sure."

"Yes," was all I said.

We spoke casually then of quotidian things: house and garden matters, as was entirely pleasant for us both. Never mind that, however subtle, there was in everything we discussed the same enigmatic quest for identity, the same acknowledgments of delicacies in relationships, the constant romanticizing of the past, and the careful interaction of each of these to our southern ethos and culture. Nothing new was made of any of it though. Sometimes, you know, it's just good to be home.

We had nearly finished our coffee together when I asked Grace about things downtown in the Vieux Carré. She told me about roof construction going on across from my shop at the old courthouse. She described it, as she often did with important things, in a certain off-handed manner she affected to elicit special attention.

"Oh well," she began gradually, "there were some men working up on the courthouse roof, but they—one of them anyway—seemed more interested in the passersby below than anything else. I went by there on my way to the French Market for your rolls yesterday."

I took in her inference and her pursed smile above her raised cup but replied, "Ah, the rolls. So you knew I was coming. Henry must have called while I slept."

"No. The Sisters did. Those gals seem to know everything going on all the time, don't they?"

"Yes," I agreed. "There's that turret, you know, up in their Key West house. I swear, and I've said it before, I do believe they've got a magical spyglass up there and keep watch all around the planet."

"Hmm," Grace intoned, finishing her coffee. "They've got Henry of the Hive in that network. That's what they've got, and Lord knows he does get around."

"To a fare thee well," I agreed and finished mine. "To a fine fare thee well."

After the rain the night before, the day was cool and bright. I was back on St. Charles in the early afternoon, buttoning the jacket of my freshly pressed cream-colored suit at the streetcar stop. I planted a brown-and-white loafer on the step up, hopping the streetcar over to Canal. The sunlit breeze through the windows felt bracing as we clacked along. I was glad and warmly reassured (heartened really) by how unaffected the world beyond the eclectic and eccentric houses and yards all along the tree-lined avenue remained.

I was off the street car when it jerked to a stop merely a block back from where I'd exited Henry's truck the night before. When the light at the crosswalk changed, I crossed Canal with a gaggle of young bridesmaids. Their giddy banter revealed that they too had slept late, though after a raucous night in which the one walking faster ahead had embarrassed them all. So now they had been drinking mimosas at another hotel and had to hurry back to dress if they were to be lined up in the atrium of the Ritz Carlton on time. All of that was revealed in trifling detail, conveyed over forty feet of crosswalk, with an alacrity that would lose the most competent court stenographer.

Chapter 17

Down Bourbon Street, at the very cusp of that vicinity where nightly the riot of excesses begins, is a narrow alcove that has the appearance of an alleyway (if it is noticed at all). There's a blackened iron security gate six feet in. On closer inspection it can be seen that this high gate, with it bulbous crown above the entry, is actually a finely casted depiction of a giant octopus. Above its mantle reads the maxim *Ultra Plus*. Below, the tentacles part to reveal a polished disk where a handle or latch might otherwise be. That disk is a security card reader.

I placed my black-and-gold card against the disk and was immediately buzzed in. During regular business hours the reading of my card would have informed select employees of the private club not only of my presence but would have noted my preferences and predilections in hospitality there as well. Just now the broad mahogany lounge was partially lit and bore a sweet scent of tobacco leaf, warm bread, and orange marmalade. I made my way to a non-conspicuous side door that opened to a carpeted stairway to the second level.

Upstairs I entered an office where a young man with a peroxide blond mop, wearing a suit that was stylishly too small, sat behind a tiger oak reception desk. He was chattering fawningly into the phone at his pierced ear. I waited while he listened impatiently then and widened his eyes up at me in a friendly gesture of recognition. His hand cupped the phone's mouthpiece.

"She's in," he said in a loud whisper with a swish of his head toward the office door behind him.

The woman in that office was also on the phone, though her distinctly foggy voice could barely be heard from behind her high-backed desk chair turned toward the wall of French doors to the balcony behind her. A willowy hand, signaling that she would be a moment longer, extended from the chair back on a luxuriously clad arm, heavily jeweled at her petite wrist.

Mounted on the wall opposite was a bank of closed circuit TV monitors. The gate off Bourbon was in full view, as was the dimly lit lounge where a barkeep now polished cocktail glasses. Then there were hallways, dining rooms (both congregate and private) where crisp white table cloths were being spread, the impressive library, the vast kitchen where prep work was occurring, and other assorted spaces with hardly a crack or crevice that could not be observed.

Elsewhere around the room hung promotional posters in fine frames and a slender dancer featured Tropicana style. One wall held black-and-white photos of various sizes in a wide assortment of frames. I'd examined them before, finding of particular interest the ones picturing prominent figures in the Cuban revolution and various celebrity types of that era. On her large provincial desk were smaller photos in sundry standing frames. I picked up the one with a pleasant looking mature woman and a young girl with her dog sitting out on the plank steps of an old house somewhere in palmetto country.

Elle Rousseau, in her trademark turban, spun back around to return the phone to its cradle. She flashed a puzzled smile and said emphatically, "So you made it back. I'm glad."

"You doubted me?" I put the family photo back, and her dark eyes narrowed as my hand parted from it.

"No," she said hauntingly. "Never. Let's go out. I want to smoke."

Leaning against the railing on the balcony over Bourbon, Elle lit a long, slender cigarette with the jeweled lighter. I put my sunglasses on and braced myself against the railing close by. Parked on a side street below was a big red Bonneville convertible. The top was down, and a trophy mount of longhorns now festooned the front grill. A drugstore cowboy dude was propped up by the front bumper. He looked away as I watched him banging on his cheesy-looking five-string for tips from disinterested passersby. There was usually an authentic cowboy guitar guy around, but this wasn't him. Everything about this one screamed surveillance.

Elle exhaled a thin trail of smoke and said abruptly, "I have another trick for you."

I didn't like the terminology and declared, "I'm not here about another assignment, Elle. I'm here about what went wrong on the last job."

"Nothing went wrong," she said with a disarming shrug. "It never happened."

"Really? I've got a hole in my shoulder, Elle. Something happened."

Chapter 17

She inhaled again and seemed more frail than I had remembered her.

"There's a yacht," she began, as if reciting, "one of the super yachts in the Bahamas now. In the stateroom on board is a specially designed case housing a small statue of a boy riding a dolphin. It's said to date back to ancient Greece. I don't know the pedigree. There's nothing documented, no verified provenance because it was purchased years ago under, let's say, questionable circumstances. It was when the underground antiquities market was much more fluid than it is now. Anyway it appears to be an exquisite bronze, rumored to have been caught and brought up in a fisherman's net."

I peered warily at Elle over the green lenses of my sunglasses.

"Yes. Yes, I know. We've heard that one before. But it doesn't matter here. It only matters that the object is thought be, represented to be, one of the finest known examples of its kind. Fully intact, with only some shell encrustation at its base, the piece could easily fetch $900,000 and upward on the black market. Who knows what it could go for at Sotheby's or Christie's if the time is right? Immaterial. The owner wants it stolen."

"*Wants* it stolen?"

"Yes. And it's not about the insurance either. It seems he's in rather a pickle. Here's a world class entrepreneur and highly respected collector, someone you'll recognize immediately if you haven't already guessed."

"I have. Guessed."

"Well ... so you know he has a stellar reputation, quite hard to come by given the company he keeps. And he'd like to keep his reputation intact, so the boy on the dolphin needs to disappear before the entirety of his collection is donated to a major museum, where the Greek boy on a dolphin will most certainly be discovered as a fake."

"So why doesn't he dispose of it himself? Toss it overboard. Say he was robbed if he prefers."

"Because he wants the robbery to be authentic," Elle says with a shrug. "He wants that much to be true. There's $300,000 as a nonrefundable retainer, more than enough cash for expenses, and another

$600,000 when we provide proof of total destruction. No chance it shows up later on the black market, gets nabbed, is exposed by some international authority, or shows up as some other embarrassment later."

"He's protecting his legacy, so to speak."

"Yes. Whatever," Elle said through the cigarette smoke.

"And just what's Bertrand Oliphant's involvement?" I asked, not intending to sound bitter.

"None. He doesn't have a clue."

"I should believe that?"

"Do you believe that silly cowboy down there is surveillance?" Elle counters drily.

"Yes. Without a doubt."

"Of course. You pegged him the moment you looked out. Let's let them think they have us. Bertrand has already made his deal with the devil. Or, I should say, it's the other way around. There's an agent—I'll tell you this much—she's been undercover but not now, I think. No, I think she is here. She and Bertrand talk. And your cowboy friend down there, I think he's a direct consequence of whatever deal Bertrand has made. Frankly, I think he may have been working with the government all along. I don't know. It's just a creepy feeling I have."

"So you play out your hand with him now, and that's it?"

"Sure. We're friends," she said with a wan smile. "Friends who lie to each other because that's become the kinder thing to do. Look, they can't get to me without taking him down. Nor you, really. After all, it was Bertrand Oliphant who set you up in the trade. You haven't forgotten that. So I say we're on our own now. Simply that. Let's do this thing. Take the boy on the dolphin. Our last episode involving Bertrand Oliphant is avenged, and we're well compensated, fifty/fifty, by this sweet little deal. What do you say?"

"Sixty/forty—my way."

Elle peered nonchalantly down at the cowboy surveillance guy. "Sure. You take sixty."

"I'll think about it," I said and left Elle out on the balcony lighting another cigarette.

Chapter 17

I crossed over to Royal past the Montelone Hotel to the shady side of the street. The roofers were in view atop the courthouse. And, just as Grace had observed, one of them seemed more interested in what was happening on the sidewalk than what he was doing on the roof.

I paused at the entrance of the gallery—an airy interior complex of specially lighted rooms featuring antique fine art and artifacts, classic furnishings from around the world, exceptional antique jewelry, and other exquisite adornments. Most remarkable was a hundred-foot-long Smithsonian museum case displaying rare coins from centuries past, dating to the time of the ancient Greeks and the Romans. I turned back into the indented entrance to look up from behind my sunglasses and flash a suspicious smile at the apparently idle roofer atop the old courthouse. I didn't really know if it was a sandwich or binoculars he'd rapidly brought down from his face. But I smiled as if I did. I turned and pushed through the heavy glass door of the marvelous place I simply referred to as "my shop."

The beautiful young woman was seated at a large Louis XVI Boulle desk by the door. She greeted me immediately.

"Good afternoon, sir! And welcome home," Rachel Perl sang out in a warm, melodious voice.

I was pleased to receive her greeting at the desk, though her duties and responsibilities now far exceeded that station. Rachel had been a busker—the real deal—a soloist virtuoso in an astonishing street performance by a traveling band of bicycle gypsies. I'd been admiring her talent for some time with handsome deposits in her shoebox when she appeared one day in the shop. I showed her around myself.

Rachel demonstrated an astonishing breadth of knowledge about the sixteenth century conquistadors, as well as Aztec and Mayan history, architecture, and the cultures of indigenous peoples "uprooted," as she would say. I teamed her up with Ducky, my resident numismatic expert. She soon demonstrated she could be a skilled negotiator. Fluent in five languages, she was also imbued with a calming sort of confidence especially useful in international acquisitions, their provenance fully discovered and disclosed. Not exactly my MO over the years. But surprisingly, all said and done, our business had prospered by the genuine credibility she'd brought. Now Rachel handles most of our international antique and collectables business as a quite able young associate of mine and, frankly, heir apparent to my shop.

So we were chatting briefly and catching up on things when two suits, a man and a woman, came in. They walked directly over to the Smithsonian table. Seated behind the wide expanse of its glass top, Ducky wheeled over to invite their interest. No surprise there. Well within earshot they were asking about the treasure coins. Rachel threw me a glance laced with an ironical smile. I excused myself to my office with a nod to her and a wink to Ducky as I went. The two at his coin display, as we both knew, were federal agents. They'd been in before.

I was back in my office, my "chart room," as I referred to it, the interior being walled and adorned with the mahogany features of an old sailing vessel salvaged in France. A schooner once owned by the swashbuckling actor, Errol Flynn. A large framed photograph of that boat under full sail in Cuban waters hung on my office wall. Close by was another of me and my smirking crew aboard our PBR (flying the Skull and Bones), tied at a fueling pier on the Mekong. Another section of wall was devoted to my collection of vintage Formula One racing, drivers and their cars at all the best European venues, including the fiery crash of my favorite driver, Sergio Castellan.

Most of the paintings, though expensively framed, were of more personal than monetary value. I bought them when I lived on apples and cheese, trekking around Europe. Most I bought at sidewalk tables where art students picked up a few coins for expenses to continue their assigned works. Nevertheless I found these fledgling pieces to be quite fascinating, holding over the years a continual increase in their intrinsic worth.

My broad captain's desk was strewn with antique and vintage maps along with stacked rare books that chronicle the early explorations and colonization of the "New World." I've always been fascinated by maps and mapmaking. The maps, hand drawn and shaded with raw colors deepening with the terrain to darker hues, I leaf through time and again. I find fascinating in the maps (as well

Chapter 17

as these fragile tomes) old words no longer in use and the names for places not presently known if they ever were.

Momentarily Rachel buzzed up to say that the Feds were asking to see me. I told her to show them in. The two suits entered before Rachel's extended hand. She offered them coffee or tea or water, but both declined and showed me their badges instead. Lim's a US Marshal. Omerlund's from the US Treasury.

"Yes, I remember," I said. "We've had the pleasure, I believe, of meeting in the last Yule Tide. I'm always more accommodating at Christmas."

"Aren't we all?" Lim quipped.

"Well, I was concerned I may have wearied you with all my meanderings. I do go on with my little stories, I know. Ask me the time of day, and I want to tell how the watch is made," I said, feigning an apology as I came from behind my desk.

"We know what time it is," Omerlund stated blandly.

We sat in the burgundy chairs by a small conference table—an elegant chart table actually—and on it more rare leather-bound books. Open was an edition I'd been reading for some time. Lim took up the book as she sat. She opened across her knees the memoir of the conquistador, Bernal Diaz del Castillo, comprising *A True and Full Account of the Discovery and Conquest of Mexico*. As it happened I'd bookmarked the pages devoted to Cortés and his conquest of Montezuma's great floating city of Tenochtitlán. Of course, Marshal Lim immediately inserted a red fingernail to turn to that section.

Omerlund spoke first. I'd reminded them as we came to the table that on their previous visit I referred them to an attorney acquaintance of mine and sometime business associate, Mercer Pendarvis, lately of Key West. He would be, I assured them, something of an expert in federal and state laws regarding salvage and found treasure. I entrusted all such acquisitions of that type to his counsel.

"I had high hopes," I said, "that Mr. Pendarvis might settle your minds on these matters that seem to trouble you so. He's far better than I am at getting to the point."

"I'm thinking *you* are the point, Mr. Redmond," Lim said, looking up coolly from the cracked and peeling leather tome in her lap.

She took a mottled cob from her black suit pocket and turned it around in her agile fingers for me to see. The octagonal cob was stamped with a heavy cross on its face, a crude octopus opposite with its legend marred and made illegible by the centuries of shifting sea sands. But I knew what it read.

"Yes, you are the point, Jack," Omerlund agreed. "Or should I say 'Irish'? Irish Bly?"

I threw back my head and laughed, actually laughed as Lim put the coin away.

"Oh, for such delights as boyhood brings," I said with glee and repeated more contemplatively then, "Oh, for such delights as boyhood brings."

"You've been away?" Omerlund said more than asked.

"I was missed?" I asked pitifully. "You know, sometimes I just have to get away. I do dream of a simpler life, living perhaps in a little bungalow down in the Keys with maybe an old bicycle to get around."

Omerlund stared at me blankly. Lim didn't look up from the book.

"Well, let's try this. Are you asking if I've been away as a matter of personal interest," I said spritely to Omerlund, "or do you inquire under the aegis of an official investigation?"

Omerlund shifted his weight in the chair uncomfortably. He clearly didn't care to answer.

Lim, entirely absorbed by the conquistador's memoir, had appeared absent from our exchange but looked up then to say, "So here's an account telling of the Spaniards first sighting of the Aztec island city of Tenochtitlán. They see it for the first time from a high pass in the ring of volcanoes surrounding the Aztec city built out into the lake below. Says here they thought that the city, with its magnificent temples, seemed to levitate above the shimmering water, and they asked each other—it says here—if they were dreaming."

"Yes. I seem to recall that from my reading."

"Was that it, Irish Bly? Were they dreaming?"

Chapter 17

I took the question under serious consideration. I was the point of her question after all.

Unhurriedly I shifted in my chair to ask, "What sort of dream? I don't know what the conquistadors saw exactly. But, as I take it from the horrors they found, it was a nightmare waiting to happen down there."

"I'm not fond of banter," Lim said scornfully. "Just what sort of nightmare do you suppose your friend Diebolt Krym has had?"

"Krym? He's not my friend," I replied earnestly. "Hardly an acquaintance, I'd say."

"A nemesis maybe?" Omerlund countered, pleased with himself to be back in the game.

"A competitor perhaps," I shrugged. "I understand he is also a collector. He's a casino man. Has some gambling boats—an offshore enterprise, is it? I understand Krym fancies himself to be an authority among salvers and collectors of all coinages transported by the Spanish treasure *flota* of the conquistadors."

"Ever gamble aboard one of his floating casinos, Mr. Redmond?" Omerlund asked snidely.

"Never set foot on one."

"Never set foot?" Lim followed up. "How about fire? Someone set fire to one of Krym's floating casinos about a month ago. Pirates hit Krym and made off with the contents of a safe on board."

"Pirates? Pirates attacked Krym's casino boat and absconded with his gambling money?"

"Well, see, that's the thing," Omerlund began to explain. "They didn't go for the gambling money really. They went for Krym's private safe box in his personal quarters. They made a play for the casino itself for cover, but that wasn't it."

"Ah, the ink of the octopus," I touted.

"Exactly," Omerland decided. "So they hit Krym's safe and faded quickly to their fast boats to make off with something or some things that were evidently more valuable than the fresh cash on board."

"You don't say? And the poor fellow—Krym—how's he taking it? Not sitting down, I bet."

An Unfinished Sunset

"That's the hell of it," Lim says curtly. "Krym made the mistake, as seems to be his habit, of trying to take things into his own hands. Seems he got himself in an altercation with some of the local law enforcement down in Florida. There was a shootout on a tidal creek with a fiery conclusion. Krym was burned severely. He's not expected to make it. It was a bad scene. A nightmare waiting to happen, as you say."

"News to me."

Lim stood up and walked over to the nautical credenza by my desk. She stood for a while, apparently to admire the sturdy trifold pirate's hat brandishing a great white plume hung there between the long blades of crossed sabers. It was the same hat I'd worn as a boy.

"Yes," she said, as if consoling, "and I don't suppose you'd ever dream up a thing like that—the piracy of a gambling boat at sea?"

"Dream?" I answered, mimicking her tone. "My dear, you must know the anecdote about the ancient Oriental gentleman who dreamed he was a butterfly, do you not?"

Lim looked at me as if I'd asked if she knew a certain dirty joke, something offensive, and said flatly with cautioning eyes, "No."

"Oh, you must," I said plowing on. "You see, the ancient one dreamed he was a butterfly. Or was it, as he wondered on awakening, that he *was* a butterfly dreaming now that he was a man?"

As if suddenly bemused, Lourdes Lim walked back over and handed me my hat. "It's yours, isn't it?"

A sudden but not unpleasant melancholy washed over me as I let the trifold with its fantastic plume roll in my hand.

"It's yours, right?"

Omerlund looked confused.

"I don't mean one of your acquisitions or some impersonal item out of one of your collections," Lim said with sympathy in her tone. "It's yours, yes?"

"Yes," I said. "I confess to the hat."

"You're an incurable," Lim said solemnly with an uncertain smile. "It's just a matter of time. The sun is setting, Irish Bly."

She signaled Omerlund and they went for the door, though Omerlund's furrowed brow suggested he wasn't quite sure why.

Chapter 17

In an act of mischief intended to emphasize her point Lim slapped off the lights as the two walked out.

I sat alone then to contemplate my fantastically plumed hat. And time. Time: I'd pirated plenty of that and now felt its weight while the graceful paw of evening light settled like the sheen over a blue-black jaguar's pelt. I mused upon the pelt of time. In the inevitable hour we are not called by name, nor does time take its toll on each the same. We never know except to say, day by living day, we choose between adventure and the mundane. Either way, as time goes, in the end it's a zero-sum game.

With a sigh I tossed this treasured gift of boyhood—my tri-fold hat with its cavalier plume—onto the ochre surface of frayed Caribbean maps, illuminated there in the unfinished sunset by which I knew full well Irish Bly would return.

Ultra Plus.

Epilogue

While darkness shrouds the adobe walls and tiled rooftops of the ancient city of Malinalco, a rooster crows from a bell tower crowned with morning stars. On the second story veranda of a hotel across the plaza Consuela Doge and C. C. Moth sit patiently at their breakfast table in the dark. A colorful macaw in a wicker cage close by stirs excitedly as the cook arrives by the back stairs. He brings seed pods in his pockets and fresh trout in his basket, taken from cold mountain pools in the shade of banana trees.

At first light smaller birds are charmed by flirtations of the sun over a Kapok tree on the plaza. A primal, if serene, sense of awe awakens in the eyes of the two old but somehow ageless companions. They lift their faces in unison to the sun, appearing now in unruly fractions above the towering sandstone cliffs that surround the town. Doge and Moth moan sweetly together while shadow and light define the precipices, stone crags, and wooded escarpments. Humankind has observed such spectacles of the sun in this valley since time immemorial. The Aztec sun was deified here in dance and worshipful summonses—earthly and astral—were sung out from the towering stones. To this day many who delight in such things know the place as *Pueblo Magico*.

"Pueblo Magico," Moth exhales as a second wave of golden light gilds the ridgeline to the Hill of Idols.

"*Cerro de los Idolos,*" Doge intones. "Up there is a complex of temples, outlying platforms, and statuary carved from the stone of that high ridge. Ah yes! It was there that the warriors of the Mexica worshipped. There they once sacrificed in communion with their high priests and sacred sorcerers in ancient ceremonies that conferred upon them the fierce prowess of their animal fetishes: the

An Unfinished Sunset

eagle and the jaguar. It was where La Malinché—the Mirror of the Jaguar Night—was made and hallowed."

"Indeed," Moth affirms solemnly. "There. The House of the Sun. Indeed so."

By the time the scent of fresh coffee, bread from brick ovens, polenta flecked with green chilies, and buttery trout grilling with coriander and lime waft from the hotel's kitchen, Dr. Harry Hollister slides hazily into a vacant chair at the Sisters' table.

Dr. Hollister is a lean young man with black bedhead hair and brilliant green eyes behind his round glasses. A Stanford archaeologist and trained architect, the Sisters had recently endowed his Archaeology and Ancient Engineering Fellowship for study of the Aztec ruins at Malinalco. So of course Harry was only too pleased to drive them down from Mexico City in his dusty Volvo.

The plan, at least in so far as he knew, was to inspect his detections and conclusions among the Malinalco ruins. Exuberant narrations as a tour guide, however, were not Harry's forte. Interestingly enough though, this Harry Hollister is a grandson of the famed garrulous Hollywood gossip, Hap Hollister, Errol Flynn's chatty pal at the Compleat Angler on Bimini. So there had been that for the Sisters to reminisce and ruminate about on the drive down.

But nothing of all *that* is of interest to young Harry. Moreover, he was already a bit put off by the Sisters' insistence that they both sit in the back seat, their luggage overflowing from the trunk stacked high in the passenger seat beside him. And then "… they start up with this Hollywood crap (he didn't say this aloud)."

Nearer to Malinalco, however, the Sisters invited Harry's description of the ancient temples and terraces they were scheduled to visit the next day.

"Tell us about Cerro de los Idolos," Consuela demanded stiffly from behind. The *Cuauhtinchan*, where the eagle and jaguar warriors raised their chant in the serpent's belly on the solstice when she swallows the sun. Oh, to witness such things!"

Hollister might as well have been speaking in algorithms by the time he pulled to a halt before the boutique hotel among usual *tiendas* on the cobbled street, along with small bohemian shops boasting *hierbas, incienso, cristale, and masaje* behind the macramé and beaded curtains over their doors. Some had already lit lamps inside by the time Hollister's Volvo rolled by in the early dusk.

But now—on the following morning—the light is bright before noon on the day of the winter solstice, a complete cooperation by the weather with the Sisters' stratagem. With Dr. Hollister in the lead they are well up the stony walk leading to the ruins. Hollister is quite surprised that, despite his long stride and the steady clomp of his hiking boots, the Sisters are keeping up. In fact, they plod after him quite well, all the while deep in discussion or debate regarding lesser gods of the Mexica. Consuela, becoming increasingly adamant, hisses like an old swan in French. She quotes from a Parisian edition of Duran's *Rivre Des Dieux et Des Rites*, insisting that it is the most authoritative source on the subject.

"As with all things delicate or discreet, these are better left to the French," Doge admonishes while Moth is only too eager instead to declare the attributes of their English walking shoes.

Ahead and behind them are any number of counterculture types who, by their tussled hair and dramatic clothing or lack thereof, Moth most conveniently identifies as "hippies," adding, "I think some lost tribe still wandering from Woodstock."

Hollister also thinks their ecstatic greeting of each another on the path is curious, as no one they encounter looks the least bit like an heir of the Mexica.

"Welcome home," they passionately hail one another in passing. "Welcome home," the others would rejoin warmly. "Welcome home."

The Sisters are no more winded at the top of the walk than they had been below. Now, at wide steps carved up to the excavated plateau on which the sculptured architecture is terraced and tiered, they climb to stand with Hollister and gaze upon the array of temple ruins as if for the first time (so far as the Sisters are concerned) by anyone since the ancient Aztec themselves.

Cut high into the ridge before them stands the House of The Sun. Thirteen steps carved with balustrade mount to the sheltered platform before its cavernous entrance, which is fashioned in elaborate Aztec detail to expose the gaping mouth of a great serpent with fangs on either side, its bifid tongue sculpted on the floor.

But the front steps are not permitted use now. So they climb sidewise upon wooden steps and boardwalk to the temple door. There a colorful and cacophonous recital has already begun among the bohemian group of fellow travelers on the path. A few give voice to an oracular hum, Doge says, to parrot some universal sound emanating from the spheres. Others perform tactile displays of tiny tones. These contribute to a great, all-encompassing sound that has the effect of cicadas in full force. This is the clinking of finger cymbals, their sound dancing like sparks in a smoke of chiffon swirling amidst the rattling plethora of small drums.

Though they are a boisterous and blissful congregation, the celebrants of the solstice are careful not to block the temple's entrance. With an acknowledging nod to Hollister the Sisters know exactly why the portal is kept clear.

From a cleft in the stone far across the valley a distinct ray of sun begins to climb the ancient steps. It passes between the two crouched jaguars on guard there. In mere moments the beam is at the entryway and upon the tongue of the great serpent. With it comes the winter's solstice, celebrated wildly by the anticipatory assemblage. Exactly as the temple was designed to receive it, the bolt of light illuminates the head of the eagle sculpture. And even more astounding is the beam of light reflecting from the jaguar seat on the crescent bench deep within, illuminating next the entire grouping of statuary beneath the sloping walls of the circular room.

The Sisters, Hollister in their wake, brush in before anyone else to find the mysterious source of this second illumination. There, against an oddly triangular fissure in the hindmost, is the Mirror—the one of black onyx, mounted between golden jaguars with emerald eyes. A male and female nuzzle at the top, their bodies angling out to form a triangular mount for the Mirror and their hind legs and long tails cast to form its base. This is the object known as La Malinché, the ancient treasure dubbed by them with mock surprise, "The Mirror of the Jaguar Night!"

Dr. Hollister carefully takes up the find, claiming without opposition the Mirror for Mexico's National Museum of Anthropology, with whom he has been closely allied in his fellowship.

Epilogue

Outside, on a nearby plat of boulder offering a spectacularly panoramic view of the valley, the Sisters nod to one another with congratulatory, if mischievous, grins. Far below, where a decrepit stone wall lines the narrow road out of Malinalco, goes a truck with a burnt-orange hood and pale blue fenders, its high side panels swaying playfully round each tight bend. What those panels boast in carnivalesque print and icon can't be read from that distance. But the Sisters know. They are witnessing the timely exit of Henry of the Hive.

Acknowledgment

I AM IMMENSELY INDEBTED TO Kendal Norris for her careful editing of this book. Where the writing is most clear and concise, her hand is in it. Her confidence in me as a writer and her unremitting support for the unfolding story were immeasurably helpful. In all, our shared enthusiasm for the right words and their right arrangement has made the writing of this book an adventure in itself.

I am most grateful to my wife, Carol, my admirable son and daughter-in-law, Wri and Kimberly, and my inordinately talented grandson, Liam, a wordsmith in his own right at age two. I'm keenly aware that the time and attention my writing takes is time and attention spent away from them. Though the loss is more mine than theirs, I'm sure, I remain entirely grateful for their love and understanding.

There are countless others to whom I also owe acknowledgment or apology. To start, I wish to thank Don and Donna Quincey, for our adventuring has become grist for many of my stories, Thaddeus G. Osborne and Paige Brookins, companions and wayfarers in this business of writing. *Ultra Plus*.

About the Author

WILL IRBY LIVES AND writes in Florida and North Carolina. A fifth generation Floridian, he credits the adventure novels and chivalric tales his mother read aloud as inspiration for his writing. He is a US Navy veteran, formerly stationed in the Mediterranean. Traveling throughout Europe, Central America, Cuba, and the Caribbean informs his creative efforts. Places such as St. Augustine, Key West, and New Orleans often appear as virtual characters in his stories. Irby studied history and English literature at Florida State University, which awarded his modest academic credentials. In the Blue Ridge Mountains of North Carolina he collected folk tales, joined a theatre troupe, and learned to buck dance. Later, his treasured students at the island school on Cedar Key, Florida revealed a rare glimpse into a way of life already fading from their view. As a private investigator and security consultant over the past twenty years he has served a discrete clientele including corporate clients, private collectors, trusts and estates. His wide-ranging experiences and extensive travels continue to color and enrich his fiction.